the Making of Maggie Munroe

an' the four men makin a meal o' it, so they are

JJ SCOTT

FIREWORDS

First published 2023 by Firewords
Copyright © JJ Scott 2023

ISBN 978-1-7393059-0-1

This book is a combination of oral family history and fiction. Names, dates, places, events, and details have been changed, invented, and altered for literary effect. The reader should not consider this book anything other than a work of literature.

Typeset in Caslon and cover designed by Dan Burgess

www.firewords.co.uk
www.jjscottauthor.com

For Maisie and George
Mind to haud yer wheesht when you're reading this together over my shoulder.

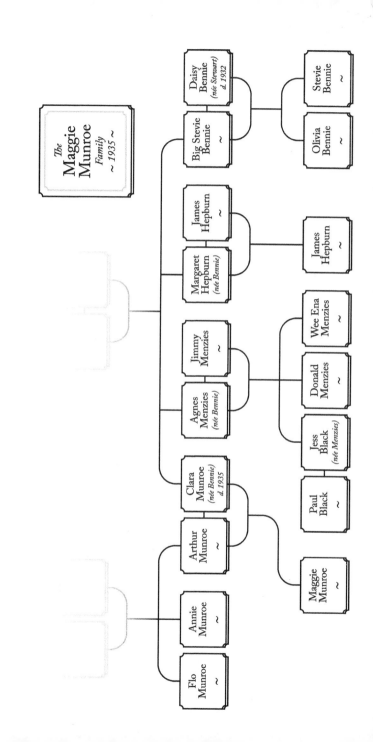

The
**Maggie
Munroe**
Family
~ 1935 ~

Flo
Munroe
~

Annie
Munroe
~

Arthur
Munroe
~

Clara
Munroe
(née Bennie)
d. 1935

Agnes
Menzies
(née Bennie)

Jimmy
Menzies
~

Margaret
Hepburn
(née Bennie)

James
Hepburn
~

Big Stevie
Bennie
~

Daisy
Bennie
(née Stewart)
d. 1932

Maggie
Munroe
~

Paul
Black

Jess
Black
(née Menzies)

Donald
Menzies
~

Wee Ena
Menzies
~

James
Hepburn
~

Olivia
Bennie
~

Stevie
Bennie
~

PART ONE

The Beginning

It's a fair tragedy, so it is. Ah jist finished telling ma Kenny and it near brought a tear tae his eye. Maggie's only twenty and when ye're that age ye're no far aff bein a wean yersel – e'en if ye think ye know awthing, so ye dae. And noo she's left wayoot her mammy. No' that we didnae see it coming. That Clara'd been ill fir years, so she hud; aff and oan, like. And noo there's Maggie left wae a' that *responsibility*. Ye know her faither's eyesight's getting awfy bad, so it is? Aye, it's true. He can hide it weil, so he can, but ah huv it oan gid authority. Ne'er mind that he's pairt crippled – couldnae shield himsel fae the de'il, nei'er he could. That Arthur Munroe, he's a gid man and a proud man, ah will testify tae both, but noo he's crippled and hauf blind wae only a wee lassie tae look efter him. It's a sin, so it is. And fir Maggie tae hae lost the maist important thing in the world. Aye, she's lost her mammy's touch. So she hus.

ONE

The First Man of Maggie Munroe

GLASGOW, JANUARY 1935

The frosty air bit around the foot of the tenement flat with gnarled teeth, like one of the wizened men with a pocketful of cash to buy the lassies down in Woodlands. It had gnawed away at her mother until nothing had been left.

A fire was crackling in the kitchen; it danced with life but Maggie refused to feel it. Instead, she found relief in the long shadows cast in the small space between the main and storm doors, free in grief and out of sight. Behind her, incoherent chatter melted into one, feeding off each other and relaxing as the drink wore on. The main door was slightly ajar and revealed the familiar faces roaming about inside. The warm glow of their words was toxic. They felt like strangers.

Beating her head against the storm door, she could not dislodge their smiles from her mind. No one had loved Clara like she had. Her daddy had been a good husband but he had seen so much pain in his long life that he could bear it. He was in there right now, over by the hearth, playing host amongst an onslaught of laughter. It was an assault on her soul and she wanted to cry but the tears would not come.

The cold, damp wall permeated her thick cotton dress as she slid towards the ground, unnoticed while her mother's love wrapped around her like an eiderdown quilt. The musty smell of the dank water that seeped from the shared lavatory was not enough to move her. Instead, she hugged her knees toward her chin and, for the briefest moment, the pressure of her thighs against her stomach filled the gaping hole that had been left.

"Och Maggie."

"Daddy?"

Looking up, she saw him outlined against the darkness, his silhouette filling the doorway. His steady treads had fallen silently but he hesitated as he stared into the blackness behind cataract eyes.

"Ye'r nae daein ony gid oot here," he told her kindly.

Instinctively, she reached out to grab his hand. He pulled her up, unflinching when her icicle fingers prickled his skin.

"Awbody's arrived. There's nae need tae wait. But thank ye hen, ye did a lovely job and ye're a credit tae yer family."

She did not want to follow but his firm grip led her slowly through the hall and into the warmth of the kitchen. So many people were squeezed into the tiny space. It had often felt too cramped for the three of them but the long table had been pushed back against the wall, its usual spot filled by the crowd. Friends and family nodded and hovered awkwardly with drinks in hand, casting her sympathetic looks when they thought she was not looking. She was lost in the sea.

"Ah'm sorry fir yer loss."

It was a small, thin man who had been lurking on the periphery. He ran a hand over the spot where his hair used to be and glanced back at his wife, although it was his children who needed minding.

"Thank you, Mr McNulty," Maggie muttered automatically.

Leaving her father, she walked further into the room and slid back amongst the living. Mrs McNulty was keeping Reverend Bowman and her husband, Doctor Bowman, deep in conversation rather than controlling the youngsters. Perhaps it was their running, flitting presence that made the kitchen seem such a mass of faces. Reverend Bowman's smile was unwavering as her pastoral gaze drifted from the blethering woman to the snow which piled high on the sill outside.

"It winnae make anything better but it'll take the edge aff it." Alec McLean, a man she knew from MacIntosh Leather Merchants, slipped a tall glass of whisky and a supportive smile into her hand. She took a sip without tasting it and then managed another.

"Can ah hae that?" She nodded at the half-smoked cigarette that hung loosely from his mouth.

Pushing up his round copper spectacles awkwardly, he rested it against the bulb of her lip. It was a day when anyone would do anything for poor wee Maggie Munroe.

The cigarette was as strange to her as the whisky. On the few previous occasions when she had sneaked one, her throat had scratched in protest and her mother had not left her wondering if she had smelled it. How she wished for the arched eyebrows and glib remark as she took a deep suck, and her exhale escaped like a sigh. It was a day for whisky and cigarettes.

Alec waited silently by her side, hands clasped behind his back and head slightly bowed. He was obliged to stay but desperate to leave, fighting the urge to fumble for a second cigarette and not knowing what on earth she would ask for next.

"Och, mammy," she muttered, searching the sea of faces for the one she had never been without. Never had she been in such a crowd; never had she been so alone, and the chasm inside her widened.

She wanted her daddy. There he was, over beside the stove with Uncle Jack. It was a testament to her mother that the man had travelled so far to say farewell for Maggie had not seen him since she was a child playing in the back court with her dollies, but he looked the same as ever. Tall and whiskered, in a smart green waistcoat with unusual embroidered lapels, he asserted his presence in every strut from stove to whisky bottle and back again, fighting to keep his wooden leg under control. When he finally came to rest, it was with one hand on Arthur Munroe's shoulder and the other across his heart. Maggie was comforted by the sorrow on his face, but she did not know what they were talking about.

Beside her, Alec wordlessly topped up her glass and reached for another cigarette.

"It was good o' ye tae come," she told him sincerely, taking a long sip and looking around. The family was there, of course. And Clara's friends. The funeral had been announced in church and it seemed the entire congregation had transposed itself into the small flat, and Maggie's friends had not let her down, either. All their chatter clamoured around her, pushing about with graceless persistence. It would overwhelm her if she let it.

She turned back to Alec, a lump in her throat, and he smiled gently.

"If ye need anything then ye know where ah am. Jist aroon' the corner. Will ye remember that?"

"Of course," she agreed.

"Tak it easy after this wan, for a while, at least, or ye'll be getting drunk."

"Ah want tae be drunk."

He had no comeback for that.

Neither of them heard the deliberate stomp of wood and were only aware of Uncle Jack's presence once he was standing over them. His chin was elevated in his struggle to look through the puffy waves of skin that ebbed across his cheeks, so all he mastered was a disdainful glower.

"Would ye mind terribly much, sir, if I steal this young lass for a word?"

His Irish lilt lifted the edges of his handlebar moustache like the inflated wings of a hawk. Addressing Alec, he eyed Maggie's long brown ringlets and clear round face as if he were seeing her for the first time. Such health and vibrancy showed an inherent resilience which he was no match for: a beautiful thing set like stone in a city of smoke and labour.

With a polite smile and his hands clasped behind his back, Alec began to move away. Maggie wanted to latch onto them to stop him from leaving.

"I was talking to him earlier. A good man," Uncle Jack said, ushering her through the hallway.

They were in the front room before she knew it and he immediately turned to address the guests.

"Can you please leave us for a minute?"

One look at Maggie and they pushed out into the hall, but he followed close behind to force them further back into the kitchen. It was a tight squeeze but he shut the door, then returned to her and smiled. She smiled back.

The front room was small and square, with a large fireplace and an old grandfather clock that had been in the Munroe family for generations. There was a bureau, and an armchair was positioned by the window, overflowing with coats and scarves. Otherwise, the room was suddenly very empty. The curtain around her bed recess had fallen open slightly and she fought the urge to go and fix it, just the way her mother would have wanted. There would be time for that later. More pressing was the coolness she felt after the warmth of the kitchen. The flames burned low on the hearth and, as she busied herself with the embers and a coal scuttle, Jack lent against the mantelpiece to watch. His back was to the recess, saving her embarrassment, and his wooden stump scratched absently at his remaining leg.

"There is not much coal left in that container there."

"The coal man comes themorra. If ye want mair, feel free tae go tae the bunker. It's ben the press. Here." She held the scuttle out to him, unsurprised when he did not take it.

It was her responsibility to run the household now, and she would do it her way. The fire sprang to life and she took a step back, dusting her free hand on her dress with as much satisfaction as her battered spirit could muster.

"Still, it's a deep winter and with your daddy unable to work. Do you really think you alone are going to be able to keep this place?"

"Aye, ah dae," she muttered.

Uncle Jack scratched his stubble and raised his eyebrows. "All I'm saying to you is that coal scuttle is looking a bit low and, after what happened to yer mammy, I thought ye'd be a bit more cautious about that kind of a thing."

"Ma mammy died o' bronchitis. She'd been suffering a' her life. You know that. It wisnae ma fault."

"Hush, hush, love. I'm not saying it's yer fault, like. Only the cold couldn't have helped things, could it? And if you don't have enough coal then you can't keep warm."

Clutching the scuttle tightly, she struggled to match the words with the man she thought she knew. Her shallow breath was louder than the blood pounding in her ears but if she had screamed louder still, she was not sure he would have heard her. Her voice grew soft.

"Ah've already telt ye, there's mair in the bunker. There wis twa feet o' snow ootside so of course it didnae help, but she was ayeways warm enough ben the kitchen. We made sure o' it."

She dumped the scuttle on the floor and the quiet thunk did her case no good at all. Her heart sank.

"I respect ye, Uncle Jack, but ye cannae staund here suggestin' ah did onythin wrang. Go and speak tae Doctor Bowman if ye dinnae believe me. Mammy wis ayeways suffering. Every winter she'd hae a lapse and every year it got worse. It wis jist a matter o' time, the doctor says."

His moustache twitched, ever so slightly at the ends, and she tried to read it as an apology but no such luck. She felt herself begin to tremble and prayed it wasn't visible to him. He stood up straighter, inched away from the mantel and pressed on.

"Please don't read too much into my words, love. The last thing I want to do is upset you. I just wanted to show you the reality of the situation. You must be awfully frightened. It's understandable to be scared of the future and doubtful at a time like this, which is why I want to give you security. Both you and your daddy will have nothing to worry about for the rest of your lives."

She stared back vacantly, sensing impending disaster.

"I want you to marry me, Maggie."

Nothing moved save the swinging pendulum of the clock. Even Jack's moustache had come to an uneasy standstill.

"Well?" he prompted, unwilling to give her time. Of all things worldly, time was not his friend.

"Why wid ye ask me to dae a stupit thing like that?"

"I'm being serious with you."

He rested his chin on his hand to cast an illusion of calm, but his salacious eyes roamed everywhere. Perhaps nothing could shock her anymore but the betrayal ran deep. Her mother was with her, she could feel her presence and her incorporeal face was thunder.

"Is it because I'm a Catholic?" he whispered, afraid of being overheard. "If that's what is worrying your wee soul then don't be afraid, I wouldn't try to turn you. I have too much respect for your mother, God rest her soul, and the grandparents we shared, may they rest in peace."

Maggie took in the marked leather of his seventy-year-old face, unpreserved by the beating of a lifetime at sea. His straw-like hair hung low over his shoulders and his hangdog expression drooped from a man reaching the end of his days. Such deterioration could not be masked by a well-tailored suit and healthy swagger, and there she was, her life spreading out unchartered before her.

"No, it's nothing tae dae wae religion, Uncle Jack. Ah'm flattered and a' but, well, we're no' really a very good match, are we?"

She turned to the mirror, hoping the polarities reflected over the mantelpiece would save her from harsh words, and rested a hand tentatively on his shoulder to soften the blow. It seemed to take an eternity for him to speak again. When he did, he did so slowly, deliberately, lifting his chin even higher.

"I see the same as you, young lady, but there is a bigger picture you must consider that cannot be mirrored back within these four walls; the one where you and your daddy are provided for the rest of your long lives. Imagine that. Where else are you likely to get it?"

He drew himself up.

"I am not a poor man, my love. My wealth is no trifle. And my age? Pah. Surely you should be grateful, only a few years with me in exchange for a lifetime of security."

As he rested his hand on top of hers, she drew back, childhood memories crashing down and demolishing themselves against his crass words and skeletal touch. He lingered over her pursed lips and furrowed brow, willing her into submission, and it made her feel sick. Never again could she innocently assume what had been going through his head when he had visited in the old days to keep the family captive audience, regaling them around that very fire with endless stories of seafaring adventures more daring and remote than the most swashbuckling of novels. Clara would foretell his arrival with anticipation, scrubbing the house from top to bottom before settling everyone in place to hear tales of ships as big as the Titanic, lands more dry than a desert and men as black as coal. The whole Bennie clan was there, listening intently. Maggie and her favourite dolly would sit cross-legged and wide-eyed, and when he had finished he would always come and spend a few moments playing with them on the floor.

Clara Munroe was standing next to her daughter at her own funeral and she would have a lot to say about the proposal, all in stark contrast with the admiration she had shown for years, and Maggie hated him for taking that away. She could hear her mammy's voice from the dark recess, strong and dauntless, *'Dinnae ever sell yersel' short Maggie. No' for ony man.'*

"Thir's security right here, Uncle. Really, I appreciate yer offer o' help but it's unnecessary and ah couldnae put ye oot. Ye've got yer ain life tae lead in Ireland and, tae be honest, I dinnae think I'd like it there, let alone fit right in. Ah dinnae want tae be so far away fae hame. So I think we'd be as weil tae forget aw aboot … ."

"But I've already asked yer daddy's permission."

She faltered, bile rising in the back of her throat.

"Whit did he say?"

"He said he would stand by whatever decision you made, that you are a big girl now and that it is your own choice, and all that. But I know he's for it. To be sure, it's a favourable situation altogether."

Noticing her hesitation, he rushed on before she could catch her breath.

"Come on Maggie. Don't be so stubborn. I'll take you home with me and that will be an end to it. It is not attractive for a young lady to be headstrong."

Panic was setting in but she fought it down, the scattered memories of childhood not enough to offset the straightjacket he was trying to force her into, market negotiating when she was at her most vulnerable.

"I've tried tae say it politely, Uncle Jack, but ye keep pushing me. I cannae mairry ye. I willnae mairry ye. No' in a million years, I swear."

Her voice rose and she had lost the will to control it. So much for the hero of her childhood.

"I dinnae luve ye and, when ah dae get mairried, it's luve, no' money, that'll be ma only motivation. It's offensive tae hear ye suggest otherwise."

"Respect for yer elders now, Maggie."

The sick feeling dissipated, leaving only anger.

"I hae respect fir ma mammy. It's her we're here fir, and we've been oot here talking aboot this nonsense lang enough."

She headed for the door.

"Stupid wee bitch," he hissed.

"Excuse me?"

She turned back. She must have misheard.

"You are the most silly, ungrateful child I've ever laid eyes on."

He attempted to draw himself up straight but his peg leg was an inch short so he stood glowering at her like a crooked scarecrow. His jacket swung open to reveal a dark stain down the middle of his shirt and his sneer unveiled previously-concealed and deeply-unsettling thoughts.

"How you expect to support yourself and your father on the wage of a message girl is beyond me but, as you have made so clear, it is not my concern. In fact, when faced with a thankless attitude like yours, I respectfully withdraw my proposal. Thank you very much."

The front door hit him as he loped out.

TWO

The Family

"Och Lordie, ah hope ah'm no' interruptin' onything here, so ah dae."

From the kitchen doorway, Mrs McNulty filled the frame like a huge oak in a forest of dwarf trees. Her breasts were as big as her stomach, and her children had to push past her in their dash for freedom. The only small things about her were the flitting blue eyes which saw everything so Maggie closed her mouth and listened, motionless, to the retreating thud of wood on concrete as her uncle strode from the building. There was nothing to do but wait out the intrusion and hope her stomach did not flip out of her body as she grappled with disaster.

"Ma Kenny's got an awfy chill, so he dis, and ah need tae be gettin him hame. Dinnae want him catching his death, neither ah dae. Oops, sorry hen, there ah go wae ma big mooth, shootin' aff aboot cauld and deein wae yer poor mammy no' ten minutes in the grund, so she is. We'd better be aff afore am saying onything else."

She paused but Maggie did not fill the silence.

"Eddie, go ben the front room and get the jaikets. But dinnae ye worry, Maggie hen. Whit e'er happened the nicht is bitween yersel an yer Uncle, so it is – or should ah say yer man? Ah'm no a blether, neither ah um. Ma lips are sealt. Ye jist go back ben there tae the body o' the kirk an dinnae be gein' ony o' this anither thocht."

She shuffled towards the door and buttoned her coat. Behind her, Kenny sneezed. His small frame was diminutive compared to his wife and he merged with his children in her shadow.

The big woman clapped her hands.

"Jimmy! Stop chasin' Eddie roon' like a loony. Molly's gettin' a' upset, so she is. Jist look at her! Kenny wid ye go an' help the weans oan wae their coats? Ah cannae dae awthin aroon' here, neither ah can. Mak it look like there wis a reason fir marryin' ye."

Shifting Molly from one hip to the other, she held out an arm and folded Maggie into a tsunami of a hug while Molly cried out and wriggled, kicking her legs uselessly against her mother's thick coat. Silently, Maggie commiserated. There was so much to protest at: the crush of body parts, the foetid smell of mothballs, the harsh fabric that scratched at her cheeks and threatened a rash. If she accepted the hug wordlessly like a good girl, if she acquiesced to this exaggerated show of affection, perhaps the woman would keep her secret, on the off chance she realised that there was a secret worth keeping.

"Richt, weans, come oan."

Mrs McNulty eventually pulled away and, with an omniscient smile, three skipping children and a beleaguered husband, headed out the door. For Maggie, there was no relief in their leaving, for Mrs McNulty had heard enough to send tongues wagging on both sides of Maryhill Road.

"Ah'm sorry, mammy," Maggie whispered, wishing beyond reason that she was sitting cross legged in her recess and leaning against the greatest comfort of her life. They would share words of outrage, and then laugh and cuddle, and everything would be set right again.

She moved away from the hall before anyone else could pass, back to the sanctuary of the front room to stomp around the hearth in solitude and quash the embers before they managed to catch. The whole scene replayed in her mind but she would not dignify it with guilt. Heat permeated the thick soles of her tough black boots but the pain was not enough to bring her to tears, no matter how much she wanted them. She hitched up her dress and soot billowed underneath, the tiny granules of ebony glass swirling in a tornado of dust. Through belching, throaty coughs she worked on, continuing her stubborn march until every prickle of light was rubbed out. Finally, she became still and all that moved was the swinging pendulum, the steady tick-tock of the grandfather clock reminding her that, still as she was, time would continue on.

"What on earth are ye dain?"

Her cousin was incredulous, her question flying with bullet speed across the room.

"Shut the door."

"There's no room fir aw'body ben there but Uncle Jack chucked us oot. Can we no' come back again?" Jess's hands were on her hips and Maggie couldn't blame her.

"In a wee minute. Jist gae me a minute. Uncle Jack's gone."

Saying it aloud, reality hit home. For the second time that day, she wanted to sink to the floor and curl into a ball.

"He is? He didnae come an' say goodbye. Are ye feeling a'right, Maggie? Come awa' and sit doon."

Jess took her arm and started guiding her towards the recess.

The cousins were as dissimilar as could be, with Maggie's clear complexion and ringlets often causing her to be mistaken for a teenager while Jess was taller, broader, and seven years older, with wavy brown hair cut tight around her ears. The only family resemblance was the vigorous determination that their mothers had passed on. In that moment, Jess was determined to comfort Maggie, and Maggie was determined not to accept the support. It was not Jess who she wanted to talk to. Gathering her strength quickly, she pulled out of her cousin's grip and headed for the kitchen.

"Thanks fir yer help," she called, kicking the last embers from her soles on the way out.

She entered a crowded kitchen that felt much emptier without the McNulty brood. Aunt Annie and Aunt Flo, her father's spinster sisters, sat straight-backed by the window, two stately grey figurines from another time. Their fingers twitched as they manoeuvred phantom needles, one sewing and one knitting in their minds, and their fast-paced chatter competed in the narrow space between them with typical urgency. Nothing could shake them from their routines, not even a funeral, and soon they would leave again for the countryside, to their own home and their own lives. Their well-meant concern would be worse than Jess's unbearable intensity and Maggie could not stand it. She turned away.

On the other side of the kitchen, her mother's family were more subdued. The sight of her Aunt Agnes, with her heart-shaped face and short curled hair, was a haunting mirror to whom Maggie could look all day and find her mother. There she fussed over her two youngest children but with less conviction than usual, her heart elsewhere. Her husband, Jimmy, rubbed her arm without anything to say. Face streaked with tears, Jess had followed Maggie to re-join her parents and stood beside her brother and sister like steps and stairs. She saw Maggie watching and whispered something to Jimmy, but Maggie shook her head and turned away.

At the far side of the range, Big Stevie sat with his small son wedged between his knees. There was as much distance between him and his living sister as there was with his dead one. He stared deep into the fire smoke, remembering his wife's funeral not long past. At last, Maggie had found someone who might understand, but his brooding was too deep. Only a few feet away, his daughter, Olivia, sat rolling pebbles on the sooty ground that Maggie had swept clean the night before. Her luscious blonde curls set her apart from all other heads in the room but no one was paying attention; only her brother looked longingly at her game from his position trapped between his father's knees. Singular and alone. So like her mother, Maggie thought. Ghosts were returning to every corner of the flat.

Faces floated past; people who had sat in the kitchen during happier times with a cup of tea and a biscuit, some of whom would become strangers now that the matriarch was gone. Others, Maggie knew, would stay. Her two childhood friends, Minnie and Rachel, kept flinging her furtive looks from a watchful distance. Their kind scrutiny bore into her like daggers until Rachel suddenly stood a little straighter, smoothed her skirt down and pushed her shoulders back, remembering to impress. Maggie had no doubt that these friends would support her through all that was to come but she could not call on them when she woke up, sweating and alone in the depths of the night, terrified by the realisation that the previous week's horror was her newfound reality.

She counted on one hand the days that would take her to her twenty-first birthday. Three. It was crass to remember but impossible to forget while the wide, midnight blue hat that they had seen in Mr Henderson's Millinery sat on the mantelpiece. They had first passed it just after church on a Sunday in November. *Jist wait til efter yer birthday. Thir's ayeways something special waiting fir ye*, her mother had told her, lifting her face to heaven. From then, it had been an open secret in a box beneath the bed in the kitchen recess, waiting to be gifted.

Protocol and age be damned. She marched across the stowed kitchen, ignored her aunt and uncle on either side, lifted the lid and put it on, bothered only about who it brought her close to. Then she wandered to the table where Arthur was sitting with Alec from the leather shop and poured herself another whisky. Their legs swung off the floor like a couple of school boys and their cheeks were flushed, and she lifted herself next to them. The hat slipped over one eye and the brew slid down her throat like syrup washing away the grime that had been caught there.

"Daddy," she whispered, the word a comfort in a world standing on its head.

"Ma wee lamb. Ye wir gone fir a long while."

"And ye know why that wis, daddy," she scolded, lacking the strength to stay angry.

He patted her hand, glancing at the top of her head. She wondered whether he was acknowledging the hat or trying to find her face, but his supportive smile meant the world.

"We'll talk aboot that later, hen. Richt noo ah wis tellin Alec here a belter o' a story."

"Aye, it was a fair laugh, Maggie," Alec agreed, pushing up his glasses and grinning.

"The wan aboot yer mammy and that bugger o' a teacher when ye wir a wean at the school. Whit wis her name again? Ah couldnae remember her name for aw the tea in China."

"Miss McDonald."

"Aye, that wis it. Weil, did she no' have it in for oor Maggie?"

Both men were laughing already. The tale had been told and retold and they knew the ending well, but for Maggie, six years after leaving school the impression left by that teacher still ran deep. She had been seeking a distraction and this was it, so she sat back and let the hat fall further down her forehead.

"Aw the weans were terrified. A right nutter, she wis, ah think on account o' her bein' an auld spinster." Arthur lowered his voice to avoid being overheard by his two sisters, who still sat in front of the window nearby. "She used tae belt aw the weans fir nae reason, an' it ayeways seemed tae be Maggie mair than most, but then maybe it jist seemed that way cause she wis oor ain. Fair tae say, awbody lived in fear o' that loony.

"So, this day oor Maggie wis at the schail an' drapped her boency baw in the class. She'd bin oan at me fir weeks tae buy that baw.

Awbody hud wan fir the summer, she telt me. Ye could see 'em oot there in the street efter school. So, ah got her wan. This bonnie blue wan. Wis it nae bonnie, Maggie? An' she was lined up at schail ready tae go in an' the baw fell oot o' her haund. Pure accidental, like. When this bloody – what's her name?"

"Miss McDonald."

"Richt, weil, she appears oot o' thin air like the de'il an' says she's keeping that baw fir gid. Then she gies Maggie a leatherin' fir gid measure. Later oan, back comes this yin, black an' blue an' greeting like a wean."

"Ah *wis* a wean."

"Tells us the whole tale. Weil!! Ye should hae seen oor Clara's face. Ragin, she wis. She marched richt up tae that school an' gave that Miss McDonald a gid seeing tae. Nae fists involved, thir wir witnesses, but fair tae say Clara got that baw back an' came hame triumphant. Seriously, efter a' the bloody shite that teacher put those weans through, she finally got her comeuppances o'er a bouncy baw. That wis my Clara. Fearless."

"Even when faced wae Miss McDonald."

Maggie smiled but was unable to laugh. Instead she removed the empty bottle from the table and looked forward to the day when she could think of her mother with humour. It was a frightening thought.

In the time that had passed, Olivia and Stevie had bridged the gap to play together on the floor amongst soot and shadow, trying to ignore their cousin, Wee Ena, who seemed oblivious to their disinterest and did her best to boss them anyway. Her hands were on her hips and her scowl was firmly in place. There were only a few months between the two girls but she claimed superiority. After all, she was almost eight. Meanwhile, Jess had moved towards Big Stevie. Even when sitting, he was the height of most other people in the room and he paid Jess little mind, his unfocused gaze loosely fastened on the three children playing on the ground, dirtying their good Sunday clothes. Frowning, Aunt Agnes watched her brother while absentmindedly fidgeting with her son's lapels. Donald was fourteen and too old to be fussed over but he hid his irritation by pestering Wee Ena from afar, poking her with a stick he had found in the coal bunker. It was a freeze frame of cyclical observation, a stagnant family tableau lacking soul or resolution.

Not long afterwards, Jess got up and left her uncle alone. His silhouette was cast in firelight, the worn blue of his emaciated body, the hair falling long and limp around his downcast face. A near-empty bottle rested on the fireplace beside him. Slowly, Maggie approached.

"Are ye awright?" she asked.

It took a moment for his gaze to leave the floor and find her, then he nodded. His dark eyes shimmered out of sunken pits. Sometimes it was difficult to remember that he was only thirty-three.

"Stevie's been a gid laddie for his daddy today, haven't ye son?" he called out languidly, and the boy left his game to stand solemnly between his father's knees.

"How are you, pet?" Maggie asked, noticing how pinched he had become over the winter months.

Stevie shrugged and Maggie followed his attention back to his sister, the wee blonde thing who displayed none of the Bennie genes and was a tormenting sight for anyone who had loved her mother or any child who was growing up with pictures of who his mother should have been. When he had lost his job along with his reason for living, Big Stevie could barely look after himself, let alone his children. Aunt Agnes would help him out, she said. She would take one of the children to make things easier for him, for a time, until he found his feet. That had been three years previously. The boy was his bloodline and namesake. He stayed. And Olivia sat dejected between them, desperate to belong. The furtive look she threw her father was filled with an uncertainty and apprehension that broke Maggie's heart. Just then, she could have throttled him.

That night in bed, sandwiched awkwardly between her two spinster Aunts, Maggie stared numbly at the ceiling. Annie snored loudly for someone so small and, on the other side, Aunt Flo stretched long, kicking and turning and muttering protests about her sister's snoring while remaining firmly asleep.

Maggie was too weary for sleep. The day's events played in her head, an endless picture show that held little reality, but she wanted to remember everything. Eventually, the reel spun to the few moments she had been able to snatch alone with her father. The guests had finally departed with many kisses and condolences, everything had been moved back to its usual place, and the Munroe sisters had left the kitchen to occupy themselves with cleaning and tidying, chatting all the while. Father and daughter had sat alone by the dying embers of the fire, still and warm while the howling wind whipped around the tenement and swept snow drifts onto their sill. His salt and pepper hair looked grey in the fading light, his shoulders rounded and his countenance weary. She stole herself to speak.

"Ah dinnae think Uncle Jack's gonnae be comin back."

She had reached tentatively for his hand, over the few grey hairs that had begun to sprout from his knuckles.

"Ah gathered that when he went tae speak wae ye, ne'er tae be seen again. Aye, ah'm proud o' ye hen."

"You are?"

"Weil, ye'r a woman noo and need tae be free tae mak yer ain choices, even the wrang yins, wae oot yer daddy bothering ye. But Jesus Mary and Joseph, if ye'd thrown yer life away goin o'er the watter wae that auld sailor the shock might hae sent me the same way as yer mammy."

"Dinnae say that! When I thought ye'd given us yer blessing, ma tummy wis in knots."

"Naw. Ye did the right thing."

He held her chin like he had when she was a child and pinched it pink. Stubbornly, he used his right hand; after all, the hand itself worked perfectly, it was the arm that was the problem. She stood it for as long as possible before wriggling free and he cackled at his own triumph.

From the hallway, Maggie's aunts could be heard clucking and cleaning between the stretched twilight shadows. It was the end of a long day in which they had all aged beyond measure. Now, in the wee small hours, the sisters slept and the house was finally at a tentative rest. Maggie wanted to turn back time and live the day again, to somehow hold onto the woman who was getting ready to slip away into the darkness.

Oblivious, Aunt Flo's snoring seemed integrated, harmonious with the mournful creak of the windows as they strained against the flurries outside, keeping time with the faithful clock in the corner, the intrinsic heartbeat of the home. That her aunts were leaving early the next day was a reminder of the lonely life that awaited her.

As the night grew old and neglected morning hours rolled round the cramped recess, snuffing out the embers of a dying fire, she cooried down into the rough surface of her blanket and shuddered. Memories were everywhere. When she caught the whiff of stewed beef she expected to see her mother's stovies; each time Rachel told a funny story there was a black hole in place of the woman who would love to hear it; if Jess wanted advice about Paul there was no one to confer with; when Auntie Annie let out a rumbling snore, it had the same deep timbre as her mother's had, rising and falling through the wall. Thoughts imploded; all that had been lost from the blackness of a kitchen recess to the eternal confinement of a heavy wooden coffin. Maggie felt four sides of the mahogany berth rise up around her, trapping her in darkness. From the crevices of her bed grew the monstrous image of her entombment; suffocating her, drawing her down in a spiral of despair.

She began to let herself fall but, with a jolt, sprang out of the grip that had been dragging her under. Snapping her brain to the present, her consciousness shifted back to reality. She rolled onto her side and drew her knees up to her chest, careful not to disturb either of the sleeping relics at her side. All the screaming was inside her head.

In the distance, birds sang out to hasten in the morning.

THREE

The Friends

January snow gave way to February slush. While the sky threatened one final onslaught before spring, red streaks finally broke through the packed clouds of morning. Muted lights blinked from shop fronts and shelves were filled behind heavy doors. A trundling tram ploughed its way up Maryhill Road, providing the only activity through streets left abandoned as Glasgow hibernated. It juddered with the effort, catching its footing on a stubborn pile of ice which defied the splattering rain. It stuttered, and started, and picked up pace again.

A lone figure could be seen crossing the tracks in its wake as it disappeared over the hill and down towards Charing Cross. She was wrapped tight in a long grey coat and gloves, and a matching scarf covered her head against the cold. The hem of a skirt was barely visible, hanging just above the knees, and the thick woollen stockings stuffed into heavy black ankle boots did little to waylay the cold. Her small mouth was pursed with solemn resolution as she tramped up the street with a brown paper bundle tucked securely under one arm. The rain was getting heavier and she wanted to get this over with quickly. She pushed her way into the sudden brightness of MacIntosh Leather Merchants and dropped her package on the counter. At the resounding thud, the two men leaning against the workbench sprung to life.

"Gid mornin laddies!"

"Weil, if it's no' Maggie Munroe! How are ye, hen?" cried Alec McLean.

Mickey, his handsome workmate, hung back slightly to finish the leather. The two men had been the backbone of the store for as long as Maggie could remember and much of the time they could be found in the back room, using it as a workshop for their own repairs. Stooped forward with cigarettes in their mouths and tools in their hands, they would flatten and soften diligently while all the saleable produce which came from tanners in town, an array of bags and shoes, was strewn around their small shop front in chaotic order.

As the smell of leather filled her nostrils, she breathed deeply to immerse herself in the musky world of trade and accidentally caught Mickey's eye. His face had the perpetually unshaven look that her mother had called unclean but which she thought was marvellous. Suddenly, she felt things that had been foreign ever since the funeral: emotions that were uncomfortable but exciting, a lifetime away from despair. Struggling to meet his gaze, she felt her muscles twitch. It was far less painful to focus on his colleague instead.

Alec moved closer to retrieve the package and she could smell the same glorious odour radiating from his clothes and his hair. Polish stains streaked his overalls, his shirt sleeves, he even had a brown smudge on his small round spectacles and she had to resist the urge to reach out and rub them clean. Under the harsh electric light, his skin resembled the tough leather he worked with – ageless and in need of softening. She hoped, for his workmate's sake, it wasn't catching.

Pecking her cheek lightly, he pulled away quickly from the clammy touch of her skin. "Och, yer frozen. Mickey, go put some watter in the kettle and brew us a wee cup o tea."

"Mr MacIntosh winnae like it if he comes in an' we're aw sittin aboot."

Mickey's brow furrowed so seriously that Alec laughed more loudly than Maggie had ever heard him speak.

"He winnae like it if he comes ben here tae find a wee lassie frozen oan the spot, either. Go ben tae yon kettle and if oor boss comes in, ah'll deal wae him."

"There's nae need fir that," Maggie said, but Mickey had already disappeared around the shelves into the back room so she lifted herself onto the countertop to wait.

"This place could burn tae the groon and ma gid uncle widnae hae ony idea, so dinnae worry yersel. Yer lookin' well, Maggie."

She sighed, carefully removed the scarf and freed her long hair. Over the past month, a large streak of her beautiful chocolate curls had been set aside for white. Not grey, not flecked, but the stark white of freshly whipped cream, lapping at her forehead without forgiveness like a fluffy albino tongue. As it tumbled down her back, she watched his reaction.

"Like wan o them skunk thingymajiggers," she said flatly, gazing at the speckles of dust on the counter as casually as she could.

"Dinnae be stupid," he scolded.

"Doctor Bowman says it's likely a reaction, stress, but he cannae be sure. Could jist be wan o those things. If it disnae stop soon ah'm gonnae look a hundred years auld."

She shifted awkwardly but glared down at him through her lashes, eyes like slits, challenging him to sympathise. Instead, she saw perverse admiration.

"Ye're certainly unique. There's no' twa o' ye in a' the world, Maggie Munroe."

"Jesus, Mary and Joseph, whit happened tae ye?"

It was Mickey, choosing that moment for a mistimed return with the tea tray but still managing to carry enough magnetism to have stepped right out of a double feature. Except for his jaw. It hung in slack amazement and Maggie told herself it made him look a wee bit glaikit. It was the reaction she was used to. Coming from anyone else, she would have left them to deal with it but, for him, she pulled her scarf back over her head.

"I just like tae mak an impact."

"Onyway, it's jist gid tae see ye, hen. Very gid. We hudnae seen ye fir a while and, weil, we thought ye'd changed yer mind and gone o'er tae Ireland efter a'."

"Mickey…." Alec warned, but his workmate's face was its usual open self.

"Noo, why wid ah be goin tae Ireland, exactly?"

Maggie's legs swung dangerously against the glass cabinet and she stared at Mickey like she had never had the courage to stare at him before.

"It wis jist that Mrs McNulty said, efter the proposal and a', ye were in a bit o' a state, and, weil …"

Suddenly aware of her glower, he played with the dirt under his fingernails.

23

"… when ye'r a' emotional like, it's easy tae change yer mind fae wan thing tae anither thing … and then back again, ae no? Ye just hae tae wait til ye settle doon, so we didnae know whit ye might decide … and I'd jist like tae say we're very happy tae keep ye in Glesga. We need tae get that light fixed."

He pointed desperately at a flickering bulb, rubbed his stubble and looked around the room at anything other than Maggie. She took her cup and raised her eyebrows at Alec. Silence descended. The sight of those two grown men, pensive naughty schoolboys who had been caught out in their gossiping, built until she could not contain her laughter. It ripped out – a true bark that she had not enjoyed since her mother died, dragged kicking and screaming from the depths of her belly until she almost felt guilty about how good it felt.

"Aye, weil, ah'm sure Mrs McNulty's been gabbin' aboot a load o' things and nane o' them wid surprise me. Uncle Jack wis wrang tae propose tae me like that, but ah'll tell ye wan thing he wisnae wrang aboot. He said ah couldnae support ma daddy oan the wage o' a message girl. So laddies, this is yer last parcel fae me. In fact, it's the last message onywan'll be getting fae me, full stop."

"Ye've quit?" Alec was shocked.

"Aye. Ah've mentioned ma predicament tae the gid Doctor Bowman and he wis looking fir a receptionist doon at the surgery. Perfect timing. Ah start there the morra."

"That's jist doon the road, then?"

"Aye, Alec, so ah'll see ye if ye get ony aches and pains. Ah'll be the wan tae help shove a thermometer in yer … mooth!"

She hopped off the counter, tucked a loose strand of hair out of sight and strutted out of the shop before Alec could compose himself to respond: a grand exit from her life as a message girl. Mickey let out a low whistle. Never before had he seen legs like that. He wondered if she did it on purpose, wearing her skirts shorter than fashion or season dictated to show the curved legs that were the talk of Maryhill. Beside him, Alec took a long slurp of tea. He was not the only one who would miss his favourite messenger. But, although he contemplated it every now and then, when the days were cold and the nights were long, he never did feign an illness to go to the doctor and visit Maggie Munroe.

~

"Ah'm no' celebrating ma birthday, Rachel."

She would not take that one, final, devastating step, especially when her twenty-first was already in the past.

The traces of good humour from earlier that day were fading fast, her last day as a message girl petering out in a damp dishcloth of 'I'll be seeing ye next week at the dancin onyways' and 'Aye, Jinnie's finishing next week in a' so jist leave it oan the sideboard'. Girls in that job came and went as quickly as it took to step through one of the many doors they opened each day and, in the end, she wasn't really going anywhere – just to the doctor's surgery a few doors down.

"Uch, it'd dae ye gid tae hae a pairty. Noo, if ye're no going tae eat that then ah am."

Rachel pushed aside her empty glass, leaned across the wide table and drew Maggie's knickerbocker glory towards her.

"Ah thought ye bought me that as a toast," Maggie muttered, but she had lost her appetite and didn't put up a fight. Instead, she clasped her hands under the table and watched.

Each booth that lined the walls of Cafe d'Jaconelli was filled to the point of bursting. It was a cacophony of clinking glass, bickering children and laughing adults that seemed loud enough to be heard all the way at the Botanic Gardens. Those who had been lucky enough to get a table did well to gloat: a queue was forming at the till for a wee pokey hat to takeaway and a few stragglers stood about hopefully, unwilling to take their ice cream into the cold.

As always, the ambiance was a warm hug on a cool plate but the company was turning the air sour. Unbeknownst to his mother, a wee boy with bright rosy cheeks was succeeding in his attempt to climb through the sweet cigarette smoke and scale the low partition of the adjoining booth. His head appeared over the wooden precipice behind Rachel but Maggie did not acknowledge his stare, for nothing existed beyond convincing her friend to leave her alone.

"Ah could ask Christopher alang," Rachel said.

"Wha's Christopher?"

"The new lodger. A doctor. At the Southern General."

"And …"

"He's thirty-twa, wae black hair – whit's left o' it – and hus a wee bit fat roon the middle, in a gid way. But I'd jist be asking him tae be polite, mind. Ah'm a lassie, I know whit's proper and a' that, but it'll be a community event."

Rachel moved to scoop some strawberry sauce from the melting ice cream with a wafer but did not get there in time. Maggie could not see where the glob landed and turned away.

"Ye sure ye dinnae want ony?"

"Where are Minnie and Davie?" she asked, craning towards the door. "Ah thought they wir meant tae be meetin us hauf an hoor ago."

"Uch, ye know whit newlyweds are like. They hae a mind o' their ain. It isnae like the gid auld days when we hud Minnie tae oorsels."

"That's ayeways the way. Ring oan the finger an' they're aff."

"It must be awfy nice, huving that," Rachel murmured, wistfully gazing at two men who were shrugging into their topcoats. They were laughing amongst themselves and paid her no mind, but Maggie followed her gaze and suddenly felt wistful, too. She was too tired and lonely to feign disinterest, and shook her head at the hopelessness of it all.

"Ah cannae imagine a laddie ah widnae get sick o' efter a week," she admitted. "Tak oor Jess. Ah've seen mair o' her since her weddin than that man o' hers. Jist as weil the rate they fight. Anymair time the gither and wan wid end up deid!"

"Wha'll end up deid?" Minnie asked.

She had just appeared at the end of the table with Davie blowing into her fine blonde hair to make her giggle. Typical, the few seconds Maggie had torn her eyes away they had landed. He guided her into the booth and she did not let go of his hand until he had helped her out of her coat and hung it on the stand beside him. Like a magazine model, her grace was effortless and she sank into the seat beside Maggie. The warm red of her heavy woollen dress contrasted perfectly with the light inflections of her hair and, even with thick grey stockings and boots, she had a sparkle that no other girl could emulate. She was glowing, yet she shuddered as if she had been completely de-robed. Clearly, her happiness did not transcend her sensibilities.

Her husband reached across the table and rubbed her shoulder in concern – the picture of true love or the truly sickening, Maggie could not decide. The only certainty was that there was enough heat going around to melt all the ice cream in the cafe.

Minnie had been her friend since school and had only met Davie two years earlier, on the Townhead tram. In the course of that twenty minute journey their fates had been sealed: the clerk and the coalman. He provided for her, followed after her, and loved her with each step. Catching the unabashed adoration in each intercepted glance, Maggie was often struck by the contrast between this relationship and the marriage of her cousin. In comparison, Jess's love seemed like a glum resignation. But then, Maggie had no experience of how love worked.

"Have ye had a gid day?" she asked.

"Weil, ah didnae see Mr Hepburn a' day so that wis gid." Forgetting she was cold, Minnie leaned forwards and grinned. "And Sandra got a wig fae Kember's that disnae sit straight. She reminds me o Daft Daisy, that wan. So we hud a right laugh."

"But ye shouldnae be workin," Davie said, so softly that the girls could hardly hear him. He cleared his throat and continued more confidently. "She knows she can dae onythin she wants tae, but it disnae look gid, ma lassie gaun oot tae work."

Minnie sighed but smiled up at him all the same. "Och, Davie, if ah didnae go oot and jist sat in the flat a' day, ah'd go batty."

"We were jist talking aboot Maggie's birthday."

"In the name o' the wee man! Gie it a rest, Rachel! Did yer mammy no' tell ye tae close yer mooth when ye eat?"

Maggie bristled. So much for finally leaving all that behind. A glob of cream was sliding down Rachel's chin and she wiped it with the heel of her hand just before it could drip onto her pink jumper.

"Is it still a bit too soon, hen?" Davie asked gently, leaning forward to take her hand, a fleeting moment that showed more kindness than Rachel or Minnie had been able to conjure between them.

Maggie nodded and pulled it back. "We wir talking aboot how ah'm no' celebratin this year. It's weeks late and ah dinnae feel like it."

"But if she leaves it ony later the hale thing'll be o'er."

"Ah've jist said ah dinnae feel like it. And it's been and gone already. The hale thing *is* o'er. Tae a'body except you."

Minnie sipped thoughtfully from the china cup that had just been delivered by a harassed looking Amelia Jaconelli, as if she hadn't heard a word her friend had just said.

"Yer twenty-first, Maggie. Rachel's right enough. Ye cannae get that back."

"Ah've telt her," Rachel agreed.

Maggie wanted to scurry away into the back kitchen with the Jaconellis and shut the door fast.

"If ye wannae hae a pairty wae oot me, dinnae let me staund in yer way. Or find some other reason fir Rachel tae go oot wae a laddie."

The couple wore blank expressions but Rachel's eyes flashed with the plans already forming in her head. There was no point in staying around any longer. The day had taken its toll and she needed to breathe.

"If ye'll excuse me, ah huv tae get up early in the morn fir ma new joab. Ye a' seem tae hae forgotten that thir's mair goin oan than sortin' a knees up."

"But it's only the back o' five."

She did not care. Fumbling with her head scarf, she rose and waited for Minnie to let her out in an awkward moment when, at last, no one spoke. The girl took her time, smoothing her dress and grabbing the table edge for support. Stuck behind, Maggie threw up her hands in frustration, a thoughtless gesture in a fleeting moment which sent her cup clattering across the table. Tea spilled everywhere. Neighbouring diners jumped at the commotion and Davie's soft apologies floated by, but the time for politeness had shattered with the china. She squeezed past quickly and flung on her coat.

"Dinnae be rude! Come sit back here fir a wee bit!"

Maggie was barely listening. She ignored their bewildered faces and frantic attempts to salvage pieces of china as she stormed out onto Maryhill Road, stumbling on the slick cobbles in her haste to leave, never once considering that they were trying to help. The weight of her burden made each step a struggle but somehow she managed to fly through the chilling February rain.

"It's tae soon, it's tae soon," she whispered, praying her mother would hear.

There was no one close, but she could feel a presence on her shoulder, watching over her, still able to protect. Pushing through each frosty breath, she wanted to halt time and stay in the moment, when they were almost together.

FOUR

The Skunk

Finally, she was home. Hours earlier she had ventured into the dark clutches of the cold winter's morning with the optimism of starting a new chapter but she returned only with frustration. Her left stocking was sodden, her boots were saturated, and her clomp was more of a squelch reverberating damply down the close. It was ten steps from the entrance to her front door, distance enough for her footfalls to herald her approach, but when the front door slammed, her father expected to see a kitten with soft paws and a feeble bite.

"How wis yer last day at work?" he asked.

"Awright."

He finished wringing a shirt through the mangle and hung it on the pulley, his right arm cranking the rope, hoisting the pulley into the air while the other hung limp by his side. The checked shirt he wore was just as crinkled as the one he hoisted, its sleeves rolled up amidst a hard day's work. She removed her stockings and hung them on the fireguard to dry, her mind still two blocks away at Jaconelli's. Her friends would still be there, laughing and talking; she dreaded to think about what.

That was where her mind remained, so she did not notice Big Stevie sitting by the range. His cough startled her and she dropped her boots to the ground.

"Bloody... I never saw ye there! Daddy didnae say ye were coming o'er the day. Can ye pass up the...?"

She held out her hand for the wooden shoe last and stuffed it in one boot, noticing straight away the sole had pulled free.

"Yer Uncle Stevie's come by tae pick up Olivia."

Big Stevie stared at the floor and twirled his flat cap.

"Aye, hen. Ye were right whit ye said tae me afore. Ah've jist been taken on doon at the docks and they have a fair workload on, what wae the new Government contracts and awthin' else, so it's lookin' up. Then I thought aboot whit ye said, aboot us taking Olivia back and I knew it wis time. Ah can support her noo and she needs tae be wae her family."

"Och, I'm happy for ye. I telt ye everything wid work oot in the end. Why are ye no o'er at Aunt Agnes's hoose getting the wean right noo?"

"Neutral territory," Arthur said, whiskers twitching, and suddenly the dark day seemed lighter.

"That's rare. Thir's nothing mair important than family."

Sitting by the range, Big Stevie was such a familiar sight, yet so different to the fine figure he had cut, slumped there at the funeral. That day, most things had passed in a blur but some God-awful moments had stayed with her, like when he had shunned everyone else and she felt obligated to stay.

"How's work going?" she had asked him then.

"Dribs and drabs." He had shrugged, ruffling his son's curly brown hair and sending him off to play once more. Then, whenever Stevie's four-year-old curiosity was back on the floor next to his sister, out of earshot, he had whispered, "Thir's jist nuthin goin. An' e'en if thir wis, wha'd wannae hire me?"

"Dinnae say that." Maggie had scolded.

"It's true. Look at me."

"Awa get a haircut then. Seriously, somethin's gonnae happen, ah can feel it. Yer luck's gonnae change and ye'll get yer wee lassie back."

It had been a stupid, baseless promise.

"Did ye see Margaret afore she left? Ah couldnae believe it. Her sister's jist died and she couldnae stay fir more than an oor afore runnin oot the door."

"She came tae the church. That's something," Maggie had murmured, grateful that here was one person who was too drunk to tiptoe around her feelings.

"Did ye see whit she wis wearing? A' that sequins and that ruffly bit at the bottom ye lassies seem tae like so much, ye'd hae thought she'd been aff tae the dancing."

Maggie had adjusted her own wide-brimmed hat self consciously.

"And she'd hae the pick o' that God-awful big shop o' hers, could hae picked onythin, onythin and she picked that."

He had leaned forwards and she recalled thinking that he might fall off his chair.

"Ah remember when we were wee and it wis ayeways Clara and Agnes who would bicker. Bicker bicker bicker. Nae stopping them. Wha had the doll first, wha wis gettin mair attention fae daddy, wha's knickers were mair twistet, oan and oan. Ah couldnae get away fae it. Ah think it wis cause they were the auldest. Margaret and me, well, we were the weans and got the attention, so didnae mak a fuss. But noo … noo it's Clara and Agnes wha look efter awbody, really like, and Margaret jist swans aboot wae this lifelong sense o'… whit's that word?"

"Entitlement."

"Ah cid hear ye talkin o'er there wae yer daddy. Dae ye know why Clara wis so quick tae get doon that schail and sort oot yer teacher?"

Maggie did. She had heard it many times. It was as familiar to her as Big Stevie's slurred speech and the rambling sentences that threatened to go nowhere.

"It wis cause o' oor Margaret. Ah mind, ah dae. Walked intae that classroom jist as Mr Leven wis bringin doon the liffey on her bare airms. No' a better or quieter wee lassie in all o' Pollockshaws. Now her airms a' black and blue. It wisnae richt, so ah picked up a slate and threw it at his heid!"

"Then legged it."

Big Stevie had ignored her and gazed into the range, finding his memories there. "Margaret, or wee Maggie back then, saw a wee drop o' blood and shouted, 'He's kilt him! Stevie's kilt him!' Aye, she wis fiert, poor lassie. He deserved it though. She hudnae done onythin wrang. Quiet as a moose, so she wis. Eager tae please, in a'. But she didnae know the name o' the river which gangs through Dublin, so there wis her clue. Bloody Liffey. Bloody bugger. Ah didnae hit him near hard enough."

He had cleared the phlegm from his throat and swallowed it.

"Clara, she wis like oor mammy afore yon alki moved in, and efter. Her and Agnes both, did awthin fir Maggie and me, but she couldnae help wae that blastet Mr Leven. She tried. Went up tae the schail when she wis barely mair than a wean hersel' and he jist shooed her richt oot again. Ah mind when ye were born and she said tae me, thir's no' gonnae be a Mr Leven fir ma Maggie. And neither thir wis."

"Sometimes it felt like thir wis," Maggie heard herself admit. "Dae ye think that's why she's the way she is?"

"Naw. Ah'm done making excuses fir her. She's auld enough tae tak care o' hersel. Ah bet that auld man she's married tae … Whit's his name?"

Just like that, the conversation had shifted from her absent aunt to the extended family, which was incrementally less hurtful.

"James."

"Aye, aye, James. Weil, ah bet he has some important business tae attend tae that couldnae wait until the morrow. Like a lassie has a run in her stocking or some such."

"I thought they might hae brought James wae them."

"James wis here. In that bloody swanky suit. Like he wis the wan at the pearly gates trying tae impress. An' that monocle. Pretentious bloody…"

"No, no' that James. Wee James. He's attending the University. Law. First wan in the whole family tae study and he's going tae be a lawyer. You remember that, don't ye, Uncle Stevie?"

"Aye, weil, the things ye can dae when yer daddy's loaded." Big Stevie had snorted deep back into his throat and spat the residual phlegm on the floor.

She had stared as the thick white pool ran into putrid yellow and the spit lay unapologetically on the ground. Clara would have been so disappointed. Grief could make people do unexpected things but, ensnared in her own heartache, she did not have to watch so had walked away, leaving the broken family in peace as she thanked Reverend Bowman for her touching service and acknowledged the commiserations of her friends, showing more grace than she felt.

It may have been that brutal dissection of her absent Aunt Margaret which kept the conversation fresh in her mind, or perhaps she was merely desperate to keep alive the memory of a woman who seemed more than happy to be forgotten. No matter, it was a changed man who sat before her, focusing on the other sister – the one who was still alive and forever making her presence known. His foot covered the same spot as his phlegm had lain weeks before. His shoes were clean and polished.

"If Agnes thinks ah cannae look efter ma ain lassie, ah'm gonnae get her telt!" he barked, slapping the knee of his blue suit while his tormented dark eyes sparkled with a clarity and focus that Maggie had not seen since the Bennie clan lost him to drink.

She turned towards the pulley and unwound all her daddy's hard work to retrieve a jumper that still felt damp to touch, desperately busying her hands while her thoughts careened backwards to the events that had brought them to that point. Thanks to her uncle's drunken ramblings, she could clearly envisage all those incidents that she had not witnessed firsthand.

It had all begun during a particularly bad influenza outbreak when the children were still so young. Beautiful, untameable Daisy Bennie had contracted the virus early that year and was admitted to Ruchill Hospital before the city had descended into such uproar and confusion that she would have been allowed to die in her own bed. Unfortunately, she caught it while there was still some semblance of order, but the hospital was filling fast. It struck, sudden as a thunder clap, her face pallid with green veins protruding high on her cheeks and her hair sticking damply to her head. It was shades darker than its normal sunny blonde, and that was all before the van from Ruchill Hospital for the Contagiously Ill had shown up, just after lunchtime, to take her away. Only Big Stevie had been allowed to remain with her in the house and had tucked her blanket more securely under her shoulders while they readied her to leave.

Maggie never saw Daisy again. Neither did Big Stevie, but the reports that slowly filtered into the *Glasgow Herald* were enough to send him diving for the bottle where the sticky residue in each glass accompanied his conjecture. It should have been his escapist haze but, instead, it made his worst fears reality. Maggie had listened through the kitchen door the first night he had lost himself to booze, when the earliest report alluding to the dire conditions had gone to print but before things had fully come to light. She had been woken by the crash as he stumbled into the hallway and ignored Clara's cries that he should have been home with the children. His ramblings were not for his children, but his wife.

"Naebody'll be explaining tae her…aye tae busy…shiverin' in a corner…in wae the usual – diphtheria, cholera an' the rest…no enough room…concoction o' disease, is whit the papers say… left tae soil themsels, in a'…no' gid at strife, oor Daisy…she winnae be able tae close her eyes tae it … tae much pain … prayin fir the weans … she'll want tae come hame…Jesus Christ."

Maggie's rounds as a message girl had made her privy to early rumours while malpractice allegations were still being hidden, hearing snippets about doctors' drinking and philandering, and the neglect. She could picture her Aunt Daisy's face amongst it all but those were not images to share with her uncle; she reported straight to Doctor Bowman, instead. Soon, detailed horrors began to filter out and the whole city united in outrage against the medics who argued that the poor souls were dying already; dying at such a rate, in fact, that it was impossible to discard one set of bodies before another batch was brought in. As if that could excuse them drinking and self-medicating the days away, fornicating amongst the anguish and decay while the patients were left untreated.

Had he known at the start, Big Stevie would not have sat by so quietly, wringing his hands in the depths of his small tenement flat with Stevie bouncing in his arms and tiny Olivia playing with her dolly on the floor. His wife had died in agony, crammed amongst strangers, completely alone. It made it tough to lay the blame at his door when he started to drink so hard and why, looking at him three years later, Maggie was heartened by the healthy flush of colour in his cheeks.

"Believe me," he continued, engaging in his enthusiasm, "if ye'd been ten years younger when oor Clara died, that bloody Agnes wid hae whisked ye aff tae live wae her afore yer daddy could say a 'haud yer horses'."

"Ah widnae be so sure aboot that." Arthur objected. "Ah'd hae marched right roond there and no' left wae oot ma wean if she'd dared try ony o' that wae me in the first place, that is."

"Miby yer right. Miby that's whit ah should hae done."

"Naw, dinnae be stupid. Yer circumstances didnae allow it. Ye did the right thing at the time, but Olivia belangs wae her faither and Agnes will respect that. Just gie her a wee bit time. She's grown awfy fond o' Olivia. It's tae be expected. She's a gid lassie."

"Aye, she is that. She is that."

Big Stevie pushed his hair behind his ears and cracked his huge knuckles impatiently. Maggie wondered where young Stevie was. Seeing her uncle sober and without his son really was a day of firsts.

~

"Weil, that's why ah'm here, onyway. So yer daddy can mak sure me and ma big sister behave oorsels and dinnae upset the wean. He's bin tellin me aboot this new job o' yours – "

A loud banging on the front door interrupted him and all three of them jumped. By the time Maggie reached the hall, Aunt Agnes had already breached the shutter entrance. Barely recognisable under a thick wool hat pulled low, her red leather shoulder bag gave her away. It shook slightly as she trembled there in the hall, but whether from the cold or funnelled agitation, it was impossible to tell.

"This is pure ridiculous," she spat.

Squeezing in behind, Olivia beamed up at her cousin. She wore an old hand-me-down of Maggie's; a long coat of sky blue with white trim on top of tough brown boots. Maggie knew it looked better on Olivia than it ever had on her, what with the light shade matching Olivia's eyes and blending with her sunny blonde hair, and when Jess entered she was a complete contrast in a sensible brown coat, with her hat pulled down to eyebrows furrowed tight against the cold. Like her mother, the weight of the world sat heavily on her shoulders.

"Come awa' in," Maggie beckoned. "Are Wee Ena and Donald no' wae ye?"

"It's a bloody miserable day tae be walking the streets like this." Aunt Agnes snapped. With the sharp tongue of the Bennie clan, she lacked the grace that others had to go with it.

Jess moved quickly to her side, glancing at Maggie as she put down the small case she had been carrying. She straightened her mother's fingers and pulled off each glove slowly. Agnes held her icy hands against Maggie's cheeks, snorting when she did not get the reaction she hoped for. Her fingers bent in on themselves, all signs pointing to the rheumatism getting worse, but Maggie squeezed her elbows lightly and turned to Olivia.

"Is that a' yer stuff, hen?" she asked.

Jess held up the small grey case again. "A'thing's in here, rarin tae go."

It appeared to have as many threads falling outside as the meagre pittance inside. Using it to usher Olivia forwards, Jess kissed Maggie on the way past and flicked her new white whisp with affection. Olivia giggled, her mouth hanging open in amazement.

"Ah'm a skunk!" Maggie teased. The young girl smiled sweetly.

"Paul's oan leave next week an' he's comin hame, so ye winnae see me fir the next wee while."

Jess's grey eyes twinkled, remembering the good times rather than the fights which were fast becoming family legend.

"How?"

She lowered her voice as Olivia was pulled into the kitchen by Aunt Agnes's inflexible fingers.

"Weil, ah'll be tae busy in the bedroom."

"Uch, dinnae. Ah dinnae want tae know," Maggie cringed but, like reading Rachel's clandestine copy of Lady Chatterley's Lover behind the bin shed, she wanted to know everything; a taste of the dangerously forbidden that made her feel so grown up and like an inexperienced child, all at the same time. She could count on one hand the number of boys she had kissed at the dancing and, until she could face it again, this was as close to living as she was going to get.

"Weil, ah'll be surprised if ah can remember onything. It's bin months, Maggie, seems mair like years since ah've seen him." Jess totted up the time on her fingers but quickly lost track.

"It cannae be that long. Ye've only been married six."

"It feels like an age. Ah'm telling ye, dinnae ever marry a merchant seaman. He's mair married tae the sea than he'll ever be tae you."

The two girls stood for a moment thinking about that, and Maggie knew that only the toughest love could possibly bear it. She had heard Rachel talk of finding the love in the foreign lands that they both read about in storybooks, of great adventures laced with peril that would leave the lovers unsure which way to turn, but Maggie was not so wistful. Her heart was a vast empty space and, when it was filled, it would be filled completely. She looked at her cousin, who was often described as handsome but rarely pretty, with the cleft chin and short hair, who never dressed up to impress like so many of her peers; the girl who had always been able to teach her so much. To Maggie, there was no one finer but she could not feel Jess's usual wisdom emanate through her current distress, only a throbbing longing that was infectious.

"Ye must come o'er again themorrow on yer ain, Jess."

She was about to say something more but was interrupted by the loud rumbling of ongoing sibling debate from the kitchen.

"Ah don't know whit yer causing a' this fuss o'er." Agnes was furious. "That lassie is fine wae me. She hus three square meals and a roof o'er her heid."

That lassie stood between her father and aunt, wide eyed and rigid.

"Ah appreciate that but she belangs wae her faither. Ye should see it, hen – ah hae a proper steady joab and ah'm getting masel a' set up noo."

"Aye, fir how lang afore yer back oan the bottle and up tae yer usual tricks? Wae twa weans relyin on ye, it's a disgrace!"

"Ah winnae dae that!"

"If ye tak her back noo, ah winnae pick up the pieces when awthin fa's apart. Ah huv ma ain family tae deal wae. An' Margaret's tae busy being rich, and she's got that James, so ye winnae find ony help there. And we dinnae hae oor Clara onymair, although no doubt she'd sort awthing oot like that."

She attempted to click her fingers and managed a loud one. Arthur shoved a cup of tea into her hands and a chair under her bottom, and her hard eyes fixed on him.

"Whit aboot you, Arthur? What dae ye make o' all this?"

"Ah'm no' becoming a pairt o' a' this arguing, and dinnae bring Clara intae it, either. She wis ma wife and better than this. Fir what it's worth ah'll tell ye, though, blood is the strongest bond thir is, Agnes. All o' us here understaund yer doubts. But the laddie just wants tae be a gid faither. It's commendable."

"Wait a wee minute here. Whit dae ye mean *wants tae be*, Arthur Munroe? Ah'll tell ye noo that I *will* be a gid faither!"

"Calm doon. Ye'll dae the best ye can and we will a' be here tae support ye. Won't we Agnes?"

But Agnes continued on her own path, her voice icily clear. "And whit happens when she grows up like her mammy? Eh? Already ye can see that woman all o'er her. The bright yella hair right doon tae her shufflin walk. And sometimes ah look at her and see the same wull glent in her een. Dinnae look at me like that, Big Stevie, ye've no seen yer daughter like ah hae these last three years. Ah'm telling ye, ah aye said her mammy wis hauf daft and the fruit disnae fa' far fae the tree."

"That's enough, Agnes." Arthur snapped, his patience spent.

Big Stevie looked as if he had been punched. He knew what people said about his wife behind his back, about the crazy wigs she wore and her habit of talking to a room rather than the people in it, but not his family. Agnes's verbal onslaught hammered into him and he spat at the fire, as if to rid himself of the words as they hit him hard, for it was not in his nature to broadcast that it was all those quirks that had made him love Daisy most.

Glancing down, Maggie saw Olivia forgotten and adrift. She gripped her dolly tightly in both hands and it hung sadly in front. Maggie knew that if she could cry then this is what it would feel like. She bent down quickly.

"Are ye awright there, hen?"

Olivia nodded slowly and Maggie pulled her into a hug; the kind of hug she dreamed of getting from her own mother every day. Squeezing the girl tight and trying to occupy her with the doll she kept so close, she knew Big Stevie was right: Olivia needed a proper family home, which was so much more than her Aunt's embittered shelter.

"Och, dinnae encourage her wae that bloody doll. She's near eight years auld aready and disnae talk or hae ony friends – jist that stupid thing. It's in her blood already. Daft, daft, daft. The lot o' them. You in a', " she turned back to her brother and spat, "Daft!"

"Dinnae you listen tae that nonsense." Maggie spoke softly, ignoring Jess's defensive scowl. "I think yer dolly's the maist bonnie wan ah've ever seen. Whit's her name?"

The child shrugged and Maggie understood the doll did not have a name. It seemed fitting.

"Are they her things?" Big Stevie asked, nodding at the near-empty suitcase.

Reluctantly, Jess brought it forward and cast a glance at her mother, but Big Stevie did not wait for the conversation to continue. He grabbed it up, took his daughter by one mittened hand and left, thanking Arthur with his whole heart and pointedly saying polite goodbyes to the rest on the way out. Naturally timid, Olivia did not look back.

It was over quickly, like a gust of wind had blown in and swept them out in a flurry. Arthur let out a low whistle as the shutter door slammed, patting his sister-in-law's hand sympathetically, but she just shook her head and glared, silently berating. She did love the girl in her own way and suddenly, thanks to Arthur, she was gone. Her twisted hand trembled as she struggled to connect tea cup with saucer and, in an instant, Maggie understood that there would not be a good outcome to any of it.

PART TWO

The Middle

FIVE

July Heat

1939

A man walked into a doctor's office. Removing his black fedora, he ran a hand over his slick dark hair, smoothed down his thin moustache and surveyed the room. Waiting females blushed and turned from his gaze, in awe of the dashing newcomer in the sharp black suit. Each felt the prickle of their spine as his eyes cast over them, begging to be noticed. They would not have felt a greater thrill had it been Clark Gable himself. He had many smiles stored in his repertoire: sincere – useful in matters of business; charming – perfect for young ladies; and endearing – which he saved for older ladies with their own boys at home. It was the latter he prepared as he crossed the waiting room and approached the bent white head of the receptionist who sat engulfed in a padded chair, slouched forward in concentration.

"Hello, I was wondering if I could have an appointment please."

"Yer name?" The woman did not look up from her paperwork.

"Tommy Gunn."

From somewhere beneath the curly white locks, the receptionist erupted, her whole body shaking with laughter. His smile froze.

"I am well aware of the connotations …"

"Awright, Mr Gunn," the woman interrupted, tapping her pen against the desk, "if ye jist gie me some details aboot the kind o' ailment we're dealing wae and then take a seat, Doctor Bowman will be wae ye as soon as he can."

"How long will that be?" he asked, looking behind at the packed waiting room.

"Aboot an hoor."

He kept his opinions tucked behind an innocent grin but she did not look up to see it.

"Oh no. See, I'm a shinty player, very good at it actually, and was in a bit of a collision on Saturday. Now I've got an awful pain in my back which will make sitting very uncomfortable. I don't know how long I can stand it, actually, so please, if there's anything at all you could do then I would be eternally grateful." He lent forwards to catch her eye. "Maybe you could move me forward a bit? I wouldn't tell anyone. It really is a terrible pain."

"Aye, and ah've got an awfy pain in my arse," the woman muttered, unaware of how her voice carried.

"Excuse me?"

"Ye're goin tae hae tae wait o'er there wae a'body else. The doctor will be wae ye as soon as he can."

She spoke slowly, deliberately and finally looked up. He had been about to change his smile to a charming one and seal the deal but, instead, he was blown away. Rather than an elderly lady, he was looking into the delicate face of a pretty young woman. He should have guessed as much from her voice, which dripped with honey-sweet disdain as she teased him. White ringlets bounced around her chin and shone in the sunlight, but her skin was smooth and healthy and her large brown eyes glinted when she saw him trying to reconcile the hair with the rest of her.

"So, Mr Tommy Gunn," she continued, prompted by his silence, "ye were playing shinty and huv a sare back fir yer efforts. Nae problem. Go and sit o'er there noo and the doctor will call ye when he's seen a' his other patients. Ah, Mrs McNulty, how are ye the day?"

Maggie turned away from him, her attention on a new patient who had arrived with a troupe of children in tow. Panting, the woman pushed her weight past him and leaned on the desk. It was a hot day and circles of sweat shone through the multi-coloured cotton print that stretched across her back.

"Ah'm no' very weil tae be honest, neither I am. Ah've jist been talkin' wae ma Kenny aboot the possibility o' the weans being sent

intae the country. It's a' this talk aboot war and bombings, ye see."
She leaned heavily on the desk.

"Whit?"

"Takin' oor kids, pied piper-like. Ah hear things, ye see. Plans
afoot. Efter seeing the state o' those air raid shelters bein built. Ah
saw them in the papers, so ah did. Ah couldnae staund the weans
hiding in there, neither ah could. Look like tin cans. If it comes tae
war, they'll huv tae go, so they will. Ah know that, but it wid be awfy
hard tae dae, so it would. The hoose wid be fair quiet wae oot them.
And noo ma wee Molly's sick tae top it a' aff! She had such a pain in
her chest this month, she cid hardly get oot o' bed an ah didnae hae
the heart tae mak her, neither ah did. Get her tae the doctor quick, I
thought."

There was coughing at the back of the troupe and the girl in
question pushed forward to mumble,

"Jist a wee drink o' watter if it isnae tae much trouble, Miss
Munroe."

Maggie complied and wrote the girl's symptoms on a piece of
card for the doctor. When she rose from her seat, Tommy craned
around the large woman for a better look. Her dress fell casually,
showing curves that had previously been hidden and the material
stopped just above the knees, but he was not at an angle to see
any further. In what seemed like a deliberate slight, its large blue
collar swooped down to spotlight her bust but her outstretched arm
blocked his view. He was smitten.

"Aye Mrs McNulty, ye were right tae bring her. The doctor wis
put here on earth tae help wae sickness and we treat every ailment
seriously."

She looked pointedly at him. He held up his palms in submission
and backed away.

"It's time to go home," Doctor Bowman said, shuffling from his office
that night. Not yet fifty, the weight of the world still managed to pull
him down and he looked ready to drop. The effort of lifting his hat to
his head was palpable.

"I'm jist putting the files away fir the morrow. Dae ye want me tae
lock up so you can get away hame?"

"Aye, Maggie, that would be grand."

Maggie was startled. They always left together. He must feel as bad as he looked, stretching into his jacket and heading out as fast as his small steps could take him. As the door shut behind him, the room took on a cavernous quality, every corner lit by the setting sun.

"The loneliest time o' day," Maggie whispered, knowing her mother was in the corner somewhere, listening.

It was quick work putting the files of the last few patients back in the cabinet where they belonged. When she had started there, the place had been a hodgepodge of paperwork, but she had quickly turned things around. Organisation was far from inherent but was a thousand times better than sitting around when patients were scarce, twiddling her thumbs and mulling over her thoughts. She ran her finger through the cabinet drawer to deposit the last one, *Hamill*, and her finger paused a few places too soon. The surname, *Gunn*, written neatly a few hours before in her own handwriting. At the time she had not given it much thought but now the place was empty.

"Should ah?" she asked aloud. There was no answer.

Her fingertips twitched, ready to flick it open. Her mother was a tangible presence at her shoulder, neck craned, hands stuffed expectantly in her pinny. It had been four years since her passing and Maggie did not like to disappoint her, but she could not bring herself to take that one final step. Instead, she deposited the Hamill file, grabbed her cardigan and headed out into the gloaming.

Two weeks later the surgery door tinkled open and a tall gentleman in cool white linens strode in, a veritable vision on Maryhill Road. His black hair was gelled back, determination was chiselled onto his long, tanned face, and more than one female patient fought past their ailments and found the resurgence of energy to fix a loose strand of hair and straighten their skirt as he sauntered past.

"So, you think Tommy Gunn's an amusing name then, Miss Munroe?"

"Not at a', Mr Gunn. Rhoda Pony left ten minutes ago, ye jist missed her."

She was surprised to see him again and he laughed too long and too hard at her mediocre joke.

"It's true. Ah never discuss the patients but ye take yer name so seriously, ah thought ye'd like tae know there are others oot there like ye."

"Well, that's reassuring." His smile wavered.

"Whit can ah dae fir ye the day? Playin shinty at the weekend, were ye?"

He ran a hand through his hair and gave her a prolonged flash of pearly whites. So much for small talk.

"Erm, I woke up this morning and my head felt like a playing field for a brass band."

"How's it noo?"

"Better. Slightly."

"I see. Did ye go oot last night?"

"What?"

"Did ye go oot. Tae the pub or the dancing? Maybe hae wan tae many?"

"Of course not."

"Awright, dinnae be offended. Ah'm jist tryin tae find the cause o' this heid o' yours. Help the gid doctor oot. After a', as ah keep telling ye, Mr Gunn, he is a Very. Busy. Man."

"Look, I just came here today to see you. Is there anything wrong with that?"

"Not at a', Mr Gunn."

She fixed him with a meaningful stare and felt vindicated by the involuntary flush beneath his eyes. Stuck behind the desk, it was liberating for her to hear his lines before he had uttered them and match them with a few of her own.

Sitting back in the huge chair, she clasped her hands on her lap. He thought she looked like an angel.

"Please don't call me Mr Gunn. It's Tommy."

When they shook hands, he felt supple skin that conflicted with her harsh tongue. It excited him; he could feel it pressing against his trousers for all the world to see. He let her go quickly.

"I'm Maggie," she admitted, going beyond the long wooden plaque on her desk that announced Miss Munroe to the world. "Ye dinnae hae a sare heid, dae ye?"

"No. My back's a lot better though. Doctor Bowman really knows what he's doing."

"Aye. He's a gid doctor. That's why we dinnae like time wasters."

"Apologies for that. But, you see, I don't know anything about you or how else I could have gotten in touch. Do you live close by? Do you go out to the dancing? Do you have a boyfriend? At least I don't see a ring on your finger."

"I like tae dance," she told him flatly, not flinching when he moved in to scrutinise her bare hands.

"I like to dance, too."

In his mind, he ran his fingers over her body, feeling her under his skin. He would test every inch of her, see how she responded, react as she wanted, even if she did not realise that she wanted anything at all. Nothing would be left unsavoured. The power of imagination was potent and was doing nothing to quell his erection. He glanced over his shoulder but the women in the waiting room all seemed to have their eyes glued to his face.

"I go to the Barrowlands most Saturday nights."

"So dae I. If ah'm no' somewhere else. It's a wonder ah've no' seen ye there afore."

"It is. I'm sure you will though. Very soon."

He threw her a wink and left her with that thought, imagining her swooning with anticipation. His confidence was palpable as he lit a cigarette and turned onto the street, heading north towards the house of a busty young chambermaid under his supervision at The Beresford Hotel.

SIX

The Barrowland Ballroom

She was there. A coincidence. Bad luck.

"Why did ye have tae say ye'd meet Minnie and Davie here?" she groaned.

Rachel shrugged. Her bent head revealed an unflattering squint in her ginger parting but all she was concerned with was tucking her new pink dress up to raise the hemline. It had the same floating skirt and short sleeves that Minnie often wore but she was determined to wear it better. She put on a fair helping of lipstick and passed it over, and Maggie grabbed at it thankfully. If her daddy could see her now, he would never approve. They puckered their lips at each other and admired the results.

"We ayeways come here," Rachel said belatedly. "How wis ah tae know ye'd hae a man tae avoid? Ah've got a run in ma stockings."

"Och, it'll be dark in there. Naewan'll notice."

"No' that it matters onyway wae legs like mine. Twa great lumps o' meat."

"Dinnae be daft. Naebody'll be bothered aboot yer run or yer legs. They'll a' be tae busy trying tae keep fae tripping o'er Jess's face."

Jess grunted. She had been standing wordlessly beside them for an age, arms folded tight across her chest. The only activity coming from her was sporadic fidgeting as she readjusted the lace trimming of her own dress. She was in a foul mood. Paul's leave had been cancelled indefinitely, with all the talk of war leading him towards a very different kind of navy training than they offered in the merchant fleet.

49

"Ye cannae take it tae heart," Maggie's voice softened. "It's no' his fault. This is oot o' his control."

"Aye, well ah'm no' so sure. Why come hame tae yer wife when ye can huv a lassie in every port?"

"Ye dinnae really think that."

"Weil, ye dae hear aboot them things. Like in the *People's Friend* jist last week," Rachel piped up enthusiastically. "True enough, it wis a story, but the idea hud tae come fae somewhere."

"That isnae helpful," Maggie groaned.

The cleft in Jess's chin deepened in rage.

"Ah knew it! It's nice tae hae someone agree wae me at last."

"Aye, but look who it is. Hardly a tower o' wisdom, is she?"

Rachel ignored her. "At least ye've got that bonnie new dress. The men'll be fa'ing a' o'er themselves fir ye."

"But *he* cannae see it." A pause. "Ah'm thinking aboot leavin him."

Jess's voice trembled as she fidgeted with the fine lace decolletage, looking uncomfortable in all the frills. Her generous makeup was not enough to mask the bitter emotions swirling beneath the facade; bright sweat overpowering the rosy cheeks and ruby lips that shone under the Barrowlands' neon glow.

Maggie hugged her cousin but she had heard all this before. She would only believe it when Jess stopped wearing her wedding band.

"He's ne'er gien ye ony reason tae doubt him."

"But I do onyway." Jess shrugged, chest heaving, unable to control the doubt that ate at her.

The hazy summer sun sunk low to the west, a smudged gaslamp up high that turned the sooty tenements and worn cobbled streets cherry red for a brief second, a blink of fire from heaven. The trundle of the Townhead tram faded in the direction of the sun while the Saturday night foot traffic continued at a steady pace. The bright lights overhead flickered slightly as they geared up for the long night ahead. Maggie looked skyward. The Man Pushing Wheelbarrow that illuminated the entrance to the Barrowland Ballroom looked down on her and winked. Maybe, if she asked politely, he would pick her up and wheel her away from an angry cousin, an unhelpful friend and a potential meeting with an ego the size of Scotland.

"Plus, noo Minnie and Davie hae moved doon the Gallowgate, comin here jist maks sense." Rachel returned to their earlier conversation, grinning at a passing group of men as she continued to hike her skirt up to levels that no one else would dare. She failed to notice that the higher she pulled, the more squint it became.

"Whit aboot the Palais? Lauri Blandford and his band are playin the nicht. Or the Locarno, even?"

"Laurie Blandford plays every nicht. Ye're bein unreasonable, Maggie."

"Ah didnae ask fir yer tuppence worth, Jess. If ah'd known ye were going tae side against me ah'd huv left ye mopin aboot at hame."

Wondering as usual where on earth Minnie and Davie could be, she kicked lightly at a cluster of pebbles on the ground. They hopped to freedom and she watched them scatter; anything rather than witness Rachel preening, pouting and systematically destroying all the natural appeal that God had given her.

"You will ruin your shoes doing that."

The voice was familiar, deep and melodic, regrettably beautiful and lilting through the air like sweet molasses. Maggie spun towards it; to Tommy Gunn, who stood slouched and smoking against the wall. From his crisp black jacket to the jaunty slant of his Fedora, he looked flawless as he walked forward to greet her, a shimmering silhouette before the setting sun. There was nowhere else to look but into his cool blue eyes.

He bent forward and planted a kiss on her cheek.

"Och, hello there," she mumbled, hoping the girls could not hear her.

"I'll meet you inside, John," he called, stepping back but keeping his attention on her. A sandy-haired man had been standing to one side unnoticed, erect and stiff in a high collar and tie. He nodded to Tommy and looked curiously at Maggie on his way past. She smiled at him and his round face brightened.

"Yer friend?" she asked.

"Yes. The best. He's visiting from the country. And these lovely ladies must be *your* friends."

"Friend and cousin," Maggie corrected, making the introductions. Both girls were unusually quiet, strict observers.

"So you made it after all?"

"Ah had nothing tae dae wae it. Rachel here made a' the plans. Ah'm jist following alang."

"Then I'm eternally grateful to Rachel."

The fluttering of the poor girl's heart at the mention of her name was palpable and her face turned the same colour as her hair and dress mixed together.

"Whatever the reason, it's good to see you Maggie. Can I take your arm inside?"

She screwed her lips. "Ah'm waiting on some mair pals. Ye'd better go in efter that John, onyway, and save the country bumpkin fae the Weegies."

"I suppose you're right. It was good to meet you, girls."

He bowed graciously and disappeared into the dance hall. As soon as he had gone Jess spoke up, and she was incredulous.

"*That's* Tommy Gunn? *He's* wha a' this fuss is aboot?"

"Ah know. Whit a belter. Ah dinnae know whit yer aw aboot, Maggie. Really ah dinnae," Rachel chimed in, hands on hips.

Both girls stared at her.

"You twa dinnae understand. A' ye see is a handsome face and ye think he's Prince Chairmin. He's tae smooth fir ma likin. Met me wan time and expected me tae fa' at his feet. And fae the looks o' ye, that's exactly whit he's used tae. Ah widnae trust him as far as ah cid throw him. Ma mammy telt me tae trust ma gut and that's whit ah intent tae dae, nae matter how gid he looks."

"At least she's admitted he's handsome." Jess nudged Rachel with her elbow and they both started laughing. Boys had always been interested in Maggie Munroe but for the first time she seemed to have let one under her skin.

"Look, look, look!" Rachel squealed, suddenly pointing at a group of men who were approaching the entrance.

"What are we gawpin at?" Maggie asked, scrutinising the group.

None was particularly tall, none particularly broad, therefore none was Rachel's usual type. Jess looked like she couldn't care less and turned away towards the Gallowgate in search of Minnie.

"That laddie, the wan in the middle, that's Sam."

"Sam yer lodger?"

"Aye."

"The wan wha's staggerin?"

It might have been a trick of the light, the way the sun's glare struck straight down from the west and bounced off the cobbles, but she saw a blonde-haired man in a tweed suit, about her own height, stumble over nothing. His tall friend seemed to grab him before he hit the street and he laughed, never glancing their way. Reluctantly,

Jess glanced over her shoulder to see who they were discussing but by then the crowd had moved inside and it was too late.

"He's a schoolie." Rachel fidgeted with her belt, pulling her back up straight. Maggie narrowed her eyes.

"Is this why we're here?" she asked suspiciously. "Why we couldnae possibly go tae the Locarno?"

"How wis ah tae know he'd turn up?"

Rachel turned round to join Jess staring the other way but Maggie was not finished. She ran full circle to stay in her friend's sight.

"This isnae a gid idea, hen."

"Whit isnae?"

"Gettin a' attached tae yer lodger." She almost added *What wid yer mammy think?*, but she knew Mrs Campbell well enough to leave that thought well alone.

"Och, but he's braw, Maggie. He's a schoolie."

She threw up her hands. "Aye, ye've said."

Their conversation was cut short by Minnie and Davie skipping down the street towards them. Davie cleaned up in a blue suit and Minnie looked beautiful in the same pink dress that Rachel wore, the shade of strawberries. Their friends could not hear what he was whispering but her laughter carried and Jess's eyes filled with tears.

"Ye're bonnie the night," Minnie told her as soon as she was within earshot.

She sucked at her cigarette, making a show of it from the long, enamelled holder. It had been a present from her man. Jess's smile was tight but Minnie slipped an arm into hers and strolled towards the entrance. Davie was right behind and Rachel linked with Maggie to follow suit, a sallow imitation of the gorgeous figure who led the way. There was no one left for Maggie to roll her eyes at but she did it anyway, passing reluctantly through the entrance to the Barrowland Ballroom.

Suddenly, a honey tobacco laced the air and the world intensified. Billy McGregor and the Gaybirds were in full swing and the hall was packed with girls lining the walls waiting to be asked and boys standing in tentative groups, preparing to do the asking. The dim light was blinding after the balmy summer night and the place was full to bursting, an Aladdin's cave of active hormones. Underlining the thumping tunes from the band came the unmistakable twitter of the crowd and the sweet whiffs of illicit drink. Maggie could already feel her spirit lift and her body sway.

The five friends claimed a spot next to the dance floor and carved out a space against the wall where they surveyed everything with feigned disinterest. They had only been there for a few moments when Jess excused herself and disappeared into the throng.

"Is she awricht?" Minnie asked.

"Aye," Maggie assured her, smiling. "But how are things wae you, anyway, doon the Gallowgate?"

"Aye, it's braw. A wee bit different but it's gid tae be close tae the toon and a' that."

Davie pulled her close and whispered in her ear, determined to be heard over the music. He wrapped his arms around her waist and she laughed.

"He says he could dae wae a wee bit male company cause he husnae seen a laddie in twa weeks! Apairt fae oan the job. Davie's ne'er been mair happy luggin coal."

"If ye want mair laddies aroon', wait til ah tell ye somethin aboot a man," Rachel shouted, leaning closer to fill them in on Tommy. The story unravelled quickly but, describing his arrival, she took liberties over Maggie's reluctance, failing to mention her own reaction, or Sam, at all.

"Ah've ne'er seen ye like this o'er a laddie," Minnie said to Maggie, giggling.

"Like whit?" She shrugged. "Ah've no' said onythin. Ah'm jist staundin here, listening tae the twa o' ye blether oan. Davie, gie's a drink."

He passed over his hip flask. Jess had been gone for a long time. Scanning the crowd, she tried to catch sight of a fawn dress but there was no sign of it.

"Ye want tae dance?" a man asked, walking up behind her and taking her hand.

His calloused fingers itched her skin but Davie was rubbing Minnie's neck while Rachel fidgeted with her belt and searched the room for a dance of her own.

"Go oan then."

"Ah'm John," he said.

She looked up into his face, half-expecting a different John, but there he was. His wrist turned limp as he led her onto the dance floor.

"Ah'm a friend o' …"

"Tommy Gunn," she finished for him. "Ah know. Fae ootside."

"Oh, aye."

He sounded relieved, as if he'd forgotten. His broad face was sweating although they had not yet danced a step and he wriggled down his collar without undoing his shirt buttons. His entire aura was moist. Running a hand through his hair, he may as well have saved his energy. It stood to attention like a line of soldiers poised and ready for action for all of five seconds before falling back down in front of his eyes.

"Shall we?" Maggie took the lead as people waltzed around them.

"Oh, aye," he said again, grabbing her waist and rushing to keep up.

Tommy was watching from the sidelines, his head visible in the middle of a small group of women. He appeared deep in conversation until their eyes met and he smiled a smile that did not quite reach his eyes. With every spin of the waltz, his position changed to observe her. It was easiest just to ignore him, to focus on the music, her swishing blue dress and John's 'One, two, three' whispered beneath a furrowed brow.

"Is there much dancing doon in Wherever Yer Fae?"

"Lanark? Aye, a wee bit, but haud on the noo. I cannae talk or… och!" He trod on her toes, stumbling. "One, two, three… One, two three."

He picked it up again and kept going, and Maggie followed, imperceptibly setting her wrist so it was she who was taking the lead. She had danced with worse but was used to an apology after being stood on, her Aunt Flo and Aunt Annie living proof that good manners were alive and well, even in the countryside.

She knew better than to push for a conversation over his counting so she stared over his shoulder into the middle distance, avoiding Tommy and praying for the song to end. That was when she saw Jess spin past her with tweed-suited Sam, not dancing in his arms as much as propping him up. The fact he was still standing was a wonder as he stumbled through the moves, his right hand low on her back. The distaste was evident in Jess's curled lip and rigid spine, so Maggie was not the only one dying to escape. But the song kept going.

"One, two, three… One, two, three."

John's sweat was extensive and there was a lot of skin for it to accumulate on. She felt her palm grow sticky and kept a polite, safe distance from his broad chest. His brown eyes were crossed in concentration, leaving the swirling small talk in her head unsaid. Meanwhile, Minnie and Davie sailed past, light on their feet, skin barely touching, and she wanted to scream.

Then, finally, the tune started to draw to a close.

"Weil, there we are, then. By, that wis rare," she said quickly and sashayed her way back to Rachel before John remembered to stop counting. Glancing over her shoulder, she saw him standing there, arms still bent in a dancing hold, and felt a pang of regret. She had never intended to be cruel.

"Is ma dress no' sitting richt?" Rachel asked.

"Och, hen, it's early and folk are still getting warmed up. Ma partner needs some practice if ye wannae dance."

Rachel snorted derisively and continued to look around the crowd. After a few moments of silence, Minnie ran over to them, eyes glistening.

"Richt, so oor Davie is awa' wae some laddies fae the work, and this other laddie jist asked me tae dance. Ah telt him ah wis only dancing wae wan man the day, but he said it wis a aboot ma moves, ye see? Hudnae seen anybody wae ma moves since Eleanor Powell, neither he hud."

She paused, and Maggie shook her head while Rachel wriggled her skirt up ever further.

"So?" Minnie pushed. "Should ah dae it?"

"Naw." Maggie kept on shaking her head, unable to stress the point enough. "Davie widnae like it!"

"Someone ought tae tell that tae your Jess." Rachel scowled.

The girl was approaching from the dance floor, guiding Sam through the crowd. He stumbled after her, looking every which way but at his feet.

"This is wan o' yours."

She deposited him with the group, unsmiling.

"Rachel!" Sam shuffled forward, arms outstretched.

Closeby, a couple cast disgusted glances their way but Rachel did not look displeased. Maggie stepped in and put her arm out to block him. He looked at her, sidelong.

"Och, no' you in a', hen, fussing aboot me like ah'm wan o' the weans."

"Dinnae behave like a wean, then," she told him, her arm firmly in place.

"Ah deal wae them every day and know a fair bit mair aboot it than you."

He batted her hand to the side and Jess held her shoulders in restraint. Minnie took that as her cue to return to the dance floor.

"Rachel, whit a bonnie lass, like ayeways. No a lassie. A wuman. A thing o' beauty."

He grabbed her waist on both sides and Maggie forced herself to look away. More people were beginning to stare. Rachel held him by the wrists, suddenly as desperate for propriety as she was for attention, but her grin outweighed her apprehension.

"Ye're awfy affectionate, Mr Belchford. So ye've met Jess?"

"We wur dancin'."

"*Ah* wis dancin'," Jess muttered.

"This is Maggie and this ... oh ... Minnie wis here a minute ago. She'll be richt back."

"Maggie and Minnie? It's a right tongue-twister. Maggie, Minnie, Maggie, Minnie, Maggie, Mingie, Mannie. Sisters?"

"So, who are ye?"

"Ah've telt ye," Rachel said slowly. "This is ma new lodger, Samuel Belchford."

Maggie wondered if the esteemed Samuel Belchford was capable of introducing himself.

"Tell us aboot yerself."

"He's a schoolie," Rachel said.

"Can he no' speak fir himsel'?"

"Ah'm a teacher."

He took a swig from his hip flask and rocked back on his heels. Maggie thought he was going to meet her gaze but, instead, he stared at her chin and shoved his hands in his waist band.

"Ah teach. Ah drink. Ah enjoy ma life, wae an easy-oasy landlady and her bonnie, bonnie daughter. Awa' ben the kitchen recess thegether. If ye ever want yer big bed back, Rachel, ah'm really gid at sharing."

Rachel giggled out from behind her hand and Maggie was too stunned to defend her. He took one final swig, grabbed the hand away from her mouth and disappeared onto the dance floor. He dragged behind him a young girl desperate to be loved, who slicked back some fly-away wisps of her bonnie orange hair and faded into the crowd, out of sight.

Maggie moved to follow. "He cannae talk aboot her like that, Jess, and stoap hauding me back. Whit if he says things like that and she's jist stauning next tae him a' giddy-like? He could say onything, that yin, and word'll get roond."

"He's a bad yin, richt enough, ah had tae watch him every second o' that dance, but he's her lodger and there's no much we can dae. Go o'er there noo, try tae drag her fae that dance flair, ye'll make a fair spectacle o' yersel and lose yer pal intae the bargain."

Jess tentatively let go of her shoulders, moving to one side and scouring the crowd. She was taller by a foot but shook her head.

"Ah cannae see them."

"Whit dae we dae?" Maggie asked.

"Nuthin."

The squeezing in Maggie's stomach did not lessen at this assurance. All she could do was cross her fingers and talk to Rachel in the morning.

Across the hall, John kept his distance. Maggie wished he would cast his eyes somewhere else, she had more important things to worry about. As time wore on, the grease on her palms came from both his sweat and her own, building slowly as her fear for Rachel grew. She talked quietly to Jess and kept her opinions to herself, but inside she was screaming.

When her friend did re-materialise, springing back through the crowd and looking decidedly pleased with herself, it did not waylay Maggie's concerns one bit. Cheeks flushed and eyes glazed, there was a story behind Rachel's demeanour that did not bear repeating. She puffed shallowly on a cigarette and jutted out her chin to avoid the smoke but kept up the pretence that she was enjoying it. Now she was in the lead.

"That's fair worn me oot," she said. "Thank you, Sam. Ye're a lovely dancer."

Jess snorted.

Over the way, Tommy appeared at John's side and soon they were deep in conversation, the thin line of John's mouth unmoving while Tommy held the floor. Maggie tried to focus on Rachel but could see him out of the corner of her eye, the girls close to him swaying a little bit harder, laughing a little bit louder; and when he asked them to dance they became the embodiment of hope. Her friends saw him, too, and their own conversation dropped away as they looked between him and their friend, waiting for action. She could feel their expectation; it was maddening. Her head grew hot under the pressure. Deliberately slitting her eyes, she turned to challenge them until, one by one, they lowered their gaze, a clowder of cats yielding their power.

He danced and cajoled on his side of the divide, but it was the small, bold girl with the shocking white hair that Tommy wanted. To hold the little body that fitted so well under its short blue dress; the very thought overwhelmed him. The lanky blonde from the night before was a grainy memory, her graceless advances quickly tiresome. All night he could have been anywhere, lying on any thin, frayed mattress and gazing out any window pane which was cracked like a spider's web. Any tenement in Glasgow, with any girl.

"Will ye dance?" asked man after man, and Maggie accepted, each face and song blending into the next. Flying around the dance floor, always just out of reach. Until The Gaybirds struck up a foxtrot. Then their eyes finally met. For the first time in a long time she was back amongst her friends without a dance partner and she did not look away. The crowd parted like the Red Sea and he beelined towards her.

"Can I have this dance?"

Maggie looked around to confirm he was talking to her. Her tired, swollen feet and the drouth that burned the back of her throat were all she could think about, but a certain etiquette made it impossible to refuse. Stepping back, she welcomed him into the group.

"Rachel's been complainin a' night aboot how Minnie hogs Davie and winnae share him wae the rest o' us. It's gid tae see anither man, isn't it Rachel?"

Rachel beamed, shifting her weight away from Sam and, for the first time that evening, wriggling her skirt down rather than up. Tommy took the hint and gave a theatrical bow, nodded briefly to the others, and led Rachel to the floor while the Schoolie looked on with passive interest, swirling his Scotch.

Aware of Maggie's stare on his back, Tommy expertly navigated through the crush of bodies and, with his mind full of Maggie, his eyes never strayed from Rachel. He thought of shimmering snow as he looked into vibrant red tresses and imagined expressive brown eyes while dancing with flitting blue ones. How graceless the movements, how clumsy the footfalls in their endless dance floor performance.

"This is rare." Rachel swooned, eyes half-closed as she forgot to pay attention. A loud *crunch* crackled from under her cuban heel. The smile froze on Tommy's face as agony spread from his toe to brain with the speed and intensity of smoke up a flue, but he did not miss a step.

From the sidelines, Maggie caught John's eye. His broad farmer's build was easily recognisable, hands stuffed in pockets and shoulders bent towards the ground like an over-stuffed scarecrow. She raised her eyebrows and laughed at Rachel's laboured attempts, but he blushed under her gaze. As for Tommy, when the song ended, there was no question of a second. His kiss on the cheek was as fleeting as his exit back to safety.

"Your turn now," he stated firmly, grabbing Maggie by the hand.

She seized Davie's hip flask and took a long swig while Minnie selected a cigarette from her enamelled case, lit up, and settled back against the wall to spectate. It turned out she had more than one friend to watch over when Sam grabbed a scowling Rachel and followed them to the dance floor. Acting as a safety net, it had become sticky as the night wore on but he squeezed her waist with startling familiarity and she stumbled nonetheless.

Maggie was pensive and eager. So far, Tommy's movements around the floor had been a showcase as smooth as his words but far more believable. The starched cotton of her summer dress crinkled as he pulled her towards him, clenching the material until he could feel the contours of her skin underneath. The tune changed once again to a waltz, something slow enough to hold her. Looking down on her perfect little face, he saw her body move impatiently to the music and he wished she would look at him rather than at his collar bone as they twirled on.

"You know, they say that if you dance round the hall at the Palais ten times you've danced a mile," he told her.

"Aye, so they say."

"Do you ever go there?"

"The Palais?"

"Yes."

"Aye, ah've been there afore. When ah wis a wee lassie. Weil, mair wee than ah am noo. Afore it burnt doon. Ah've no been since it opened up again, though."

"Maybe I can take you there some other time." He pulled her tighter and they spun. "And the Locarno? What do you think of the dancing there?"

"Aye, it's braw."

She did not elaborate. He sighed.

Her feet felt like two wooden spoons that had been dropped into a big mixing bowl and stirred just right to create something magical. Although the same floor was being trodden and the same beat was being played, the waltz she had shambled through with John was a universe away. Things had suddenly fallen into place, as if they were meant to be.

Up close, his black suit was pristine save for a solitary white hair on his lapel. It was her own. Mentally, she dusted it off but physically kept her hands in place, fixating on it as she twirled round without a care. Finally, she looked up into his thoughtful stare and wondered if she was imagining the glassy adulation in his eyes; a look of intense meaning that was hard to ignore. Dismissing it as a trick, her stomach grew tight. It was unnerving.

Hopelessly, she reverted back to a careful study of his collar while his hand moved down her back. His feet slowed and his face drew closer. A stifling heat surrounded them. She was running out of places to hide. His head bent and his lips parted. They slowed to a shuffle.

The band stopped. Maggie jerked back, drew breath and looked towards the stage. A spotlight shimmied its way over the crowd.

"Ladies an' Gentlemen o' Glesga!" The brittle voice of Billy McGregor rang out around the hall. "Wan lucky couple is aboot tae be chosen fir the game o' their lives!"

The spotlight flicked and flitted across the room, fixing on one couple near the back. The man swiftly removed his wandering hands when he realised that all eyes were on him and a raucous applause reverberated up into the rafters and out into the warm night.

"It's time to see what's in the mystery box. C'mone up here you twa. We huv the box a' waitin."

"Och, I love this pairt!" Maggie pulled further away, leaving Tommy floundering mid-embrace.

The winning couple made their way onto the stage and stared around like startled rabbits. Their host stood arms wide in welcome, grinning out from under his curly moustache.

"Rather them than us," Tommy laughed.

"Och, shoosh."

A drum roll started softly and reached a crescendo just as the couple opened the box.

"AND IT'S A ..."

A communal gasp from the spectators.

"... ROTTEN EGG!" Billy McGregor announced, his maniacal laugh shaking his whole, substantial being, from his jovial belly right down to his shiny patent shoes.

Maggie didn't usually have much time for the man but, right then, she could have kissed him. The crowd was in hysterics as the band struck up a pacey number and the night flew by once more. By the time Tommy had turned around, she was already walking back towards her friends.

"Thir gonnae be disappointed by that wan," she called as he ran to catch up. "The pair last week wan 20 pounds. Each!"

"Jings."

Rachel bounded up beside her to hook arms, and the two girls escorted each other back to Jess. Minnie gave them a small round of applause as they approached.

"Are ye huvin a gid night, girls?" she asked, pushing herself away from the wall.

"Weil, it certainly looks like oor Maggie's hud a ball," Jess said dryly, folding her arms.

Rachel's little green monster lurked close by and she snorted loudly, her lipstick running at the side to give a hangdog expression as she measured her lot. For Jess, a Paul replacement was nowhere in sight, and John had edged closer, standing to one side with his sandy hair stuck fast across his forehead. He chewed on his lip but his awkwardness counted for nothing. Looking around, Maggie hoped she presented better to others than the exhausted, hot mess she felt inside.

"So, wha'sh lookin efterz the weansh," Sam slurred at Minnie.

"Och, ah thought ye'd gone awa' hame!" she said, smiling as Davie put his arm around her waist.

"Nawz, mes and Rachelsh wer like bugsh oan a lavvy. But yer weansh…"

"We dinnae hae ony weans," Davie said.

"Whit? Ahz cannae hear yesh."

"We dinnae hae ony weans," Davie repeated louder, gripping Minnie tighter.

"But ye're mairried."

"Aye."

"Whit? Are yesh a poof or some'in?"

Silence.

"Eh?"

Silence.

"Och, ah'm awa' tae finds ma folkshwa string twa wordsh thegether. Rachel, shbin braw. See ye't hame."

And, with a wink that made Maggie want to punch him, he ambled back towards the rabble he had arrived with, oblivious to Minnie doubled over like she had been struck. Whether she was clutching her stomach or struggling to breathe, in the end it did not matter.

"Ah'll kill him," Davie promised, his voice carrying over the music for once. His face was red and his fists were clenched, but his target had sauntered into thin air.

"He had no right calling you a poof. How terrible," Tommy agreed.

"Ah couldnae gie twa hoots aboot that. Oor family's nane o' his business."

"We've been trying," Minnie gasped, leaning into Davie.

"Let's no' talk aboot it." Her husband grew wary. "Dinnae empty yer mooth tae fill someone else's."

"Dinnae bother aboot that Sam Belchford," Maggie interjected. "He's a bad yin wae a face tae match."

"Whit's that suppost tae mean?" Rachel asked.

"Whit he is is staring richt oot o' him," Maggie said quickly before Jess could stop her.

"But it's been a gid night," her cousin stepped in.

Maggie sighed, duty bound to play along.

"Aye, it turns oot Tommy here's quite the dancer. Thanks awfy much. Ah've had a wonderful evening."

She had to stand on her tiptoes to reach his cheek, but he turned his head at the last moment. Their lips met, warm and soft, startling her. She stumbled back to see him grinning.

"Progress," he whispered.

Nodding to John to follow, he walked away; two men as different as black and white and, with the night still swirling in her mind, she could not decide which was which.

"Ah need some air."

"Efter a' that dancin'?"

"Aye, something like that."

Maggie grabbed Jess's hand and led the way out of the main hall and into the street beyond. The night was wearing on and the crowd was thinning out, with only a small handful of partygoers clinging on to the cobbles.

"Ah need ma bed," Maggie said, walking towards a small lane that ran down the side of the building.

In the late hours, her voice cut through the stillness like Olivso through dirt so she kept it down and they cleaved out a space of their own in the shadows. The lane was empty and they would not be overheard.

"Are ye awright?" she asked.

"Ah should be askin you that, awa all night wae the toast o' Glesga. And whit were ye thinkin, setting aboot Samuel like that?"

"Aye, it's been eventful, but afore a' that ye wernae yersel, gaun awa tae dance wae that Sam. Weil."

"Ah didnae know ah wis gonnae dance wae him. Ah didnae plan it."

"Naw, but wae a face like that ye should hae known better. Thin features fir a mean spirit. Besides, Sam or no Sam, ye were awa tae dance wae someone. It's no jist Rachel wha'll hae tongues waggin the night."

Jess's voice changed. "Weil, whit dae ye expect me tae dae? Jist hing oan like yer bloody chaperone? Ma Paul's no' Davie. He cannae come wae me. Whit am ah meant tae dae? Sit and wait while ma hale life passes me by?"

Three young boys by the doorway glanced at them and headed back inside.

"Naw, ah dinnae, but you're no' Rachel. Ye're ma ain blood so ah huv tae tell ye the truth. Whit yer dain, gaun aboot like a single lassie, weil, it isnae proper. Ye're getting a kinds o' attention."

"Really? Dae ye think this is some kind o' an education?"

Struggling to keep the volume under control, Jess's voice broke completely, telling a story that was agonising for Maggie to hear. She sagged against the hot bricks and buried her face in her hands.

"Ah'm sorry." Maggie was defeated. "Ah didnae want tae mak ye feel like this. Surely it's better ah let ye know?"

"Ah saw ye kissing him."

Maggie shrugged. There was a beat, her cousin waiting for an explanation that did not come. It was too much. Never before had they spoken to each other that way. Jess barged past, back inside. She did not know how things had gone so wrong but, beleaguered, Maggie followed, wondering what she should have kept to herself and if she could have lived with herself if she had.

The crowd had thinned inside and the air was tepid at best. It was time to go home.

"Where's Minnie?" she asked Rachel, who had been keeping their spot. Jess had arrived first but didn't say a word.

"Awa wae Davie. Where else? Ah stood here watchin them kissin like twa lovers straight fae the pictures afore they finally took aff."

"I dinnae see why they come oot wae us if that's all they're gonnae dae," Jess muttered, grabbing her bag to leave. She wound her way through the crowd, with Maggie reaching the exit a few seconds behind. The street was deserted but if they hurried they could still make the last tram home.

Rachel scoured the hall for Sam one last time and ran after them, filling their ears with what she thought they wanted to hear.

"Yer tune's fairly changed towards that Tommy Gunn," she said vehemently, feeling liberated after a few gins and oblivious to the subtext. "If ye dinnae want him, I'll hae him. Jist dinnae play aboot a' selfish like and keep him tae yerself if ye've no intention o' seeing it through."

"He's awright as long as ye know how tae take him," Maggie admitted. "And it's awfy important tae know a man wha can dance."

Her tongue was softened by the same gins that hardened Rachel. She climbed on the tram and deliberately took her seat next to Jess while Rachel squeezed in across the aisle. Her eyes sparkled, the jewels of the Gallowgate. Ignoring her, Jess stared out of the window as the city tumbled past and the sound of the big band faded into the peaceful rumblings of the night.

SEVEN

The Flitting

On a sunny morning in early August, an optimistic man walked into a doctor's surgery on Maryhill Road looking for a pretty young receptionist with curling white hair, but the girl was nowhere to be seen.

"Move it gently, Big Stevie!" Maggie shouted.

The grandfather clock was tilting precariously and she peeked through her fingers, imagining it lying smashed across the floor. Her uncle had done so well moving the writing bureau earlier that day. It had been her great grandfather's desk when he had been headmaster so it would have been a sacrilege if anything happened to it, but he had risen to the challenge. Moving the grandfather clock, however, was progressing less smoothly.

"Donald, will ye go help Big Stevie wae that clock afore it fa's oan his hied? It's awfy heavy. Ah cannae hae his remains smeared o'er the flair the very day ah'm leavin'. Wha'd move in then?"

"Ye fair exaggerate," Big Stevie muttered, resting it on his back to wipe the sweat from his nose.

With him at the bottom end and Donald at the top, they made the colossal structure move in pushes and shoves.

"Ye're a slave driver, Maggie," Donald admonished, "but at least ye live on the grund flair."

"Aye, but wait til ye see the other end. It's twa flairs up!"

Donald groaned, and with good reason; it was an immense task for an overworked thirty-seven-year-old and a strong lad of eighteen.

At the kitchen table, Uncle Jimmy listened closely but did not look up from the sack he was packing with china. His pot belly rested on the bench top and his greying beard no longer detracted from his balding crown. Maggie noticed his whole frame lower as he gathered himself to speak.

"Where's Margaret?"

"She isnae coming." Maggie sighed.

The two men hoisting the clock ceased their patter. Jess was on her way past with an armful of clothes and stopped.

"Whit?"

"Ah went tae see her the other day but she wis awfy busy."

"Did ye tell her we'd a' be here?"

For some reason Jess was disbelieving, and Jimmy knew his daughter well enough to change the subject.

"How's she getting oan?"

"Aye, she's gid, ah think. She likes tae talk aboot a load o' office chat that's way o'er ma heid."

"It'll be way o'er hers, in a'."

"Be nice," Jimmy warned, putting a plate in the sack with a crash.

"Eh, Uncle Jimmy ..." Maggie whispered, her hand rising automatically to break the fall.

"Ah jist wish she wis here tae see oor Donald. Look at him."

Donald grinned. He put the clock down so quickly that Big Stevie nearly dropped his end and, while his uncle scrambled to stand it upright, bellowed, "A strapping young laddie!"

He pointed gleefully at himself, his black hair hanging limp around a wide grin that stretched across thick lips, inviting everyone to join in. His father wasn't enjoying the joke.

"Aye, but fir how much longer? It winnae ayeways be like this. Ask yer daddy, Maggie. A' that talk o Germany and war."

"They've been talking like that fir months, daddy," Jess placated. "Ayeways this story and that, but that disnae mean onything'll come o' it."

"It only hisnae happened cos it hisnae happened yet. Ah've seen it. The first time roon'. Ye're a changed man efter, in every way. And how d'they come hame? Buckelt in the body like Arthur, or worse, buckelt in the heid like aw them loonies doon the docks, or they dinnae come hame at a'... ."

He let his voice trail off and the two girls looked at each other. Jimmy never spoke about his brother, and especially not his death. They understood, or thought they understood, the pain that kept him hidden in the recesses of Jimmy's mind, a memory too precious for the consumption of even those closest to him, but his haggart expression and hunched back suddenly brought his lost sibling hurtling into the present. He let another plate fall into the sack with a crash. Maggie let it rest unchallenged.

"He wis strong and brave and a that, jist like Donald. Margaret ne'er knew him, right enough, but it would hae been nice if she'd come tae see him. Afore."

His voice trembled and it was all Maggie could do not to hug him, but that was Jess's place so she stayed put. Big Stevie shook his head sadly and looked at Donald but the boy just shrugged, stuck half-way between embarrassment and annoyance. Still, he kept grinning and said,

"It's exciting. Tae be aboot something bigger than masel. Ma conscription'll be coming through shortly. That's whit ah want." He bent over to pick up the clock again. "Now, enough o' this. Dinnae leave it a' tae the young wans, Uncle Stevie."

"Ya wee bugger," Big Stevie replied, unable to look his nephew in the eye.

"Watch yerself wae them boxes, Wee Ena, yer tilting them awfy far. They're gonnae land on the flair!"

"Uch, gie it a rest, Jess," Donald's voice snapped from behind the clock, already halfway out the door. "Mammy's at hame wae her sare knee. We dinnae need a replacement."

Wee Ena stuck out her tongue as she stumbled forwards after her big brother, the top edge of her pile of boxes tucked securely under her chin, so Jess sucked in her breath and bit her tongue, letting both of her siblings escape. There was no ally to be found in her father; his mind remained elsewhere.

When Maggie followed them out of the kitchen a few minutes later, she allowed herself one last look over her shoulder. The bed recess lay stripped to its bones, the floor was brushed and the fireplace was empty. Already it felt lifeless.

Just then, a huge crash reverberated from the front room. The gaslamp careened in its cradle overhead and she ran to see what was happening. Her Aunt Annie was over by the window, huddled peacefully with her needlework. It was over at the recess that the action was happening. Arthur was there, wrestling a box out of Aunt Flo's arms while his eldest sister continued to pack it higher, and a chamber pot spun fast in the middle of the floor, coming to a conspicuous standstill in the centre of the room.

"We cid get a few mair things in there," she grumbled, but he would not listen, wrangling it away from her and accidentally knocking the light felt hat off her head. It was not the time to apologise. Struggling under the weight with his one good arm, he used his thigh to hoist it onto his hip and bolted for the door.

"Ah cid jist add them candles!" she called after him as he hurried out into the close, moving faster than Maggie had seen since her mother died.

By the window, Aunt Annie hummed a Highland jig to herself and peered outside to see when he would stomp past, but the only occupants of the cobbles were the neighbourhood children playing tig.

"Aw, gie it a rest," Aunt Flo told her haughtily, grabbing the bed pan and hat and following Arthur out.

It had been a long day. As predicted, the two sisters had sat in the kitchen for the majority, organising boxes and pedantically telling everyone how to do everything exactly the wrong way. Until Jimmy Menzies had arrived with his brood. Then they had gone to the front room to fold some linens and escape the congestion, but their presence was always felt.

"We'd hae finished already if it wisnae fir those twa." Arthur had grumbled to Maggie. *"We're only movin roon the bloody corner."*

Aunt Annie stopped humming. "Is a'body gone?"

"Aye, gie me yer haund."

Together, they angled her out of the chair, first one side, then the other, grunting all the while. Nothing more could be done to take the pain away.

"Ah'm awright, hen," Annie said, leaving her needlework on the chair, and they made their way slowly after the rest.

In the hallway, Annie bent lower to collect the sweep and dustpan, unwilling to leave them behind, but Maggie took them gently and passed her over to Jimmy at the front door.

"Ye haud oan here," he said, offering his arm.

She took it gratefully but there was no need to rush; the close was congested. No one had made it outside and the whole family queued up as Big Stevie and Donald worked out angles and strategies to manoeuvre the huge grandfather clock out of the entrance. They appeared as silhouettes – murky shadows contained within the damp close walls cut out against the bright summer backdrop, and if Aunt Annie had stayed put to see her brother stomp past then she would have been waiting for quite some time.

Jess and Arthur stood patiently behind but Wee Ena pushed stubbornly forward, holding the box in front of her like a battering ram. Her brother kicked out at her as he struggled under the weight.

"Keep her ahin, Jess!" he shouted, glaring over his shoulder.

Raised up on her tiptoes, Maggie was at the back of the line and held no sway. Her frustration mingled with excitement and all she could do was wait until, eventually, Donald and Big Stevie slotted themselves through the entranceway and spilled out into the light.

Set free, Wee Ena took off down the street, skipping and weaving her course around ball games and hoops, the busy playground of a quiet summer's day. It was a short walk down the road to the new flat, but the whole street moulded itself into an obstacle course as the group struggled on. Neighbours hung from windows to watch the show and shouted down to offer their help.

"We hae tae many helpers already," Maggie shouted back.

"Should we jist go hame then?" Big Stevie asked.

"Hud yer wheesht, Maggie," Arthur warned, "Can ye really see the twa o' us movin' that thing?"

"No' wae yer dodgy airm."

"Aye, or those stupit wee shoes ye ayeways wear."

"They're Cuban heels, daddy."

The new brown pair she wore added a spring to her step as she set the pace and her face turned upwards to welcome the sun.

"How's the flitting?" a voice called down.

If her eyes had been open, she would have noticed, three floors up, wee Mrs Murphy poking her tiny hawk head over her window ledge to see the spectacle below. The sound of her squawking caused the entire moving party to look to the sky, to her expectant hands clutching the sill and beady black eyes flickering rapidly over them all. Everyone knew wee Mrs Murphy. She would ensnare them for hours if they let her while the boxes grew increasingly heavy in their arms, so Big Stevie and Donald offered her a smile, a nod, and soldiered on. They were struggling and breathless, and that precarious cargo, that irreplaceable heirloom, teetered on the brink of disaster. Maggie grinned, waved the dustpan and kept on going behind them.

"This is it," Arthur told them, stopping short and pointing straight ahead.

They congregated in a tight band to stare at the open door. After a second, the peace was shattered by a call from behind.

"Weil ah never. There's a sight fir sair eyes!"

A young woman was exiting the close across the street. From a distance, her mottled green eyes were noticeably serpentine, and her strides were long and assured as she walked towards them. She certainly cut a striking figure, with her jet black hair pulled into a tight bun that contrasted sharply with her floating white dress. From her fixed gaze, it was unclear whether her comment was directed at the grandfather clock or Big Stevie.

"Hello, we'r jist movin intae number ten," Maggie called back.

"Whit, all o' ye?" The girl laughed at her own joke. "Ah'm Sarah Gibb."

"It's nice tae meet ye," Arthur stepped forward. "It's me wha's movin. Me and ma daughter."

"Oh, hello." Sarah sounded disappointed and walked closer, revealing the sharp features and appraising stare of a woman in her thirties.

"Dae ye live o'er the road wae yer man?"

It was Donald who had asked but Sarah answered to Stevie, "Och, ah'm no' mairried."

She carried a black clutch in front of her like it was her dowry, ripe for the taking. Under the strain, Big Stevie grunted and focused all his energy on keeping the clock erect. Stare as she might, he would not meet her gaze.

"Weil, it's awfy nice tae meet ye," she said, letting her eyes roam up and down, and the next moment she was off again, striding smoothly down the street towards Woodlands. Donald watched her, grinning, and Big Stevie stared at his shoes.

Maggie turned her attention back to the facade.

"It's a two room and kitchen, and bathroom and scullery," she told them. Although she had never been inside, when she looked up at the second floor she could pick out her new windows easily.

"And press," Arthur added.

"Are ye afftakin me, daddy?"

"Naw, it does hae a press," he said, fooling no one.

The tenement was set back from the road by a low railing and a small garden bloomed with pink and white roses under the dutiful maintenance of Mrs McNulty. Her boys were already standing by and rushed out to lend a hand, relieving the women of their burdens while the lady herself stood surveying their progress. Her hands were clasped loosely atop her wide bosom and her white fingers twitched, as though she was holding a secret close to her chest but was about to open up and let it fly. Wee Ena had been awaiting their arrival but right then she was nowhere to be seen – innocent Ena who had many stories that she would willingly impart to receptive ears.

With the clock still leading the way, everyone traipsed inside. The walls were painted a stark white, refreshing after the damp and peeling plaster of the old stairwell. Even the air seemed cleaner, and Maggie put that down to a diligent Mrs McNulty and inside toilets.

"It's a braw place ye have here," she told Mrs McNulty, stopping at her door while the others heaved boxes up the stairs.

The woman grunted and rubbed her chest. "Ah see ye've met Sarah Gibb. She's a right floozy."

"Oh aye? Ah've seen her aroon but we've ne'er been introduced."

Wee Ena scurried past and Aunt Annie took her time, focusing on one step, then another, until she was out of sight and enveloped into the distant, infuriating laughter overhead. Every inch of Maggie wanted to be up the stairs with her family, but Mrs McNulty filled her ears with tales of a girl she did not care about and details of minor indiscretions and neighbourhood gossip that were disastrous to a woman but would have a badge of honour to men such as Tommy Gunn. The words sailed over her head while her mind flew up to the second floor and everything she was missing. Long moments seemed to pass until, finally, Arthur reappeared at her side.

"Donald's awa back noo fir that last chair in the front room. Time tae go lock up," he told her.

He nodded to Mrs McNulty, took a firm grip of his daughter's arm and they walked together, up the street to their old house, one last time.

Donald had been and gone by the time they arrived and the rooms shifted silently in the faint breeze, awaiting their new family. She stood in the hall for a moment, her palms against the thick walls that had listened to all her secrets, while her father moved past her into the front room. It was time.

Deviating to the kitchen, she looked out through the stained net curtains to the familiar patchy grass and middens that she would never see again. It had been her mother who had loved the houses on Wilton Drive, ogling their large bay windows and indoor bathrooms, and it was for her they were moving to the second storey location where high windows would let the light stream in, even on the darkest day in winter. It was fulfilling her dream; not their own. When the new place became available, it had felt like fate, but Maggie moved to the bed where her mammy had struggled in the end and felt as though she was leaving her behind.

Her father was elsewhere so she picked up the pillow that was permanently dented by two heads. When she was younger, sometimes she had added her own head to that pillow, in good times and in bad, like at four years old when she had lain sick with fever and with little hope of recovery, yet she had sat up, straight-backed and wide-eyed in the middle of the night with words of a psalm tumbling out as easily as the sweat which trickled down her forehead. It was a beautiful song that rang out and haunted her distraught parents, sure that it sounded her end. Wee Maggie had never heard that song before in her life. When her fever broke the next day, it had been a miracle in the tiny kitchen recess that she was soon to leave forever … in every crevice of the room, the ghost of Sooty the mouse-catcher ran in circles as it chased its tail and elusive mice into eternity, meowing and baring its claws with feral menace … she was two years old, in the front room, looking out the window as her daddy left for war. Her very first memory was watching from that window as he strode down the street, kilt swishing at his knees. At the corner he stopped and looked back and gave his daughter a slow, final wave. To Maggie he looked heroic and proud and she could not understand why her mother's grip tightened around her small fingers or why she was crying … she was eight years old … eleven years old … fourteen years old and Mammy was screaming. She had been a bad lassie. The list was long of fights she had lost but secretly thought she had won, like when she was home late after playing in the back green despite being told that it was a school night; the bad words she had used amongst friends when she thought no adult was listening and the language she had used against that blasted Miss McDonald when the whole household was unanimous that the old bugger deserved it … she was eighteen and it was the first time she went to the dancing, sneaking into the kitchen drawer to remove the lipstick hidden there, slipping it into her bag.

The memories were coming thick and fast and she panicked, jumping up to check the drawer underneath the workbench. It looked empty except for a thin layer of dust, but she had kept a postcard in there, a beautifully embroidered thing that her father had sent her from France during the Great War. Her mother had sat her on her knees and read the words aloud so that tiny wee Maggie could understand, and had continued to do so every night until he returned. At twenty-six, she could still recite the words; her first connection to a man she barely knew. She could not remember seeing it in any box or bag being packed earlier that day. Her heart thudded harder until she felt sick.

"Daddy?"

She heard him approach from the front room but she was not done yet. Desperately, she felt around the edges of the drawer, just in case, and her fingers hit a thin piece of cardboard. Slowly, she peeled it away from the side. It was a photograph that had been stuck, wedged up against the back. Grabbing it, she held it against her chest.

"Whit's that, hen?" He hugged her hard and led her back to the bed. His grip was firm and her shoulders smarted, but she did not want him to let go. Until then, neither of them had appreciated how hard this moment would be. Side by side, they took a closer look.

"Ah."

The photograph had been taken in 1916, two days before he had left. Arthur stood tall and determined in his uniform, an awkward smile breaking under his cap, and baby Maggie was on a chair beside him in a pretty white dress. He held onto her lovingly to be sure she would not fall; it was Clara, seated on his other side, that showed the photograph for what it really was. They had been lucky they could afford the expense of going to a photography studio but she glared into the lens like it had come to take her husband away. The epicentre of the photograph was those eyes; black pools of fear. Taut and pensive, she radiated pain, speaking her emotion louder than words ever would.

Once he returned, the photograph had been banished to the drawer with the other wartime memories and locked away forever. In that one image, Clara seemed alive.

"Yer mammy is wae us where'er we are. Can ye no' feel her at work?" Arthur stroked his daughter's hair until she nodded her agreement. He did not know the half of it.

"It'll be the same in the new place. Tak that photae wae ye and we'll reunite it wae the rest. This hoose has a load o' memories and a load o' ghosts but ye cannae live yer life wae ghosts, hen. It's whit's oot that windae that counts."

"Miby we shouldnae hae flitted," Maggie murmured desperately, unhelpfully, now the flat was empty and awaiting a new history.

"Naw, it's time tae go. A' we're leavin is bricks and mortar. Ah'll tell ye something. The light in the new hoose is different somehow. Ah see clearer. The world is lichter."

"Truly?"

"Aye."

They stayed until it felt like they might remain there forever. Then, with Arthur's arm locked tightly in her own, she stood up and made her way slowly to the door. This time, she did not look back. Her hands shook but she kept moving forward.

EIGHT

The Big Room

The slant of the concrete steps and the subtle undulations of the bannister between her fingers filled Maggie with fáilte on the long climb to the second floor and she savoured every moment. Everyone was waiting. The storm door was thrown open in welcome and the front door was also ajar, the indistinct orders of Aunt Flo echoed out with Donald's light laughter overriding her insistence and, with that, Maggie stepped over the threshold for the very first time.

A flick of a switch was all it took to illuminate her new, modern home. The weak electric sizzled above to reveal the long, narrow hallway that Arthur had told her so much about. This was it, their very own two room and kitchen, bathroom and scullery. Ignoring the chatter from the front room, she allowed herself a few moments to absorb it all. On the right was the second room: a proper bedroom with a real bed already set up in its centre, its large frame and thick mattress a looming mountain of cosiness; she would most definitely need Donald's help to push it back against the wall. Her clothes chest was set in one corner, thrown open for a pile of blouses and jumpers to escape across the floor, and the space in the other corner was perfectly sized for the dresser that she had seen in the window of a new shop that had just opened next to MacIntosh Leather. Things were coming together. As for the rest of the room, it was large enough to dance in. There had been a wardrobe in the shop window, too, but she had never imagined that she would have room for both. Picturing them in her own private space was a dream. Suddenly, dreams were coming true, a realisation that was confirmed when she keeked into the open doorway opposite to find a real inside bathroom with running water. And the bath itself looked huge. Already, the old flat on Dunard Street was beginning to fade.

She ignored the escalating babble from the front room and moved to the kitchen where a new sound greeted her: the thud of a ball stoating against pavers outside. She moved quickly to the window. The lace curtain was surprisingly heavy but she held it firmly aside and leant far over the sideboard to gaze down onto the large back green, where colourful foliage and children coexisted in flourishing life. The boy was there, recognisable by his light blue flat cap as Jimmy McNulty. From her elevated position, far away from the midden, the wash house and the ball games, she felt at peace.

"Maggie, hen," Arthur's voice prodded from the hallway, but there was another room off the kitchen. It looked like it should lead to a press but she knew from her father's reports that there was a whole other space she was yet to discover. She couldn't help herself. She heard Arthur's loud sigh from the hall but she only wanted to peek.

It was there that she discovered the tiny scullery, complete with a cooker and sink big enough to fit a mangle. Like so much else in the flat, keeping her washing away from prying eyes was a luxury she had never believed would be hers. She caught her reflection in the kitchen range; it was grinning.

"Ye huvnae seen the parlour yet and yer missin oot oan the blether," Arthur called impatiently.

"No' a front room?" she asked as she joined him and linked his arm.

Arthur laughed. "We can call it white'er we like."

"The Big Room then," Maggie said as they pushed through the door to the biggest room in the house.

Everyone was there. Having reacquired the armchair, Aunt Annie had advantage, while Aunt Flo perched on a tall stool and Jimmy and Jess contented themselves with one rickety old chair each. The others sat cross-legged on a large blue rug that Maggie had never seen before.

"Whit's this?" she asked, toeing it suspiciously on her way to the bureau to deposit the sacred photograph, never to be lost again. It was a stitched-together medley of cushion covers, a mosaic of intertwining patterns and styles that complemented the fireplace tiles and contrasted dramatically with the expansive dark-stained floor.

"Dae ye like it, hen?" Aunt Annie asked.

"We made it fir ye!" Aunt Flo said before she could answer. "Ye know ah'd rather be knitting, but ah helped."

"Thank you," Maggie said, kneeling down to inspect it. "It's an awfy bonnie rug. Ah'll be scairt tae staund oan it."

"Aye, thanks hen," Arthur agreed.

There was no doubt, it was beautiful. And unique.

"How did ye know whit colours tae use?" asked Big Stevie, picking at the cyan stitching from his position on the ground.

"We didnae." Aunt Flo's frank indignation proved her truthfulness.

"It's the room o' gid fortune," Wee Ena said.

Everyone turned to look at the high voice of childish wisdom in the back corner, playing absently with a wooden stork. Its long legs were agile, moving and clicking together as she repositioned it, over and over again, in a mantra of boredom.

"Ye didnae think ah wis listening," she said, "but ah'm a bit big fir a wee lassie's toy like this, daddy. Gonnae mak me a sojer next time? Like we'll hae in the war? Then ah winnae hae tae listen tae a' the talk o' parlours and rugs."

"Did ye mak that?" Jess asked her father, not surprised but impressed.

Jimmy cleared his throat. "Aye."

"Olivia and Stevie hae wans in a'," said Donald. "They wir playin wae them when we left, ae no daddy? Stevie hud the caterpillar and Olivia hud the cat, and mammy looked like she wanted her knee tae get better so she could get on the flair and play wae them. Olivia wis hayin a ball and she's the same age as you are, Wee Ena, so dinnae mak oot like ye're a big lassie. Yer jist a big pain in the heid."

"Jimmy, son, yer talents are wasted," Aunt Annie told him kindly.

"Och, naw. Ah like bein a factor and helpin folks oot. It's gid. Besides," he cleared his throat, "there's a load mair talent than me in the Menzies clan."

"Thir is?" Flo was doubting.

"Donald?" Jimmy prodded his son in the side until he stood up. The boy seemed to remember something and grinned.

"Weil, ah made ye a wee something in a'," he said, hopping to his other foot in excitement. "It isnae much but it's the quality o the thing, like."

Maggie and Arthur nodded and looked at each other, but nothing was forthcoming.

"Err…" Donald looked awkwardly down to one side and Aunt Flo stared back.

"The stool," he whispered.

"Oh!" She jumped up. "Is that whit ye went a' the way back tae yer hoose fir?"

"Aye. Uncle Arthur, Maggie, ah asked ma boss if ah could mak this fir ye and he said aye."

"As lang as he did it in his ain time, efter a lang, hard day at work," Jimmy added, thick with pride.

"And didnae use the gid wood," Donald admitted.

"Yer boss let ye dae that?" Arthur walked over to take a better look at his gift.

"If ah paid fir the wood. A gid price. And strong!"

He picked it up in one hand and bashed the seat, grinning at the sturdy sound of his knocking against wood.

"Ah made it fir the kitchen table. Or sitting at the jaw box while ye'r working the press. But it's no heavy so ye can move it wherever ye want. And right noo, it maks mair sense in the body o' the kirk."

"Where ah can sit oan it," Aunt Flo added.

Arthur ignored her and ran his hand over the seat in appreciation.

Jimmy said, "Donald is wan o the best carpenters that Glesga's ever seen."

"Daddy's a wee bit biased," Jess added.

Jimmy stroked his beard. "No, ah'm no'. Proud. And wae every reason."

Arthur set the stool back down for his sister and Jess gave up the old chair for him, folding her skirt and sinking to the floor. Maggie swivelled to the ground next to her and looked up.

"We're a' proud o' ye, Donald. Turning fae a wee laddie intae a man wha can mak things."

"It's fair exciting. And it's why ah cannae feel bad aboot a' this talk o' war," he admitted, taking the stork from his sister and fidgeting absently with its legs. She crossed her arms and scowled.

"Ah jist think, if ah get in quick-like then there'll be things ah can dae, wae wood and a' that, that they'll be crying oot fir, and ah can mak a right place fir masel. Whit dae ye think? The opportunity …"

The look that came over Jimmy was the same as earlier, with a ghost standing right in his way but, caught up in his own anticipation, Donald could not see anything past his own bright future.

"The only thing getting made fae wood will be a' them coffins," Arthur muttered.

Donald shook his head, taking him literally.

"Naw. It winnae be like the last time. We've learnt oor lessons and we'll be unstoppable. It'll be the fun o' it. New ways o' building stuff. New ways o' carryin stuff. New awthin. It's whit we need tae get things moving. And ah can help."

"Ah didnae bring onything," Big Stevie stated, knowing fine well that his interruption was gift enough.

"Ye brought yersel and twa gid pairs o' haunds," Maggie told him.

"Aye, weil, if it maks ye feel ony better, these twa haunds'll be sufferin' a' week, red raw fae that bloody great clock o' yours."

"Go get Sarah Gibb tae kiss them better, then," Donald said and Wee Ena laughed so hard she rolled on the floor with her skirt caught around her knickers.

"Big lassie, indeed," Big Stevie admonished, but Donald would not be distracted.

"Ah'm jist jealous. If she wanted tae gie me a wee kiss, ah widnae stop her."

"Whit are ye talkin' aboot?" Aunt Annie said archly from the armchair, cheeks drawing close as she processed the insinuations.

"Donald!" Jimmy warned, scowling as he rose to leave. He had had enough.

Big Stevie joined him. "Listen, ah'm away tae pick up ma weans fae oor Agnes. Ah hope she's no' been tired oot."

"We'll come back wae ye," Jimmy said, ushering Donald and Ena and kissing Maggie goodbye.

"Arthur," he said with a wave. "Ah'm sure Agnes will be o'er soon. Her nose'll be botherin her. Come oan, Jess."

Taking Wee Ena's hand, he headed out the door.

As she moved to follow, Jess bent down and clasped Maggie's elbows for strength.

"Ah cannae be daein wae this," she whispered. "Ordered aboot by ma faither, and wae ma Paul o'er the water ready tae ficht, but wha cares aboot him? He's no the wan gein the orders. And neither am I. It's like ah'm no even a woman grown."

She followed the rest of her family with leaden feet and Donald could be heard berating her all the way down the stairs.

~

Once everyone had left, Flo retrieved her knitting and opened the window wide to welcome in the refreshing summer air. It whipped around each crack and crevice to wash away the old and clear space for the new. Aunt Annie pulled her chair far forward, saying it gave her light by which to do her needlework, but her focus was on the street and all the people in it.

"It's a rare rug," Arthur said again although he was unable to appreciate the pattern.

Maggie agreed but there was nothing left for her to do so she grabbed the stool and made for the kitchen. Soon she would have her friends over, and Aunt Agnes and the Bennie children, and the whole place would be filled with laughter but, for now, the peace and quiet suited her just fine. She plonked the stool at the window and gazed out at a view all of her own.

In his own time, Arthur followed and stretched out on his new bed with a contented groan, kicking aside the pile of clothes at his feet. It was a modest lump in comparison with his daughter's trunkful, but the bed was far smaller than the one he had just left.

"Are ye sure ye dinnae want the bedroom, daddy? It's rare. Ah'm gonnae get some drawers and a wardrobe and awthin. Ye'll hae mair space."

"Naw, hen, you enjoy it. Ah've lived in a kitchen recess a' ma life and dinnae intend tae change noo. Ah might get a wee settee for the parlour, though, and a table... ." He was quiet for a moment. "Hen, look here."

He pointed to the foot of his bed. Behind the curtain, there was a long wooden shelf which slanted at an angle towards him. Until that moment, his failing eyesight had missed it.

"Mak sure ye dinnae put yer heid at that side, then, or onythin heavy up there. That'll gie ye a fright in the wee sma' hoors!"

"Daddy, that scullery ben there is awfy gid but, say we needed mair money anytime, like Rachel and Mrs Campbell? Weil, ah cid sleep ben the big room and we could let oot ma room. Tae a lodger. We'd mak a fair bit o money that way."

"Dinnae be daft, Maggie. This is a dream, no' a nightmare. Ah jist wish yer mammy cid see it."

"She can."

Pulling himself up slowly, Arthur rose and walked cautiously round the room, feeling everything in its place, using both hands, leaving nothing untouched. His cataracts were spreading to his peripherals, but he was game. His limbs were heavy and his left arm hung at his side, but he was not weary. He was barely fifty and this was just another in a long line of challenges during a lifetime of being old. It had been that way since he had returned from the Great War, worn and broken by the horrors of life.

Maggie watched, her throat tight. The air was thick and the sunlight streamed through the window. She saw Donald in his place, then Tommy, who she had been trying not to think about all day. Try as she might, she could not see who they would be when they were old.

NINE

The Other Hauf

Two weeks later, Maggie stood with Arthur on a wide curved pavement in the city's West End, gazing up at a building that reminded her where opulence truly lay. It was a free standing block, narrowing at one end like a grand coffin, and its smooth, sandstone exterior carried an air far loftier than the tired grey stones of Maryhill. She had walked past many times but had never before had reason to stop.

They edged slowly onto the road. Behind them, the large expanse of the Botanic Gardens sprawled over the hill but, despite the reflective panes of the majestic Kibble Palace spurting radiance through the gates, it was far from her mind. It was an iron masterpiece shining on from the Victorian era and sent threads of sunlight dancing across the grass, but Maggie walked in that park weekly and her gaze was fixed solely on the property ahead.

A solitary DuPont sat at a crisp parallel to the tenement, its tanned leather interior encased in obtrusive burgundy paintwork. She smiled at the chauffeur, hoping to engage, but the man sat straight-backed and uptight, hiding behind his navy blue cap as he awaited his employer's return. Safely behind his glass barrier and proud pencil moustache, he gave her nothing, just drummed his gloved fingers on the wheel. Her smile wavered and she felt her friendliness turn desperate but, rather than beat on the windshield until his head turned, she took Arthur's elbow and led him inside.

The entrance was beige marble bordered by green and red leaf but, with all the tiling and disinfectant, it reminded her of a bathtub.

Still, the smoothness of the stairs underfoot was impossible to criticise.

"And here, ah thought oor close wis braw," Arthur muttered, his quiet voice reverberating up the walls.

"Is that you, Arthur?" Mrs Campbell sang from above like a bell from a tower. "I saw ye both fae the window. Are ye managing the stairs awright?"

"I have stairs in ma ain hoose noo, Mrs Campbell," he reminded her, ascending the last few steps with surprising agility and leaving Maggie three steps behind.

"Come ben here. It's bin a fair trek fir ye and we've got tea brewin'."

They followed her through a set of majestic oak shutters on which a large brass knocker growled. Rachel waited off to one side and grabbed Maggie's arm as soon as she crossed the threshold.

"You take Mr Munroe ben tae sit doon, mammy. Ah'll get the tea wae Maggie."

Mrs Campbell nodded and looked incredibly pleased with herself as she ushered Arthur further into an entrance hall that seemed as large and as bright as all the greenhouses across the road combined. Helping him out of his jacket, she hung it over a tall coat stand with practised nonchalance, then guided him through the wide parlour door. The two china dogs that book-ended the display cabinet watched her go.

The two girls forked off to the kitchen on the other side of the hallway. Maggie felt the thick carpet give way underfoot and glanced up at the gold leaf that adorned the cornicing overhead. This was a splendour that would never be hers but she could not tell herself that she did not want it.

"Are ye awright, Rachel?" she asked, struggling to refocus.

Her friend moved in small, fitful steps, repeatedly clenching her fists by her sides but refusing to answer. They entered the kitchen in silence and the only activity was water brewing on the range. How a kitchen could be impressive was beyond Maggie, but she knew she had found herself in a special kind of workroom. If it was not for the bag of coal sitting to one side, she would have sworn the fire was redundant, for no flyaway soot escaped past the fireguard and the whole place was more pristine than she would ever have given Rachel credit for. The pulley hung vacant overhead and the large preparation table was impeccably set for three. Everything was in order. She could not see what the problem was.

"Right," she said, at a loss.

"The tea's no ready. Come tae ma room," Rachel ordered.

Her friend was in charge so they traipsed back through the hall and Maggie smoothed down her good dress in case one of the grand family portraits was watching. The place was turning into a maze. Finally, in the bedroom, there was some familiarity with signs of Rachel everywhere. From the shoes by the bed to the perfume on the vanity table, she had made herself at home.

"This is ma room, while mammy sleeps ben there."

Rachel nodded back into the hall towards another door. The two women were certainly acting like they owned the place and if her employers saw their housekeeper taking such liberties while they were away, there would be an explosion.

"Aye, that's braw, but whit's wrang wae yer face?"

"It's Sam."

"Och, Lord, whit's he done noo?"

Rachel chewed her lip so hard she drew blood and Maggie took hold of her chin gently to stop her.

"He didnae come hame the other night. Ah wis listenin oot fir him."

"That's no' surprising. Shocking, aye, but no' surprising."

The long silence was filled only with Mrs Campbell's distant laughter.

"Ah dinnae know whit ye mean by that," Rachel said at last, "but it's ne'er happened afore. Ah can tell ye that right noo."

"And since?"

"Weil, ah huvnae been there. Moved oot the next day so wha knows whit he's dain. Maks me sick, Maggie. Ah cannae shake it. Ah feel it richt here."

She held her stomach, clenching at it as if there was something missing that she could put back, if only she squeezed hard enough.

"Yer mammy's here in a', so he's probably in yer flat, right enough."

"That isnae helpful! In ma bed. Ma bed, Maggie! It's mine and noo ah huv tae share it wae some wee hoor. Fir the rest o' ma life, she'll ayeways be there. And ah dinnae e'en know her name!"

Tears streamed down her cheeks and she paced from the bed to the dresser and back again, pulling at the thick green collar of her dress. Maggie had never seen her act that way before and she was in no place to be told to keep her voice down. Maggie glanced at the door, feeling her own stomach contract.

Just then, another burst of laughter came from the parlour. It seemed like the thick brick walls had saved them. She tried again.

"It's no right, morally speaking and a' that, but why dae ye care? Really?"

Rachel stood in front of the dressing table and looked at Maggie in the reflection, fingering her orange curls. "He said ma hair wis bonnie. Naebody's said onything wis bonnie afore. No' ma hair, no' ma clathes, no' ma face, nuthin. Ah liked tae hear it, Maggie. And ah thought he meant it. But how cid he mean it and then go awa' wae another lassie while ah'm waiting at hame?"

"Sometimes, there are twa bonnie lassies and … the new wan disnae cancel the first wan oot? Or miby … miby there wisnae ony lassie. Miby he wis just oot wae his friends. Or he likes a gid drink. Miby wan dram tae many and he fell asleep up a close."

Rachel stared back, disbelieving, and Maggie didn't blame her.

"Should we go mak that tea?"

Straining the last dregs into Arthur's china cup, Mrs Campbell put the teapot back on the large oak dining table and offered round some scones. Her daughter took hers first, back straight, finger raised.

Maggie's attention split between her hosts and the luxurious mint room, its wallpaper a diamante gold motif above a delicate white picture rail and majestic furnishings somehow managing to sit unobtrusively beneath. The nonchalance of it all was half the fun. She settled into the low undulations of the cobalt banana settee and admired the nest of tables with their Streamline Moderne edge – she and her daddy had thought they were posh when they bought one beech wood table for their own front room at the barras the week before.

"Aye, they huv three bedrooms. Ah dinnae see the need fir aw that space masel', but jist tak a wee look aroond. It's bonnie, isn't it? An' it gets the sun in the forenoon so helps oor Rachel wake up. A wee workaholic like naebody else."

The trusting couple was in Moray, far away from their bakery chain and leaving the real work to their lackeys for a while. When they asked their housekeeper to live in during their absence, they had been quite unaware that her mother would be coming, too. Looking around at how comfortable the Campbell's were, Maggie did not admire the morality but could appreciate the outcome.

"How lang are they away fir?" she asked.

"Anither week. Rachel'll mak sure everythin's in order afore they get hame."

"Miby yer ain hoose'll be missin' ye. Dae ye no think aboot goin back there tae get that hale bed tae yersel waeoot Rachel?"

She kept her eyes trained on Mrs Campbell, avoiding the grandeur around them as she spoke.

"Och naw, ah pop in noo and then but why hae that bed there when ah can hae this wan?"

"Ah widnae leave ma stuff aroond unchecked wae a stranger. E'en if he is a teacher. What dae ye think, Rachel?"

Rachel ignored her lifeline and shrugged, detracting their attention with some high notes on the piano forte. The discord worked. She was sitting at the centrepiece of the parlour, the spotless bay windows creating a perfect backdrop – spectacular views over the Botanic Gardens and the deep red sandstone of the illustrious residences beyond. With thick velvet curtains hung straight to the floor, these windows looked like grand doorways into another world, and Rachel was at its centre. No matter how tuneless, the effect was striking.

Galvanised by all eyes on her, she flounced from the piano to a satin zebra-print futon and morphed into Queen Bee. Gone was the depleted girl who had sat biting her nails a few moments before. She pulled herself tall in her best green dress and let her mother fuss over a few rogue wrinkles, finding it easy to pretend that this was where she belonged. Nothing else existed and Maggie was happy for her. It was a fun game to play.

"Mammy's bin hearing stories ye might be interested in, Maggie Munroe."

Whenever a story started with her first and surname, Maggie knew it would not be good.

"Aye, ah've bin hearin' a' aboot ye, Maggie." Mrs Campbell took over in excitement. "Ye know yer neighbour, Mrs McNulty? She wis up oan Maryhill Road this Wednesday tae get her hair set, mindin' her ain business and jist stopped at Jaconelli's windae fir a look. It wis somewhere atween the ice-cream and the raspberry sauce, ah think, that her attention wis taken, pure captivated, she wis, by Tommy

Gunn. He wis sittin in wan o' the quiet booths right at the back where ye can smell Mario makin' it a' up.

"Efter a second look – fir he is awfy handsome – she wis gonnae go oan her way again when she saw a lassie. She recognised her straight away, whit wae the hair and the laugh she cid hear right doon the street. Wis it no oor freend, Maggie Munroe?"

She was as animated on the subject of men as her daughter and sat forward until her knees were touching Maggie's in unreciprocated intimacy. Maggie's heart skipped.

"So whit? Ah wis huvin an ice-cream wae a laddie. Is that ok way ye?"

Arthur stretched forward. "Wha's this? Ah've ne'er heard his name afore, an' ah'm yer faither."

"He's a patient fae work."

Rising gracelessly, Maggie fetched a chocolate eclair from the spread. Comfort food. Acting aloof did not come naturally to her.

"Dae ye take a' yer patients tae Jaconelli's?" Mrs Campbell asked innocently.

"Naw, only the wans wae the stupit names."

"Dinnae be like that, a' serious and hoity-toity. We're jist hayin' a laugh an' here ye are acting like ye've got something tae hide."

"Ah've got nothing tae hide! He came in a few weeks past wae a sare back, and then ah bumped intae him at the dancing."

"Accidentally?"

"Aye, of course. Fir ma pairt. Rachel can tell ye, daddy, when she's finished windin' me up. Ye were there, weren't ye, Rachel? And then he came in tae work again, his back a' healed, an took me tae Jaconelli's tae say thank you. An awfy nice gesture, so ah thought."

"Should he no' be taking Doctor Bowman oot tae say thank you?"

"That wid hardly be appropriate."

But Rachel was not finished with her. She twirled a rose stem in the arrangement beside her. "According tae Mrs McNulty, her freend is quite the ladies' man. She's an endless source, that wumman, and fae a' the stories aboot that wan … weil, ah'd be wary of him if ah were you."

"Whit stories huv ye heard?"

Rachel leaned back with her feet up, still holding the rose. "Och, nothin' specific. Apparently he likes tae spend a lot o' time doon Woodlands, filled wae its dark streets and nefarious characters."

Maggie blanched, not convinced that Rachel even knew what the word nefarious meant, but she held her tongue.

"There's been a list o' lassies as long as ma airm, in a'. No' jist the immoral sort but proper ladies wha's decency disappeared efter twa words fae that man."

"Ah saw a bit o' that when ye danced wae him, yersel." Maggie interjected, throwing herself back into her seat and fighting for control. Her conjecture about Sam would blow all the Tommy stories out of the water but they would hit too close to home.

"The details are vague but needless tae say a litter o' broken hairts are strewn behind him. And when Mickey saw it wis you now being courted, he wouldnae keep quiet about whit you were gettin intae. Seriously, it looks like a'body hus an interest in that laddie!"

"Whit an honour."

Sarcasm only barely masked the hurt that Mickey was involved in all this and loyalty for Rachel was threatening to give way to self-preservation, but she remembered her friend, tearful in the bedroom half an hour before, and bit her tongue, an angry whipping boy.

Arthur's face was set hard but now was not the time to put him right. She would explain later that the meeting at Jaconelli's had been innocent enough, but her intuition told her all the stories were true. There had been a glint of more than friendship in his eye and now tongues were wagging. She was going to have to talk to Mr Gunn.

TEN

Three Craws

'…sat upon a wa', on a cold and frosty morning,'

~

'the first craw wis greetin fir his maw, on a cold and frosty morning'

At the start of September, it finally happened. There had been an air of inevitability over the few days since blackout regulations were imposed, heralding the immediacy of bad times ahead and, just like that, the pillars started to fall.

Maggie looked up to the pulpit for guidance, sandwiched in her crowded pew between Arthur and a large man whose acrid sweat was less annoying than his drumming fingers. Reverend Bowman struck a commanding figure as she delivered her sermon and surveyed the congregation down her long, straight nose, gathering up their bleak incomprehension and whittling it into something that gave peace. She had a strength that took Maggie's breath away and could reach each individual personally while addressing the whole. Although Maggie found it difficult to focus on the words, they washed over her and gave some relief.

Even the Reverend's fiercest critics, who delighted in questioning a woman's ability in such a role, were quietened by the words that bounced around them, expounding the need for calm. But darkness was creeping in from the sidelines.

The pews were overflowing, with an entire community seeking solace. To the right, Maggie could just distinguish the bowed head of Doctor Bowman, nodding gently to the words of his wife. His stocky, rectangular body crammed in a tight corner of the first row, wedged within the stiffness of his stretched brown suit. As the Reverend talked about faith and endurance, her eyes found his and the rest of the church was suspended between them for an intimate moment. Maggie was not sure if anyone else had noticed but it made her tune in to what was about to be said.

It was a commendation for all those who had already chosen to enlist. It was an open secret in Maryhill that the Bowmans' son was a member of the No Conscription League, but she supported her congregation and the desire to stabilise the continent, choosing her words carefully as she acknowledged the outstanding bravery of their chosen path. Mickey from MacIntosh Leather Merchants, magnificent and clean shaven, looked almost baby-faced in his uniform and he nodded along from his standing position against the wall. Maggie's guts shook at the sight of him. How she wished he was rough and sweating, hammering nails into soles, rather than the scrubbed-up man in front of her who her mother would have approved of. His eyes were glassy as he listened but it was she who wanted to cry for him.

So many men in uniform already. Glancing over her shoulder, she could see them all, many late arrivals but there they were, layers of cannon fodder that the Government had been recruiting since April. Donald had received his letter the week before and her heart clenched thinking about it. There he was at the back with Agnes and Jimmy, and the rest would be there somewhere; she would catch him later.

It was almost impossible to believe the madness in the world. Only the cool wooden pew pushing behind the thin loose fabric of her dress seemed real, only the immediacy of her father's rugged profile close on her left. Looking down in prayer, she realised she had been wringing her hands. She caged them in a firm, safe clasp. Reverend Bowman's words retreated once more and the whole nightmare seemed dreamlike around her.

When the service finished and they returned silently to their flat, the first thing to do was to switch on the radio, just in time to hear the distinctive voice of Neville Chamberlain crackle to life like he was sitting talking to them from the fireside chair. It was 11:15 am on a peaceful Sunday and Europe was at war.

~

'the second craw fell and broke his jaw, on a cold and frosty morning'

By the end of the week, the city was on fire and it was a scorcher on the Barrowlands dance floor, electrified by the nervous energy that kept everyone awake. Even Billy McGregor and the Gaybirds seemed to play at an incredible pace, aware, perhaps, that time was running out.

Maggie met Tommy under the ballroom's neon sign, the beats from within raising her heart rate as Rachel quickly disappeared inside. Jess was not with them. She had discovered that Paul was on his way to Norway on the HMS Highlander and, suddenly, their marital warfare was blown out of the water and all she could do was wait for him to come home. Davie had decided not to wait for conscription and had enlisted first thing the previous Monday, and Minnie was too busy preparing for him to go to be bothered about the dancing. Normalcy was slipping away fast. So, Maggie Munroe was alone when Tommy stooped to kiss her, feeling from the adrenalin like she was back in her early twenties and feeling from the weight of the world a hundred years old, all at the same time.

She cocked her chin to the side and he brushed her cheek, smiling wanly at her habitual coyness. Her lipstick shone a deep red and her cheeks were rubbed the same colour, but she stayed fresh in a light lemon frock, her own way of beating the gloom. The way she had pulled one side of her thick white hair back, all the better to blink up at him from beneath her lowered gaze, was not entirely coincidental.

"You look beautiful."

Linking his arm, she ignored the implicit insult of his surprise and together they strode inside, away from the burning haze of the street. The wood-lined entrance hall was cool and a group of men had congregated beyond the reaches of the big band noise. Tommy's friend, John Anderson, was at the epicentre, arms stretched to regale the crowd with epic tales of heroic feats he was yet to accomplish, but was sure to unravel whenever he got to the front line. The crowd pressed together as it listened, nodding in agreement and impatiently waiting for its own turn to talk. As Maggie watched his theatrics, she imagined him destroying the entire German army with only the hoe and scythe from his Lanarkshire farm.

"So when are ye aff, John?" someone called to him from the back.

"Weil, noo – ah huv a couple o' loose ends tae sort oot here. But then ah'll be aff, you mark ma words."

As Maggie and Tommy walked towards him, the crowd muttered amongst themselves and dissipated. There were plenty of real heroes to be found in the room that night amongst the young boys who had signed up in their droves, undeterred by stories from the last time round and chatting excitedly as they rushed forward to offer their services: a generation in a hurry to die.

Tommy patted his friend on the shoulder and John sagged down like a newly burst balloon.

"It's true. Jist a couple mair months an' ah'll be aff, Tommy."

"Yes, and maybe I'll come with you."

"Dinnae say that!" Maggie said, grabbing his arm as she forgot to stay strong.

"What's wrong with me going to serve my country and fight with the rest of the lads? Surely it's my duty."

"It's a stupit idea. Fir you in a', Johnny, so dinnae be lookin' at me like that. They stairted a' that conscription business afore the bloody war hud even begun they were so anxious, and oor Donald wis called up twa weeks ago. His mammy and daddy are worried sick. When that letter came in he wis gey feart, though he covert it well. Ye may no' be the age they're lookin' fir the noo, but when the deid and wounded start rolling in ye'll be whisked awa soon enough and dragged oot there tae serve whae'er and whitever they want ye tae defend. Ye'll live and die yer days o' glory. Nae need tae hasten them alang."

"Och, we need fighting talk, hen. We're at war. Yer wallowing's no' gonnae dae us ony good, is it? Leave it tae the men tae sort oot."

She was silenced and John rose back to full height, quick to forget his own inaction when he could hide behind strong words. Neither man noticed her as they decided, quite resolutely, that when John had finished his business in the city they would go and join up together. Tommy wore his usual smirk, a performer wooing his audience, but John was grave as he considered his options. For all he had dismissed her, she could not bear it.

"Want a dance?" she asked.

John looked to Tommy for permission and, still smirking, he stood back to let them pass. Pushing his hair off his face, John led her by the elbow, avoiding her hand. Still, he seemed more confident than he had been during that first waltz. The memory was suddenly a distant fragment, lost in time. Now it was a reel and she was being carried around the floor by the muscular arms of a labourer.

"Are ye counting?"

"In ma heid."

He smiled, keeping time, and her dress felt light as it birled around her thighs. No one looked at her with envy or appreciation, not the way they did when she was with Tommy. For the first time in a month, she had stepped out of his shadow and into a light which paled in comparison. Every face on the dance floor was following its own path but she did not have a path of her own. The addictive energy that existed with Tommy, the energy they both fed off, linked them together. He was standing off to the side, his face a blur with each passing spin, but she could see he was smiling.

"Ye're no' paying attention," John scolded. "Ah've been tryin' tae dance wae ye again fir weeks noo, Maggie. E'er since ah met ye that first night and we hud that waltz. Ah wis wae Tommy. Dae ye remember, Maggie?"

"Of course ah dae," she snapped. "It's no' like that's the only time ah've met ye."

His mouth fell open as though she had slapped him. "Ah'm sorry ah asked. It's jist, Tommy's such a … weil … he's got a big braw personality. It's like thir's nae room fir onywan else so it's gid tae talk tae ye for a bit."

"Ah've never hud any problem getting ma tuppence-worth in," she told him.

He shrugged. Standing so close, she could smell a mixture of cigarettes and whisky through his crooked yellowed teeth. He was sweating again, heavy circles gathering in the pits of his shirt. He stopped abruptly and pulled a tiny hip flask from his pocket. Adorned like a fabulous piece of jewellery, it was muted silver covered with the intricate embellishments of the Anderson family crest.

"Will ye hae a drink wae me?"

"Whit is it?"

"Whisky."

"Go oan then," she said.

She exited the dance floor and wound in front of a couple who had been so absorbed that she caused the woman to stumble. Angry shouts followed her.

"Sorry!" she shouted back and beckoned across the hall. "C'mone Tommy!"

John caught up with her quickly and grabbed her shoulders, twirling her round with such force that she kept spinning all the way to the floor. He grabbed her wrists and pulled her forwards before she hit the ground, whispering urgently, "It's only a wee drop. Maybe we should jist tak it oot there, the twa o' us – mair tae go roond that way."

"That's no' the Christian spirit," she said, pushing herself free. "Besides, here comes Tommy."

A trail of appreciative gazes followed the man himself as he sauntered up, put his arm around her shoulder and squeezed. He immediately caught sight of the hip flask, gave a small nod and headed for the door, and she was happy to be dragged behind.

They escaped through the crowds, slipping into the street and the narrow lane between the buildings. Streetlamps could not reach them and she glanced quickly over her shoulder, questioning his choice, for she could smell the waste that ran through the central drain even if she could not see it. The last time she had stood there, her argument with Jess must have been really awful if it had managed to mask the stench.

She kept flush to the wall and shuffled forward a few paces, stopping before the light from the gas lamps was extinguished entirely. Close beside her, Tommy was unperturbed. He moved in deeper and sparked a hissing match, leaning against the wall while his cigarette shone red in the darkness.

"Are ye dancing wae onywan else the night or keepin a' yer moves fir Maggie?" John spat as he finally caught up.

Tommy laughed loud and long. The layered shadows allowed his friend's face to twist and contort in private, and Maggie was surprised the two were still talking. She waved away the cigarette, took the hip flask from John and gulped. The whisky was hot and rough on the back of her throat. Ever since the funeral, it took her back there, and even after four years she could imagine what her mother would say about these men.

"Slainte, mammy," she whispered.

"What's wrong?" Tommy asked.

"Whit maks ye think somethin's wrang?"

"I just know." He put his arm around her shoulder again, familiar and warming as the drink.

Clearing his throat, John said, "Get some o' that doon ye. Ye'll feel much better."

"There's nothing wrang wae me," Maggie laughed, taking a long swig. It rushed to her head and prickled her brain. "There, see? Noo it's your turn."

Half an hour later, she re-entered the party, giddy and giggling although nothing in the real world gave her cause to celebrate. She rushed forward to find everything as she had left it, a hot tin full of beans, and for once it was Tommy who followed. With his arm slung casually around John's shoulder, he was ever watchful for his girl.

Time flew with them around the dance floor. One, then the other, then back again. She had never spent such an evening before, in the company of two strange men on the opposite side of town. She could not decide which desire to listen to most, the mellowing of the alcohol or the urge to dance. Casting around for Rachel, she realised just how alone she was. There was a fever in the air. It was liberating.

"Ah'm awa tae find Rachel. The time for gang hame's fast approachin."

"Take that way ye," John said.

"Naw!"

Maggie tried to give back the hip flask but he crossed his arms stubbornly, so she slipped it into her bag, out of sight.

"If Rachel wanted to be found she would be here already," Tommy told her.

"So whit?"

"It is not for me to give the indelible Maggie Munroe any pointers."

"Jist shut yer mooth then."

She spun around to walk away. The floor tilted. The lights glared suspiciously into her raw eyes and she struggled on, each step precarious, each victory making her giggle. Two metres or two minutes, she could not tell how far she had travelled or how long it had been since she had turned her back, but she had seen Big Stevie too drunk to walk, slipping to the floor; she had heard him talk nonsense and Arthur pretend that he could understand. She had never imagined that she would ever be in the same position but she recognised the truth. It was time to take control.

She fled into the ladies toilet, to the privacy of the first cubicle she could find and poured every drop of whisky down the pan, the action alone making her feel better. Shaking it twice to make sure it was all out, she sighed with relief and shoved it back in her bag. The liquid lay there, invisible amongst the sour water, but she pulled the chain anyway to make sure it got sucked into the abyss. If only the alcohol in her system could be flushed out so easily.

She did not know how long she sat there with a barrier between herself and the world but eventually she rose and went out to the sinks. Her self-inspection in the mirror, imagining that it were the reflection that was real and she who was a figment in yellow and white, a daffodil fresh out of season, was interrupted by the cloakroom attendant coming into the toilet on her break.

"Are ye awricht, hen?" the assistant asked.

"Erm," Maggie floundered, turning to look at her but struggling to focus. Her eyes could acclimatise far more easily to the mirror world than the thick makeup, starched striped blouse and shocking green pencil skirt.

"Jist tak a wee moment afore ye go ben there. Splash some watter oan yer face and ye'll be grand. Oh, hello!"

The assistant turned to greet someone else, determined to get into a good conversation, and Maggie took that as her cue to leave. She was fine, she told herself, and cloakroom assistants were always paid to see more than they were meant to. She wanted to go back to the toilet and sit down or, better still, be lying in bed with her careening head safely under a pillow, but she had a friend to find, so she gathered herself and pushed back out onto the floor.

All she could see were the blurred forms of passing strangers. Rachel's pink dress and flaming hair would have been impossible to miss but she was not on the dance floor or the surrounding lounge areas. It was unnerving. Maggie's desire to go back to the ladies and the safety of the mirror world grew.

A firm grip tightened on her shoulder. It was Tommy, smiling and alone.

"Where's Johnny gone?"

"I sent him packing. A lovely boy but I wanted to spend some time with you tonight. Alone."

"But ah still hae his hip flask!"

"It's alright, he knows! Told me that you should keep it for him and he will collect it when he comes back from war. How about that?"

He paused and his lip curled unkindly.

"It looks like you have yourself quite an admirer."

"And ye sound awfy surprised."

"I'm not shocked, I'm jealous. You know I can't stand when another man looks at you, even if that man is John Anderson."

"Dinnae talk aboot yer friend like that." She reached out to stop herself from swaying. "Besides, ye dinnae git jealous. Ye love it when ony laddie looks at me. It makes ye feel like the big man."

"Well, suppose I do? It's easy when I am standing beside a girl like you." He stood close and took her tiny chin in his long fingers. "I take one look at you and feel like the cat who's got the cream. Which is funny because I haven't even had you yet."

His dark eyes mocked her but she was too drunk to trust it and he held all the cards on his pinky finger as he turned to leave.

"Get yer arse back here. Sayin somethin' like that an' then jist walkin' away fae a girl isnae very gentlemanly, is it?"

"I'm not very gentlemanly."

Stumbling after him, her feet felt like rubber, slipping from one version of reality to another. He stalked out of the dance hall, aware of the soft footfalls rushing to keep up and, together, they plunged into the tender night and the shadows which kept them hidden from an extraordinary world.

"If I'm such a rascal then why are you rushing out here to be with me?"

"Wis getting awfy hot in there."

"Yes, you look a bit peaky. Come on, lean here."

He guided her back towards the lane, thick with the smell of smoke and stale urine. There was only a trickle of people and no one noticed.

"Here."

He pushed her against the cold brick wall and she sank back, grateful for the support. Turning, she saw a blurred shape at the far end of the lane; two people struggling to separate. The round outline of curled hair was Rachel and the other, short, stocky and pulling down his cuffs. Sam. Maggie stared hard. The two had sprung apart the moment she arrived. Perhaps they had recognised her, for they were leaving quickly from the other end, Rachel hitching down her dress.

"She cannae…" Maggie started, grappling with the implications.

The girls had read Lady Chatterley's Lover many times, passing the book between them in secret, but it was compelling for its sordid vice rather than something to be emulated, or so she had thought. In a lane at the dancing, not even Rachel would truly consider that a good idea. And if anyone else saw her …

"Miby ah drank a wee bit quickly," she said, telling herself that her eyes were playing tricks.

Tommy placed his hand on the small of her back and pulled her up from her slouch.

"Maybe you did."

It started as a soft kiss, like the one he had surprised her with weeks before, but grew prolonged as he gently prised her mouth open with the unrelenting force of his lips. It slowly engulfed her as the energy pushed her back against the cold, moist wall. Her head flew somewhere with the stars and she could not rein it down tightly enough to combat the hand that moved around her waist and found the bone of her pelvis. His touch was as light as that first kiss but the sensation that shot through her was electric, and his wet tongue was in her mouth and he was throbbing. Never before had she experienced anything like it.

As he moved his mouth slowly down to her neck, she knew how exposed her chest was, could feel the air around it slowly begin to close, and all the while his hands continued to work around her waist, coming to rest on her backside as if they belonged there. He squeezed. It was horrid, she knew. It was stifling and disrespectful. But she could not ignore how agreeable it felt.

Words of protest flew around her head and she knew she must catch them.

"Get aff," she muttered at last, trying to remember what she would do if she were sober.

"Take this and just relax, would you?"

A cigarette was suddenly in her mouth, pushed so hard that she bit her tongue.

"Argh!" The warning signal in her scattered mind had just flicked from amber to red. "We cannae be seen doon a lane like this."

Wriggling under his grasp, she only seemed to move further into him.

"You weren't complaining when we were down here earlier."

"Whit? Wae Johnny? That wis different."

"Not really, darling. Have a smoke and you will feel much better."

The familiar nicotine rush flooded into her brain but did not shift her unease. When she looked up, she expected to see Tommy with a long wooden spoon, reaching deep into her stomach to stir her insides out. Instead, he stood a few feet away, looking like the ring leader at a carnival, both sceptical and anticipating great things to come.

Her mind was pulled from the sky and dragged earthward by the acidic, burning vomit, which rose in her throat and threatened to add to the stench of rotten Glasgow. It did not get past her gullet but the near miss landed with a thud. The spinning world was pulled together as her mind focused, calling on her scattered senses to work together. All at once, she saw her situation for what it was.

Swallowing deeply, she sidestepped out of his way. He paused, taken aback as she wobbled to the street. Glancing around, everyone was concerned with themselves, talking and laughing as they bustled in and out. Blinkered by their own activity, no one had seen.

"Maggie, wait a moment!"

His voice echoed after her as she tottered forward to join a swarm making their way home. The fizz of his lips and his warm touch lingered, and an angry part of her wished she did not have the baseless sense of propriety that made her walk away.

He jogged up to her side. "We did get a bit carried away round there, didn't we?"

"We?"

"Ok, maybe I did, but only because you are so beautiful. Unique. And funny. Then, with all the whisky… You must know how I feel about you."

He smiled his best smile and she swung round to face him.

"Ah may be hauf-cut but ah'm no' goin back tae yer hoose, Tommy. Or daein onythin up a lane. Ah'm gonnae find Rachel and ah'm gonnae get hame afore it's midnight. It's Sunday themorra."

Truly exasperated, he threw up his hands.

"Who is talking about sex?"

"Ssssshhh! Ye were all o'er me back there!"

"Of course I was. You are beautiful, Maggie Munroe. These are uncertain times we live in but the one thing I am certain about is you."

"Aye, right."

"Will you be my girl, Maggie? Official like? I've been courting you for weeks now. All you need to do is say yes. And then maybe you can start trusting me."

Whisky still drained from her brain and the touch of his hand was a memory that lingered on a multitude of places she had never been touched before.

"Aye, awright then."

She felt coy, almost shy, as he moved in to sweep her off her feet, but this time she did not move her chin to the side.

~

'the third craw couldnae flee ata', on a cold and frosty morning'

"Ye did whit?" Jess was incredulous.

"Sssshh. Keep yer voice doon."

Stopping still in the middle of the path, her cousin's eyes were so wide that the whites ran thick and her nostrils flared.

"Ah cannae believe it! And we shouldnae be discussin' ony o' this oan a Sunday! Ye're gaun straight tae hell, Maggie, and takin' me wae ye."

In Maggie's opinion, she was grossly exaggerating.

"There's nae need tae lecture me. Listen, ah jist hae tae get this oot afore Rachel gets here."

Jess shifted position uncomfortably. "Can we no jist wait fir her?"

"It's like Davie wis telling Minnie yon time – dinnae empty yer mooth tae fill someone elses."

"Ooo. But Maggie, hen, ah hate tae say it but ah'm someone else yer fillin."

"Naw yer no'. Yer family."

It was a relief to share but some things were hard to put into words, like the way he had touched her and the warmth she had felt even when she knew she ought to be screaming bloody murder. On a see-saw of shock and satisfaction, she could not decide if she had gone too far or not far enough.

As usual, the Munroes, Bennies and Menzies's had met for a Sunday stroll through the Botanic Gardens. Arthur, Agnes, Jimmy and Big Stevie were the grown-ups at the front, while Stevie, Olivia and Wee Ena pushed and shoved their way behind in their Sunday bests. Jess and Maggie had been trailing at the rear for a while but soon their luck would run out.

Maggie looked around to make sure they were alone. It was an overcast day in mid-September and the air was warm and threatening thunder. The whole place was abuzz. Workers from the docks cut a fine sight with their families, pressed clean despite the pressing storm clouds gurgling overhead, lecturers who taught just a few blocks away within the cloisters of the University contemplated the beauty around them whilst nursing hangovers of their own, and aristocrats ambled arm in arm while their nannies kept apace behind them. A calm had settled over the city. There was still the talk of war, audible in every passing conversation; of dreaded air raid shelters in the back greens and barrage balloons in the playgrounds, of political strategy and the unknown duration of conflict, but church had left everyone in a precarious state of peace.

Most importantly, no one was near enough to hear them talk. Steeling herself, she kept her voice low.

"Ah think ah made it sound worse than it wis, really. Aye, we were up the lane, and aye, his hands were wandering, but ayeways oan top. Ah think."

She had awoken that morning with a cracking headache but a clear memory, although memory loss would have been preferable to the uncomfortable flashbacks that came hurtling at her through an alcoholic haze. Slowly, she began to recount the whole tale.

Once she started, she could not stop describing each insidious touch and, try as she might, she could not pretend that it had all been bad. Unbidden, her lips curled into a smile. This dangerous undercurrent was not lost on Jess, who was unable to contain herself with sporadic interruptions of, "He did whit?" and "Yer kidding me oan," and, "Yer filthy, Maggie Munroe."

"And that's how ah came tae be the lassie o' Tommy Gunn," she finished. "It's official, he's my beau and there's nothin' ah can dae aboot it wae oot condemnin' masel' as a filthy wee slut."

"Och, dinnae be daft. Lassies are daein a lot worse than a wee kiss every weekend doon that dancing. It disnae mean ye owe him onything. Besides, a' claes intact. Nae big deal, hen. Yer secret's safe wae me," Jess said, petting her hand with more condescension than she felt was necessary.

She tried to regain control of the narrative.

"But it wis wonderful. Near impossible tae tell him tae stop. And tae be honest, ah dinnae mind stepping oot way him official like if it means a couple mair kisses like that."

With her mind whirling back to the night before, she perched on a bench and leant dreamily against the wooden arm. The Gardens lay below her on the cusp of working and gentrified Glasgow, two worlds combined. Spread across a small hill of grassy swathes and ambling pathways, it was a haven from industry, soot and toil. The pond at its entrance was a mere trickle in late summer, but the leaves on the surrounding trees were colouring, a sign of wetter things to come, and the large greenhouse by the boundary wall was the mirage of a fairytale palace, shimmering through the most dreich Scottish day.

Maggie wanted to sit awhile on that bench halfway up the hill and take it all in, but Jess had other ideas.

"We hae tae keep up. Mammy's no' been daein well since oor Donald went awa'. Ah dinnae want tae leave her."

The rest of the family was further up the path, at the crest of the hill. The children had run ahead into the dense shrubs and the backs of Arthur, Agnes, Jimmy and Big Stevie were almost lost amongst the foliage. Maggie jumped up to follow.

Favouring her right leg, Aunt Agnes appeared years older than the rest, more of a grandmother to Wee Ena, and the sight of her made them walk faster to catch up. Despite the protestations of the adults, the children were flying over the brae to a more secluded section of the park where, nestled amongst the trees, a youngster's paradise lay waiting. The swings and chutes were chained up in deference to it being Sunday but a small group of children were already there, using the play area to twirl their skipping ropes and kick their balls.

"Get yersel back here!" Agnes called, limping quickly after her daughter.

Big Stevie picked up his pace beside her, no easy feat in his starch-pressed trousers. The siblings were determined to stop their children from making a spectacle of themselves.

"We're jist gaun tae hae a wee look, mammy," Wee Ena called over her shoulder, slowing slightly at the sound of her mother's approach. This was the pause Agnes needed to catch up and grab her slender arm, pulling the girl roughly into her side.

"Naw ye dinnae," she hissed so quietly that the others could barely hear her. "Ye're no gaun tae hae a look at onything. Whit have ah telt ye aboot playing on a Sunday? This is a day fir reflection, hen. Ye should be thinking aboot God."

"But whit aboot a' the other weans up there having a go?"

"They're the Catholics fae up the road. No morality in them."

"Ah wish ah wis a Catholic and could play on a Sunday!" She was shrill and angry, and more than a few heads turned to stare.

"Ah swear, yer going tae get a right leatherin when we get hame, young lady. Yer wee bahoochy's going tae be so sare yer no' gonnae be able tae sit doon fir a week."

"Oh aye? Why no' gae me a leatherin the noo?" Petulant and headstrong, she began to wriggle out of her thick white stockings.

"Because it's a Sunday!" Agnes exploded, a cotton ball of dynamite.

As her fate was sealed with a strike on her backside, the poor girl howled, more at the thought of pain still to be endured than the feeble sting of the whack just delivered. She looked such a sorry sight with her pretty straw bonnet falling askew over her tear soaked face, Maggie could barely stifle a laugh.

At the capture of their accomplice, Stevie and Olivia hesitated, giving Big Stevie the opportunity to catch up and let them off with an understanding shake of the head.

"Weans will ayeways be weans," he muttered to Arthur, and Agnes whirled towards him like he was the next one she was going to skelp.

Arthur looked around for an escape. "Och, look wha it is. Is it no yer friend Rachel, hen? Fancy meeting her here!"

The girl and her mother approached over the crest of the hill in identical lilac jackets, and Maggie was delighted that Arthur had been able to pick them out from a distance. They were continuing a tradition that had started when Rachel had taken up residence at her employer's flat and continued long after she had returned home.

"Och, look who it is mammy!" Rachel cried theatrically, mirroring him with a wink of her own. "Ye remember Maggie and Jess, don't ye?"

Mrs Campbell scowled. "Of course ah dae, lassie. We meet them here every week."

"Ye exaggerate something awful mammy. Look, go ben and talk wae Mr Munroe fir a bit and ah'll be right behind ye."

"Ma pleasure, hen. Whit a fine looking big fella he is."

Mrs Cambell's voice carried past her own deaf ears in a shout that crinkled the corner of her eyes. Aunt Agnes gave an ill-concealed shudder and turned back the way they had come, veering away from a confrontation with her brother and, instead, pushing a still-sniffling Wee Ena in front of her. They fell into step that way, Big Stevie taking Olivia and Stevie protectively under each arm and Mrs Campbell and Arthur Munroe, one deaf and one blind, walking arm in arm behind.

"Dinnae leave mammy alone," Jess told her father.

He moved forward dutifully but kept a distance from the argument, stroking his beard as he tried to keep out of it. At that moment, Jimmy Menzies was the image of Kenny McNulty.

Turning back to her friends, Jess was scowling and dissatisfied.

"Ah might leave ye both if they need ma help."

"She seems tae be daein a'right tae me," Maggie assured her, but Jess clicked her tongue, shook her head and sank down onto the nearest bench.

"She's quick o' the mooth tae hide the ways she's slowing doon."

"Weil, we'd better get oor talkin done fast, then," Maggie said, slumping down next to her. "Like efter ah got tae the dancin' last night, Rachel went missing. Where did ye go onyway?"

"Ah met Sam. You know Sam."

"Aye, we dae know Sam. Why didnae ye introduce me?"

"Ah couldnae see ye onywhere."

"Ah wis right there. Hard tae miss."

"Were ye?"

Rachel was being reticent, and Rachel was never reticent. She took the seat on the far side of Jess and crossed her arms. Clearly Maggie had not been the only one listening to Davie's advice.

"So, whit did you and Sam dae a' nicht?"

"Had a great chat and a wee dance. Aye, it's funny ah didnae see ye 'til the end."

Jess's eyes did not leave her parents. "It's lucky ye both met up again, onyway. It isnae safe tae be oot yersels like that."

Rachel groaned. "It wisnae the witching hoor yet. We got hame by midnight, respectful-like, tae welcome in the Lord's day. Ae no', Maggie?"

"Aye, true enough."

Maggie looked hard at her friend and willed her to confide but, unable to bring herself to ask about what she had witnessed up the lane, hurried the conversation along.

"So ah met Tommy as usual and we got thegether wae John Anderson."

"Wha's John Anderson?" Jess interjected.

"The big laddie fae oot Lanark way wha's ayeways hanging aroon'. Gentle big fella, red face, sandy hair wae a tub o' Bryl Creem oan. Ayeways flopping o'er wan eye."

"Oh aye, the butcher wha talks funny?"

"Naw, he's a fairmer."

"Ah think he used tae be a fairmer but his sick uncle's a butcher here," Rachel interrupted. "That's why he came tae the city, tae learn the trade and a' that."

For a moment there was a stunned silence at the unprecedented voice of wisdom from the end of the bench.

"Onyway, the point is, we wir aw haeing a right laugh. It wis a braw night and Johnny hud a wee flask o' whisky …"

"It sounds like yer decision wis made there and then." Jess smiled. "No' like ye've been forced intae onythin."

Maggie could have throttled her and nipped her in the arm but it was too late.

"Whit decision?" Rachel asked.

"Weil, ah've agreed tae be Tommy's girl," she admitted, missing out the details which led her there.

"Tommy likes the lassies."

"Aye. So ye've telt me."

"Dae ye think ye'll be able tae keep it civilised, then?" Rachel asked, looking disappointed.

Jess snorted and Maggie almost stamped on her toes.

"Aye. Definitely."

"Ah need some romance in ma life," Rachel sighed, ignoring the implications and eyeing a man who strolled past while his wife followed with their brood and threw daggers at her yearning. "Look at you twa a' happy wae men fa'ing at yer feet. Wha wants me?"

Maggie was confused. Maybe she had been seeing things, after all.

"Ah can see masel in the mirror and ah know whit's looking back at me. Ah've been telt ah'm bonnie, ah've been kissed, ah've been mair than kissed but …"

She stopped. Maggie and Jess waited for her to continue.

"Ah've been mair than kissed," she repeated. "But naebody's ever telt me they want me tae be their girl. Ah'd cut aff ma airm fir it!"

"It'll happen fir ye wan day, hen. And ye can talk tae me aboot onythin."

Maggie leaned forward to peer around Jess, but Rachel stared wistfully up into the trees, unwilling to meet her gaze. She gave up and slumped back.

"It feels gid, but it'll feel even better when it's wae somewan ah love and wha really loves me, rather than Tommy, who jist wants tae get in ma knickers."

"But until that day, ony bugger'll dae." Jess concluded. "Well, lassies, I may as well tell ye, I have some news o' my ain."

"Ye're pregnant," Maggie joked.

Jess's face broke into a grin and she almost jumped out of her seat. "Ye are no!"

"Aye. It's gonnae be ma wee ray o' sunshine. Ma wartime baby!"

"Och hen, congratulations."

"It's been a month, right afore Paul left. Mammy plans tae tell a'body this efternoon but ah wanted ye tae hear it first."

Her eyes welled with the relief of confiding, already a ticking time bomb of pregnant emotion.

"Dae ye think it'll be a lassie or a laddie?" Rachel asked.

"It disnae matter tae me as long as it's healthy wae ten fingers and ten toes. Paul would love a wee laddie though. Ah'm telling' ye, it's the best thing that bugger's done his hale life."

"Does he know yet?"

"Probably no'. Ah sent him a letter but no one can say when he'll get it."

"That wis fast work. He wis only hame fir five minutes."

"Och, it'll be lovely tae hae a wee wartime wean running aboot the place. Ye huv tae mak sure its Scottish roots are strong though."

"Aye, we cannae hae a wee Sassenach in oor midst."

"Aye, very funny." She cut them off and rubbed the flat stomach beneath her fawn overcoat with affection, as if the embryo were breathing life into her soul already.

"Ah'm so happy right noo. Really ah am. If only Paul wis here tae share it wae me. He's oot there in the middle o' the ocean wae nowhere tae run. Nowhere tae escape. Jist storms and waves and screaming torpedoes."

Seeing the tears coming, Maggie scrambled for something meaningful to say. "Ye cannae think like that, especially no wae a wean on the way, hen. And when Paul finds oot aboot it, a' the fires o' hell widnae stop him fae coming hame safe and sound."

"But what if he doesnae get ma letter, Maggie? What if he dies oot there at sea and he never knows aboot his son? Whit if he disnae e'en know that ah love him?"

There was no substance to her smile as she continued to nod a social greeting at the Sunday strollers who passed. Maggie grabbed her hand but fell short of meaningless promises.

"No matter whit happens oot there, we'll aye' be thegether, you and I. And Rachel, too."

"Right," a meek voice concurred from behind a shroud of supposed inexperience.

They sat like three crows on a wall until the clouds finally broke overhead. Droplets pattered around them and, suddenly, there was a chill in the air.

ELEVEN

The Floosy

Her belly was flat; boring and shapeless. Prodding it through her pleated brown skirt, she stared in the mirror and imagined she was her cousin – smiling, happy, carefree Jess: a completely different girl to the one she had grown up with. Two months in, with Jess adamant that her bump was starting to show, Rachel said it was the thick jumpers she was wearing. No matter, all that it took to create the difference was a baby.

They were borrowing clothes already, yellow and white ones mostly but some blue, and on the day Donald's letter arrived to tell her there was no sign of conscripted soldiers being moved to the front line, Aunt Agnes had gone to town to celebrate, buying a new shining pram although it was Jimmy who had to carry it home. It was a family affair and there was talk of nothing else but, standing there staring in the mirror, Maggie saw possibilities for herself that were so far out of reach she could cry. Children were a dream that had eluded her since childhood. She could watch siblings squabble from afar, she could imagine what it would be like to share everything with someone and have someone to play with until there were no games left to play, but she had never known what it was truly like. As for the future, she could only keep dreaming while it all became a reality for others.

Taking a blue bow from her dresser, she attached it to her hair and sighed. Tommy would be there soon and she must look like she had made an effort. The thought of him did not bring the fantasy any closer. In her daydream, there she was, standing with a hand placed over her bump and a smile on her lips. He was not in the picture at all. She visualised the scene hard, what her belly would actually look like if she were changing into her nightgown. Would it turn blue, she wondered. Would her belly button get pushed out the wrong way? Would it be sore? Would she be able to see her baby getting bigger and bigger inside? It was almost unimaginable, yet the picture was so vivid that at first she did not notice the physical naked flesh across the street. Something moving so slowly and confidently that she was eased out of her daze to watch.

It was Sarah Gibb in nightwear that Maggie had never seen before, not even in the movies: black lace lingerie and suspenders over stretched white flesh. The room was empty yet she was all poise and focus, sliding towards a full length mirror propped against the far wall. In increments, Maggie realised she was not still imagining things, she was watching a rehearsal. The woman stopped side on, facing the mirror. Her reflection bounced back, a perfect image towards the street. One leg bent on tiptoe, she admired herself, pursing her lips together and running her fingers up through her thick dark hair. She stretched towards the ceiling, legs splayed, and bounced on her left foot before her imaginary audience. Her underarms were hairless.

Maggie crossed her own arms self-consciously and flew to the window to scour the street. Tommy should be arriving any moment and, sure enough, there he was strolling down the pavement in the already-fading light. Behind a thick scarf, his light, purposeful stride was instantly recognisable. If he glanced up now, even for a moment, he would see things that she did not want him to see, on her or on anyone else.

Glancing back at Sarah's flat, she jumped. The floosy was there, looking straight back at her. It was indecent. Maggie had spent all morning trying to imagine the human body but not like that, flaunted in sparse lace, and any curiosity was dispelled by the woman's challenging stare. Fighting for composure, she tried to smile and wave. The clouds between them drew close but Sarah did not show any sign that she felt the cold. Instead, she sneered and drew her flimsy curtains shut, leaving a huge tear down the middle to flap in the draft.

~

"Come awa' in son, tak a seat." Arthur's voice was loud in the hallway.

"Thank you, Mr Munroe. It's good to get inside. Early October and chilly already."

She did not know how he had climbed the stairs so quickly. Readjusting her clasp, she rushed to meet him.

"Aye, weil, we've got the fire goin' ben the parlour so no need tae worry aboot that."

"Sorry ah didnae hear the door," she said, taking Tommy's coat.

It was thick wool and soaked through from the water that hung in the air. She hung it behind the press door, glad to be rid of it, then followed them into the big room where the raging fire warmed the bleakness of October away. They only used it on formal occasions and Arthur had not called it the parlour since that first day, so her day did not appear to be getting any better.

"So, daddy, this is Tommy Gunn. Tommy, this is my daddy, Arthur."

The words formed awkwardly, leaving so much unsaid. Arthur knew she was Tommy's girl; it had been that way for over a month already. Tommy knew he knew, she knew Tommy knew Arthur knew, yet all lay unmentioned before them like a big unnecessary secret. To make matters worse, she did not know how to act in front of her father and her beau at the same time. Neither did Arthur, but it was not a situation in which Tommy should take the lead.

As both men summed each other up, she plopped herself onto the settee and kept a safe distance, allowing the fire to smoke the image of Sarah Gibb from her mind. In its place came Tommy, sitting down next to her with those reptilian eyes that could stare right through her. Remembering his hands on her, she shuddered involuntarily and focused desperately on the film of grit under her nails.

Arthur manoeuvred himself into his armchair at the opposite side of the mantelpiece, unwilling to let anything get past him. He had been waiting for this day for weeks. He smiled pleasantly and got started.

"Noo, that's a fine proper accent ye've got there. Straight aff the wireless. Tell me, where did ye get that fae? Maggie says yer family's fae doon the Gallowgate."

"Yes, but I live on Raebury Street now. It's a beautiful spot and so close to Maggie," he threw her a wink which, thankfully, Arthur missed, "and my accent is self-taught, I'm afraid."

"Why wid ye want tae dae a thing like that?"

Arthur's face wore a look of such open perplexity that Tommy laughed aloud.

"My job."

"In the hotel business. Maggie mentioned that."

"Not just any hotel. The new Beresford. I'm only twenty-eight but I'm looking at management already. A place like that only employs the best."

Arthur nodded silently, feeling like he really was listening to a radio commercial.

"When I was fifteen I started at the Grand Hotel, you know. I was there for ten years, until the Beresford opened last year."

"Oh?"

Tommy sat up straighter and clasped his hands in front of him. Gone was the suave leader that Maggie had come to know. In his place was a young man desperate to impress.

"I was a bellboy to start with, doing the dog's work but always with a smile and good conversation. I'm sure you can imagine. And I worked my way up. Quite successfully. Which would not have been possible if no one had listened to me when I had something to say. I have a lot to say."

Listening quietly, Maggie wondered if he always sounded so phoney or if the pressure of the occasion was besting him, but when Arthur continued he was serious.

"That's a terrible statement aboot oor position in today's society."

"True. But it is also true that, if I hadn't changed, I would not be where I am now. Sometimes the high ground gets you nowhere. Instead, I taught myself the type of English that people want to hear, and it's quite easy. The Beresford and the Grand are both top establishments, as I'm sure you know. There's only the best to learn from."

"Ah suppose that's true enough. Ye hae tae decide whit kind o' laddie ye want tae be."

"I may be a fake, Mr Munroe, but I am an honest fake."

Tommy bowed his head respectfully but Maggie had never heard such nonsense in all her life and the lines on Arthur's forehead warned that his careful exterior was cracking. That was the final straw for Maggie. She burst out laughing at the ridiculousness of the whole situation and everything that had preceded it. Her tears flowed freely and she tried to stem them with the heels of her hands, but the force of her laughter was enough to drown out the grandfather clock which had inexplicably chosen that moment to chime an hour. Both she and it were united in uncontrollable and completely inappropriate noise.

"Excuse me," she said, making a swift exit from the room.

The crisp air hit her as she passed down the hallway, not stopping to draw breath. Only once safely inside her room did she let the wall take her weight and the laughter erupt. With her legs splayed, she was almost horizontal, but things felt easier that way when two worlds were colliding and she was in the middle. She remained there, breathing heavily long after her composure returned, and noticed a tiny brown spider dangling on its thread. He took a break from spinning his web to watch her there, smiling up at him. Was he smiling back? Was she losing her mind? Nothing felt real. It was not yet four but already the wan daylight seemed to beat a retreat against the heavy onslaught of dusk. Taking a deep breath, she pushed herself up. She would shut the curtains, brew some tea and return to the big room – as close to normalcy as she was going to get.

She moved to the window. Across the street, the huge tear flapped open to reveal Sarah in front of the mirror. She had changed into a red leather fascinator and shoes with four inch heels. Apart from that, her appearance was unchanged. Swivelling her hips this way and that, she performed to her reflection; her eyes smouldered longingly and her shoulders heaved with each intake of breath. She held her hands out towards the make-believe audience, beckoning them towards her. Maggie had heard talk that she was a singer but had always imagined it being with more clothes on.

There was no way she could tell her neighbour that she needed to get her curtains fixed; her mother would have told her it was disrespectful and her father would point out that perhaps the poor girl was in no position to fix them. Besides, she knew she could learn something from this unwitting mentor. The way Sarah held herself, unsuspecting of being watched, showed none of Maggie's insecurities and she could not decide whether to laugh or cry.

"Maggie?" Arthur had a hand on the door frame.

"Daddy, it's tae cauld fir ye tae be staundin ben here."

She walked to meet him but he had already turned back down the hall, calling, "Where did ah put that wee drop whisky Big Stevie brought o'er, hen? Can ye mind?"

"Aye, ah've been waiting fir ye tae finish it aff. Ah'll get it fir ye."

The kitchen fire was empty save for the previous night's charred disappointment and her full skirt whipped around her legs as she rushed to find the bottle, tunnelling fresh air up past her thick boots and a shudder down her neckline.

"He isnae whit ah expected," Arthur said, holding his hand out for the bottle as she retrieved it.

"Dinnae be silly. Go and sit doon. Ah've got it."

"Ye're a good lass," he said, pausing to say something else, but Tommy was too close for that so she led the way back to the big room, tea forgotten in favour of something stronger.

With Arthur settled back into position in his armchair, she passed one glass to him and another to Tommy, trying to detect any tension in the room but it only seemed to come from her. Bunching up her skirt, she sat cross-legged on the hearth before the raging fire. Its thick brown folds were muted against the shining turquoise tiles but she felt the heat searing through the filmy white cotton of her blouse and was invigorated. It may become more than she could stand, but not yet.

Gathering her courage, she disentangled her legs and jutted her pelvis forward, moving her hips towards Tommy and willing him to look at her, but he was too busy lighting up. If only she had Sarah's mirror, but each action felt heavy and wrong and all she could imagine was her face morphed into a sultry clown. Still, she would finish what she started. Her hip began to bob and her lips puckered like a fish. She could not, however, imagine what was supposed to happen next.

Her movements were imperceptible, she told herself; they were easily forgotten. If she did not want to be noticed by her father then she could not expect to be noticed by Tommy. It was this thought that saved her when the dawning realisation of how ridiculous she must look threw her off kilter and she fell back dangerously close to the fireguard. She yelped. She had been a fool to think her inexperienced form could compare with the seasoned professional across the street. Tommy looked up slowly.

"You aren't joining us?"

"Maggie disnae drink whisky."

"Oh really?"

That smirk again.

"An' ah winnae be smoking any o' yer cigarettes, either," she muttered.

Tommy drew on the end of the paper, releasing the sweet smoke from inside. It rose up in a misty plume, thick and impenetrable. For a moment, his straight nose and twisted moustache were lost, but he wafted away her annoyance before it could manifest.

"It's an acquired taste," he told her.

"Ah bet ye've seen some right characters at that hotel," Arthur urged, getting back to business. "Film stars, celebrities, an' are the survivors o' the Athenia still there?"

"Oh yes, but we're not encouraged to talk about them and we're still not good enough for some."

"Oh aye?"

"Yes, like the bloody U.S Ambassador who sent his son to comfort his own people. Not my idea of security, but that's isolationists for you, trying to set the boy up as a big shot, as if he'll amount to anything. They gave that child a right earful though, which was good to see. No, and film stars and celebrities are off limits, too, but I *can* tell you both about the time Lady Blane came to stay."

"She's married tae Laird Blane?"

"Precisely. He was in Perthshire hunting and she preferred to stay in the city. A beautiful woman, but likes her drink. Not whisky either. Vodka. Pure Russian. But never before midday, that was her rule. And no matter when we saw her, or how many of Russia's finest she'd had, she was immaculate. And so sociable. It was part of my job to keep her entertained."

So the evening continued, and many a reputation never knew how lucky it was that the stories fell on discerning ears.

"Ye see a lot fae the shadows," Arthur observed.

"If you keep your head down and work hard then people forget you're there," Tommy responded, leaning close to knock his cigarette ash into the fire.

Maggie thought it unlikely that anyone would forget Tommy Gunn. More likely, he had been the cause of one or two scandals of his own.

"Ah wager ah cid tell ye a few things aboot Maggie which wid make yer hair staund oan end."

"Oh yes?" Tommy leaned forward for the whisky bottle but Maggie nudged it away.

Arthur grinned, leaning far back in his armchair with arms stretched wide to begin his story.

"Och, look at the time! Long past ten. Ah winnae be ony use at work themorra," Maggie interrupted.

"Quite right."

Tommy rose to leave but sounded disappointed. He smiled with his lips closed. Arthur struggled to get up so the two men could shake hands.

"Cheerio, son."

To Maggie, it seemed so final. She fetched his still-damp coat and walked him to the door, and he bent to kiss her but she took a step back, her confidence shot. He recovered with an innocuous kiss on the hand and a wink which implied so much more.

Pulling his collar up under his chin, he headed out, footsteps echoing loudly as he jogged down the stairs. Everything seemed lighter once he was gone. Closing the door, she bobbed her hip slowly, imagining him standing in her thrall. In the darkness of the hall, she had all the confidence in the world.

"Hello," she said to the vestibule, puckering tight. One shoulder forward, one back. It was easy to be ridiculous when she was alone.

"Enough of that."

She set water to boil on the range, in need of something warm to settle her churning stomach, and her father came to join her just as it began to whistle.

"What did ye think, daddy?" she asked.

He frowned and put his glass next to the sink.

"He's a smooth wan. And slippery tae go wae it. But he's good company. In fact, he minds me o' the lads ah see doon the Garscube."

"So ye approve then?"

"Maggie hen, ye've met those boys doon the pub."

She had, and she could feel her daddy whisper close in her ear, *"They're good company right enough but ah widnae let them near ma wee lassie fir a' the tea in China."*

"Ah love ye, Maggie."

TWELVE

The Wee Bitch and the
Strawberry Tart

"Come oan, come oan."

Maggie glanced at the clock above the counter. Ten to Twelve. Tommy would be arriving any moment. While their first introduction had not been a disaster, she did not want to leave him alone with Arthur for too long.

The queue for Jaconelli's was typically long for a Saturday, a mask of faces stifling her progress. There were rumblings that care may be needed over food provisions such as sugar, just in case the war ran on longer than expected, but Mario had a knack of acquiring the good stuff and no one wanted to miss out. Ignoring the small heads of the children in front, she craned her neck to see how quickly Teresa and Amelia were working. Teresa was laboriously slow and had given up on trying to stop her son from blethering. Amelia's arms were working overtime as she scooped and packaged and wiped, but was getting nowhere fast. Each time Mario called, she was off to help him tend the tables. Hearing a baby crying close behind, Maggie instantly regretted her long cream coat. She did not want to dress up for a man but baby sick and ice-cream spattered garments might be taking things too far. She looked at the ceiling and sighed.

"Maggie! Gillian, Gillian, it's ma cousin, Maggie!"

Wee Ena had been in front of her the whole minute she had been there but she had not been able to see past the ticking of the clock.

A large girl stood beside her with folded arms and an upturned nose, her small eyes mere slits of appraisal. While Maggie was unsure what she had done to deserve the attention, she was sure that she would have been better off without it.

"Ah didnae see ye there," she said, trying her hardest to ignore Gillian. "Ye look so grown up, awa tae the shops on yer ain."

"Mammy says ah need tae grow up now there's a wean on the way."

"Are ye no' bein a' grown up helpin aboot the hoose?"

"Does it look like she is?"

"Oh, hello. Wha're ye?"

"Ena already telt ye."

"Technically, that's no' true," Maggie said, taking in the girl's threadbare coat, holed stockings and trying to find some compassion.

"Are ye daft?" Gillian stuck her chin forward and moved her hands to her hips.

Wee Ena stood silent, watching them. In her wide, startled eyes, Maggie lost sight of the bossy wee powerhouse who could hold her own. She turned to face Gillian, determined to lead by example.

"Ye'd better watch wha yer speaking tae. Respect yer elders."

"Respect yer betters."

The queue inched forward and Gillian turned back to face the line, leaving Maggie stunned. If this was the friend Wee Ena was choosing, she was in trouble. Her cousin opened her mouth but shut it again quickly.

"Are ye having a gid day?" Maggie asked her, keeping close behind in the moving line, now two customers from the front.

"It's a'right."

"We're ha'in a braw time," Gillian told her. Maggie decided it best not to point out that she had not been asked.

Teresa Jaconelli leaned over the counter.

"Whit can ah get ye?"

"Ah'll get the lassies whitever they want," Maggie said.

"Ah'll hae a pokey hat," Gillian said immediately.

"Ah'm no sure whit ah want." Wee Ena scowled.

On the back shelf next to the raspberry sauce, a half empty tub of sweeties sat, conspicuous in their isolation. Even with things beginning to tighten, perhaps this was a sign of things to come. Mario was a resourceful man indeed.

"Can ah hae a poke o bonbons?" Maggie said, veering away from ice-cream in a bid to save her coat.

Old Teresa smiled thinly at the choice and turned to call in the order. Her daughter-in-law ran to keep up.

"Ah'll hae a poke o bonbons, in a'," Wee Ena slipped in quickly before it was too late.

Aye, Maggie thought, *leading by example.*

Gillian grabbed her ice cream without thanks and began wolfing it down, not bothering to use her napkin to wipe the mess that slowly began to drip down her chin. Maggie had never seen one disappear so fast, and she was friends with Rachel.

Teresa's face crumpled in distaste and she wiped her hands carefully on her apron. Maggie felt like apologising but doing so would be taking responsibility for the wee wretch. Finally, the bonbons arrived.

"Thank you, Teresa," she said cheerfully but Wee Ena lived up to her name; she was too small.

When her bag came, she did not stretch far enough, or perhaps Teresa did not lean over far enough, or perhaps one of their hands shook from the momentousness of the occasion. All Maggie saw was the bonbons toppling out of the bag, rolling their dusting of pink sugar all over the pristine glass countertop. It was not with the hopes of being a good Samaritan that Gillian grabbed at them, shoving them in her mouth as quickly as she could with one hand while holding her ice cream safely out of the way with the other. The bonbons kept on rolling. Down onto the floor they dropped, clinking like coins in a coffer, and Gillian was down there after them on hands and knees, shovelling them into her mouth. A woman behind her gasped and a man sitting with his family tutted loudly, leading by example in his own way.

Maggie turned to Wee Ena with a smile.

"Dinnae worry, hen. Ah'll buy ye anither."

She bent close to Gillian, almost to the ground so their upturned noses nearly touched.

"And *you're* no' getting ony!"

She made it home, hot and angry, just in time. She dropped the bonbons on the hall dresser, called out to her father and ran to her room. The bed was unmade, the drawers lay open and hose littered the sheets from her earlier search for a pair without a run. Eventually she had been successful, but she could not say as much for her housekeeping. Throwing up her hands, she kept going, smoothing and tidying a room that no one would see. Then she caught her reflection in the dresser; pink and flushed, but not untidy. She would do.

She was reaching into the bowl on the dresser for a clasp when the doorbell rang. Heavy footsteps clomped across the floor.

"Hello, Arthur."

"It's yersel'! Come away in, son."

Maggie rushed faster, fumbling her clasp.

"So ye're taking Maggie fir a picnic. It's a bit cauld oot."

"Only in the shade. There's good warmth in the sun," Tommy replied confidently. "Isn't she ready yet?"

"Is she chooch. It takes her ten oors tae mak it oot the door. I swear she gets mair and mair like her mammy every day."

"Ah can hear ye!" Maggie's voice snapped from behind the closed bedroom door.

Arthur guided Tommy into the kitchen where they could not be overheard. Moving was awkward for Tommy, carrying a picnic basket one handed while its broad and tilted weave banged against his leg, and both men ignored the fact that a shopping bag would have done just as well. Opening it, he retrieved a sandwich and handed it across.

"What kind is it?"

"Cheese and coleslaw."

Arthur bit down and smacked his lips. "It's a feast."

"Nothing is too good for Maggie. It's important for me to provide for her. I hope you realise that."

"Son, when it comes tae Maggie, ah try no' tae think tae much. She does enough o' that hersel'."

Tommy laughed. The floorboard in the hall creaked but neither man noticed. Maggie held her breath, leaning against the wall to stop her legs from shifting. She needed a moment. The morning had left her flustered and she was not ready to dive straight into another saga. In hindsight, she should have stayed in her room until she was ready. In reality, she was stuck in a void, unable to move forward or back without giving herself away. What she could not see was Tommy, elevated in position to a guest worthy of the kitchen, eyeing the table where the remnants of Mrs Murphy's tea cried out to him, the watery dregs reflected at the bottom. It was another thing that Maggie had failed to tidy away, but he was none the wiser of the gender of the visitor or their intent. Ignorance gnawed at him, jealousy incapacitated him, and the possibility that the prize might not feel as satisfying as the struggle did not enter his thoughts.

"Do you remember when I told you I am working hard to secure my future? Well, there might be a few bumps along the way, but whatever happens from now on, I'll get there."

Silence; just the tick-tock of the clock and muffled cries of children playing in the back green. Maggie strained to hear if she was missing something. Had she seen through the walls, her father would have been there, his fingers digging so violently into the chair arms that the upholstery might tear. His visitor was starting to feel uncomfortable.

"Ah hope ye cherish yer future as much as ye're letting on tae me."

"Oh, of course, sir...."

Raising his hand, Arthur hushed his guest.

"Ye're a bright laddie. Tae bright tae get muddled up wae a' the hysteria goin' aroond."

"Some would call it Patriotism, sir."

"Aye, weil, you jist ask some o' the lads doon the Garscube Bar aboot that. Ye see the plaque oan the wa' and ken ye're amangst the bravest folk in the country, Mr Gunn. It's no lie that Lyon Street, wee as it is, hud the maist deaths in Scotland during the Great War, and wis decorated the maist fir it! But wis it worth it? The brave young laddies wha made it hame are noo cripplet auld men and wid likely gie it back if the could. Jist try tae keep oot o' it as long as possible."

"What happened to you over there?"

"Ma airm? We wir in a stand aff." He smiled thinly.

"Was it shot? Were you injured? I mean, clearly you were injured," Tommy stumbled, not used to losing control.

"Ye wannae know? Weil, it isnae ony different tae hunners o' other times, wae hunners o' other men, that noo-adays folks cannae walk past. And we're the lucky wans.

"Onyway, it hud been a brutal day, jist like the wan afore. Stalemate, they called it. It hud been like that fir a week. A' we were da'in wis loosin' gid men. The days were spent deeing and the nights were spent waiting tae dee. It wis so dark. We'd built some huts, quick-like, but it wis frozen in a'. We couldnae talk in case we were heard. There wis nothing tae dae but think."

Arthur sat forward in his chair, clenching his hands in front of him. His voice was low and calm, as if he were reciting a story that had happened to someone else. Maggie strained to hear. She had been told the story from her mother, but never from her father's own lips.

"It wis Iain MacKee wha stairted it. We couldnae blame him, fir we'd a' been thinking the same thing. Still, when he lit that match a hail different war broke oot in that wee room. Some o' us hissing fir him tae put it oot and others near shouting tae gie him a wee minute. He wis writing a letter tae his wife, ye see, and many o' us had been wanting tae dae the same thing. It wid help mak us feel a wee bit normal. But we hudnae. He wis the only wan stupit enough t'dae it. In the end, whether it wis the light or the racket, it didnae take long fir hell tae crash doon oan us.

"First, the Gerries threw a grenade. It destroyed most things right aff, and whit wisnae shent soon caught fire, so then a' us wha cid walk hud tae run ootside intae a load o' fleein' bullets. Came doon like rain. We helped oor pals, no leavin onybody breathin back there, but fir most it wis tae late. We wha could, carried them wae us and legged it."

His face had turned grey as the memories hit him fast. "Many were shot doon oan the way; we were a' stumbling through the mud. Anither regiment wis close and wis quick wae a counter attack."

"Thank God," Tommy said.

Arthur took a deep breath and closed his eyes. When he opened them again, he sat forwards with his elbows on his knees, his voice animated. He had managed to climb out of his head and back into the real world.

"Finally a small group o' us reached a first aid post. By this time, there were far mair casualties than gid wans and the nurses needed a' the help they could get. We got the injured in an ambulance and at first ah wis confused when wan o' the medics told me tae get in wae them. In a' the panic, I hudnae realised ah'd been shot. Ah couldnae e'en tell ye when it happened. Ah didnae feel onything."

He lifted his arm up as far as he could, knowing it was worse to look at than to experience. The injury might well have saved his life and he had always been grateful for that.

"The bullet went clean in wan side and oot the other, through ma muscle just above the elbow. Ah wis ne'er able tae straighten my airm, ne'er able tae go back an' fight. The wounds in there on the other haund," he tapped his head, "are no' so easy tae explain, son."

Tommy looked up at the cornicing, unable to meet the old man's eyes, and Maggie could feel the silence.

"Ah'm ready!"

She burst through the kitchen door like an autumnal wind blowing in to dispel an uncomfortable heat. Tommy jumped up, ready to go.

"Weil, you twa hae a gid time. Dinnae sit aroond tae long and catch a cauld. It's November remember."

"It's no' been November lang enough tae e'en ca' it November. No' really."

"Ye're bloody daft."

With her low-heeled shoes and long woollen coat fastened tightly and hanging just above her knees, she was immaculate. The only addition since that morning was a strawberry red scarf, thrown on loosely to act as a barrier between the clashing cream clothes and her hair.

"Are ye no' wearing a bonnet?"

"Naw."

"Jist mak sure ye dinnae get a draft. Mind whit happened tae yer mammy."

"Wir jist gaun fir a wee bit. It's mair aboot a walk and a blether," she told him quietly, stooping to kiss him goodbye.

"Ah saw Wee Ena when ah wis up the road," she added. "We're gonnae hae tae watch her while Jess and Aunt Agnes are tae busy tae pay her ony mind."

Arthur patted her hand.

"Can ye put the wireless oan, hen?"

She flicked the switch on the new machine and it crackled to life.

"I'll see you soon, I'm sure, Mr Munroe."

They shook hands again.

"Gid tae see ye, laddie," Arthur called as Maggie led the way out into the fresh afternoon light.

"Who are you going to have to watch out for?" Tommy asked.

"Och, ne'er mind. Ma cousin's jist got mair friends than sense."

"You just follow me, Maggie love, and you'll forget about everything for a bit."

Tommy enjoyed the way her shoulders relaxed and allowed themselves to be guided under his grip. Lace twitched as Mrs McNulty marked their progress down the street, two retreating figures gravitating together in the blue light of approaching winter.

Later that afternoon, Maggie looked up to see Tommy silhouetted by the distant sun, which radiated directly behind his head like a halo. Swinging her feet freely, she knew he was the perfect backdrop to a perfect day.

They had arrived at Kelvingrove Park as the temperature dipped, crunching loudly through fallen leaves and wrapping their jackets tighter. She had linked his arm firmly and he had looked down at the top of her head.

"Are you alright?"

She had nodded. "Fir a wee bit. Ah'm no sittin oan the grass, though. Then ah really will get a chill, just like ma daddy said."

They had headed to the fountain, out in the open as a cloud shifted to wash the park in light. The heat from the sun was part-imagined but Maggie took the opportunity to bask. She would have preferred to be in the shelter of the Kibble Palace, hot behind a protective glass wall, but that was a fifteen minute walk to the west. So there they sat in Kelvingrove, a meandering urban playground where soot-caked tenements towered close to the perimeter and brought the city crashing inside.

"If it gets any colder we can go into the Art Gallery and I will show you the beehive," he said, opening the picnic basket and waving to a puzzled couple who strolled past. Maggie had not told him that she had seen it all before. He seemed deflated enough already without her help.

Looking up now into the featureless smudge that was his face, it was as if she was seeing the future, that one day he would fade into shadow, and she grabbed both his hands in hers. The force of her touch rocked him forward and his face turned toward the sun, the light illuminating his features. With that, the illusion was broken.

"You missed a bit."

He wiped a stray bobble of mayonnaise from the corner of her lips and followed it with one of the kisses she was becoming increasingly used to and reluctant to push away. She was sensitive to the coleslaw on her breath, but the sweet taste of his cigarettes overwhelmed all else. He nudged closer until there was no air between their thighs, pressed tight while the whole universe seemed to exist between their lips. Usually, he would have tried to push it further. Usually, his roaming fingers would have worked their way lower until, finally, she would seem to realise the danger and push him away. But Tommy had not been acting like usual since his conversation with Arthur. Instead, he cupped her chin with a reticence that chilled her.

Eventually she broke the kiss. A young woman walked briskly past, hands thrust deep into her pockets while her eyes flitted toward the handsome couple cuddling on the bench. She smiled but the woman reddened and hurried on her way.

"I like this," he told her. "It's my favourite time, out and about with you. Don't get me wrong, I like the dancing, but this is better, I think. Something I've never experienced with a girl before."

"Yer supposed tae tell me there husnae e'er been a lassie afore me."

The raised eyebrows told him she was joking but it set him on edge.

"There hasn't been another girl like you before, anywhere in the world."

The feeling that he was slipping away returned more forcefully than she could have imagined. She needed to lift the mood.

"Right, whit's next?"

She reached into the picnic basket for a strawberry tart.

"Ma favourite." As if he didn't know.

It wobbled high with cream and, combatting the tiny pastry, she could feel some of the cloud lift from him as he watched. He even managed a short laugh. In a battle to retain her dignity, it was a fight she could not win. She emerged with a line of cream streaked across her cheek.

"It was lucky ye brought these hankies."

She dug one out from the basket, wiped herself clean and reached for another tart.

"Weil, dinnae jist sit there watching me," she told him, holding out a chocolate éclair.

He covered her hand to guide it to his mouth and suddenly felt the cool cream squidge against the tip of his nose. It was Maggie's turn to laugh.

"I felt you push it!" His voice rose. "I was just about to take a lovely bite, really looking forward to it actually, and then you ruined it for me."

"Stop yer whinging and eat up."

He did as he was told.

"Puddin's the best part o' ony meal. They should put it at the stairt o' dinner so we arnae aw full o' ham and coleslaw sandwiches."

"You seem to have managed very well for one so full."

They sat in silence for a moment, his superficial intensity replaced for once by something real.

"It's nice to see you all cheered up from earlier. What was that about? Your cousin?"

"She's jist a wean," Maggie said. "Ah'm surprised ye remembered."

"Is she in some kind of trouble?"

He turned towards her. If Wee Ena was in trouble, she had a feeling that something would be done about it.

"Naw, naw, no yit, onyway." She fell silent. "It's jist ... she hus this pal and ah dinnae like her."

"Is that all?"

He sat back again as if it wasn't a big deal but they both knew better.

"She's only wee and easily led. Ayeways acting like a wee bloody know-it-aw, but it's jist the attention she wants. If she's impressed then she wavers, and that's whit's worryin me. This bloody Gillian, she's a bad yin, but Wee Ena seems fair taken wae her. Ah'd dae onythin tae mak sure ma wee cousin disnae turn oot like that torag! Ah want tae find the lassie's mammy and tell her, commiserations oan the wean but ye really should hae shut yer legs!"

"I remember my sister going about with some right wee hairies when she was wee."

Hearing Tommy slip accidentally back into his old way of speaking, Maggie took note.

"I mean..."

"It's awright," she told him. "Bad memories can dae funny things."

"I just mean, I understand the worry. Not personally. My mammy, she worried awfully."

"And awthin turned oot a'richt in the end?"

"I feel like I can talk to you, Maggie, and you'll be discreet?"

She nodded.

"My sister, she got herself in a bad way. She only told my parents, but I was young and their shouts travelled through the wall. My father is a man you do not want to cross, and, so, one way or another, she was married before long."

She sighed. "Well, that's a gid ending."

"Is it?"

His head hung low, confiding and staring into the fountain as he became lost in family memories, but she wondered how many girls he had been responsible for getting in a bad way without a backwards glance.

"I have to ask, does this Gillian come from Woodlands, by any chance?"

"Whit?"

"Just, if she did, that would explain a lot."

"Whit's wrang wae Woodlands, like?"

He laughed. "As if you don't know. Full of poofs and prostitutes. I know that's really why you prefer the Botanics, but you made it here alright and your wee cousin can deal with the heat down there just fine."

"Rubbish. It's wha ye are, no' where ye're fae. Dinnae put yer ain sorry sel' oan me. Naw, ah want the end o' yer story. Whit happened tae yer sister efter she got married?"

"Don't listen to me. Everyone has to follow their own path."

"Ah didnae even know ye hud a sister," she muttered. "And John. How did ye meet him?"

"His uncle is my family butcher. It's as exciting as that. He always came to Glasgow on holiday when he was a boy. Don't look so startled, I know it's usually the other way round, but he would come up here. He used to love helping out in the shop and I'd tear him away to come play on the middens. Always an awkward big lump. I was just what he needed."

"Hus he no' rubbed aff on you?"

"I am not easily swayed."

This was not an adequate answer. "Whit's been bothering ye theday? Hus there been something on yer mind?"

"Everyone always has something on their mind these days."

"Och, dinnae gie me that! Ye know whit ah mean."

There was a flash of that easy grin he wore so well and the casual arm swung naturally over her shoulder.

"It won't do you any good sitting around here thinking of me. No good at all."

"Ah know that – an' you luve it!"

She shuddered and retrieved her gloves, wondering if he had kept her out too long, after all. He took the empty picnic basket in one hand and her gloved hand in the other, leading the way over hardened earth and dead leaves. She noticed he was heading towards Woodlands, but she did not miss a step and followed him, always with something to prove. He left the light wane in the sky behind him, like a candle about to be snuffed out. As winter tumbled over the city and the night was drawing in, they walked through the main, tree-lined avenue of Kelvingrove towards the north exit, cocooned from the approaching blast by the high eastern incline. Their lunch had been cut short but it felt like something was just starting. Sometimes they walked hand in hand, other times they were too animated for such intimacy but their smiles sought to drive away the approaching shadows. The quick wind whistled through naked branches and tousled their hair and they pretended it was not blowing their future away.

THIRTEEN

Out With The Old

Auld Lang Syne echoed around the tenement and bounced out of the window, mingling with the chorus of voices that ricocheted down the snow-clogged street. The sentiment resonated in the hearts of the city and even the most tuneless voice was carried high into the night. Jettisoned from their usual spot in the kitchen, the hosts were insatiable; the fires in the kitchen and the big room were stoked and the shutter door was flung open in welcome. So the old year flew out and the new one banged to be let in. No amount of warmongering could stifle the singing that accompanied the Scottish Hogmanay and, when the Munroe's grandfather clock eventually decided to catch up and chime in the New Year five minutes late, there was laughter as people rushed around, spontaneously looking for a second dose. More kisses were given and the sentiment of the words were just as heartfelt as the first time round.

"What we certainly dinnae want is tae repeat *this* year twice," Big Stevie joked as Arthur poured them a round of whisky.

Rearranging the dumpling on the beech wood table that had been dragged back against the big room wall, Maggie tried to flash her father a warning. The red veins in the corner of her uncle's eyes took her back to times past but her daddy had already turned away, and it was likely that he would not have seen if he had been looking. At least Stevie and Olivia were safely over at the bay window, stationed at the card table that Aunt Annie and Aunt Flo had set up and so involved in their game that they seemed oblivious to everything else.

Wee Ena, on the other hand, had a long face, watching the adults laughing around the room from her place with the children.

"Here y'are," Maggie said, walking over and setting the dumpling before her.

"Should the weans be getting a' that in a oner?" Aunt Flo asked.

Maggie pretended not to hear. Wringing her hands, she cast around for an ally. Jess was sitting by the fire out of reach and, hunched near the wall, Aunt Agnes was telling Uncle Jimmy something which he was pretending to listen to. She could not bring herself to interrupt.

"Look at her, how could ah ever hae let ma wee lassie oot o' ma sight? Ye should hae telt me whit a fool ah wis being."

From the food table to the card table, Big Stevie's voice carried. Although Olivia pretended not to hear, her back straightened and she ordered Stevie to shuffle the playing cards faster, clearly not as intent on her game as Maggie had thought. With sunshine tresses and soft ceramic skin, she still bore a physical resemblance to her mother, but an assertiveness had replaced any weakness. Maggie studied her quietly from the other end of the table and wondered if her flighty nature had been blown away or merely covered up with entitlement. Meanwhile, Stevie swung his legs and kicked the table.

"She's such a clever wee lassie in a'. Stevie struggles a bit wae his numbers but Olivia helps him oot. Ye're a gid big sister tae that brother o' yours, aren't ye hen?"

The girl turned to grin, glowing in the warmth of his attention.

"It's noo the son wha's left oot in the cauld," Maggie muttered to Flo, who sat silently beside her and witnessed the same.

Arthur's scowl showed that he shared their misgivings. He believed the capacity for paternal love was great enough to encompass all children with equal fervour but, then again, he only had one, so he swallowed his disapproval, lit his pipe and tilted his head back to blow. He thought about what to say next but, in his inebriated state, the topic did little to lift the mood.

"It's pure terrible, a' this war. Efter the first time roon ah didnae think ah'd huv tae live through it again and yet here we are, same auld routine only noo wae them blasted monstrosities oot in the back court. Ah widnae trust them tae keep staundin when a tramcar goes by, let alone a bomb."

"Eye-sores, that's whit they are. And yon great balloons arnae much better. At least ye cannae see. Think aboot whit it's like fir the rest o' us!"

"Ha ha. Very gid, Big Stevie, rub it in, why don't ye. Still, there's plenty ah hear tae be fiert o."

Both men's voices carried easily around the room, overriding the other conversations that struggled on. Maggie perched beside Stevie to help him shuffle the cards with an expert flick, but it was impossible to block them out.

"Wan o' Maggie's girlfriends has been married tae this laddie fir five years. Childhood sweethearts, they were. Minnie and Davie fae doon the Gallowgate, mind ye met them last Hogmanay when they came by and spent the hale nicht like luve's young dream?"

"O' aye. Braw lassie that, e'en if she wis a bit young fir me. The voice o' an angel. And her man Davie wis doon the docks deliverin that coal o' his. Ah saw him a couple o' times later in the year, the nicest laddie ye cid meet. Ayeways a friendly word and a bit o' banter. Probably due tae going hame tae that wife o' his. Mind, ah huvnae seen him fir a few months."

"Naw, ye wouldnae hae. He's aff tae war. Wan o' the first wans awa and caught up in the madness. Twenty-eight and auld enough tae escape the draft but his wee brother hud tae go so aff he went, tae protect him like. Wis doon that office oan the Monday. Minnie's fair distraught, keepin tae hersel' like a loony. We asked her here the nicht but ye winnae be seeing her."

"Ssshh. Keep yer voice doon or the weans winnae be able tae sleep fir a week. Pity that, though. I'd hae liked t'hae seen her."

"Aye, but stories like that are just the stairt. Mark ma words. Ah hae a feeling we're gonnae be hearing a lot mair o them afore this calamity's finished wae us."

"Ah'm saving ma prayers fir Donald. Oor Agnes is beside hersel' wae worry," Big Stevie said, patting his stomach to drive home the point.

Maggie jumped up fast and stumbled over the rug.

"Maybe you shouldnae be talkin aboot this right noo!" she called across to where her feet wouldn't take her.

"Ah telt him tae be a conscie, conscription or no conscription," Big Stevie said. Agnes's face was thunder and the room grew silent. "Ah telt him he wis a gid boy wha went tae church every Sunday and Reverend Bowman would testify tae that. There's nothing wrang wae the will tae live. Ah thought ah saw some sense in his eens, but he didnae listen and noo he's awa' wae a' the rest o' them."

"Still thir's a lot fir us tae be thankful for, wae yer weans being so young and ma Maggie being a lassie, at least they cannae get muddled up in it."

"Daddy, ah'm staundin right here," she said, finally making it over and nudging both men towards the door. Arthur rocked slightly on his feet but would not budge.

"People dae funny things in wartime. Maggie's a braw example, taking up wae that beau of hers."

"Ye dinnae approve then, Arthur? The protective faither speaks oot?"

"It's no' that. Ah said lang ago ma lassie can mak her ain decisions and ah'll stand squarely by her. It just seems odd, is a'. Afore the war she telt me the twa o' them were jist friends and noo she cannae get enough o' the laddie. It's as though she's been caught up in a' this fever goin roon, the young wans aw thinking time's running oot."

"Maybe they're no far wrang."

"Aye, but it disnae dae ony gid tae lose yer sense o' decorum. Ah've met the laddie. He'd charm the pants aff Adolf Hitler and end the war if he hud the chance, ah'm tellin' ye."

They stopped and Maggie knew she had gone red. People were listening.

"Daddy, can ah hae thruppence tae run up tae Jaconelli's fir a bottle o' ginger?"

Transparent and beguiling, Olivia ran across the room to tug on Big Stevie's shirt. Her small grasp had surprising strength and Maggie could have kissed her for the distraction.

"It isnae open the now!"

"Can ah go themorra then?"

"Whene'er it's open, ye can go, hen. Ah promise."

"Hello!" a strange voice called out.

It was Sarah Gibb. She threw open the door so hard that it hit Arthur's arm and walked in without apology, but she had a fruit loaf in hand so all was forgiven. Maggie had no idea who had let her in. She untied her coat to reveal a short black dress with a ruffled neckline and the high red shoes that Maggie had seen from her bedroom window. Maggie turned a darker red, angry at the injustice that she was the one who was blushing.

"Och, look at a'body here," the woman said, but once her eyes settled on Big Stevie they did not move. "Dae ye still love me, Stevie?"

"Jings!" Aunt Agnes exclaimed, rubbing her arm and glaring as if she were the one who was hit.

Big Stevie, already pink from drink, flushed with delight, and Maggie could see the intoxicated glint in his eyes but could not think of how to save him.

"Is someone gonnae dae a turn?" she called out at last to no one in particular, surprised when it was the man himself who started.

Settling back to listen, she tried to relax. In the year since their last Hogmanay, she had not forgotten how well her uncle could sing. He held a captive audience with a soulful baritone that sent shivers up the spine and, with his shirt sleeves rolled to the elbows, he meant business, drink be damned. Hearing him, guests started pushing in from the kitchen, swelling the numbers of the big room further. Everyone knew the words to *Will Ye No' Come Back Again* but nobody wanted to join in and spoil it.

Halfway through, Tommy entered. Heads turned. He nodded to Sarah who perched on the arm of the settee and made straight for Maggie, knotting his hands around her waist. She pushed his forearms down and inched away.

"What's wrong?" he whispered.

"Ma family cannae see me like this," she muttered. "Ye know her?" She nodded towards Sarah.

"Fleetingly. Work."

Just then, Big Stevie stopped singing and Tommy cleared his throat to take the reins. He did not sing quite so well but with just as much passion. His voice was high and tinny, and his emphatic nature shone. His choice of *They Can't Take That Away From Me* made Maggie smile for, where one man had left them wistful and mellow, the other was raising the spirits of the room, each having chosen a song to perfectly encapsulate his spirit.

She felt like she was back at the picture house on a Saturday afternoon with Olivia on her knee and Jess and Wee Ena beside her watching the film, and suddenly it seemed that Fred Astaire was right in front of her. She would not have been surprised if he had broken into a spontaneous dance routine. At the other side of the room, Sarah twirled her long hair around a finger and swayed in time. If she had been so enthralled by her uncle's rendition, Maggie had not noticed. Everybody loved Tommy except Maggie.

A tight knot shifted in the pit of her stomach. At twenty-five, she had never felt the gnawing clutch of jealousy before. It did not sit well. She told herself that anyone else was welcome to him but, even as she thought it, she did not quite believe it. His attention towards her had been constant and she looked forward to the bubbling tension each time they met. Whatever liberties she let him take, he had taken very, very well. She did not for one minute believe that he was faithful but, in that moment, she found herself beginning to hope.

She cleared her throat as the company joined in his singing, limbering their vocal chords ready to take the next turn. He looked sideways at her and winked.

The whole gang was there, packed together like fizz in a ginger bottle. After the Bells, their numbers had doubled, with old friends and new neighbours popping by to First Foot. No one would risk being the first over the threshold without a gift to bring good luck and prosperity for the year ahead and mindings ranged from a piece of dumpling to a pot of jam, whatever could be spared as pursestrings tightened. Arthur thanked each for their kindness with an illicit dram.

Disgruntled, Maggie stepped over resting legs to squat down at Jess's feet.

"Dae ye think daddy's awright wae a' these folk?"

"Aye, he's grand. Look at him. He's glowin'." Jess nodded to where he stood with a hand on Big Stevie's shoulder, roaring with laughter. The power of the joke, and something stronger, was knocking him off kilter. "And if somethin wis tae happen then ah'll be here tae look efter him."

"Are ye no' comin first-footin' wae us?" Disappointment mixed with jealousy was a horrible combination.

"Ah didn't think ah wis invited," Jess sniffed, rubbing her bump.

"Ye're family. Family disnae get an invitation because they huv nae choice, hen. Yer comin."

"Och, tae be honest, Maggie, ah dinnae really want tae."

Jess lowered her voice so Maggie had to lean even closer.

"It's a bittie uncomfy, see. Ah didnae think ah'd feel like this fir a wee while yet, but ah jist wannae sit here wae ma feet up, wae ma mammy."

She looked embarrassed, realising that her cousin did not have her own mother close by; not realising that Maggie took her mother with her, everywhere.

Maggie smiled for her cousin's sake, standing up to stretch just as Tommy's song came to an end and Aunt Agnes heaved herself onto the settee next to Jess. She and Jimmy had finally separated to rally around their daughters.

"Jings Fred, that wis grande," Jimmy called from the card table. He stood over Wee Ena, encouraging her to take part. However, despite his best efforts, while Olivia was using every inch of her small frame to block her cards from view as she separated the pairs for a game of Auld Maid and Stevie had moved onto the floor for more room, Wee Ena just looked bored.

"Whit aboot something fir the lassies?" Maggie called out, remembering her promise to look out for the girl and determined to find her a distraction. "Ah've just hud a turn twa minutes ago, but how aboot you, Sarah?"

"Och, naw. Ah couldnae." Sarah shook her head and raised a hand in abdication.

"Why no'?" Aunt Agnes asked, but Sarah had no answer.

"Miby she only sings when she's paid fir it," Jess muttered.

No one knew much about Sarah Gibb, only that she was a performer. Apart from that, there was what Maggie had seen from her bedroom window, which suggested that perhaps her talents lay elsewhere.

"Ye know me, a'body – ah'm oan the game. Ah'm jist no' feeling weil."

"On the game?" Tommy laughed.

"Ah'm game. Ah meant ah'm game fir onything. Get yer heid oot the gutter, Tommy Gunn."

Aunt Annie gasped loudly from the corner and some guests tittered.

Maggie whispered, "Let's get goin afore this goes ony further."

"Ah wisnae joking, Maggie. Ah'm staying here."

"Ye'r sure?"

"Ah couldnae. Please, dinnae ask me again."

Maggie looked long at Jess and saw the truth of it.

"Jess is stayin here wae me," Aunt Agnes piped up, stretching her fingers slowly.

"Go wae Tommy. He's waiting." Jess nodded to the end of the room where he stood talking to Arthur and Big Stevie.

"Ye're sure?"

Jess nodded, rubbing her stomach once more, her new way of underlining any statement.

"Gie it laldy," Aunt Agnes told her, grimacing through her pain.

It did not take long to get a group together. Big Stevie was drunk and eager to get away. His two children did not look up from their game as they asked for one more song. He smiled a crooked apology and downed the last of his drink.

"Are a' the coats in the press?" Maggie asked. She could hear the distant echoes of the McNultys in the close and was eager to get out before they made their way inside. New Year was a time to welcome friends and neighbours with open arms but, although her hospitality was boundless, her patience was not.

"Can ah come?" Wee Ena asked, jumping up and running to her, leaving her father behind, but Maggie's efforts to distract her wee cousin would not extend that far.

"Miby in a few years," she said, patting her head.

Wee Ena skulked back to Jimmy, just as Sarah Gibb slid off her perch.

"Ah'll come wae ye."

"But ye've only jist got here! Ye're no' in til ye're oot again!" Wee Ena yelped, too distraught to remember her place.

Maggie would have enveloped her in a hug right there if the girl had not been bouncing towards a temper tantrum.

"It's a'right, hen," she consoled, but Wee Ena started crying so loudly that Jess, who had started a rendition of *Ay Fond Kiss* from her position on the settee, had to stop. She glared at her sister but it was not enough to stop the flow.

"If yer wee enough tae stairt greetin' o'er a stupid wee thing like this, ye've jist gone and proven yer tae young tae First Foot." Aunt Agnes called over without getting up, to which the girl pushed her fists into her father's thigh and cried harder.

An audience watched the impromptu show, thankful that the spectacle was someone else, and Maggie used the interlude to go kiss all her visitors one last time and follow the others into the hall.

"Jist ask oor Jess if ye need help wae onythin," she told Arthur.

His face was blank and confused by drink, and she hugged him tight.

"I'm sure that isn't the turn Wee Ena expected to take tonight," Tommy said, heading to the press. He helped Maggie on with her coat and led her out into the night.

The close was empty, not a McNulty in sight. She breathed in the cold night air and hurried to keep up with the shadowy figures of Big Stevie and Sarah who were disappearing into the gloom. As usual, Tommy slung an arm around her shoulder to protect her from the pitch black as they picked their way up Wilton Drive, cautious and giggling in the dark. She was reminded of similar scenes from the year before: the biting weather and her giddy head. But she was also reminded of everything that had changed. The gas lamps had been snuffed out, sinking the street into obscurity, the full moon reflecting off the fallen snow a shimmering, welcome relief from the dark. No light sparkled from windows, the blackout curtains were drawn tight despite the festivities, but the barrage balloons were visible through the gloom, ready and waiting for action in the playground of the school at the top of the street. Jess had been replaced beside her, downgraded to a girl whose morals ran as low as the ladder in her stockings; Donald no longer taunted her mercilessly, nor was he there to stick up for his wee sister against the wrath of their mother, propelled instead into some unknown nightmare far removed from the warm scenes of a Glasgow tenement; and Davie was long gone, having welcomed in 1939 carefree and in love. Now his wife was spending New Year with her parents on the south side.

Maggie wriggled out from under Tommy and linked his arm instead, their boots sinking into the white ground.

"Where are we going?" he asked, trying to walk in the wrong direction.

"Rachel's hoose. Jist the next street o'er."

"Are you sad it's me you're with and not Jess?"

"A wee bit, but if she wis oot the night she'd jist worry til the cows come hame, let alone Paul."

She did not look up to see the disappointment on his face.

"She'll be awright efter she has that wean. She got a cot aff Mrs McNulty which is jist plain wood, like, but ah just hope it's no' a wee lassie, since she and ma auntie hae been doon the shoaps stockin up fir a boy. She thinks she's dain it fir Paul, fir his memory like. Ah keep telling her he's no deid yet."

"Look at these two!" Tommy changed the subject, pointing up the street to where Big Stevie and Sarah were linked tight together like they had known each other an age.

"Big Stevie knows the way," she said. "Surely he's no steamin enough tae get lost."

An elderly couple strolled towards them and they greeted each other with a *Happy New Year!*, a kiss and a handshake. Maggie offered her salutation enthusiastically and waited until they had passed, then hung back slightly as Big Stevie reached the top of Wilton Drive to see which way he would go. Left for Lyndhurst Gardens, right for anywhere else. Big Stevie paused. Snow landed gently on her rosy cheeks like prickling fairy dust and she thrust her face upwards. It was a generous gift on a night when happiness was as transitory as the gift itself. Then Big Stevie turned left.

Maggie nudged Tommy. "Ye seem tae know her awfy well."

"Who?"

"Sarah," she whispered.

"Not awfully well. I've seen her around."

She stopped and turned to look at him. The drifts of snow did light the night up better than she could have imagined on a blackout night. He held her gaze frankly and shrugged.

"We used to work at the Grand together. She was the nightly singer there for as long as I can remember. Still is, so I'm told. A favourite with all the regulars, especially Mr MacIntosh the leather man."

"But he's married!"

"When has that ever stopped a man from looking?"

"Awa' tae buggery. So, she dis sing, then?"

"Oh yes, but apparently not at New Year."

"So she's no' oan the game, then?"

"Not as far as I know," he muttered, and flung his arm back around her shoulder.

Rachel's house was parallel to Wilton Drive and another left took them there. Although the windows were covered, the laughter inside called to them as they trudged forwards. Big Stevie staggered as he led the way up the stairs. The fresh air had sent his head spinning and the wooden bannister bent precariously under his weight. Sarah giggled and Maggie mouthed over her shoulder, but Tommy only shrugged. Neither of them knew what had gotten into the big man – after years of practice, he could hold his drink better than succumbing to the first blast of cold.

At the top, Rachel was waiting in a low-cut red dress that she looked set to flop out of and a thoughtless grin.

"The sights ye see when ye don't hae a gun," Sarah whispered back to Maggie, then to Rachel, "Lovely tae meet ye. Ah'm Sarah."

She planted two air kisses beside Rachel's cheek and strode inside with confidence, breaking first footing tradition. Maggie was incredulous. The more she saw of Sarah Gibb, the less she liked.

Oblivious to the slight, Rachel's grin widened when Maggie thrust some shortbread into her arms.

"The tall dark and handsome man we brought tae First Foot ye is half cut so a wee white-haired lassie'll huv t'dae instead."

Ignoring Maggie, Big Stevie let go of the bannister and planted a wet kiss on Rachel's cheek. Her face turned the same colour as her hair and, laughing, he pushed into the hallway and out of sight.

"You do have a Gunn; you have me, but if I'd done the honours, it would not have been our good friend here whom I'd be shooting," Tommy said mildly, attaching his colours to her ineffectual flag, then, "Lovely girl, how are you tonight?"

He bent down to kiss the other cheek. Rachel grinned at his closeness.

"Right, in ye get."

A two-handed push from Maggie sent him falling in the door, straight into a hallway full of people and alcohol. The party was well underway. He righted himself and headed straight for the kitchen.

Quickly scanning around for a familiar face, Maggie found only strangers until she stopped on Alec McLean. Mickey was long gone, but it was comforting to see that one half of the MacIntosh's leather team remained. He saw her at the same time and held out his packet of cigarettes in offering, but at that moment Sarah took the neighbouring seat and his attention was taken. Maggie wondered if rumours were true and they knew each other through his uncle.

"Dae ye still love me, Alec?" she heard Sarah ask.

She watched Alec sit back in his seat, unable to put more distance between them, while Sarah crossed her legs and touched his arm. Around them was a sea of faces that she did not recognise, older people Mrs Campbell had known her whole life and some younger friends of Sam. It was a small mercy that he was nowhere to be seen.

She did not want to witness what Sarah might do next and had lost sight of Big Stevie so she ambled into the big room, to a table piled high with food. Helping herself to some fruitcake, she struck up a conversation with a like-minded woman in a long green coat. Mrs Lawlor was far too cold to remove her outer clothing but was in good spirits nonetheless and time passed quickly. When Mrs Campbell joined them in a mid-calf frock with puffy puce sleeves, Maggie was happy to stand back and watch the friendship before her; two women who had known each other for longer than she had been alive.

"And how's yer daddy?" Mrs Campbell asked eventually.

"Aye, gid."

"Is this the man ah've been hearing all aboot?" Mrs Lawlor asked, and Maggie laughed. With age, some things did not change.

"Come over here, Maggie!"

Loud and clear for all to hear, Tommy staggered in with Rachel close behind. He veered left and collapsed into an armchair, completely oblivious to the people parting to make room.

"Come on!" he persisted when she ignored him, throwing his arms wide.

He had only been in the kitchen for a few moments but the difference in him was astonishing. She dragged her feet, in no rush to join him, but he pulled her onto his knee and folded tight arms around her. She was caught.

"Gie us a song, Rachel," Mrs Lawlor called out. "Gie it laldy!!"

The rest of the company agreed, shouting encouragement and suggestions, and pure mortification burrowed its way into Rachel until it seemed she was folding in on herself. Maggie felt useless as everyone carried on their encouragement, and Tommy was gyrating in such excitement that she was in danger of bouncing off his knee into the middle of the floor. For the first time, she thought that perhaps First Footing was not such a good idea, after all. Rachel was a fox cornered by hunting hounds.

Then a male voice started softly from the edge of the room. It rose steadily as everyone hushed, realising that a song was underway.

"Oh Danny Boy, the pipes, the pipes are calling."

Sometimes it did not quite reach the notes, shaky and feigning as breath ran out and then back to full force as the lungs filled just in time for the chorus. It was an imperfectly perfect rendition. It was Alec McLean singing from the doorway, hands clasped behind his back, and Rachel gaped at her shiny white knight. He stared at the floor, avoiding the gazes of all those around him, but he did not stop. As the song wore on, Tommy joined in with a flourish of dubious harmonies that warranted rapturous cheering. Soon everyone was singing along, any initial embarrassment forgotten as Rachel slipped away from sight.

The sensitive deliberateness of Alec's actions surprised Maggie. There was a tenderness in his actions, but then Maggie remembered another tender moment five years ago when he comforted a young girl as she grieved for her mother.

"What are you staring over there for?" Tommy asked her.

She did not answer. Faced with her silence, he grew restless and his knee jittered – a sure warning sign that he had fallen madly in love with Maggie Munroe, but she was too distracted to notice. Mrs Campbell walked over to hand him a cup of tea and bent forward for a cheeky kiss as repayment. He played along and its sobering effects hit him almost as suddenly as the drink. The world stilled. Following Maggie's gaze, he recognised the man from that shop he went to when he needed to get his shoes repaired.

"They say he tried to sign up whenever the declaration was made," he whispered in her ear, biting playfully at her lobe. She whipped around to face him.

"Wha's 'they'?"

"You know what it's like around here. Everyone's arse deep in everyone else's business. Anyway, I think I heard it from a woman at your surgery one day when I was standing waiting for you to finish. Your neighbour. The one with all the children and a bit of a moustache who never shuts her mouth, neither she does."

"Mrs McNulty! Ah should hae known, the wee clipe."

"She was saying that he was first one down at the registration office the afternoon war broke out – which might be a bit of an exaggeration – but he failed his medical exam. His heart skips every now and then, hardly a serious condition, but they won't let him leave the country!"

"How dae ye remember that?"

Tommy shrugged.

"Typical. They drag some laddies awa kicking and screaming tae god-knows-whit, and then the wans wha wannae go, cannae go."

"I'd have thought they wouldn't have let him join on account of his age! "

"Shut yer face Tommy, yer terrible. Ah bet folks are saying a whole lot worse aboot me way ma hair aw white like a Granny. Onyway, ah only wish oor Donald hud been so lucky. Ah'm tellin ye, sometimes it pays tae be sick."

"Now that we're on the subject, there's something I need to talk to you about. Let's go out into the close for a minute."

They hung on until Alec had stopped singing and then made their exit, bending low to creep out unnoticed.

"Ah'll get ye some ginger," Maggie told him, relieving him of his tea cup and shoving him towards the door. "Ah'll meet ye oot there."

She walked into the kitchen and beelined for the bottle on the workbench. If he was going to talk to her about anything, she needed him sober, and she did not trust that one cup of tea was enough.

"Och, yer no' on the ginger," Big Stevie derided.

Over at the range with a group of men she had never seen before, he rocked back on his heels and eyeballed her. Their suits were well-pressed but drab; everything, in her opinion, that a good teacher should be. Sam stood a few feet away with Rachel, talking and gesticulating while she hung on every word. Maggie could not imagine that conversation being an improvement on the good old sing-song in the front room. She remembered Rachel's tears, her doubt, and knew they were not over yet.

"That's her," one man whispered.

"Excuse me?" Maggie looked back towards the range and the gentleman in question was staring brazenly at her, his toothy sneer nothing but unkind. She had never seen him before but wanted to punch him in the face as soon as look at him.

"Ne'er you mind, hen," he said, pointing as if he were making a threat.

Big Stevie cleared his throat and made it to her side in one long stride, turning her round so they both faced the corner.

"Whit wis a' that aboot? Ah huvnae talked tae them in ma life. Ah couldnae e'en tell ye their names."

"Weil ..." Big Stevie paused, embarrassed.

Maggie was worried. It did not sit well that her uncle could feel uncomfortable when his mind was muddled and his spirits high.

"The thing is, Maggie, ah widnae want tae tell ye this – ah dinnae want tae tell ye this noo – but ye're family so..."

"Whit?"

"Weil, thir's been some talk the nicht aboot a conversation some o' the laddies were huvin doon the Garscube a couple o' days ago."

He paused again. Maggie could imagine that a conversation arising from the pub would be just as colourful as the ones that were currently taking place. The way Big Stevie was looking at her, sidelong and apologetic, was frightening.

"Weil?"

"Apparently…I didnae hear this mind you, it's jist *apparently*, yon Tommy Gunn wis there. And he said," Big Stevie lowered his voice so Maggie could only just make out what he was saying, "'That Maggie Munroe is a right wan. Ah'm goin tae bow her head fir her afore nineteen forty is done.'"

"Whit?"

Big Stevie was quoting Tommy, but the words from her uncle's mouth was a compound horror. That was what these strangers had been referring to; that is what she would be known for.

"Wha telt ye?" she asked, spinning back round and grabbing his forearm.

The desperation in her voice was impossible to control. She needed to find out if these rumours were true. Perhaps she would never know for sure, but if that was all Tommy had in store for her then she would not be able to believe anything that came out of his mouth. Everyone was talking about her, thinking about her, judging her character, drawing conclusions. A laughing stock to some, a floosy to others, she felt sick.

"Wha telt ye?" she asked more loudly.

Big Stevie shook his head. He could not bring himself to say, but his eyes flickered to the back wall. The young couple had raised their heads at Maggie's shout and, as their eyes met, Sam quickly turned away. There was no surer sign of guilt, and it did not escape Rachel. She scowled in confusion and turned to whisper in his ear. The group of men watched intently, looking forward to a show, but Maggie would not give it to them.

"It wis lovely tae meet ye," she called over, grabbing her cup and shaking her head at Big Stevie as she hurried from the room. He may have been dealing with things the best he could but it was easier to point a finger at him when there was no one else to confront.

Reaching the front door, the man at the centre of the scandal sat right in front of her. He was on the top step, back towards her, drawing lines in the dust at his feet. There were some things she would not talk to him about. Perhaps Sam had been lying about the entire conversation but that was something she would never know for sure. Instead, she decided then and there that she would not have her head bowed by him, not in nineteen forty or any time after that. But, even as she thought it, the memory of his touch lingered.

Approaching him slowly, she tried to organise her thoughts but all she could see was the barrier between them, invisible yet robust. He heard her coming and turned, as handsome as ever.

"There you are. I thought you'd got lost."

"Couldnae find a glass."

Tommy sat quietly and she settled on the step next to him. He took a long gulp of ginger.

"I had word from John last week."

"Oh aye? Next time ye see him, tell him ah still hae his flask."

"He got in touch with me because the work he was doing for his uncle has finally concluded and he remembered the pact we made at the Barrowlands. He said he was ready for war if I was."

"Dinnae ye dare, Tommy Gunn. Ah'll ne'er speak tae ye again."

"It's too late, I'm afraid. I met him on Sauchiehall Street yesterday and we did it. I'm going to France."

"Ye bloody idiot."

"I am not. You said yourself, they are coming for me sooner or later so at least this way it's on my own terms."

"In the name o' the wee man ..."

"And I'm not afraid to go, Maggie. How can I let all those terrified young men march off while I stay here, perfectly willing to go in their place? In truth, if I stayed it would just be for you."

"Is that no' enough reason?"

"It is for me."

His look was meaningful but she did not ask him to stay. It was all academic now. Even if she claimed to love him despite all the lies he was spreading, his name had been given over to the ultimate power and he would be sent away. Besides, the promise she had made to herself stuck fast; he would never touch her again.

"How lang?"

"I leave Glasgow in two weeks"

"So soon?"

"They are desperate for men. The sooner I get over there and sort this mess out the better."

He struck a heroic pose and laughed but she could not make herself join in. No amount of propaganda and patriotism would save the lives of the men who were given over to the bombs.

"Weil, at least ye've got yer name gaun fir ye. Naewan's gaunae mess wae a Tommy Gunn."

"No truer word. Think on that when I'm gone."

His kiss was soft and lingering but she imagined she was taking a walk along the Kelvin; her body was not his. She felt he was trying to lead her somewhere. If she could have seen inside him, she would have known that he wanted so much to ask her if she loved him, to hear from her lips that he meant everything to her. He wanted her to be destroyed by his departure; he wanted to know that he had her always, that he had had her since that night at the Barrowlands when she had finally agreed to be his girl. He was afraid of the answer.

They walked back into the party, hand in hand. Maggie felt that two bricks were being ground together inside her chest, crushing down to nothing. She felt eyes on them but whenever she looked, people had already averted their gaze.

"Please don't say anything," Tommy asked. It was not like him to hide but Maggie knew it was not her story to tell.

"Gie's yer cup. Ah'm gaun hame."

He joined Big Stevie and Sarah, and Maggie pushed her way into the kitchen.

"Oh, yer still here," she said, faced with Sam and Rachel again.

"Absolutely legless, he wis. But we hud tae get him hame somehow. So that's when we took a crutch aff old Ed, sittin oan the corner like usual, and telt him we'd only be a minute. Propped him oan it, slobberin and yelling, and took him hame. Tell oor Helen ah love her, the right eejit said. So we did, and six months later she's aff tae the country visiting an aunt. Weil, it'll no' be an aunt popping oot o her if ye ask me," Sam continued as if no one else was there. "In fact, she's sellin hersel' short. Tak a look at yon Sarah. Ah've heard stories, ye know. At least she gets paid fir a gid time. Ma mammy ayeways says every lassie's sittin' oan a fortune and disnae e'en know it!"

"Is that mair stories yer spreadin?" Maggie spat, the scraping inside her chest getting harder. He glared back but she put the cup beside the sink and turned to leave.

"Are ye having a gid night?" Rachel asked.

She had almost made it to the door but the question made her turn back and look at Sam, smug and smiling at Rachel's side. She'd had enough.

"Naw," she said. "I've hud somewan saying horrible things aboot me. Things ah couldnae e'en repeat."

"Weil, it wisnae me wha said them in the first place. A'body likes a gid story. Ah'm just giein the people whit they ask fir."

"Ye're no' even denying it?"

"Naw. Huv ye asked yer man?"

"It's nothin t'dae wae him," Maggie cried helplessly, not believing her own words. "Things said amongst friends are private, especially when ye've hud a drink. Ah think it's worse tae be the spreader o' gossip, no' caring aboot a lassie's feelings, all fir a quick laugh."

Rachel looked between them, upset but not surprised. She had known about this all along. Sam was not finished.

"Weil, ah thought it wid dae ye some gid."

"Whit's that supposed tae mean?"

Looking her up and down, his curled lip was clammy and maleficent.

"If you thought a bittie mair aboot keeping him happy it might dae ye some gid, so tae speak. Noo poor Tommy'll be getting his satisfaction elsewhere. No' wae a ... whit wis it Rachel? Oh aye ... wae a frigid bitch like you!"

FOURTEEN

The Gobshite

1940

Barrelling past the few guests who clung on at Wilton Drive, Maggie crashed into her bedroom and slammed the door. It was too much.

She hoisted herself onto the bed, drawing her knees up tight. It was impossible to deal with everything at once: Tommy going to war, Tommy who had told the whole of Maryhill that he would get her into bed and left it for Sam to pass around to anyone who would listen. And that was the least of it. Frigid bitch. It cut her to the quick.

Putting her head between her knees, she could not squeeze the memory out. The hurt was so long and hard that she should finally be able to cry; the tears falling behind dry eyes. She rolled onto her side, pulled up the blanket and fell into a fitful sleep.

When she materialised the following morning, her father was already sitting in the kitchen with a pot of tea. He was on the scullery stool, left there by guests the night before and serving as a reminder that Donald was no longer with them. That this was more important than the words being slung around to hang her out to dry gave little comfort. She was still wearing the blue wool dress from the night before but Arthur paid no attention.

"How wis yer night?" he asked. "Ah heard ye come in and thought ye'd hae come tae see me."

"Ah'm sorry, daddy," she said, unable to think of anything else to add.

"Is it Tommy?"

"He's going awa tae fight."

"Truly?"

"He's registered awready."

Silence.

"Weil, ah can see why ye jist want yer ain space, hen."

The doorbell went. She jumped.

"Ah cannae get that. Ah need tae get dressed."

She ran into her room and threw on a plain brown skirt and white blouse, defying the tradition of dressing up on New Year's Day by telling herself it would do, for now. Only when she was halfway down the hall again did she pause long enough to pay attention to the voices that had arrived. It was the laugh that clinched it; high and throaty. Mrs Campbell. Without thinking, she pushed back into the kitchen.

"Hello," she greeted the visitors who were dressed in their matching Sunday bests and smiling in unison as they turned to her. Internally, she fought a raging battle to stay calm.

"Ye left awfy fast last night," Rachel said.

"Didnae come tae say gidbye," her mother agreed.

"She hud some news," Arthur mitigated and Maggie could hear an apology in his voice.

"Excuse me. Ah've jist remembered…"

She left the kitchen as fast as she had entered. It had been a mistake. She should have turned around as soon as she heard that laugh.

Quickly, she made it back to the bedroom; the only safe haven she had left. The dressing table reflected back a pale shadow of who she had been the day before, gay and radiant as she pushed 1939 out the door and unaware of what she was welcoming in. She put a hand to her cheek and tried to rub some life back in, but her eyes were large and vacant, reflecting the space in her head where thoughts and disappointments jostled everything else out.

"Are ye no' getting dressed already?"

Rachel pushed through the doorway after her, not bothering to knock. Her right to such liberties had fast worn away so Maggie kept her eyes on her own face, banishing her tormentor to the peripheries. The outline was a blurred figure with a hand on her hip.

"Whit are ye daein here?" she snapped. "Why dae ye e'en want tae look at this frigid bitch?"

"Keep yer voice doon." Rachel moved inside and closed the door. "Is that why ye ran oot last night? That's daft, Maggie."

Maggie's fingers curled around the dresser, unable to believe what she was hearing. She had not anticipated their conversation but had, somehow, imagined an apology. A cracking headache was coming on.

"Whit aboot a' ye were sayin aboot me last night. Ah'd ne'er hae believed it, no fae you."

"Ye've clearly hud tae much tae drink. Ye're misremembering, Maggie. It wis Sam wha said that aboot ye. Sam wha says a load o' things. Ah think he'd hud a bittie much tae drink in a'."

"Oh aye? Then why wis he lookin tae you fir support?"

Rachel's silence spoke the thousand truths she would never admit.

"Frigid? Whit maks me frigid? That ah'm no' up a lane liftin ma dress fir ma drunkard bidy-in?"

The startled squeal from the doorway gave little satisfaction. If she had shared everything that had happened between herself and Tommy that night then perhaps the frigid insult would not have been slung, but then the whole neighbourhood would be talking about her for different reasons and Tommy's plans for her would have acquired frightening significance. In the mouth of Rachel, truth was a flimsy friend and she sent a silent prayer to Davie, wherever he was, for the words of advice that had saved her.

"Ye dinnae know whit ye saw." Rachel shrank back into herself.

"Whit ah saw is nae mair than ye've telt me yersel. Ah hope a' ye've said aboot me's impressed him enough tae get him intae yer bed, rather than staundin up a back lane like a bandy-legged hoor. Or *his* bed, ah should say.

"Did yer mammy hae ony idea o' this when she wis sleepin in the next room? When she put food oot in the mornin', no' realising whit her lodger wis up tae? Did ye manage tae shag a' those other lassies oot o' his heid, or is he jist biding his time afore moving oan tae something better?"

Open-mouthed, Rachel searched for a comeback but nothing came, lost as she was in the muddle of imagining the worst; so Maggie ploughed on, side-stepping the precipice that she had come dangerously close to falling off.

"If it's frigid tae hae mair respect fir yer parents than that, huv mair respect fir yersel than that, and hae mair faith in yer man than that, then aye, ah'm frigid, but the only bitch here is you!"

The tears that came thick and fast from Rachel only angered Maggie more.

"Get oot." She held the door open and wondered who there was in life to depend on other than her daddy. "Ah huv tae get dressed. It's New Year. It deserves something better than the auld shite ah saved fir you."

Rachel paused, disbelieving. Eventually she shuffled out, allowing Maggie to slam the door in her face.

"We're still friends," came a hopeful voice from the other side, but the bricks returned to Maggie's chest, rubbing hard, daring her to cry.

Friendship had fled and what had happened would stay right there between them. She would not explain any of this to Jess or Minnie – as far as they were concerned, they were all great friends and always would be. For Maggie, this was as much as they would ever be again.

FIFTEEN

The Thing That Comes In Threes

The year did not get any better. News had arrived that conscripts and volunteers were finally needed on the frontlines and they were being transported from training facilities to Belgium. Nobody spoke the obvious – that the official army regiments were starting to run out.

The replacements of the replacements had a newfound importance and Central Station was a morbid site, sickening in its grandeur. Caught helplessly in a cloud of steam, distraught families tried to pull themselves together as composed young soldiers headed south on a train to England, the first stop in an endless journey. Some of those who remained on the platforms ran after them as they departed, as if they had decided to put a stop to the madness and keep their child, husband, brother at home, only to find that it was too late.

Tommy and John had agreed not to have family by their sides at the end. It was much better, they had decided, to enlist the company of three girls that Maggie did not ever remember meeting before, who talked about old times that she did not know about and did not want to know about. There was Evie, a pensive blonde; Charlotte, a pretty brunette; and Grace, the prettiest of them all. The day could not get any worse.

Each group was cocooned in their own small world, and Maggie felt misplaced in hers as she skipped by Tommy's side, feeling the steady swish of his kilt against her hip. On his other side, Grace kept close. The navy headscarf she had used to tie up her thick brown hair was covered in bright red love hearts and Maggie wondered uneasily who had bowed that head before. With the two girls by his side, he appeared dashing and jubilant, and Maggie longed to ask how he was really feeling. She need only wait. Once he boarded that train, the truth about so many things would no longer matter.

"Dae ye still hae ma hip flask, Maggie?"

"Aye, Johnny, ah'm keeping it safe fir ye."

He had Evie and Charlotte on each arm, everyone playing the role that was expected of them. Things were difficult enough without failing to conform, so Maggie pulled the flask from her bag with a flourish and proceeded to swig, staggering under the influence of dead air. It had been that way for weeks; deflecting attention to keep from confronting reality. Everyone laughed at her antics and she smiled back, offering it first to John and then Tommy. Soon it had been passed round the other girls and they lurched and laughed their way up the central platform, intoxicated on engine steam.

Halfway up the platform, Maggie stumbled for real and gripped onto Tommy's coat to keep from falling, drawing looks from passersby.

"Pull yersel' thegether or we'll get arrested," Evie snapped.

"Och naw, dinnae say that," John petitioned. "We're awa tae fight the huns. Nae polis wid try tae stoap us noo!!"

He had risen to the occasion and looked dashing in his bonnet and kilt. She had long been of the opinion that men with girth carried a kilt better than the rest and, for once, Tommy did not surpass him. He was pulling ahead and came to a stop at the front carriage, just before the train ended and there was nothing but rail tracks in sight. There was nowhere left to go.

"Aye, miby it'd be gid if these twa did get arrested right noo."

Maggie's smile faltered and time continued to march its steady beat.

"Are ye tryin tae mak oor spirits flag, Maggie?" John asked.

She didn't have time to answer. Young men began boarding the train surrounded by tearful farewells. It was no longer something that was happening to other people. Tommy stooped low to kiss Maggie on the cheek, then grinned wickedly at her bemusement.

"Only kidding."

He bent forward again and kissed her hard on her lips. Grace turned her back and, for the briefest moment clinging onto his arms, Maggie did not care if he had threatened to bow her head or not.

"Now you won't forget me," he whispered, taking her hands in his own as he pulled away.

Waving to the rest, he climbed the steps into the carriage but John suddenly seemed hesitant. He stooped to kiss her cheek but could not meet her eye. Conflicting emotions raged across his broad face and she could feel his ragged breath against her skin. Looking down at her trembling hands, she couldn't stand to watch him embark. Instead, she gripped them in front of her and told herself that she would see them both again soon.

With a low whistle and the gentle chug of building momentum, the train pulled away. Grinning, Tommy ran down the aisle faster than the train was moving, from carriage to carriage, keeping her in sight.

At the back, he swung out of the rear door and called out over the din,

"Maggie, will you marry me? When I come back! Wait for me…"

The rest of his words were drowned in speed and wind, but his silhouette remained visible, waving wildly as the train sped out of sight. Strangers in the crowd around her clapped and cheered, smiling through their tears as they held onto anything to banish the pain. Evie grabbed her close in a spontaneous hug, Charlotte jumped up and down and Grace was all teeth and no feeling. Almost everyone was happy for her.

Outwardly Maggie was in a state of stunned silence but inwardly she was cursing the man who, even then, could be seen waving his farewells. He had no right to publicly claim her without her consent. Had he whispered to her quietly in the ear, a private swearing of lasting affection, she would have rejected him but at least his request would have appeared sincere. As it was, he had merely performed the final act in a long-played game in which she was the loser.

"Ye must be awfy happy hen, tae hae made a match like that, right enough. Ah knew it fae the first time ah laid eyes on the twa o' ye thegether in this here surgery, so ah did. The way he was staunding o'er ye, all protective like, as if ye need protecting from wee auld me! Weil, ah thought he'd be a right keeper for ye, so ah did. Noo ye huv tae keep yer chin up for his sake, no matter how much ye want him hame, so ye dae."

Yes, she did want him home, so she could give him a good skelp for all the drama he had thrust on her. Once again, the whole neighbourhood knew about the proposal and, in one stupid statement, Tommy had made her a prisoner of propriety. Her blood boiled every time she thought about it. He was not desperate to have her on his return; he just did not want anyone else to have her while he was away.

"How are ye, Mrs McNulty? Huv ye heard how yer weans are getting on?"

"Aye, they're getting on great wae aw that country air but ah miss them terrible like, so ah dae. The hoose jist isnae the same, neither it is. They are living on a fairm up near Perth and are ha'in an absolute baw, especially ma boys, so they are. The fairmer must be going doolally. Onyway, it's kept me away fae the doctors fir a while, no' ha'in weans aroon getting themsels intae bother, so it has. But here ah um the day, so ah um."

"Weil, ah hope ye get weil soon. If ye wannae tak a seat, Doctor Bowman will only be a wee minute."

"Ah'm no sick. Can ah let ye in on a wee secret, Maggie?" "

"Of course, ah'm ayeways listening."

"I'm huving anuther wean."

"Och, congratulations!"

"Ah couldnae be happier, neither ah could. But ah dinnae think ah cid take anuther laddie. Take ma cousin, Elsa. Awbody knows cousin Elsa, so they dae. She hud three laddies under six at aboot twa year intervals and noo she's jist gi'en birth tae twins, so she hus. She didnae e'en know she wis pregnant, neither she did. So these twins pop oot and guess whit?"

"A wee laddie?"

"Aye. Laddies. So noo there's five o' them under six years auld. Can ye imagine that? Wee monsters, so they are. Naw, this yin's a lassie, ah can feel it, so ah can. Got a kick like oor Molly in it, so she does. Onyway, how are ye hen? How are ye coping wae Tommy gone?"

"Everyone's just getting on wae life as best they can," Maggie muttered, shuffling her appointment cards.

"Aye, the best they can, so they ur," the woman agreed, rubbing her stomach as if it was growing already. Maggie was reminded of Jess doing the same thing six months earlier and smiled, for she remembered there was still joy in the world, after all.

"The church is gid, a place we can go tae feel human again, so we can. Ah need tae speak tae the gid doctor aboot that wife o' his, so ah dae. Reverend Bowman's daein a terrific job, so she is. Fair keeping up morale. It shouldnae pass unnoticed, neither it should."

"Ah think he'd appreciate that a lot, Mrs McNulty."

"Aye, hen. Weil, ah'm sure ye'll be seeing far more o' me doon here, so ye will. Onyway, jist keep yer chin up, eh? Afore ye know whits happening, Tommy'll be back here putting that ring oan yer finger, jist like he promised, so he will."

Maggie's smile vanished.

Bad things come in threes and Tommy's proposal was only the beginning. For the end of March, the day was so unseasonably hot that it took Maggie and Arthur several minutes to understand the outburst that Jimmy spat out onto their doorstep. Panting and pale, he reached for Maggie's hand to drag her after him and, once she realised what he was trying to tell her, she was right there behind him, leaving Arthur to make his own slow way down the close. Still, as much as they hurried, nothing could be done. Jess lost her baby.

When she had started going into premature labour, her parents' fear had been immediate and Jimmy had gone for Doctor Bowman. By the time Maggie got there, the baby had been delivered and the doctor was trying to revive the child. Whenever he heard her in the hall, he called his receptionist into the room to clean around him, but no amount of shaking or slapping could produce a scream from lips that were already turning a grey shade of blue. The boy had never drawn breath in the world.

"Did he suffer?" Jess cried, too weak to sit up but refusing to let go of the tiny body in her arms.

"Look at his face there, Jess. He's at peace."

In truth, the doctor did not know when the death had occurred or for how long she had been carrying a dead weight in her stomach. He would have asked how long it had been since she felt a kick, but Jess was already broken. As Aunt Agnes cradled her daughter's sweat-sodden head and stared at the remains of her grandson incredulously, a cruel fire lit the room, still strewn with toys, clothes, and the hand-me-down cradle that would never be filled. Feeling like a grotesque imposter, Maggie glanced at Doctor Bowman and stepped back to join Jimmy and Arthur in the kitchen.

The days wore on. Maggie visited the Bennie house often but Jess wanted no one but her mother, so she and Jimmy sat in the kitchen for long moments with nothing to say. He would bring out his chisel to lose himself silently in carving another wooden figurine, and she would watch him and think on it for a while, always wondering if he was imagining the grandson he might have been whittling for. Only when the sobbing from the bedroom became unbearable would he slowly pack away his tools and wait until she headed for the door.

As the real news from the front came trickling through the propaganda, Jess fitted in to the unspoken heartache with terrifying ease. There was not enough pain to go round so, when her own heart broke, Maggie felt selfish, like she did not deserve a place amongst those who truly suffered – she was too far removed.

The third tragedy came two weeks later, on the day when the April showers arrived in earnest. After a fortnight's seclusion, Aunt Agnes decided to open her doors in the hope of jolting Jess out of her misery and, to this end, Big Stevie brought along his children to inject some energy into the day. Olivia arrived with her pigtails tied in sunny pink ribbons, Stevie in a sailor shirt that was striped in the brightest blue his father could find.

Agnes ushered them in and took a seat in the corner with a hopeful smile, content to observe from a distance. Olivia squirmed in discomfort as she absorbed the bleakness of the dimly lit room. Save for the burial, Jess had not left her bed since the pregnancy ended, curled tight with a toy soldier clutched to her chest. She had not washed, barely lifted her head from her pillow, and even a young girl could smell the despair.

Big Stevie pulled up a bench and pushed his daughter down by the shoulder, while his son sat himself on the floor before he was designated somewhere else. When he reached out for her clammy hand, Jess peered up from beneath the covers and the children were stunned. For five minutes they sat there, wide-eyed and still, as they got used to the spectacle before them.

Finally, Olivia whispered, "Daddy, ah wannae go tae Jaconellli's for a pokey hat."

"Naw, it's ma go, daddy. Olivia went last time."

"Neither o' ye are gaun. We're here tae visit yer cousin."

Olivia jumped out of her seat and pointed down at Jess like she was a grotesque.

"Aye but she's no' e'en movin. Why don't ah go an' get her some ice cream? Ye ayeways say a wee pokey hat makes a'thin better. Ye'd like that, wouldn't ye, Jess?"

Jess blinked.

"See! Did ye see that, daddy? Jess wants a pokey hat."

"Right enough, hen. Ye're a good lassie wantin' tae help oot yer big cousin, but Mario's in the tally camp the noo so ye'd be waitin an age."

She knew she was close and stomped her foot, and she was right. With a sigh, he dropped a coin into her palm.

"A'right, a'right. That's ma wee angel. Run alang and dinnae get wet."

"But da', it's ma go! Ah'll go get a pokey hat fir awbody!" Wee Stevie protested, but it was no use, his sister was already skipping out of the door with her blonde pigtails flying.

"It's no' fair. Ah could hae gone in a'."

He scooted away from his father and crossed his arms tightly.

"Ye shouldnae mak favourites o' yer weans like that," Agnes scolded, battling with her stiffness to pass him a cup of tea. "Look at Stevie there. He's a braw wee laddie."

"Huv ye no' learned yer lesson aboot commentin' oan ma weans?" Big Stevie grumbled.

Agnes shrugged, completely disregarding what affect her words had on the boy who sat grimly to one side.

It was a thunderous day and the doors of the doctor's surgery stood open to alleviate the muggy oppression in the air. When the tram hit and Maryhill Road became an uproar of screaming brakes and unearthly shouts, the noise of the furore carried swiftly through the doorway and hit Maggie full force. She dropped the stack of results she had been filing and snapped to attention just in time to see Doctor Bowman stride past, clutching his black case.

Jumping up, she ran to join him. They reached the street just as Auld Miller from the Garscube Bar hobbled up with a red face and blurry eyes and, not pausing to speak, grabbed the doctor's wrists and dragged him a hundred yards down the road. A crowd had already gathered.

Maggie was close behind, shivering as the heavy rain soaked into her bones. To their right, an elderly tram driver stood against the door of his vehicle, clutching his head and being consoled by two matronly women. Shopping bags were strewn around their feet, their rain-mates askew as all their efforts went into giving comfort. As Maggie passed, she saw the shame and shock in the driver's eyes, two small black ghosts, and her heart ached with pity for his suffering.

Twenty yards beyond them stood the majority of the crowd, many of whom had disembarked from the tram to stare aghast at the object lying on the tracks. Doctor Bowman got there before her and "Oh my God!" escaped before he could contain his emotion. He threw his jacket over it but not quickly enough to save Maggie a flash of blonde pigtail tied in delicate pink lace.

"I'm so sorry you had to see that."

He moved the crowd back quickly and, darting a quick warning, removed the jacket to examine the body. Maggie moved closer, knowing this would not be reality until there was no doubt left.

Olivia had been hit directly, her broken body bent back until her head touched her heels. Blood was congealing down her left side and hideous injuries were visible within but, for Maggie, it was her mangled face that held most power. The blue eyes stared wide, blank and unsurprised. Everything had happened too fast to register.

Doctor Bowman replaced the jacket. In the space of a fortnight he had witnessed the deaths of two members of Maggie Munroe's family and his wife had another funeral to preside over. But she did not scream or cry. She stood there, staring down, ringing her hands.

"Ah didnae see her," the driver approached on unsteady feet, palms open and happy to be purged by whatever consequences befell him. "She jist ran right in front o' me."

"Ah saw it," a bystander piped up. "She wis running tae get oot o' the rain. Came right roon the corner and didnae e'en look afore heading oot ontae the road. Head full o' sugar, no doot."

The man nodded meaningfully toward Jaconelli's where Teresa and Amelia stood watching from the doorway.

Maggie could not listen to their dissecting who was to blame.

"If ye dinnae need me fir the rest o' the day doctor, ah'm gonnae find ma uncle."

SIXTEEN

The Cut

"It's a tug o' war noo between Big Stevie and his demons an ah really cannae tell wha's gonnae win."

Aunt Agnes spoke quietly to Arthur and fussed ineffectually with the teapot, but her words carried easily to Maggie and Jess at the other side of the room. Her face was ghastly pale, not the usual hard wall she erected against her brother. It had sapped all Jess's strength to get out of bed, she had nothing left to contribute, and it broke Maggie's heart to sit in silence knowing every comment about Big Stevie Bennie was a sharp reflection of pain. She cooried down on the windowsill, pulled the thick, crocheted blanked up high and gazed out at the rain which stoated off the cobble river beyond.

It was a conference of sorts – a vain attempt to find a road out of the heartache. Futile. Unwilling to take his eyes off of his daughter for a moment, Jimmy had taken Wee Ena for a walk, but the room remained crowded with immovable emotions. They all knew that any progress would have to come from Big Stevie himself and no one could expect him to reach a catharsis soon.

Arthur spoke as quietly as Agnes, his face hidden.

"If ah lost Maggie, ah tell ye, ah'd ne'er recover."

As his family sat considering his future, Big Stevie slumped over the worktop of his small flat, surrounded by empty whisky bottles on all sides. It was not the drink, but memories, that haunted him and kept him stuck in the past. Long shadows spoke from the corner of the room: the voices of Daisy and Olivia freezing the blood in his veins, yet the most terrifying thing would be if his shackles were broken and he was free to forget.

"Will ye no' go oot and play?"

He was gruffer than he had intended, but it was unnerving the way his son stood watching his breakdown, absorbing the chaos, one arm hanging forgotten while the other gripped on the pulley rope, hard down then release. It obeyed his commands like a reluctant weapon high overhead.

"Go oot and play!" he ordered again, but his voice was weary.

They stayed like that, threatening to be lost forever amongst the insipid blues that washed down a cold and unquenchable tenement night.

SEVENTEEN

The Tear

It was getting late when Maggie jumped off the back of the tram and ran towards the Gallowgate as fast as her Cuban heels would take her. Batting a swarm of midgies from her face, she battled on. The sun would soon be going down and no lights would show her way home, but she couldn't be anywhere else. She was needed right there. She put her head down and ran faster.

Everything seemed unfamiliar. Minnie had taken her there a few times but the street names looked foreign, full of unknown landmarks, and her head was too scrambled to deal with it. Her heart was full but her mind was a void.

"Orr Street?" she asked a little old man who was hobbling towards her with a paper in one hand and a cigarette in the other.

"Next street o'er, hen."

"Thank you!"

She ran up the middle of the cobbles, desperate to avoid the baffle walls that had sprung up. Trying to dodge them would delay her. She needed a clean run. She needed to get to Minnie immediately.

Earlier that day, she and Arthur had sat side by side, sipping their tea in silence while the wireless played stage tunes. It was midday and Sarah Gibb's curtains were still drawn – everything was at rest. She picked up the *Glasgow Herald* from the crack between the cushions.

"Is it tae loud tae hear me o'er this racket?"

"Naw, ah can hear ye, hen."

Sipping his tea, he turned his face towards the fire and closed his eyes. In a world accelerated by extraordinary events, Winston Churchill's appointment as Prime Minister had already become old news but, as she read about the Axis movement through France, she felt that something was intensifying; something that had been missing when the fighting was concentrated on distant shores. Now it felt close enough to touch.

She felt a presence behind her; her mother was there, reading over her shoulder.

"Do ye feel that, Daddy?" she asked.

"Aye, hen, it's awfy sad," he said, leaning his head against the back of the armchair and keeping his eyes shut tight.

She glanced over her shoulder at the large framed picture of a fluffy white cat that Arthur loved so well. There was no one there. No one other than her mother, who had been with her in every moment of her adult life; a calming, watchful presence; but this time the air suddenly felt disrupted, as if Clara were holding her breath.

"Ah'll hae a wee look at the deiths an'll just let ye know if – aw bloody hell!"

At Orr Street, she pelted up the close two steps at a time and banged hard on the solid blue door.

"Minnie!" she called. "Minnie, it's Maggie! Open up. Ah'm no gaun onywhere!"

She banged and banged and banged, determined to bash a hole in the door if it meant she would get in faster. Minnie sounded faint and far away on the other side.

"Go away."

"Please, Minnie." Maggie lowered her voice, struggling to regain control. "Please open the door."

After a moment, it opened a crack and Minnie stared out, waxen and depleted. It was as if she were a walking corpse, the dark flat her coffin. She sank down on her knees and bent her head to the floor.

"Wha telt ye?"

"It wis in the papers."

All the things Maggie thought she would ask, about why Minnie had not told her about Davie and why she had not called on her for help, drifted away. Instead, she knelt down and hugged her friend, stroking the limp blonde hair as if she were a child. It had not been washed in so long that it stuck together in matted, moist clumps, and they were so close that Maggie could smell the florally sweetness of body odour. A child could be heard crying in a neighbouring flat but there was no sound from within.

"Is onywan here wae ye?" she asked.

"Naw. Naebody'll be wae me ever again."

Maggie drew Minnie up, keeping her close, and guided her through to the kitchen, wishing she could offer better comfort. The stool by the range was backless and she worried that Minnie would topple right over, but kept on following the plan to keep her close while the tea was brewing, not willing to let her out of her sight.

"Are ye alricht there?" she asked, propping her up sideways so at least she was resting against the wall.

The girl raised her eyes without moving her head, looking at Maggie with disdain. There was nothing alright about any of this. She turned away to put the kettle on the stove and took a deep breath.

"Yer haunds are shakin," Minnie told her.

"Dinnae ye worry aboot a wee thing like that. Where are yer folks?"

"At their hoose."

"Ye should hae somewan wae ye."

She was fussing but she couldn't help it and took two perfectly clean cups from the workbench to wash them all over again, just to give her shaking hands something to do.

"It isnae their fault," Minnie said quietly. "Ah went tae stay wae them, you know. But ah couldnae staund it. Ah wannae be here, wae Davie."

It was a fitful night, full of tears and shame, and all Maggie could contribute was cups of tea and useless words. The world outside grew dark and she closed the blackout curtains, but Minnie would not sleep. She took herself to the bed recess she had shared with Davie, lay on her side and cried for the shape she imagined was still with her.

Maggie sat on the kitchen stool to watch over her as she clawed at her blanket and pulled it high to her chin, trying to fill the abyss that a soul had left.

~

Through the murk of the pond, goldfish bumped together and scattered as quickly, their shocked mouths rounding in unanswered questions, all the way home. They were Maggie's only company save for the drizzle that tapped at the glass of the Kibble Palace, asking to get in.

"Procrastination," she mumbled, staring down at her reflection between the speckled scales of her companions. She had heard that word before but had never used it. It was not in her makeup; she would always act first and think later. Until the news about Davie.

She had filled Minnie a basin and stoked the fire while her friend washed herself clean; she had looked out fresh clothes and scoured the old ones; she had gone to a phone box on Orr Street to phone Minnie's parents; she had heard how Minnie was set to go to Skye the following week to live with Davie's sister; and she was not ready to share any of that information with anyone. After all, she had once heard someone very important to her say, *Dinnae empty yer ain mooth tae fill somebody else's.*

Now Davie was dead and a dog tag was all that remained to identify him from the thousands of other bodies trampled into the red mud. He left a broken woman behind whose long years would be spent scavenging at the carcass of their love. The nightmares that Maggie had heard about from before were becoming real again and what had seemed like fables now crashed on her doorstep. She remembered that first memory of her father's kilt sashaying down the street to war, around the corner and out of sight. She had been so young that she had never been certain if it was a real memory or the power of suggestion, but the difference did not matter anymore. She had been there. And he had come back.

She took a deep breath and tried to steady herself. The Botanic Gardens was the best place for comfort, filling her with that Sunday feeling and centring her in all that was important. That was what she had told herself on the tram from the Gallowgate. Sitting on the low stone wall surrounding the fish pond, sheltered from the rain by the streaked glass walls, she prayed.

EIGHTEEN

Fracture

In June, after three months of death, Maggie's world was taking on the colours of Europe. Every day she walked past the spot where she had last seen Olivia splayed in disturbed sleep, news from Belgium was bleak and the position of France looked set to follow, and the list of injured from Dunkirk was finally filtering home. Somewhere, lost in the fog, the names kept rolling in, flitting past so quickly they were nearly missed. When news came that Mickey, with his gorgeous face and constant manner, would no longer serve at MacIntosh Leather Merchants, she hoped that he had left the world just as he had lived in it.

"Have ye heard fae Tommy?" Jess asked.

Maggie shook her head. His last letter was dated March.

"He telt me he isnae gonnae write letters hame. But he'll be thinkin' aboot me waiting fir him. Expectin me tae feel grateful, like."

"Ye ne'er telt me!"

"Whit wis ah tae say? The hale thing stinks o' shite."

It was not proper to speak badly of a soldier so she left it there, keeping her thoughts to herself. There she was, left unwillingly under his umbrella for all the world to see when, in reality, she had absolutely nothing. Disappointment and frustration barely began to cover her feelings towards the man, her future a loveless hole that propriety would not let her to fill until he came home. Then she could end things to his face. In the meantime, as she felt the straightjacket tighten, all she could do was fantasise about screaming at all those who spoke to her about the heroic Tommy Gunn.

She and Jess walked slowly up to the park that sat at the top of the road between Wilton Drive and Lyndhurst Gardens. Jess was still not herself but some colour had returned to her cheeks and she was more talkative than Maggie had seen in a long time.

"Did ye see Minnie aff?"

"Aye."

"Wis Rachel there?"

Maggie looked away. "Aye."

"And Sam?"

"He's aff tae fight. At last."

"Did ye tell her?"

"Minnie? Aye. And ah telt her whit a lovely writer ye are and tae expect a letter soon. She telt me she's fair lookin forward tae receivin' them."

"Is she ony better?"

"Naw. Last she heard he wis in Namsos and the fighting stoaped there ages ago, so she thought he wis safe, but he wis deid already."

"Bad news gangs fair slowly, sometimes. It maks me feel awfy silly," Jess confided. "Ah've loast ma wee laddie, and ah luve him mair than onthing, but how many other mammies are goin through the same thing? Tae many. And there's Davie gone. And Big Stevie wha's trying tae carry oan regardless – and he's loast a wife *and* a wean. Nae wonder he's taken tae the bottle, but at least he's tryin tae fight. Then here's me. Ah jist gave up."

Maggie linked into her cousin's arm and leaned towards her to keep their conversation private.

"Dinnae be so hard oan yersel', isnae that whit ye're ayeways telling me? Listen tae yer ain advice. Besides, the minute Olivia died ye were oot o' that bed tae help. Yer mammy couldnae cope waeoot ye."

"Or waeoot oor Maggie. Ye're a rock, truly. Ah jist wanted tae apologise." A pause. "Dae ye wannae know the really awful thing? The thing that keeps me awake so ah jist cannae forget, no e'en fir a second?"

"Whit's that, hen?" Maggie asked reluctantly.

"Ah didnae jist lose a wean, ah've lost Paul in a'. He's no comin' hame, Maggie. Ah can feel it. Thir's nothing left."

"Ye're talkin' tripe."

"How else am ah gonnae get close tae him, Maggie? How can ah feel him fir wan last time?"

The words fell dully around them and Maggie wished she had the power to wash them away, for Death was having enough of a banquet without inviting him to the table.

Life continued. No one knew if the barrage balloons going up in playgrounds across the city were being tested or if an attack was imminent; the body and mind could only prepare and wait. By the time the bombs finally fell over George Square at the end of June, a numbness had settled over their hardened hearts.

Soon, the air raid siren was a common sound, peeling over the city like a maniacal vulture. Many a weary step traipsed down blackened close stairs and into the monstrous shelters that promised to save them. There was a direct hit on a shelter on Dumbarton Road which obliterated the structure and all of its occupants including three young girls from the same family, quickly followed by the scandalous claims that the whole construction was substandard, but the method of building in Partick was totally different to the robust structures in the north of the city. So Maggie told herself as she led Arthur by the hand, down the stairwell into the back green while the air raid sirens shrieked overhead, ignoring the stark likelihood that their own brick structure would not fair any better under a direct hit.

Time flew by. Mrs McNulty's fifth child, a daughter, was born healthy and happy and her mother took her north for safety, leaving Kenny behind. That was the same month as her garden railing was confiscated for war metal so she never did get a better view of the neighbours. In the end, there was no room in Perthshire with the rest of her children so she took refuge in Fife. Suddenly, the city felt more empty.

Like Mrs McNulty, many farsighted families had taken measures to protect their children before the war started but others waited for the bombs to drop before swinging into action. The countryside was filling up fast, slowly closing its doors on desperate urban neighbours. Wee Ena and Stevie were two of the lucky ones, although Wee Ena certainly did not see it that way as she was dragged kicking and screaming from Glasgow. Her tiny suitcase hung limply from one hand as she stretched into the air, trying to make herself as heavy as possible, but her mother's grip was unbreakable.

"Ah'm no gaun! Ah'm no gaun!" she yelled, splaying her legs at each side to stop herself.

"Aye yer gaun! Aye yer gaun!" Aunt Agnes yelled back, dragging her out of the close to a tram that would take her to the train station and far away.

Big Stevie waited on the pavement with Stevie under one arm and a tiny suitcase in the other. They had their own farewell to get through, but first they had to stand back and endure the spectacle of the niece. Maggie had arrived just in time to see them off and stood beside him, laughing at the sight of Wee Ena, her brown curls strewn across her face in a soggy mess but her iron will rivalling her mother's. Luckily, Jess was too distracted to notice; her patchy face had no space for humour.

"Ye'll be hame in nae time," Maggie said impulsively.

The scowl on Wee Ena's face showed she was not believed.

"Weil, at least ye winnae be stuck wae Gillian, the wee bitch!"

Wee Ena shrieked and cried harder.

Jess bent quickly to give her comfort but Aunt Agnes would not be slowed down while momentum was on her side. Wee Ena was yanked away, staring over her shoulder in anguish until she rounded the corner, out of sight.

"She's a right wan," Jess muttered. "Greetin' now she's gaun when every air raid she's bin greetin at the sirens and yon big mask mammy makes her wear. That's a' she likes. Tae hae a greet."

Big Stevie shrugged. "Ah guess we'll be aff in a'."

It was always a bit of a shock to see the wee man without his big sister. On their own, he and his daddy were two bendy spokes in an ineffectual wheel, trying their hardest to turn but getting nowhere fast. Maggie hugged him long and hard, willing all the goodness she could muster to be passed from her bones and protect him on the long journey to Strathaven. He stiffened like the awkward nine-year-old he had become.

"Ye're aff tae see ma Aunts. They're as close tae me as yer own mammy," she told him, although he knew that. To him, they were as close as family of his own.

"He'll be oan his best behaviour. Won't ye, laddie?"

Stevie nodded wordlessly. Father and son both seemed as resigned to this as they had become to life.

Looking away, Maggie's only option was to face Jess and try to ignore the silent tears being shed. The Munroe sisters had come up with this plan on their own, an illustration of their steady tempers and kind hearts, but that did not make the leaving any easier. The year changed inconspicuously, stealthy, waiting to reveal all that 1941 would bring.

NINETEEN

In For A Penny

APRIL, 1941

The scoured jumpers were piling up in the scullery but Maggie would not stop, perching high on Donald's stool and scrubbing down hard on the washboard.

"Ye'll wear a hole in them," her father called from the recess, whistling quietly to himself as he turned the radio up louder to block himself from the horrors of the world.

She paid him no mind, scrubbing harder; there was a lot to think about. First aid posts had sprung up as quickly as the air raid shelters had done and the whole street was talking about little else. There were calls for girls to help out and, from her work at the doctor's surgery, she knew she would be good at it, but Jess had told her that Rachel was going. At the weekly Red Cross training classes, that girl would be there, talking, smiling, *laughing* as if everything were normal. With that kind of company, Maggie's community spirit lay thin on the ground.

Then she thought of the real trials that her family had dealt with, and the nameless others whose tag had not yet found its way into the *Glasgow Herald*, and hated herself for her weakness. Closer to home, the Blitz had obliterated the lives of those she had, until weeks before, passed in the street every day, smiling, unsuspecting victims of a horror that was always just around the corner. On Kilmun Street, whole families had been wiped out with one blow and the few lucky survivors were left to pick through the debris of rubble and tea packets from a hoard of rations that they knew they did not deserve. Further west, news travelled from Dudley Drive that a woman had simply vanished along with her front room, turning to dust with everything else. Maggie knew it could have been her daddy who did not make it to a shelter in time, and suddenly she had a real chance to help.

"Thir's still no word fae Tommy?" Arthur called, louder this time.

"Naw."

"Thir's been word fae Ireland, hen. It's yer Uncle Jack."

"Is he deid?"

There was silence from the kitchen. It had been six years since her mother's funeral but there was little chance of her attending his. Wiping her hands on her skirt, she sat deep in thought. No word from Tommy, terrible words from Rachel, her neighbourhood crumbling and, through it all, time was passing her by. Each morning, it took a little more effort to draw herself from bed and a little more time to gather herself, and any contribution to the city's efforts would be better than wasting her days staring out of her bedroom window at someone else's freedom.

Jess had started classes the week before, feeling closer to Paul with each piece of gauze and each stitch she learned. Girls came from all over the north of the city to take part and Maggie wanted to experience it herself. She could be good at it. She could truly help people. Every side of the argument led to the same answer, and Rachel was not important enough to stop her. She told herself that and started the mangle again.

Beginning a week late, Maggie felt back-footed, like the reluctant pupil she had been in the past. She met Jess outside her old school, rubbing her hands together and feigning excitement.

"Yer fooling naebody," Jess told her, holding her arm out so she could link in, and they entered together.

The smell was the same, a pungent mix of chalk and lemon. The lights were dim but the silhouette of each individual desk and a-line blackboard were those emblazoned on her memory and the slow clench of her stomach was as familiar as it was unwelcome.

Jess knew where she was going, following the route she had taken the previous week up the squelching stairwell to the first floor. Three doors down, a light shone bright in welcome, but Maggie was having none of it. The cramps in her stomach were getting worse. Now the past really was near enough to touch. Not only was this the school where Maggie had dragged herself every day until her fourteenth birthday, this was the very classroom where she had sat at the torment of the infamous Miss McDonald.

Adolf's got nothing on her, Maggie heard her mum whisper as she entered the room slowly, unlinking from Jess and looking around to see that it was exactly the same as it had been thirteen years before. The desk stood sandwiched, as always, between a dusty blackboard thick with chalk and a small metallic waste bin. Rows of tiny chairs and uneasy easels stood to attention, facing the larger table with the rigid respect it deserved.

She jumped. No, it was not Miss McDonald. Just a tall coat stand behind the desk.

It was evening, the children were long gone, but with simple imagination their shapes could still be seen at their desks as a lesson progressed. In reality, Miss McDonald would be long gone, but it was still her face Maggie saw at the front of the classroom, harsh bun intact and woollen cardigan pulled tight around her stick-thin waist. Menacing her ruler against one palm, she growled at her students until she got the complete silence to assure her that nothing was going to disrupt her classroom. Only then did she take a seat behind her mammoth desk and stare into space, neck craned like a contemplative turtle out of the window and into the black street. She wore that wretched scowl, the favourite look in her limited ensemble, to assure all her subjects that nothing would be alright, ever again.

The wind changed wan day an' her face stuck like that, Clara interjected.

Maggie continued to stare at Miss McDonald, and at the distant look in the woman's eyes as she faded from reality and entered her own private world of insanity. It was a very different madness to the exuberance of Daisy Bennie, a lunacy that was dark and untouchable, a demented beast that everyone crept around in fear of waking.

For a second, the scene froze, with the children mid-poise and their teacher caught within her own haunting, and then....

"Come out!"

Everything fell into time and Miss McDonald spoke, her gaze unmoving as it floated beyond the classroom window. The children looked at one another, looked at their teacher, looked back at each other again. No one moved.

"Come out!"

Louder this time. A few of the older boys shrugged and left their seats, only to be followed by the younger, more timid members of the class.

Even at the approach of fifteen children, the woman did not flinch. Some of them followed her gaze expectantly but saw only bricks and chimney pots sending smoke into the air. No one saw the visions that appeared, only the deep creases that wrinkled up her neck and shifted slightly as she continued to breathe.

They stood still beside her, lined up so obediently and expectantly that one could have heard a pin drop on the thick wooden floor. A vein above her right eye twitched. A few feet scuffled in agitation, sensing danger, but no one dared move. Like a war drum, the twitching intensified. A crescendo was reached. Her piercing blue eyes refocused. They held nothing but unbridled fury as they whipped this way and that.

"WHAT," she bellowed wildly, "are you all doing here?"

"Ye telt us tae, miss," a brave voice said from the back.

"Ridiculous! GET to your seats!"

She flung her arms back wide and knocked over the children who stood closest to her. The result was a room full of dominos, falling with stifled yelps. They had all crushed forward at the summons so now there was nowhere to go; all they could do was careen back into the person behind. One unfortunate child crashed into the blackboard before being helped to his seat by a friend, but a chubby girl on the other side was not so lucky and landed in the waste bin. Everyone else scampered off and left her there, bottom firmly wedged in the bucket with her red hair shaking nervously and arms and legs flailing round the side, and Miss McDonald stood up, tall and erect, and bore down on her, growing redder and redder...

In 1941, the vivid memory was dissipated by a tug at her blouse sleeve.

"Sit doon," Jess hissed.

She sank into the nearest chair and looked around at a room filling up with women, all eager and interesting enough to dispel the ghosts that chased after her.

"It must be aboot tae start. Rachel's here."

In the far corner, the girl was giving her apologies for being late. She was emphatic. She leaned on the desk, ever so close to the waste bucket. That was the day she and Maggie had become firm friends, united over a mutual foe, but when she took a seat at the other side of the room, it was clear that Sam's leaving had not removed the distance between them.

Och Rachel, Maggie thought, *is yer arse still rimmed by the basket and are yer wrists still raw fae the beltin' ye took?*

Mrs Haggarty led the class and kept her coaching team in high spirits as they performed their last duty before they left to join the ambulance teams on the front. She called order and Maggie settled down to her first night of lessons, the nervous grip in her stomach dissipating as she fought to stay awake.

"Thir's gid numbers here the night," Mrs Haggarty started. "However, we a' know that the ferocity o' the recent attacks. Ah've been hearing reports that at least a thousand bombs fell. Jist tak a wee moment tae consider a' the worlds left flattened tae rubble and ash. Blitz is no longer a word used by other folk and the soond o' the air raid siren isnae jist a mild inconvenience takin us fae oor beds. And dae ye know some o' the first folk tae help oot when a' that wis happening? Lassies like you, wae a wee bit training and gid hairts. So, lassies, this is yer chance tae mak a difference."

Maggie woke up. It might have been a rehearsed speech but it filled her soul. Finally, there was some way she could contribute. She could do more than sit at home, torn between the feelings that she ought to feel and the emotions that welled up inside but she did not understand.

The following week was even more engaging when the group began to deal with the practical side of their training. It involved pair work and, when Rachel and Jess turned towards each other leaving her partnerless and floundering, Maggie really did feel like she was back at school. She turned to the girl on her left; a stick thin, fair-haired thing who looked to Maggie like a child. The girl's smile was small but strong.

"Whit's yer name?" Maggie asked, organising the paraphernalia in front of her.

"Penny Sinclair," the girl said. Her voice was surprisingly low and scratched against her throat like a bag of coal being dragged over earth.

"Ah'm Maggie. Ah dinnae mind seeing ye here last week."

"Ah sat at the back."

They got started. Penny successfully dressed a wound on her first attempt.

"Are ye sure ye've ne'er done this afore?" Maggie joked.

"Aye."

"Ah ayeways thought ah'd be tae squeemish fir things like this, but ah work at the doctor's and see a' kinds o' things. No' that ah hae tae deal wae it masel, like. Ah'm no a patch on you."

Penny smiled and continued to work diligently, not wasting her time with words as she set about her task and using a table leg to practise. Knot after knot, as easy as clicking her fingers. Maggie watched in admiration, looking at her own shabby work and unsure how she could keep up. She bit her lip in concentration.

"Ah!"

Penny laughed.

"Nae blood," she assured her.

By the fourth week, spurred on by this new partnership, Maggie had made quick progress. The self-conscious tumbling in her stomach subsided and the medical world that had surrounded her for years finally made sense. It was a strange comfort when Jess teased her for practising her suturing skills at home – it meant she was doing something right.

On the fifth week, Maggie left the house with a skip in her step.

"Ah'm gonnae ask some lassies back here the night," she warned Arthur, kissing him on the cheek. "Dinnae worry yersel though. It'll likely jist be Jess and wan lassie wha's so quiet she'll blend intae the wa' paper and ye winnae e'en know she's here."

"So ah'll see you and Jess later then?" Arthur chuckled and turned up the radio.

The class sped past. As Penny tucked a gauze expertly around Maggie's forearm, the patient focused on making a list of all the conversation points she could use later to fill the silence when Penny and Arthur sat in quiet indifference. She would find out more about the girl's family, that was sure, and the hobbies that must have made her so nimble. They would have time, and tea.

"Are ye coming tae Maggie's the night fir oor post-meeting cuppa?"

She could hear Jess, somewhere behind her, speak to Rachel. Mortified, she turned in her seat but it was too late.

"Dinnae move," Penny warned softly, grabbing her arm to keep it still.

"That wid be grand," Rachel said brightly, fixing her eyes on her own gauze and tightening it until Jess's arm turned pink.

"Oh, did ye no' know aboot it awready?" Jess was confused.

"Ah cannae mind. We talk aboot so much stuff, it's hard tae keep track."

Maggie stared ahead, trembling in fury, and Penny squeezed her shaking arm to try to regain purchase. All she had to do was pretend everything was alright. Taking a deep breath, she focused on being still and allowed the gauze to be wrapped and re-wrapped, but inside her blood was boiling. She had never believed that Rachel would have the audacity to set foot in her home again. Still, it was an inevitable repercussion of playing her cards close to her chest. If she could not share what had happened to Jess then she would pay the price for her silence.

When the class finished half an hour later, she mustered her courage and walked in silence as Rachel chattered the whole way from the school to her house. Down one short street, the journey seemed endless, idle gossip filling their ears with the misfortunes of others. What Rachel did not know for sure, she liked to imagine.

"So whit dae ye think aboot that?" she finished, just outside number ten.

"Tae be honest, hen, ye lost me when her man went aff seven years ago." Jess grimaced and walked towards the close, eager for her cup of tea.

"But wae her sister?" Rachel followed after her.

"Are ye alright?" Penny asked when the other two were out of earshot.

Maggie shrugged. "Ah couldnae care less aboot a' that, and ah cannae be arsed listenin tae it."

Across the way, Sarah Gibb's curtains were open but there was no sign of anyone inside. At least that was one worry that could be tossed aside.

"Can ye listen tae me?" Penny asked unexpectedly. "Jist fir a wee minute, on yer ain, like?"

"Of course! Here?"

"Naw. It's a wee bit cauld. Let's get in."

Rachel had followed Jess up already and, climbing the stairs after them, Maggie could hear her father in the kitchen.

"Aw Rachel, hen, it's lovely tae see ye. Ye huvnae been here since…since…wae yer mammy that New Year's day!"

"Aye, time's fair flying, Mr Munroe."

"Ah'm gonnae show Penny ma room," Maggie called.

It was a lame excuse but the chatter was so loud that she could not be sure they would have heard her.

"How long dae ye think we have?" Penny asked, following close behind.

"Afore the sun goes doon and ye hae tae go?"

"Afore we hae tae go ben the kitchen."

"Och, dinnae worry aboot them."

"Awright. Well, ah dinnae really know … ."

They pushed into the room and Penny perched onto the bed, completely poised in her pressed plaid trousers and crisp white blouse. The mattress sank beneath her and her top lip stretched to one side, considering her next move. She looked expectantly at Maggie, although she was the one who had called the meeting and she was the one who was talking. Maggie stared back.

"Right," the girl tried again, shuffling to the edge of the bed. "Ah've hud a wee sense that ye're, well … that thir's somethin oan yer mind. And ah've thought miby, miby it's Rachel. Ah dinnae wannae get involved, like, but it looks like miby there's something ah cid help wae."

Maggie just stared, thunderstruck. She thought she had been covering it so well but it turned out that a stranger could notice.

Penny fidgeted with her fingers, staring at the floor.

"It's probably jist me being stupit," she said. "Ye jist ne'er meet each other's eye. And ah dinnae think ye've e'er addressed her. It's ayeways Jess, polite like, and then you follow alang. And yer so friendly, Maggie, it's no' like ye. Ye'd talk tae onywan. So ah jist wanted tae check ye were awright."

"Thank you," Maggie said, at a loss for anything else. Then, eventually, "It's nothing t'dae wae Rachel,"

When she thought about it, which she did more than she would have liked, it felt shameful. She was starting to believe that she had done something wrong, like she should have gone further with Tommy, like he had expected it, like she really was a frigid bitch and deserved to be called it. Now he was at war and she would never know what he truly thought of her, if indeed he thought of her at all.

So she paused, unwilling to open that canister of shame for anyone else to have a poke at.

Penny cocked her head sadly and smiled. "Weil, if ye ever wannae talk, ah'm a gid listener."

"If ah've been seemin a bit funny then ah'm sorry," Maggie said, walking over to her dresser on the pretence of finding a hairclip. In reality, she could feel her face crumbling under the weight of Penny's helpful gaze. She needed a distraction, and quickly.

"Ma gid friend's jist flitted," she said.

It was an easy excuse and she decided to run with it. Penny helped her along.

"Oh aye, Jess wis tellin me the other week. It's Skye she's aff tae?"

"Aye. Ah'm awfy worried aboot her up there."

"Oh aye? Why's that?" Penny, attentive and listening.

"Weil," she sighed, "she's moved in wae her husband's sister, oan a croft, like. Thir must no' be much t'dae cos ah've hud aboot a letter a week fae her already. Oh, apart fae, thir's … Thir's a' kinds o' goings oan up there. Aeroplanes oan thir way here-there-and-a'where. And that sister, weil, she isnae used tae it. Every time the aeroplanes fly o'er, oot o the croft she runs, a' the way tae the bottom o' the field wae her jook o'er her heid! Minnie ayeways goes efter her and tells her thir's nothing tae be feirt o', but it ne'er does ony gid."

"Sounds like the maist fun she can hae," Penny laughed.

Maggie hoped so and smiled at the thought of Minnie running after Davie's sister, assuring her there was nothing to worry about while she became knee deep in mud and pelted through the fields with only the heifers and the aeroplanes for company. It was miles better than the thought of Rachel Campbell.

"Ah'm getting awfy used tae this letter writing malarkey. Ah write tae Minnie every week in a', and then thirs ma wee cousins awa' in the country, feelin a' grown up. It's much mair funny reading aboot their adventures in a letter than huvin tae see it fir masel."

Maggie found a clip and shoved her hair out of her face. "Whit aboot you. Are ye writing tae onywan?"

"Aye, thir is somewan. Ah think." Penny was wistful.

"Ye think?"

"Whit's that?"

It seemed like Penny was changing the subject until Maggie turned round and saw Sarah Gibb facing them in her lingerie, running a hand through her long hair.

"Jesus, Mary and Joseph!" she shrieked.

Penny's young mouth hung open in amazement, and Maggie grabbed her hand and dragged her from the room.

"Is that … ?"

"Normal? Naw. But ye cannae pick yer neighbours."

Rachel's voice rang out across the hallway, calling them to the kitchen. Maggie hesitated. If she was going to tell anyone about what had happened, Penny seemed discreet, detached from the situation. She really could be depended on – Maggie was almost sure of it.

No. The time for confidence had been and gone. Breathing deeply, she pushed inside to see Arthur sitting on Donald's stool and the two other girls standing guard over the kettle.

"Daddy." Maggie interrupted Rachel's flow. "This is Penny."

Arthur moved to stand, grabbing the dining table to haul himself up, but Penny got to his side quickly and held out her hand.

"It's lovely tae meet ye, Mr Munroe," she said.

"Aye hen, you too. Ma back's killin me the day. Let's go ben the big room."

She took his arm as to help him up, and kept at his side as he led the way.

"So, tell me a bit aboot yersel," he said as the door swung shut.

"As ah wis sayin," Rachel continued, shaking her head at the interruption.

Jess's head drooped and Maggie fled into the hall where she could still hear the unrelenting monologue and felt vindicated. After all, it was Jess's fault that Rachel had joined them in the first place.

The parlour door had just swung shut and she followed slowly, praying silently that Sarah Gibb had put herself away. Pushing inside, she was met by a whole room filled with the red glow of the sun dipping over the rooftops, bright and crisp like a warming fire on a cold day. From the table by the window to the cushions on the settee nothing was left untouched, it was a maharaja's palace and suddenly she felt richer. For the first time that year, the nights were growing long, the blues in the decor seemed balmy and the Gibb home was in shadow behind the sun. Maggie could not remember ever seeing anything so beautiful.

On the settee, Penny and Arthur spoke quietly. She could hear snippets from her new friend: the only child of a welder, the small flat close to the city boundary, and she leaned forward to hear more.

"Ma daddy's tae auld fir conscription, so that's a wee blessing," she explained openly. "But he's needed in Glesga fir his work."

"Ye're disappointed?"

"Weil, we'd been talkin aboot flittin tae the country. That wis the dream, afore."

"Yer close tae the country onyway, awa' oot yonder."

Penny shrugged and laughed. Their conversation wore on and Maggie went to the kitchen to help with the tea.

"It looks like we're ben the big room theday," she told Jess, leading the way with the tea tray. The two girls followed and Rachel sat beside Maggie at the table, turning her back to the settee.

"It's great tae be back here," she said in an unsuccessful attempt at a whisper. Maggie's eyes narrowed. "You and me, Maggie, we huvnae spoken in so long and…"

Jess slumped down beside her and she clammed up. Behind them, Penny and Arthur continued their conversation in private so Maggie stirred her tea and stared out at the sunlight as it started to dip lower and fade. Propping her cheek upon her fist, she stared through the glass and hunkered down for the long wait for a certain someone to go away. On her right, that someone would not be ignored. She swivelled towards Jess and her scratching, nasally whinges soon dominated any other sound in the room while the sun continued to drop and the glare gave way to shapes and shadows. Maggie stood to draw the curtain over the north window and save them from Sarah Gibb, then grabbed the teapot. It was her chance at freedom. She topped everyone up and came to settle on the arm of the settee, far enough from the bay to be able to breathe.

Before she knew it, the visit had ended and the guests rose to leave. She stood with Arthur at the window and waved as the three girls walked off into the gloaming. Then, together, they closed the last blackout curtain to shut themselves in for the night.

"Dae ye think they'll get home in time?" Arthur asked, squinting to determine how much of the murk was real. "Weil, ah know the other twa will, but whit aboot Penny? She hus tae go oot west!"

"She's got hauf an hoor yet."

"Hmmm." Arthur chewed the dry skin around his finger thoughtfully. "What happened tae that other friend o' yours?"

"Eh?"

"The wee lassie wha disnae say a peep. Wis she here a' the time and ah ne'er saw her?"

He was only half joking. Unbreakable bonds were made quickly in wartime.

On the sixth and seventh weeks, Penny continued to excel and Maggie was not far behind – by week eight, she could set a splint and dress a wound without biting her lip bloody in concentration. They held a small celebration in Jaconelli's in the end and were joined by the first aiders who had trained them. Some of the experts chatted enthusiastically about what lay ahead, the soldiers and the excitement if they managed to get deployed abroad, while their students were filled with flitting, fanciful ideas of their own. It was lucky for The Cause that they were needed at home.

All the while, no one sat quite so rigidly or listened quite so intently as Rachel. Her mouth twitched, her eyes widened with desire, but her fingers were graceless. In class, they had stumbled over gauze and splints and produced results which, she had been assured kindly, would do well enough in an emergency. Still, she saw herself a flaming light descending. Call to her and she would be there. Her time had arrived.

"Should we rein her in?" Jess asked, looking across to where Rachel was quizzing two of the women from the Red Cross.

"You can if ye want."

Maggie was dismissive but Penny was interested.

"How cid we dae it?" she asked.

Jess shrugged and chuckled to herself. The deep lines which creased her face would never leave her and her hair was shot with grey, but her eyes had regained some of their sparkle. It had been a year since she lost her baby and it was good to see her laugh again.

Maggie breathed deeply to capture the moment. Looking around, she caught Penny's eye and stuck out her tongue. Penny flapped emphatically, looking meaningfully at the experts from the Red Cross, batting her away in case the antics were spotted. Maggie did it again and was thankful that she had managed to slip into a hassle-free friendship that covered her like a warm bath drawn by the hand of fate, and neither Rachel Campbell nor Tommy Gunn would ever take it away from her. She would make sure of that.

TWENTY

Across The City

The steam engine laboured out of Maryhill station and rocked down the line as the sun shone tenaciously and the world lengthened into summer. Big Stevie sat opposite. His dishevelled clothes were clean but his puffy eyes and sweat soaked forehead betrayed him. His eyes darted around the carriage like a caged animal awaiting any chance of escape. Fidgeting with his breast pocket, his eyes finally came to rest on the floor.

"What did she gae ye?" Maggie asked, hugging her bag close.

"Jist a wee minding."

She glared at him but bit her tongue. It was more than a wee minding, to make his cheeks turn so pink.

"Are ye happy aboot the wee minding, or aboot something else?"

"Ah'm happy that ah'm gonnae see Stevie."

At least she could be grateful for that. And thankful that, when they were leaving for the station and Sarah Gibb ran down from her flat with the mysterious gift that now sat small and circular in Big Stevie's pocket, she'd had clothes on for a change. Shouting after them and running to catch up in her nightdress, she had almost been respectable. Her loose hair had flailed, her slippers nearly tripped her and the performer's confidence waned on the street corner under Big Stevie's puzzled gaze. Maggie had fallen back.

"Jist fir you," Sarah had whispered, reaching out her hand.

Just before Maggie turned away, she caught a glimpse of a thin white tissue wrapped with something inside. Clara would have said her nose was bothering her.

"It's jist, ah heard ye were aff, and…" For once, Sarah Gibb did not know what to say.

"Aye, ah'm no auld enough. Ah ne'er thought ah'd say that."

A nervous laugh.

"Aye, but it's a great honour tae be called up. Ye're aff tae save ye're country."

"And if ah dinnae come back?"

Sarah Gibb was quiet for a few moments but Maggie could sense a change in the air behind her, something stifled, a kiss or a sob, and she walked away. For the briefest moment, her thoughts turned to Tommy Gunn. If only he would write to her, just once, and let her know he was alright.

At the street corner, she stopped and turned. Her neighbour was grabbing onto her uncle's arm like she would never let go. He was speaking quietly, his words lost to the wind. Sarah Gibb nodded slowly and walked back to her close, turning briefly with a sad smile before disappearing inside.

As the train rolled away from the station, she squirmed in the uncomfortable wooden bench and gave up trying to elicit any more information. A minding it was, and forever would be.

When the train stopped at Pollockshields, two strangers embarked. An elderly man hobbled into the booth beside Maggie, noisily readying himself to read a crumpled broadsheet and a girl, weary with exhaustion, fell onto the bench beside Big Stevie just as the train pulled away. Her plain black dress and small cap identified her as a maid returning home after a long slog in some Southside townhouse and, although her haggard face could have been anything from nineteen to thirty-nine years old, Maggie could see the obstinance of youth, still undefeated by the world, in her pale eyes. Maggie idly hoped she had a better prospect than an old, lecherous uncle.

Neither man nor maid seemed interested in conversation and Maggie was left to watch Big Stevie whet his lips as the drouth set in. Urban blocks quickly turned into large houses surrounded by equally large gardens, which turned into green fields where the only buildings were those which housed cattle. For Maggie, the rural scenes only added to the nightmare of the day.

"Wid ye stop wringing yer haunds like that, Maggie? Ye're fair making me nervous."

She looked down and saw that he was right. Her palms were rubbed pink.

"Ye're wan tae talk," she retorted quickly, "spinning yer cap in yer fingers, roond and roond like a top. It's meant tae go on yer heid!"

He returned it there bashfully. The old man coughed pointedly from behind the *Glasgow Herald*, then silence reigned once more. Steam pulled the carriage on and Maggie wrung her hands harder, ashamed that lessons once learned were so quickly swept away.

Outside church the day before, Big Stevie had asked her to go with him to Strathaven. There had been rumblings about it for weeks but, still, when they finally heard that conscription was being raised to forty, it was like a bolt of thunder. Yet, instead of being supportive, Maggie had done what she always did. She had spoken.

"Ye want me tae come?"

"Aye. The weans love ye. And Agnes telt me ah'm no aff tae see the Munroe sisters wae oot ye. They're respectable, apparently, and so are you. Ye're a link in some chain. Dinnae know whit that maks me."

"Dae ye ayeways dae whit yer sister tells ye?"

She had been kidding, but Big Stevie's stricken face left her grappling. In the depths of the night, she had seen its haunting likeness etched on the ceiling plaster. When he was in vital combat in a world far from home, it was the harsh words that he would remember, and there she was less than twenty-four hours later providing even more fodder.

The man gave up on his paper and folded it neatly away; the maid's head drooped and slipped into the weary sleep of one already grown old; the countryside continued by, beyond the unrelenting clatter of wheel on track, a continuous stream of green.

When at last the view changed to the red bricks of Strathaven, Big Stevie jumped from his seat and twirled his hat faster. The commotion roused the sleeping maid and the old man grunted when the big man lurched past so Maggie apologised quickly and slipped into the corridor behind him. The train chugged slower. She stumbled. They had reached the station.

She could see her aunts on the platform, one tall, one stooped, eyes flitting across the windows of the approaching train to catch a glimpse of its load. She waved out at them and smiled. Suddenly, everything was well; the two women would gladly share the burden of the day.

Still following her uncle down the steps and onto the congested platform, she remembered childhood holidays in Strathaven when everything was big and exciting around her, including the people because she had not yet made friends and had to survey her doman from the height of her mother's waist. It was a different life where people moved slower and talked so quietly that she struggled to hear them. Her own secret world away from the city.

"Maggie!"

"Wee Ena!"

It was the glove Maggie noticed first, materialising through the thick engine steam and bobbing up and down like a defunct yoyo. It was made from an unmistakable lime green and edged with cheap pink gems, one of the pair that Donald had bought his sister before leaving for France. An early Christmas present, he had said, and now it waved out despite the heat of summer, a disjointed appendage protruding from an invisible torso.

As the train stammered off, sucking its pollution back under itself like a vacuum, a lithe body attached itself to the glove and ran so close to the track that Maggie's heart nearly stopped.

"Be careful!" she shouted.

The girl catapulted forward with fearless abandon, tumbling into a hug with such gusto that Maggie stumbled against the embrace.

"It's awfy gid tae see ye, Maggie," Wee Ena cried as she buried herself against her cousin's pale blue cotton jacket, almost knocking the bonnet off her head. When she looked up, her face was wide and grinning.

"And where's Stevie?"

"Och aye!"

She turned and ran helter-skelter back the way she had come, only to return seconds later, dragging Stevie behind her and forcing him to move faster than his small legs could carry him. His eyes darted around the platform, then his whole face brightened. Big Stevie had appeared at Maggie's shoulder.

Relief made Big Stevie smile. He went to his child and rubbed his hair.

"Ah swear ye've grown," he declared, oblivious to his son's Sunday Best on a Monday morning, with the long trousers rolled up in a vain attempt to fit. "Ah mind the day ah could pick ye up on ma knee. It wisnae that long past, but ah bet ye're tae auld fir that noo. Whit a fine, strapping country laddie ye've become."

Flinging his arm over his son's shoulder, the two of them led the way outside, past crates of parcels and milling travellers. Stevie's childish voice flew in the other direction but Maggie would have sworn she heard him reply, "Och naw, Daddy. The country's nothing like hame."

"Oh aye? Tell me, then, whit hae ye been up tae?"

They walked on ahead to join the aunts. Steps behind, Maggie looked Wee Ena up and down.

"It's you wha's a' grown up" she commented.

From curly brown locks to black patent shoes, Wee Ena suddenly reminded Maggie of herself. She smiled. There were other changes, too. The light fawn jacket was plain and functional and reeked of Aunt Annie's seamstress skills. Gone were Wee Ena's usual hand-me-downs.

"Whit happened tae yer auld coat?"

"The sleeves were up tae ma elbows, so Aunt Flo said. Aunt Annie's gonnae teach me so ah can mak ma ain next time. And ah gettae choose the colours masel'."

"Ye can mak something nice fir yer mammy, then. She's missing the lot o' ye but couldnae come cause she's tae busy runnin aroon Maryhill like a blue-arsed fly. She telt me tae gae ye a clip roond the ear if ye've been gein' ma Aunts ony trouble."

"Oh, ye widnae!"

"Of course ah widnae." She hugged her cousin tight. "And ah dinnae believe fir a second ye've been bad. If ye hud, the twa o' them would hae written straight tae ma daddy."

Wee Ena giggled and hugged back, allowing Maggie to feel how sturdy she had become, how naturally her grin seemed to lighten up her face. There was no sign of the tiny wee wisp of a thing with the big mouth and pinched eyebrows.

"Are ye likin' it oot here in the country?"

"Erm ... ah've learnt tae swim in the river. And ah'm teachin Stevie. He cin tak his feet aff the grund but screams oot when a fish swims past. He says it tickles. It disnae. And ah hae ma favourite hill tae roll doon. That's anither thing jist fir summer. If ah went hame noo covered in grass, Aunt Flo's face'd be a scream. She can be awfy scary when she wants tae be."

"Sssshhh, she'll hear ye. Come oan."

They had been talking fast but there was not enough time in the day and they had to run to catch up with the men who were already reuniting with the aunts under the clock. Seeing them juxtaposed like the straight back and slanted seat of a comfortable armchair, Maggie felt only love for the two old women and their watchful, pensive ways, and hugged and kissed them so hard that she knocked Flo's bonnet off. She dusted a patch of grit from the pink felt, but her apologies were quickly brushed away. Flo fluffed out her hair and popped the bonnet on Maggie's head, instead. It was good to be home.

Although everyone knew the way, it was only a short walk to the house and they let the sisters strike out in front; down past the park which rang with the laughter of children that had been absent from the big city for far too long, round the corner, past the bakers to the river. They rounded the bend and the house was there, the middle home in a line of identical, white-washed cottages, indistinguishable from each other save from the bright colour of the doors. Just beyond, the road narrowed into a footpath that curved round to join a boo-backet bridge, over a river that gurgled peacefully into the distance, but there would be time for that later. First thing, everyone stopped where they were supposed to – the Munroe house was the one with the blue door – and clambered inside.

Maggie felt the same thrill at walking through a proper front door as she had when she was a girl. In the tight space, Big Stevie appeared meek next to the bustling doyennes. He shuffled back as they inspected his son's clothes and sent Stevie out to the bucket at the back to wash his hands before lunch, and looked ready to follow until the Munroe sisters called him back into the living room.

They seated him beside the fire and started their barrage. Did he have an exact date for deployment? Did he know anyone who was going to be in his regiment? How was he feeling? Had he known it was coming?

He tried to push himself down into the insignificance of his worn brown armchair, keeping his answers short. Maggie bit her tongue to stop from adding a question about the minding. Instead, she helped Wee Ena bring in high stools from the kitchen. Aunt Flo knitted ferociously, listening with her ears, while Annie listened with her whole body bent forward to absorb every detail. While Aunt Flo had never found a love to lose, Annie's one true love had been stolen from her by the first war, and every nod was an acknowledgement of a desperate memory of happiness that had existed as a tangible reality before being banished to the confines of her mind.

The carriage clock on the mantelpiece struck twelve. Wee Ena rose automatically and went to the kitchen. She returned moments later with Stevie, each carrying a tray of sandwiches. Maggie felt a bunion flare and was glad to have passed that mantle on.

"Is there a wee dram tae go wae this?" Big Stevie asked, a dog on the trail of opportunity.

"Naw. It's hard enough tae get a loaf and decent meat fir yer pieces."

It was a convincing explanation from Aunt Annie but Maggie knew that she would find their private stash if she went to the cupboard under the shelves. Big Stevie's mouth twisted with suspicion and his nose twitched, catching the scent. She held her breath.

A pause. He stroked the long hairs of his knuckles to quell whatever had been brewing and threw a vague, distracted smile across the room.

Aunt Flo rolled her eyes. "Ye winnae last twa minutes o'er there if ye keep downin' that stuff. At the rate ye've been going, ye'll be meetin' that wee lassie and wifie o' yours afore the year's oot!"

She did not take her eyes from her knitting, all the easier to ignore young Stevie's instant pallor. Big Stevie was too stunned to speak.

"Ye know," she continued, "it's as if that's whit ye want, the way ye go aboot life. And let me jist say, yer prayer'll be answered if yer awa escaping the bullets so legless ye cannae e'en see straight."

"Ah'm sure ye'll be fine. Ye know how tae handle yersel."

Even to herself, Maggie did not sound convincing. In the dappled light that fought its way through the heavy lace curtains, the boy's tears glistened shamefully against his rosy cheeks. Wee Ena caught her big cousin's eye in panic, and she rushed over and pushed him to the ground.

"Tig, ye'r it!" she called desperately.

"Och, away ootside if ye're gonnae play that nonsense." Aunt Flo grumbled, but Wee Ena was already halfway through the kitchen and out the door. Stevie looked up at his father, a knot of questions, but his cousin called him again. Finally his attention was taken and he unravelled himself to run after her.

Maggie waited a beat but no one reacted so she rose to clear away the dishes. Slowly, normal conversation resumed behind her; about Aunt Agnes and Jimmy, and Agnes's irritations when there were no children left to bother her. She stood in the kitchen, looking out at the two wee ones chasing each other round and round the back court like hamsters on a wheel. Wee Ena was all bony limbs, her hair flying behind her as she darted away from Stevie's desperate attacks. In a few years, she would be too big for these childhood games. They were growing fast, out of sight, and they would never get the lost time back. She would not get it back. Overcome, she was angry at the war all over again.

Her thoughts still rested under a melancholy cloud when she stood in the hallway and kissed her Aunts goodbye. On the walk to the station, the shadows grew long and the sunlight turned blue. The cusp of the day – usually her favourite but, in that moment, it was marred by all the things that were slowly coming to an end. Father and son walked in front and she and Wee Ena followed slowly behind, trying to drag out time.

"Ah'll look efter him until Uncle Stevie comes back," Wee Ena promised.

"Ah know ye will, hen."

The train was ready to leave when they arrived, no time for prolonged goodbyes, just a quick kiss and a tight embrace.

"Damn. Yer daddy made these fir ye." Big Stevie sighed and held out two wooden figurines. One was a steam engine and the other was a girl with red lips and black hair. Wee Ena grabbed hers.

"Snow White!" Her shrill excitement was good to hear. "Please tell daddy, thank you."

"Thank you, Uncle Jimmy," Stevie said sincerely, although Jimmy was not there to hear.

"Miby, when ye both go hame the night, ye cid write him a wee letter and tell him that yersels?" Maggie suggested.

There was a hiss of steam from the train and she knew it was time to go.

Big Stevie set his shoulder square as he ruffled his son's hair. Then he boarded the train. The wee man tried to be strong but his shoulders quivered as he thrust them back, chin out, an imitation of his father. Wee Ena stood behind him and wrapped him in a hug. Catching sight of them from the carriage steps, for a second Maggie saw a blonde girl standing with him, her big eyes shining out through the crowd, her pale skin and gentle eyes peering out curiously above a soft blue coat and her emerald green hand waving high. When she blinked, the image vanished but, even as the scene settled and the two blended clearly back into focus, the haunting picture remained.

As the whistle blew, she made it up the last step and collapsed into the berth. Big Stevie remained at the doorway, waving until the train had pulled out of sight.

Later that night, the black city was suffocated by a crushing blanket of cloud, and then the sirens came. Across the city, people hurried to the uncertain safety of their shelters. It was too black for shadows and only Arthur navigated his way downstairs with any confidence: he was used to living in the dark. Maggie followed close, using her palms to guide her. The sound of the sirens clenched around her heart and she fought against the fear, unwilling to let it immobilise her. The accounts of the Clydeside Blitz had percolated and she knew nowhere was safe when the Luftwaffe had a base to get home to, unweighted by bombs. If she could have grabbed on to Clara then she would have never let go. Instead, the intangible woman beside her was speeding up, willing her on.

On the first floor landing, one of the wee girls from the flat on the top floor knocked past in her rush to move forward, bumped painfully at Maggie's leg with the snout of her Mickey Mouse. Still, better the discomfort than no gas mask. Her mother kept her hand clasped tight and kept her in line, but everyone felt the pushing wave of terror that was never spoken about during the day.

Down they went again and reached the ground floor. A dense shape rushed out of the McNulty's door and banged into Arthur, almost knocking him from his feet. It was Kenny. He grabbed hold of Arthur's dressing gown to keep himself upright.

"Ah'm no' as fast as ah used tae be, noo ah'm oan ma ain," he whispered in apology,

"Sssssh!" came a voice from behind. Everyone was listening for the sound of the first bombs to drop, praying that, if it came, it would only be a soft thud in the distance.

"Sorry!" Kenny called.

Maggie took Arthur's arm and he led her outside, across the back green to the brick shelter that had been erected beside the washhouse. It was already half full of shivering bodies wrapped tight with blankets and neighbours whispered greetings as their eyes adjusted to their surroundings. The eyes of the Munroe home, Maggie was glad of something to do besides worry.

Within minutes, the steady stream of people had ceased, the room was rammed with bodies, and everyone hunkered down under a solitary, sickly lightbulb to wait out the bombardment. Then silence. Time lost all meaning. In the middle of the night, there was only room for the suppression of dark thoughts, and distress was passed back and forward like a football. Until the steel roof started shaking. Until the door was thumped hard and long, and the shaking intensified. The weak light jolted overhead, casting dancing shadows like ghoulies across the wall. It defied reason, but the whole shelter seemed close to collapse.

"In the name o' the wee man!" wee Mrs Murphy shouted.

Maggie jumped up. Kenny McNulty moved to pull open the door. Others shouted in protest but he was in his late forties and strong. No one could challenge him as he pulled the door back to reveal a young woman in a long black coat. Her hair was plastered across her face and her body shook as hard as the walls. Her bloodied face and terrified eyes spoke to everyone through the gloom. Shouts of *bomb* reverberated against the walls, catching like wildfire.

Kenny pulled the woman inside, hurriedly shut the door again and someone, somewhere, started to cry. Still, Maggie told herself, they had not heard an explosion. She rushed forward.

"Whit happened tae ye? Where are ye hurt?" she asked, guiding the woman onto a bench.

The woman sat stupefied, her silence at odds with the cacophony around her. Maggie gently pried the hands away from the face for a better look, slowly focusing through the darkness. She saw no sign of outward injuries, but the copious amount of blood must have come from somewhere.

Gently, she took the woman's wrists and guided them downwards, away from her face to reveal the injury. Beyond all the gore and tears, the woman's nose was pushed flat against her head, the force bending the cartilage downwards until her nostrils were obscured and much of the flesh was compressed into meaningless pulp around her lips. The crowd moved back. Only Arthur stepped forwards but there was no support he could give.

"Whit hit ye?" Maggie asked, imagining flying debris from an explosion closeby.

Silence. Taking a cloth and iodine vile from the first aid kit, she gently washed around the injury. The girl pulled back and stiffened.

"It's awright," she said, lightening her touch.

She remembered Mrs Haggarty on the first day of her training: *'Wan o' the most important things we cin teach ye. Keep the wound clean.'*

"Did somewan dae this tae ye?" she whispered.

The other occupants in the shelter were moving forward again in fear that their own homes had been destroyed along with the girl's face but, if that was not the reason, any offender could be in the room with them. The stranger shook her head, denying the assumption and wincing at the sudden pain of movement.

"Move back and gie the lassie a wee bit room."

Maggie had not heard her father sound so authoritative since he had caught her playing on the wash house roof. The crowd obliged as much as possible in the confined space, and she was thankful, not wanting a room full of witnesses to see her fail. She had to focus. She pushed down the fear that she might not be up to the task and held on to the woman's wellbeing. It was in her hands.

"Noo hen," she tried again, "jist tell me a wee bit aboot whit happened tae ye."

"It wis dark and ah wis runnin'," the woman wheezed, grabbing desperately at the loose strands of her hair. "The sirens were goin' aff but ah only hud twa mair blocks tae go until ah wis hame. Ah thought ah cid make it."

"Where dae ye stay?"

"Druthven Street."

Casting her eyes to the ceiling, the woman stopped for a moment to regain her composure. She gritted her teeth.

"Ah wis near when ah ran intae the blastet baffle wa'. Ah didnae see it comin', it wis that dark, and then ah knew ah jist hud tae get intae the first shelter aboot. Those stupid wa's are suppost tae protect oor hooses, no bust oor noses!"

Wee Mrs Murphy laughed. Inappropriate, but Maggie knew where she was coming from. People had imagined their houses destroyed but, in the end, the only thing that had been broken was the woman's nose.

"Stupid wee bitch," someone muttered unfairly when the thing they were most angry at was their own fear. Then music as an accordion started up and all the relief came out in a flood of songs that would last the long hours until they were free to escape.

As she dressed the wound and strapped it up, Maggie noticed her hands were shaking. It had been a false alarm. This time.

TWENTY-ONE

The Minding

"The nights are fair drawing in," Doctor Bowman commented, glancing at the darkening sky.

"Aye, and the rain clouds dinnae help," Maggie sighed.

The keys jammed and he fumbled with the surgery door as she pulled on her gloves and stamped twice to get her blood flowing. Penny stood waiting, close against the building to avoid a light, invisible drizzle. Her loose linen trousers were tucked tight into her socks, out of the rain.

"Ah'm sorry tae keep ye."

"No a problem."

"There we are then," the doctor said, finally locking up.

Penny smiled, straightened her waistband and turned to leave, and Maggie was all set to follow when a familiar figure caught her eye across Maryhill Road. He was walking towards St George's Cross, hands folded behind his back. She wanted to leap across to say hello but the trundling of a tram car held her back.

"Come oan, Penny," she said. "Ah wannae introduce ye tae someone ah used tae know."

Waiting for the tram to pass, she lost sight of Alec on the other side. Bobbing up and down, she wished it would go faster, incline be damned.

"Wha's it?" Penny asked.

"Someone ah used tae deliver tae. He ayeways hud something nice tae say."

"And that's unusual?" Doctor Bowman asked. He sounded truly surprised and Maggie bit her tongue. It must be a sheltered life being married to a minister.

The tram moved up the line and Alec was almost parallel to them when another familiar figure cut in front. It was Sarah Gibb, strutting forward urgently and making a beeline directly for Alec. She was unmistakable in a thick brown coat with the hood down. Her chin was thrust forward determinedly and Maggie was taken back to the day she gave Big Stevie a wee minding before going to war. If this was a repeat performance, she would not be keeping the secret from her uncle.

Two other women, strangers to Maggie, scurried after her. To stop her from making a mistake? To goad her on? In a heartbeat, they had fallen on him. Sarah Gibb reached into her coat pocket as if she was going to give him a minding but, instead, drew out a large white feather.

"Oh no," Maggie gasped.

Doctor Bowman gave a low rumble but held her back when she tried to dart forwards.

"But those lassies are witches!" she shouted, squirming in his grasp. "She knows him. Ah've seen her talk tae him. How cin she dae this tae him?"

"I know, Maggie. I thought their lot had learned their lesson the last time. But there's no use getting involved. Sometimes it's best to keep your head down. You never know what's going to be asked of you. It's better this way."

"But whit if it wis yer son?"

"I'd be saying the same."

The man on the other side of the road gazed down at the feather in his hand while the women spoke harsh words that were lost to the rain. If they heard her shouts, they ignored her, too focused on their own entertainment.

It was half past five, the street was thronging and she could see people pointing as they witnessed the drama unfold. Some looked angry, and it was Alec, not Sarah, who was the focus of their blame. Maggie had heard of this in the Great War but had thought those days had passed.

"Ah cannae...he needs tae know somewan's oan his side."

She tried to move again but Doctor Bowman's hand was still on her shoulder. Penny held her hand in solidarity, perhaps also to hold her back, in a muddling moment that she would never make sense of. By the time she had made up her mind to step up and help, Alec McLean had slipped the feather into his pocket and was striding away, his even steps taking him to some unknown destination, all alone.

"I'll see you girls tomorrow." Doctor Bowman touched his hat and took his leave, then turned back once more. "And have a good night. Don't give this any more thought."

Maggie did not say a word but squeezed Penny's hand tight. It was not her own thoughts that mattered, but where Alec was going and what he might do.

The flat was dry and cosy, but she could not shake herself clean.

"Dae ye want a towel tae get yer hair dry?"

"Naw, yer grand," Penny said, taking off her rainmate. A fountain of water cascaded across the floor but neither girl was in the mood to care.

Maggie took the biggest towel from the press and rubbed her hair dry, moving slowly and gently as if her skin was glass that was prone to break. Going to the bathroom, she leant on the sink and traced the fine lines that ran from the corner of her eyes all the way to her hairline. She was getting older, but none of that mattered when men were being goaded into an early grave. She had heard that wisdom came to replace fading looks but that maxim was a lie. All she wanted was to be the best person she could and, that day, she had let Alec down. She would never forget that.

Tearing her eyes from the mirror, she crossed her fingers. Maybe remembering what had happened would be enough; she would be with him in spirit and, maybe if he felt her there, it would be enough to stop him from doing whatever he might be considering. Maybe.

The cold ceramic pushed through the cotton of her dress and she stood back, looking up again and judging the girl in the mirror for all the things she had not done. The rain beat against the window so loudly that it seemed to be breaking in, the flickering light overhead sent a cascade of shadows over the cluster of vials that festooned the sill, and the small world of the bathroom was a sanctuary that protected Maggie more than she deserved.

"Whit dae ye think, Tommy?" she asked, as if his reflection might appear beside her own.

He had not written to her in months, she did not love him and could not marry him, so she did not understand her longing to hear him say that she had done nothing wrong. It would have been cathartic to cry but it did not come. Instead, she stared at herself and compared what once was to what might have been. The towel fell to the floor at her feet.

"Ah'm sorry," she whispered.

Her father would know what to do. Taking a deep breath, she left the towel where it lay and headed back to the kitchen.

"Daddy … " she began, pushing inside.

She stopped short. Penny and Arthur were sitting together at the table, as they always did, but her father was different. Straight away she could see his shoulders were more rounded, his jowls drawn down.

"Penny telt me," he said. "That thing is terrible. It hus nae place here."

"Bloody Sarah Gibb." The animal inside of her was snarling to get out, "He cannae e'en fight, ye know. A dicky hert. But he cannae walk aroon wae a badge tae let a'body know, and they dinnae care! A' they see is a man where a man shouldnae be!"

"Maggie, hen…"

"Whit?"

"Stoap shouting."

"But ah didnae dae onything. Ah didnae go o'er tae help."

"And ye couldnae dae onything. No' really. Jist like ye cidnae dae onything aboot Donald."

Silence. Penny looked between them, confused.

"We dinnae know he's gone." Maggie's own words seemed hollow as she looked to her friend in explanation. It had been two weeks with no news, but until there was a body there was hope.

Penny knew better than that, and understood that whatever words she said would not do the situation justice.

"Ah'll brew us some tea," she whispered, slipping from her chair to give them some room.

Arthur grabbed Maggie's elbow and took her into the hall.

"She didnae know?" he asked as the door swung shut. "Maggie, hen, ye've gottae talk tae somewan."

"Wha? Jess?"

"Maggie … ah went tae see yer Aunt Agnes the day. She isnae ony better."

"And Jimmy?"

"Oot at the work. Keeping himsel' busy. Agnes disnae get that chance."

He drew himself in and she wished he would turn his head so she did not have to witness the full whammy of his pain.

"Ah dinnae … Ah'd better go help Penny wae that tea."

His hand went to the wall for support. "A'richt, hen. A'richt."

The guilt at leaving him mingled uncomfortably with the other acrid emotions that gathered in her gut, but he was in no rush to follow. He was weighed down by his own share of self-reproach, but she was too upset to glance back and see it.

Back in the kitchen, Penny was busying herself by the range. Saucer of tea leaves, cups; there was nothing unusual about the scene.

"Milk?" she asked without turning.

"No' fir me. But you hae a wee bit."

"Naw, naw. Ah'll save yer rations. Whit's wrang?"

Arthur had said she needed to talk to someone.

"Donald. Ah cannae …"

It had only been three words, not the outpouring she had intended, but it was enough. She choked up and couldn't continue.

Penny put down the kettle and gave her a long hug, which meant the world when Maggie knew that she did not dole out affection easily. Neither girl could find words so one stood remembering her cousin and the other remembered someone else far away. Eventually, the embrace grew awkward.

"Ah'll tak this tae yer faither," Penny said, picking up a cup and leaving Maggie with her thoughts.

Left alone, the air grew dense and expectant. Her mother had a visitor. She waited long moments but it did not dissipate.

"Ah cannae talk aboot it," she whispered.

"Richt, then, we winnae," Penny said.

"Christ! You were fast."

Penny walked in to reclaim her position by the range. She could have been an archeologist on a dig in her pressed trousers and she instantaneously took control, just what Maggie needed. She smiled thinly.

"We'll leave it behind, but ye can talk tae me ony time, Maggie. Jist let me know if ye wannae sit and remember. And if ye dinnae, we can ayeways find ye a distraction."

She reached into her pocket and drew out a tightly-folded letter.

"Ah hae this tae show ye, actually. It's nuthin important – silly really – but we cid ayeways hae a wee look? Ah want ye tae read this and tell me whit ye think."

Maggie took the letter and read the scrawl. It sloped across the crinkled page but was entirely legible so she read aloud.

"My Penny. Your face has been with me from the beginning here. I know it will be so at the end when I return to my beloved Scotland and see you again. The men write home to their wives and girlfriends and I write to you with hope. Your Willie"

"Well? Whit dae ye think?"

"Ah think he's in love wae ye," she said.

"Dae ye really think so?"

This must be the same person that Penny had admitted writing to before. Mystery solved.

"Aye. *Your* Willie. *Beloved* Scotland. That last sentence there." She pointed to it with force. "Why, it's practically a proposal."

"Naw!" The young girl rose halfway out of her seat, showing her age as her hopes were confirmed. "Ah didnae want tae read tae much in tae it but – och – dae ye really think so?"

"It's a' he could dae wae oot coming right oot and saying it. Jist be careful though, hen. These are uncertain times and we cannae see whit's aroond the corner."

"Ah hae these other letters, tae," Penny admitted, ignoring the warning.

With that, she produced the entire history of her correspondence, multiple letters falling from her pockets onto the table. Either she had been planning to show Maggie these from the start or the pocket was their permanent home, kept close to her always.

"The tone o' them's changed since the stairt. Look at this first wan, here."

Obediently, Maggie looked at the paper Penny thrust under her nose. Sure enough, it was merely a few friendly lines. The tea lay forgotten between them. She read aloud once more.

"Dear Penny, as I expected, France is a lot different to home. They really do wear berets here like in the movies. Maybe I will be able to bring you one. Yours sincerely, Willie."

A few letters followed in a similar vein until, gradually, the writing became more familiar, filled with I-love-yous and remember-mes.

"Ah dinnae understaund how he can grow tae love me a' the way o'er there when he cannae see me and we cannae hae a proper conversation. Whit's changed?"

This was something Maggie felt confident about because it was not happening to her. "Nothing's changed. He's ayeways felt that way. Why else wid he spend a' his time writin' tae a lassie at home?"

Seeing her friend's flummoxed incomprehension, she tried to be more clear.

"Miby he's been encouraged by yer ain letters, so he knows he's no' makin a bloody fool o' himself. Pride in a man can be a terrible thing."

"Ah dinnae think ah've been o'erly encouragin," Penny said, shoving her hands deep into her pockets to keep herself grounded. Soon she was stuck fast, chewing at her lip like a rabbit gnawing ineffectually at its cage. The intrepid explorer had vanished, and Maggie was grateful for the distraction.

"Oh naw?" she said. "Look here."

She grabbed a letter from the pile, cleared her throat and stood up to read it to the grand audience of her imagination, feeling her spirits lift to her ankles as she lowered her voice to imitate the male announcers on the wireless.

"My dear Penny, I received your letter dated the fourth of November and it gladdened me to know you have been writing, even when the correspondence does not always reach me. But rest assured that whatever letters I do receive find me well. All of your sentiments I return to you a hundred times over so do not be sad and do not cry."

Here she paused, building the emotion.

"I will come home soon, my love."

She thrust a hand across her forehead and fell back onto Donald's stool, imagining him there with her, laughing.

"I will come home soon my love. I will, I will come home soon, my love!"

"Stop it!" Penny cried, growing pinker than Maggie had ever seen her.

"Ah'm sorry. It's jist beautiful. Honestly. Yer luve's a wonderful thing. Forgive me fir windin' ye up. Ah'm jist jealous."

That was true, but she was also nervous for her friend. Anything beautiful that grew in the world at that moment could just as suddenly be ripped away and she would swap their happiness for Donald in a heartbeat.

"Why are ye jealous efter a'thing that everyone tells me aboot Tommy Gunn? Apparently there's ne'er been a mair charmin' or handsome man tae walk doon Maryhill Road."

This was not where she wanted the conversation to go. Thoroughly fed up, she groaned and threw her head to the ceiling.

"Looks dinnae add up tae much. It's a' folk talk tae me aboot, Tommy this and Tommy that, but ah dinnae want tae be his bloody wife. Ah want tae spend ma life wae someone ah can feel safe wae, someone wha'd ne'er hurt me or look elsewhere." She slapped the table in frustration. "Someone wha's at least a wee bit reliable."

As she stomped down against the woman he wanted her to become, she hoped he could not hear her in France but the release felt good. The rug rumpled underfoot.

"Ye think a lot aboot luve?" asked Penny softly.

"When it's everywhere, it's hard no' tae."

"So whit's yer advice? Ah'm so confused. Ah know how ah feel aboot Willie, but it's been so long since ah've seen him! How do ah know if ma feelings are real or jist memories?"

"Ah think and ah think, Penny, hen. Ah cannae figure oot whit luve is. Ah only know what it isnae. That's ma problem."

She paused.

"He wrote tae me a wee while ago. Wait a wee minute."

She rooted around in the drawer of the table, knowing she'd thrown it in there somewhere, and finally her fingers clenched around the short one page sheet that she had folded tight and tucked out of sight. She pulled it out. There was no going back.

"At the start o' the fechtin he'd telt me he wisnae gonnae write tae me, but then this letter came. Ah'm sure he thought ah'd be awfy impressed but when ah got that letter … in the name o' the wee man! Jist listen tae this."

She did not hand it over but cleared her throat and read it herself, all trace of humour gone. In her head, it was his voice she heard.

"'Dear Maggie, I can still see your face the last time our eyes met. You were standing on the platform of the station with hands clenched looking like you were ready to run after me and finish me off before I'd even reached France! That's my girl. By now the shock will have worn off and you will be as excited as I am for my return and married life. I have been in Bournemouth since returning from Dunkirk and it's one hell of a party. Talk says we'll be back in the thick of it soon enough, so I am making the most of my time here. Miss me and cry for me. Your Tommy.' That's it. Can ye believe it? Precocious bloody git."

"Ah cannae wait tae meet him."

Maggie snorted. "The female will is awfy easily blown awa by the sight and sound o a Gunn."

TWENTY-TWO

The Letter

Time ticked on.

From the way Arthur dithered in the hall, something was clearly amiss.

"Whit's wrang?" Maggie asked, letting her hand fall from the knob. She had been so close.

"Come here an' see this."

She did.

"Tell me, is it awfy bad? Ah can feel the hole but cannae tell how far back the frayin' goes. See it? Right there by ma pocket, where ma fingers are?"

He grabbed her hand to show her but she could see the problem quite clearly. There was no shortage of threadbare patches on her pink blouse or brown skirt either, but her pleats provided some cover.

"Och, daddy. Efter the war we'll go tae Bremners and pick oot the best clothes they hae."

"Ah'm no' bothered aboot that, hen. It's jist the nicht."

"The hole really isnae that bad."

"But ah hae tae look ma best. Ah'm going fir tea wae the Minister!"

"It's tae late tae cancel."

"Ah didnae suggest we cancel."

"Weil, whit'll we dae, then? They're expectin' us at hauf past and ah dinnae want tae hurt their feelins. Jist imagine the effort they're gaun tae"

"Aye, ye're right," Arthur sighed, "Well, come oan then. We'd best get movin."

Arm in arm, they walked around the corner to the manse. It was early evening but the streets were deserted, the war on the Continent making Glasgow appear calmer, somehow, when the bombs were not falling. The sky was clear and bright with frost, and the distant rumble of a tram car was as detached from the peaceful reality as a wireless programme.

Toying nervously with the edges of the letter in her pocket, Maggie reminded herself of what she must do. It was the real reason she did not want to be late for tea. She did not care if the pages crumpled and the corners curled; she was giving it back to Doctor Bowman. She was almost sure of it.

He met them at the door, the orange light from the hallway creating a halo around the spot where his hair used to be. With a hearty handshake, he stood aside and welcomed them into his home.

"You're looking well, Arthur. Come away into the body o' the kirk, so to speak."

The worn pocket was on the side where Arthur's arm hung limp, shielding the hole from view. It was only Maggie who noticed his fingers clench and flex.

"Where's the Reverend?" she asked.

"I'm here, I'm here." the woman said, emerging from the kitchen. "Sorry about that. Had a bit of trouble getting my pinny off but it's lovely to see you both."

Reverend Bowman stooped low to plant a quick kiss on Maggie's cheek, then Arthur's. Her hair was pulled back in a simple clasp and her starched blouse and straight skirt were plain and neat, but that simplicity belayed a long struggle, for she had fought to lead in a patriarchal world and had become the first female minister to be ordained in Scotland. The United Free Church was the progressive antithesis to the similarly-named Free Church of the Highlands where authoritarianism and repression ran strong, but it was still a significant step forwards and, to Maggie and many girls like her, Reverend Bowman was a hero.

"It's nothing fancy, mind you. Just mince and tatties."

"With a wee drop of custard for dessert."

This was more than Maggie could have wished for and she appreciated the sentiment, especially when, since rationing had been brought in, it took hours every week to queue for a loaf of bread. The doctor squeezed his wife's hand before she could swing into the kitchen again.

"Can ah gie ye a hand in there, Reverend?"

"No, Maggie, you just take a seat."

As she spoke, her husband was already ushering them through a small door to an equally small room set up for dining. From one small window came narrow slants of light, attributed to a quickly blackening sky. The darkest days of winter were long gone but summer was still a distant dream. Days flicked from clear and crisp to dark and bleak as quickly as God snuffing out a candle.

She helped her father ease into the nearest chair and turned to notice that her favourite painting, Belshazaar's Feast, was missing.

"The painting, Doctor…"

He was busy setting the table and did not respond. If he had not been her boss, she may have pushed it further.

The letter was heavy as a sack of coal in her pocket and she itched to set it down. She tried to catch his eye but after the comment he laid the cutlery and avoided her gaze. She needed to get rid of it. As long as it was no longer in her hands, it would not matter who it was with.

"Ah'll go ben the kitchen and help the Reverend."

But the words had barely left her when her host re-entered and she had to sit while tea was served. Grace was said, the Reverend encouraged everyone to tuck in, but Maggie picked anxiously at her peas. She would have to leave it for the moment. After all, it was Arthur's sight that was failing, not his hearing. Perhaps it could be returned at work on Monday. That seemed sensible.

Taking a deep breath, she tried to relax and focused on the conversation: the sermon the next day, sure it was going to be a belter, the mince was braw and the ingredients scarce, a fine feat and finer achievement, at least they still had their Jesus painting hanging on, the one and only, and should they have had more? not very Christianly but could have hedged their bets so to speak, although the Doctor preferred the old testament, no no don't give me that, there's only one of him, anyway, so how many pairs of eyes does he need? On and on. Anything rather than the letter. And she minded her language, something else to think about – a bloody here and a bugger there had never hurt anyone, but the current setting was not one in which to test the theory.

"And how is Tommy?"

"He's well, ah think. Ah huvnae been telt otherwise."

"And Jess?"

"Aye, Jess is grand. She's loving it doon there in Yorkshire. It's where her Paul's fae, you know?"

"Is it? I thought he was from Manchester."

"Naw. Pontefract. Which is so close tae the offices she's working at she can ayemost smell him."

"Casting aspersions, Maggie?"

She chuckled. "The offices are a training school, fir the airforce, like. So ah guess there's lots o' stuff fir her tae be smelling."

"That must be nice for her."

"Aye, but it maks her miss him a he-ck of a lot."

"It's a wonder they can eat so fast with all that gabbing going on," Doctor Bowman commented as he watched the women talk and laugh and scrape their plates clean.

Arthur chuckled, reminded of the good old days when the jokes would have been his. Feigning outrage, Reverend Bowman rose to clear the table and Maggie joined her. Now was the time.

"What are you doing?"

"Ah'm gy'ing ye a haund."

"No, you just sit down there. You're our guest."

"But ye've done enough an' tea wis delicious. Ah'd really feel better tae help."

"We'd really rather you didn't," the Doctor joined in, and Maggie spun towards him, surprised by the double-edged obstruction.

"It's the least ah can dae," she assured them both, grabbing some empty plates and striding to the kitchen before either could say anything else.

Reverend Bowman followed, laden with dirty serving dishes, and Doctor Bowman rose to join them. Drawing the letter from her pocket, she held it low.

"Ah." Doctor Bowman sighed.

"Ah'm a bloody idiot," she whispered. "Ah should hae joined wae Penny and Rachel, and got masel' intae a factory in Glasgow. As it is, they can send me God-knows-where. But ah cannae leave the hard work tae others just a'cause ah didnae get aff my arse in time."

"Like I said, you could go away with the Land Army, but it doesn't make any sense. We'd just have to employ two more people here in your place – one to be my receptionist and the other to look after your daddy. The letter says it all. Just take it to the powers that be and you'll be fine."

He pushed his glasses further up his nose and patted the crest of his shiny bald head. He was not usually a nervous man. The Reverend spoke up as she busied around him.

"Try not to worry about it, Maggie."

Maggie's hands shook as she held out the letter. The image of the white feather had haunted her for weeks and the hatred it symbolised was not any less potent just because she would not be putting her life on the line. She may never be sure where it would come from, but the judgement would be worse than anything she could do for her father.

"Ah dinnae want tae leave ma daddy, but …"

There was a clatter from behind, down the narrow corridor to where Arthur sat alone. He was scrambling with an upturned cup, his tea spilled across the table in front of him.

"Don't worry about that," the Reverend called kindly, but Maggie grabbed a cloth from the workbench and rushed through to help. In the last few months, he had deteriorated fast.

"It's awright, daddy," she said, wiping up quickly. "It didnae get ye. Jist the table. There's a wee chip in the cup though. Ah'll get you anither."

"Ah cannae believe ah wis so stupid."

"It's awricht. Ah'll get ye anither wan," she repeated.

She hurried past the bare walls to the kitchen where her apologies were brushed quickly to the side.

"Accidents happen."

The Reverend took both her hands and relieved her of the cup, and then the doctor spoke, his voice suddenly carrying the same authority as when he spoke to patients at the surgery.

"What will he do when the blitz comes again and he has to make it all the way down the stairs by himself? It only takes one thing to be out of place, one obstruction. Then who'd help him, if everybody's running for shelter?"

Maggie sighed. "Ah'd been thinking he cid move in wae Uncle Jimmy and Aunt Agnes. They huv an empty hoose noo Jess's aff, but Aunt Agnes is a mess. She went oot tae clean the close stairs wae the bottle and rag she uses fir the windays and the neighbour nearly went skiting on her bahoochy. Daddy's safer livin' on his ain while she's in this bloody state."

"Here. Take this." Reverend Bowman gave her a bowl that still held a meagre sliver of custard. "And take this." She pushed the letter back into Maggie's pocket.

Turning around, Maggie saw her father was staring blankly ahead, alert yet adrift. He deserved so much better. As they settled down to pudding, no one mentioned the little brown envelope which had once weighed down Maggie's pocket but now rested in the blue handbag at her feet.

"Ah dinnae believe it. Well, naw, that isnae true, ah dae believe it. Could hae seen it comin'."

"Whit are ye talking aboot?" Maggie asked, keeping her voice light.

It had been a near-impossible decision to make and, now it was done, she could finally breathe. Out of everything in the world, the most important thing was family.

Rachel slopped up the loose leaves that had escaped into her cup with a smirk.

"Och." She shook her head and pressed her lips tight.

"Naw, come oan, ah'm a' ears. Dae ye know whit she's oan aboot, Penny?"

In the rear of the booth, Penny shrugged and sunk lower into the frayed upholstery, eager to dissolve into the fabric and disappear.

On the day of her appointment, Maggie had taken the tram to the offices at Charing Cross although her feet did not want to move. It was the first snowfall of the season, the flurry followed closely by rain which turned the streets into inhospitable rivers of mud. The day was so hopeless and bleak that leaving Glasgow would have appeared a Godsend to anyone else, but not to Maggie. She would have dug into the grey mush until her heels burned with heat from the Earth's core. She would have held on to her native terrain while her nails cracked and her fingers bled with the effort. Any thought she had once fancied of returning the letter to the doctor had faded deep into the past.

She had disembarked outside the building, its red brick looming above her. Snow gathered thick in her hair, unchecked and unnoticed, and she stared upwards. Somewhere within these walls her fate would be decided.

"Efter you, hen."

A kindly man with a harried countenance and a bulging suitcase held the door open and she had mustered a smile. There was a long queue of girls, all waiting in a line of white plastic chairs, already indistinguishable but for the unique identification number pinned on their blouses. Some carried a blasé scowl, some filed their nails to distraction, and others wore only their fears.

"How did ye feel?" Rachel demanded.

"Fine," Maggie lied.

She could barely recall how she had felt sitting in that hallway with the rest of them, becoming one as their emotions merged. Amongst the thick shroud of shared experience seeped individual trauma that she could not begin to fathom. Some girls had lost families, their lives changed forever, but they fell into step with the rest and took their place to be called. Their pain was invisible. At a glance, she could not tell a Kilmun Street girl from a Knowetap; they may as well have all been children of the rubble. All she would remember clearly was the pale green light and crackling fan which spun shapes from shadows overhead. Her wringing hands kneaded gently on her lap, her breath was laboured but her squared shoulders challenged anyone to approach. If they so much as looked at her the wrong way, her resolve would crumble.

Eventually she was called through the swinging doors where she had watched many girls disappear before. Behind lay the small office where decisions were made, the worn wooden desk and two chairs underplaying its importance. She took a deep breath, withdrew the letter from her bag, and handed it to the thin-lipped official who frowned and did not say a word.

His scowl deepened. There was no end to the silence. Against the rising fear that she should apologise and grab it back, she sat firm and stared ahead.

He read it, looked down, then up at her curiously.

"I will hand this to my superior for consideration. You will hear from us in a few days."

He did not elaborate or escort her out, but leaned across the desk to tick one box in the high pile of forms. She leaned forward to see what it was and he cleared his throat loudly. She reined in the urge to salute.

In the end, after five anxious days, a letter arrived, pushed carelessly under her front door. It bore an official stamp and that was all that mattered. She was officially excused from duty, but to share her inner turmoil up to that point was more than Rachel was worth.

Facing each other at the table, Rachel glowered at Maggie and Penny could taste the spark of danger in the air like a navvy down a mine shaft. Her gaze roamed between the two, caught in a standoff straight out of *West of Carson City*. For a few long moments, no one spoke.

"Whit, exactly, could ye see comin', Rachel?"

Penny cringed at the sound of Maggie's voice – svelte, smooth and barely above a whisper.

"That ah widnae join the WLA? Because ah'm nae shirking ma responsibilities and ah winnae hae ye suggesting utherwise."

"Ach naw, Maggie. Ah dinnae doubt *your* motives. Ye huv tae look efter yer faither. Although, sayin that, the likelihood is ye'd hae ended up at a south-side factory like me or doon the docks like Penny. We're in the Third City o' the Empire so ye could hae done yer bit wae oot the worry o' flittin'."

"Whit, like Jess?"

Rachel ignored Maggie and drew herself higher.

"When ah joint the Women's Land Airmy, ah decided that it wis time t'dae ma bit fir the war. Why leave it a' tae the laddies? Are they no' daein enough? Unpatriotic. It's somethin ah cannae abide."

"Well done, Rachel. Ye put yer name doon the day afore conscription. Ah didnae. Ah'd no' hae bin able tae choose a wee south-side factory or welding doon the docks. Ah'd be flung intae a melting pot wae no idea where ah wis gonnae come oot. Like a training camp in Yorkshire. Can ye no' see that?"

"Tae be honest, ah dinnae know how you can sit by and dae nothing. Where's yer conscience?"

"Wae ma daddy."

"Ah think it's admirable. Tae belang tae somethin'. Tae matter," Penny added clumsily. Every day she headed to the docks with her father, mending the ships that would help to win the war. The goggles left deep red marks against her skin like a failed experiment and her muscles ached, but she would not change it.

"Ah might train tae be a nurse efter the fighting's o'er."

Neither friend was listening.

"Onyway, it's the other wans ah'm oan aboot."

Rachel got back on track. Her orange hair curled amongst her crowded floral dress and it was difficult to process her words amongst the swirling cacophony of distress, but as hard as Maggie tried, she could not block them out completely. It had been that way for over two years and showed no sign of abating as long as Penny was around to keep asking her along. Maggie would far rather have left her in 1939.

"The Bowmans?"

Rachel smirked into her tea and Penny groaned.

"Exactly. Ye've heard those sermons o' the Reverend, a closet Conscie only she isnae really making ony secret aboot it! That's whit ye get bein in the United Free, Maggie Munroe, lassie ministers and questionable ethics."

"Watch whit ye're saying," Penny warned, eyes on both friends as they darkened simultaneously.

"When ah want yer opinion, Penny Sinclair, ah'll ask fir it – and when dae I *ever* ask fir it? Ye're jist a wee lassie wae a big mooth."

"That's enough," Maggie snapped, but Rachel was on a roll.

"Ah've heard all aboot it fae ma pals up the road. Every-bloody-Sunday it's peace-this and pacifism-that and ah'm a' fir peace, dinnae get me wrang,"

"Aye, right."

"But the only way tae get peace noo is tae win this bloody war. Which isnae gonnae happen if there's naebody left tae fight cause a' the men are busy crying Conscie in the name o' God."

"Ah think yer reliable witnesses need tae listen tae the Reverend a wee bit mair closely. They've no' understood whit she's been sayin'."

"Dinnae patronise me, Maggie."

"Even if they're right, which they arenae, whit's that t'dae wae me? It's hardly like ah wis aboot tae be shipped aff tae the front lines, is it?"

For a moment Rachel looked like she accepted this, but then the old suspicion crept back in; an ugly mask that she did not have the will to dispel.

"But it's the same *principle*, Maggie."

Throwing her hands in exasperation, Maggie was ready to leave. If Rachel had been worth it then she would have clearly laid out all the small yet vital tasks that she carried out each day, and the resources that would be needed to replace her. She would have done that for someone who was worth it, but she could not bring herself to walk out while Penny was still on the receiving end.

"Ah think it's gid, both fir Arthur and a' the patients at the surgery," her good friend said in her defence. If looks could kill then it would have spelt the end for Penny right then but, smiling in innocence, she sipped her tea.

TWENTY-THREE

The Yanks

MARCH, 1944

"Shove them in like this."

Maggie hitched her skirt up to her waist and demonstrated with four pennies, placing them in the narrowest parts between her legs. Penny looked suitably impressed and Maggie was thankful Rachel was not there to comment. It was just the two of them in her bedroom, enjoying some peace.

"The idea is tae show aff the perfect shape. If ye can haud them, right here at the curves, but wae a gap showin' in between, it's said ye hae the perfect pair."

"Betty Grable's got nothing oan ye, does she? And her legs are insured fir a million dollars, so the papers say."

Spinning on the spot, Maggie kept the coins in place and enjoyed the compliment while Penny groaned at her own. It was unusual that she wore a skirt, and this was more of a punishment than a reward. Between her skinny legs, her skin was squeezed tight in an unflattering, gapless stretch that she would have been happier to ignore…

"It's tricky," Maggie told her, putting her friend's weight loss down to months of rationing. "Rachel showed me how tae dae it twa weeks ago and couldnae get wan tae stick. The coins fair tinkled tae the flair and she picked wan up and threw it oot the windae! We cid hear it landin' oan the street. A gid thing there wisnae a wee lassie walkin past or she'd hae a sare heid."

Penny laughed but Maggie kicked herself. Each time Rachel came over to pretend it was like the old days, she let her hackles rise, always allowing the girl to bring out the worst in her no matter what she promised her mammy.

"Ah think we should go tae the Locarno the night."

"You ayeways think we should go tae the Locarno."

Shrugging, Maggie let the coins fall from her legs and plopped down onto the floor. "Dancing and laddies."

"Even wae the irony of gaun' there when it's named efter the very place where the powers o' Europe stabilised the borders o' the West after the Great War?" Penny raised her eyebrows, knowing that there was no need for an answer, she had already won. "Noo the soldiers wha dance there'll be first tae tell ye how that Treaty wis fed tae the wind."

She sat on the floor next to Maggie and crossed her legs.

"A gid pairty's a gid pairty, no matter whit's the name o' the bloody place."

"Weil, it's nae mair depressin' than the Barrowlands these days. Did ye hear they wir made tae tak doon their sign?"

"Come oan, that isnae the same thing," Maggie groaned, stretching back against the bed frame. "It's jist gid common sense. We'd hae been blown fae here tae Timbuktu if those lights'd stayed up tae welcome the Gerry planes tae Glasgow."

"Ye're right. Ah wis jist being silly."

"Ye're the least silly person ah know."

Both girls were silent.

"Ah do want tae go tae the Locarno." Penny admitted, her voice a whisper although it was only the two of them in the room. "Ye've just gottae be careful aroon these boys, especially the Yanks. Dinnae look at me like that! Ma mammy heard a story of wan girl doon the road wha'd tae much o' a gid time and noo she's awa' tae live wae her Aunt near Falkirk until she hus the wean and the scandal passes."

Maggie didn't fill the silence but thought about the correlation of local gossip and ambiguous visits to Doctor Bowman's surgery. It was left to Penny to speak again.

"Dae ye ever wonder aboot that look in Rachel's eye? It's saucy; like she'd teach us both a thing or twa."

Her friend was more accurate than she would ever know but, despite everything, some things were not meant to be shared and she bit her tongue.

"Weil, ah'm no interested in a laddie the night. Willie and I, we've been … " Penny stuttered, showing the one chink in her armour of confidence as she glided through life. "Ah'm sorry. It's hard tae talk aboot."

"Ye dinnae need tae tell me onything," Maggie said, clasping her friend's hand and preparing to wipe away the tears. Her thoughts returned briefly to Tommy. His memory appeared less often to her these days and had never been accompanied by the kind of pain that wrenched at Penny. A small part of her longed to know what that kind of love felt like but it would never be that way with him. Just the usual nothing. Just the reminder of what he was keeping her from.

"Naw. But he says we cid be thegether. Forever, like. When he gets hame."

"And ye're happy?"

"So happy. If it happens. If he gets hame."

Maggie was looking at a drowning woman, swimming against a tide of hope and fear, so she was unprepared for the question that, by then, she should have expected.

"Huv ye heard onything fae Tommy?"

She shook her head. Inside, she was screaming.

"But Jess is huvin a rare time doon in Yorkshire. Oor legs run in the family and she's oot in Wakefield every weekend wae the lassies fae the office and the sergeants wha're daein the training."

"Tell me." Penny wiped her eyes and sat forward, the embodiment of a successful deflection.

"Weil, she's made a few friends doon there. Ah swear, it's like she feels young again. Thir's wan lassie fae Glesga, doon Hyndland way…"

"Oh aye, so awfy…" Penny flicked her nose.

"Aye, but braw, like. So onyway, this lassie showed up, homesick and lonely. Her name's Dolly and she's ayeways been sheltered. Weil, Jess and her made friends right away. She gets sent wee parcels fae hame and shares it a' wae Jess, so desperate she is tae mak friends. An only child and quiet tae boot. Jess is happy tae oblige. Weil, she hud a beau, this Dolly. He turns up wan day at Bretton Hall, unannounced. A wee laddie. Came tae see her afore heading aff tae some regiment or other. And Dolly comes back e'en mair sick than when she left fir the day. Did it no' turn oot she wis in luve wae wan o' the trainers; no' her beau at all!"

"Whit did she dae?"

"She broke aff wae her beau, right afore he left fir the fighting. That's why, when she came back, it looked like she'd caught the plague."

"Dramatic."

"Indeed."

"And did she get wae that other man?"

"Weil, no' straight away. That's the gid bit. Ah hud a couple o' other letters fae Jess and nothing wis said. Then, a week ago, it comes oot that she'd been in a terrible accident – this lassie Dolly, no' Jess."

"Thank Christ."

"Aye, but it's awright, see? She wis in an army van and it went roond a corner, but thir wis a bump in the road, thir were nae doors so oot she pops, right oot the van on tae the road!"

"Is she alive?"

"Aye but she broke her wrist. The minute this laddie heard aboot it, doon tae the doctors he ran. He didnae know how bad it wis, and he wisnae hangin' aboot tae find oot. A' the way fae the training school. And that wis that."

"Och, that's romantic."

"Aye, no fir the wee guy fae Glesga."

"So Jess bonded wae her o'er their Englishmen?"

"Naw, the man's fae Aberdeen!"

"Ah swear, Maggie, the world's got awfy sma' o'er these last couple o' years. It's a shame though. All the way doon in Yorkshire and she's no' ony closer tae Paul."

"But she is!" Maggie cried, realising she had missed out the most important part of the story. "It's not just the workers she's aboot wae. Ye see, she goes oot e'ery Saturday night, apparently, doon the Wakefield Bullring. She knows how they live now, where he's fae. Ye cannae get closer than that. And that is plenty close enough. Ah'm happy wae a' the stories ah hear aboot Dolly fae Hyndland. As lang as she's makin Weegie friends, thir's a chance she'll come hame."

"Dinnae be daft."

"Daft? Really? Whit aboot a' the locals she's getting close wae. She cannae stop tellin me aboot them. There's this wee lassie. Jess was oan a bus wan day, goin tae the shops, and there wis this shoutin fae the front o' the bus! Weil, if it wisnae this wee lassie wae blood a' o'er her face, like some ghoulie. A laddie hud turned aroond and walloped her in the face wae his elbow. An accident, like. Lucky fir her, her mammy wis the bus conductor. So she directs the bus doon this wee street and aroond the back o' the hooses, right tae the doctor's door. A hale bus full o' folk wha're just awa' tae dae their shopping! She hud tae keep her heid lifted wae a' that blood so Jess went tae guide her. And they've been firm friends ever since. A local.

"Jess writes screeds and screeds aboot it. Like, fir example, wha really cares, but it turns oot this Rose knows mair aboot the war than she needs tae. Her beau's a miner, ye see. Dangerous stuff. He works wae them Bevin Boys ye hear aboot, but he isnae a Conshie, although he gets slagged fir it. Maks me mad hearin aboot it; like yon Alec McLean. A good hert wae a bad reputation. Onyway, they'll be oot fir a night and then he'll walk her hame. She gets oan his bike and he walks a' the way beside her, and then jumps oan the bike to ride a' the way hame, four miles in the other direction! That's true luve, that is."

"Ye seem excited jist talkin aboot it."

"Aye, and that's exactly the problem. It shows me how luve's supposed tae be, but whit dae I hae? A laddie attachin himsel' wha disnae e'en like me enough tae write me a bloody letter, but ah cannae get shot o' him. It's been four *years*, Penny, and he's still managin tae hing aboot fae a distance like a bad smell."

Glancing quickly at the awkward scowl on her friend's face, she changed the subject.

"Ah've jist telt ye this lassie's hale life story and whit de ye think she knows aboot us? How much is she hearing aboot life in Glesga? No much, I'd bet."

"Dinnae get jealous. Ah luve a gid story. Especially a gid romance. And Jess hus them comin oot her ears. Ah'd love a man tae run fir me efter ah broke ma wrist, or walk oot his way tae mak sure ah wis awright. It's just braw. Ah want whit a' these other lassies hae and whit Jess is jist realising she hus. Sometimes ah think it'll ne'er happen fir me."

So it wasn't just Maggie who felt that way, but some people were a lot closer to reaching their dreams.

"Miby Jess winnae want tae come back, onyway, and we'll be visiting her doon there. I'll tak you wae me so we can talk aboot them thegether."

223

Smiling as if she were joking, Maggie was crying inside. It was unbearable to feel her cousin drift away but she would not share how Jess poured her heart out over a lost brother or the fear of history repeating itself. It was true that she felt closer to Paul than ever before, but with every breath she was hammering a nail into his coffin and mourning the loss of someone she had never truly found. Maggie would not share the nights she lay awake. With Minnie to the north and Jess to the south, there was nothing in between but heartache and uncertainty. If she could envelop them all and give them comfort she would, but her reach only went as far as her father. As long as he was around, she would not exchange Glasgow for anywhere else, but how she wished she were a magnet and all the others could just ping to her side, where they were supposed to be.

Taking a deep breath, she asked, "Dae ye think Rachel will be there the night?"

"Of course. There'll be Joshua. Mind Joshua?"

"He's the wan fae last week?"

"Aye. They met up this week an' apparently it wis wonderful. He telt her she's his girl. Can ye believe it?"

Yes, Maggie could. And she could believe Rachel believing it.

"Ah know ye said thir isnae a problem between the twa o' ye, but sometimes, Maggie Munroe, ah'd swear that whit ye're thinkin is written a' o'er yer face. Like ye'd just tasted tripe when ye were expecting a nice deviled egg. And yer no' like that wae onywan else."

"Dinnae be silly, hen. Ye shouldnae see so much. It's no' gid fir ye. Let's go o'er tae her hoose and help her pick somethin' bonnie tae wear."

Music thumped hard. Feet hit the floor, heavier on the beat. Bright lights birled heads, all the glamour of Glasgow; skirts slashed and shirt sleeves rolled; wedding rings lay forgotten on mantles at home. With the Americans came the raucous swing and fast jives that left old foxtrots and waltzes forgotten as quickly as old lovers, and people spoke just as quickly to hurry them on their way. It was the Locarno welcome.

All thoughts left her mind as she was swung roughly from the waist by a burly Major from Portland. He planted a kiss on her lips when she passed by, a funny way to keep time, and she thought she could hear some of the crowd clapping. Or else it was just the music, she could not be sure. There were definitely some giggles, though, most likely from a group of young girls who barely looked in their teens, dressed to the nines to see the American men first hand.

"What are you thinking about?" he asked her, lifting her up and challenging her to answer.

"Ma cousin, wha'd better no' be daein this at the Bullring," she croaked, her voice and lungs competing for air. The Major laughed without understanding and moved her faster.

The trick was to go with it, to let him lead while her blue dress clung uncomfortably tight around the knees. She had hiked the waistband to help, his hands all over her, giving additional support that she did not quite need, and his handsome face belay a whiff of body odour each time she passed under his arm. She put up with it. There was another man, two dancers over, who she wanted to impress, he of the sparkling eyes who took the time to enjoy each turn but was so intent on his own partner that he had not once looked her way. Under the bright lights of the dance floor, she felt strangely isolated and safe from inspection. There were shorter skirts and friskier moves to capture the attention of onlookers, so she thought.

The music stopped abruptly. Stumbling against the Major, the floor rushed up to meet her but he caught her inches from the ground and pulled her close. The sweat marks under his arms were pungent, too much to be set aside by his lopsided smile and floppy hair. The parallels with a dancefloor stumble she had taken a few years before overwhelmed her. She scrambled up and pushed herself away.

"You are hell of a nimble for an old lady."

Portland's chuckle was deep and throaty, and her hands flew to the new curve of wrinkles around her eyes, but he was twirling her hair, clearly believing his joke to be an original. She had a feeling the stench around him came from more than sweat.

"That's no' yer idea o' a line, is it? Ah'm aff. Nice dancin' wae ye."

She strode away, leaving him there. Her dress bounced high but she did not bother to hitch it down; not with the twinkling man up ahead, talking to one of the munitions girls from Rachel's factory. It was a different blonde to the girl he had been dancing with before and her friends huddled close by. He was listening intently but his perfect face gave nothing away. Her heart flipped and she finally understood what jealousy felt like; and she prayed that Penny had been exaggerating that she was easy to read.

"Nae doobt decidin' which wan o' them'll be next," Penny commented as Maggie joined her.

"At least Rachel's no there. She needs anither man like a hole in the heid!"

Her face was burning, a hot flash to the head. If anyone looked at her, she would die.

"And here she comes," Penny warned with a nod to the door.

Their friend appeared like a vision in red, searching the crowds. Spotting them, she started elbowing her way through the throng. At first they did not see the man she towed behind, two inches shorter and all sallow skin and bones. The flash of carrot hair cut short beneath his cap. The wide grin of perpetual amazement displayed a crowded set of teeth, crossing one over the other and threatening to slice his bottom lip clean off. His eyes sat low and his forehead high, and the sunspots dotting his skin resembled those of a dappled pony. They pinched each other playfully as they trotted forwards, bubbling with pride.

"If it wisnae fir that uniform o' his …"

"… he'd look like a character fae Dickens?" Maggie suggested.

"Or a ginger Bugs Bunny."

Metres away, the factory girls descended like buzzing wasps cutting off the couple's advance. Introductions were made with handshakes and kisses, and the friends inched closer to hear what was being said.

"You will all be welcome at my cabin," the boy was announcing to the group while Rachel stood in full plume at his side. "It lies right on the lake and in winter we go ice skating. In summer, it's fishing and hiking. Really, you girls would love it."

He tipped his hat.

"There's enough wood lying on the ground to create a great burning fire every night, without the need to cut any. There would be room for you all, I'm sure."

"Ah bet there wid," Maggie whispered.

"Can you imagine that? Hands off my man," Rachel joked, dusting the shoulder of his shirt and beaming, but Joshua was not finished.

"You have to be hardy to survive where I'm from. None of your modern luxuries. If you all come to my cabin, are you going to be tough enough to take it?"

He drew in his eyebrows from the far reaches of his head, but his mouth kept on grinning and the girls nodded as if they truly believed the dream they were being sold. Penny grabbed Maggie's hand and bit her lip.

The boy did not waver. "Of course you would. After all, it's army girls I'm talking to. You all know plenty about hard work."

Maggie was too incredulous to laugh at the girls who concentrated on the packaging rather than the present. They drew closer around him. She could not make out what they were saying, all talking over each other to be heard, but lost sight of the small man in the middle. Then some youngsters bounded up, elbowing each other in encouragement and pretending to play it cool. A pretty teenager in a floral dress adopted a swagger and broke ranks.

"Got any gum, chum?" she drawled, adopting the accent she had heard so often at the picture house.

Joshua reemerged. Separating himself from the group, he fished in his pockets and tossed her a piece. She grabbed it one-handed and started to chew slowly, one hand on jutted hip, exactly what Clara would have called a gallus-wee-madam pose. In her mind, she was an international film star with all the glitz of the Locarno behind her.

Rachel elaborately grew tired of the attention and nudged her man forwards. Brushing off an imaginary strand of hair, Penny camouflaged a warning to Maggie against smart remarks.

"Girls, I would like tae introduce you both tae Joshua Jarvis."

"It's lovely tae see ye again," Maggie greeted him politely and, to be fair, if he had demons then she could not smell them. None apart from Rachel. She stood expectantly next to him in the plunging red dress that had been her pièce de résistance for a year or so, an ill-fated vampire ready to move on to another unsuspecting victim. How unfair that her scurrilous lover had left and they were each free to spoil another couple.

"Where aboots in America are ye fae?" she asked, artlessly.

"I'm not," he answered, his grin faltering. "I'm from Manitoba, Canada. From a small farm near Winnipeg. We've been in the war since the beginning, but now I can't move without getting confused for a Yank. A fine bit of gratitude for all my country's done."

"Sorry, ah didnae mean tae offend."

227

"I'm not offended, just repeating a slice of my moma's old bitterness. She's ancient and miserable and isn't happy until everyone else is dragged down with her but the fact is, it works well with the ladies. You girls all seem to love the Americans. A lot of fuss over nothing, if you ask me. We Canadians are tougher, living in real wild country, that's for sure."

He nodded once and squared his shoulders dramatically. Maggie laughed. He was jovial, and serious, and she liked him.

"Joshy could rip apart a bear with his bare hands."

"Weil that's braw. Ah'll know wha tae come tae if ah e'er get stuck wae a bear."

Rachel adjusted her deep neckline, pulling it lower while whispering in Joshua's ear until realisation dawned in those eyes of his, which were not on her face.

"Well, goodnight ladies. I hope to see you again soon."

He tipped his hat and skipped quickly out of the hall.

"I'd better say goodnight in a'," Rachel said, not bothering to wait a beat for appearance's sake. A toothy grin had spread across her face; it appeared her new beau's attributes were infectious.

"But ye only jist arrived!" Penny cried.

"I have a prior engagement."

She fanned herself to leave no doubt about what that tryst might entail and turned to the door. Maggie was glad to see her go.

"If Rachel talks wae yon American accent wan mair time, ah'm gonnae belt her."

"Hey there, lovely lady. Would you like to dance?"

It was the man with the twinkling eyes and the stories to tell. Maggie's insides somersaulted into her throat. Blonde hair, white hair, no difference to a yank, and the only Tommy Gunn he knew was made of metal. Her wide smile answered everything, which was just as well because, suddenly, her vocal chords refused to work.

TWENTY-FOUR

The Returned

1946

And just like that, the war ended. Most men had gone into it whole and came out broken, but Big Stevie went in broken and came out whole. Arriving in Maryhill early in the New Year, he stumbled off the train into a world that felt so familiar that it warmed him inside. With his tote bag swung over one shoulder, he loped down the street from the station and a young woman, out beating a rug and wrapped tight against the cold, stopped to watch him pass. He threw her a wink – could not resist – and she pretended not to see. The winter chill did not freeze him as deeply as the front lines of battle and there was no rush to start afresh so he strolled easily down Lyndhurst Gardens, rubbing his hands together. He even began to whistle.

Inside her aunt's flat, Maggie heard the song float in. She stopped darning, put Wee Ena's sock on the cabinet and walked slowly to the window. The last time she had heard that song was at the blasted Hogmanay she would rather forget but, hearing it again, it was the memories of the man who sang it which flooded her. Peeling back the curtain, she peered over the hedge. It looked like the street was deserted. Still, the whistling was getting louder.

"Awa' and wash yer haunds," she called to Stevie, who was on his hands and knees, sweeping the hearth.

Obediently, he left the room and the hope that spread through her felt like somebody else's. She hopped on the spot to get a better view but the street was empty save for a few stray children. She removed her shoes and launched herself up higher, knowing that she would not be able to see much further over the hedge but itching beyond logic to find the source. The balls of her feet whacked painfully on the floor but, still, there was nothing to see. She glanced towards the hallway, trying to control her emotions, and was thankful when the pipes creaked with Stevie turning on the water.

Back to the window, her heart lurched. Big Stevie was there, visible through a scraggly gap in the branches. He was fighting his way through a renegade group of children, looking her way, but her recognition came from the tune he was whistling rather than the sallow body that carried him. It was too much.

The water pipe still gurgled. Chapping furiously on the window, she caught his attention. Stumbling over a young girl, he waved back with a grin. She laughed, beckoning him so vehemently that he broke into a jog to comply, and a few moments later there was banging on the storm doors. Silence. Banging again.

"Wid ye go and get that?" she called shrilly to Stevie. "Wha'ever's oot here winnae wait a' day!"

Celebrating to herself, she slid into the kitchen. There was a laborious creak as the heavy storm door dragged back. Her heart flipped into her stomach and she got the tea brewing on the range.

Glasgow was changing quickly. Maggie and Arthur spent most evenings with the Bennies and Menzies's at one house or the other. Jess returned with technicolour stories that jumped from the written page onto her lips. Jimmy quizzed her and listened with keen interest to safer tales than the ones Big Stevie had, and Maggie listened too, holding her cousin's hand in case she let go and she slipped all the way back down to Yorkshire. Each recounting of the daily routine, the recurring faces, the officious characters and the amenable ones, did not fill the gap left by Donald, but Maggie imagined she could hear her cousin's cackle from the corner. He would have little sympathy for the garrulous girlfriend of the residing sergeant, whose legendary affair grew while his wife sat lonely at home. He would find no redemption for them, not even when the sergeant was run over by an army truck just before the war ended, or when the girlfriend's tears were overrun by the arrival of the wife for the funeral. He would have choice words to say about the mourning, holding his sister complicit and laughing through it all. Maggie could hear him, the great guffaw from the corner which Agnes would admonish and enjoy in equal measure but, glancing around, she saw that everyone else was listening intensely to Jess's story unfold, no longer able to hear the joker's attempts to lift the mood.

Two weeks later, Paul was released from hospital.

"Ah'm scared." Jess admitted quietly that night, walking Maggie and Arthur to the door. "He's no' going back tae sea. Tae many problems up here and in here."

She pointed to her head and her stomach.

"We've been married fir twelve years but we've never really hud tae be husband and wife. How dae ah become a gid wife tae a deaf man? And look at ma hair, it's turning grey already. I'm thirty-eight years auld. Ah'm no' the lassie he married."

Maggie did not point out that Arthur's hearing was fine. He stared down at his shoes but could not pretend to be anywhere else.

"He's no' the same man, either. It'll be worse fir him so ye need tae be gentle."

"Gid night, hen." Arthur tucked his scarf into his coat and pulled Maggie discreetly down the close.

When Paul returned, the Bennie household cleared out to give them space. Wee Ena's grumblings could be heard nightly coming up the street as Aunt Agnes dragged her to the Munroe house through relentless February sleet. Big Stevie joined them, careful not to slip on the way downhill from Garrioch Lane and casting a careful eye to the dark, empty windows across the street.

At the kitchen table, Aunt Agnes's stories were centred on the unwitting people who Jimmy factored for. As interesting as they were, Maggie prayed that no one had such good gossip about her so she joined Stevie and Wee Ena on the hearth with a pack of cards while the grownups talked. They were at an interesting stage, old enough to tell her a thing or two. Perching on a wicker chair, she leant down and dealt fast.

"Dinnae stair ony o' yer cheating," Wee Ena warned Stevie, pinching him on the arm.

"Enough. Remember ye're a team. Ye might no' be in Strathaven ony mair but ye hae tae work thegether."

The two youngsters looked at each other and grinned.

"We're gonnae beat ye," Stevie told her, collecting his cards.

"Ma friend, Gillian, she ayeways cheats at cairds."

"Really, hen? Then why dae ye play wae her?"

Wee Ena shrugged. "Ah've tried tae ignore her a couple o' times but she jist stairts bletherin. Ayeways aboot wan o' oor friends. Which is fine until ah think miby folk'll think ah've been sayin it, tae."

"Or wonder whit she's sayin aboot you." Maggie finished dealing and sat back. She could understand the predicament. "Ye'll jist ne'er know whit she's saying. That's the truth. But dae ye know whit ma mammy wid say?"

"Ayeways expect the worst?" Stevie guessed.

"Exactly. That way, ye winnae be disappointed."

"Sometimes ah miss Strathaven."

"Weil, Aunt Annie telt me she goat yer letter. And yours in a', Wee Ena. She telt me she felt forty years younger."

"Jist forty years? No' sixty?"

"Haud yer wheesht, Stevie Bennie!"

"Ah'll write them some gid letters noo oor Paul's back," said Wee Ena

"He's only been back twa days."

"Aye, but it's hard work, already. Sometimes in the middle o' the night we can hear him crying and the like but we pretend no' tae notice."

"Ye dinnae know whit he's dreaming. It'll be the likes o' which ye cannae imagine."

Wee Ena nodded and bit her nail. "Ah dinnae want tae imagine."

She and all her pals had heard of some horrors, keeping their ears close to the ground, but she knew better than to ask any questions. Her wee cousin copied her by wrinkling his nose but was more interested in the game he was winning.

"And how's oor Jess getting oan wae it all?" Maggie asked.

"Let's just say, between you and me, that Paul crying wae nightmares arenae the only noise we're hearing at night."

"Ena!" Stevie turned red and clamped a hand over his mouth.

Agnes cast an irritated look at her daughter.

"Ye dinnae gossip aboot yer ain," she called over, tutting deeply before turning back to the adults. "They argue like cat and dog sometimes during the day, which is an achievement seeing as how Paul cannae hear onything. And they definitely like tae mak up afterwards, but she disnae know how he likes this done and that done and then she gets a' upset. Still, we'll see how they get oan."

There was silence for a moment and Stevie dealt another hand.

"Hus thir been any talk o' them going tae England tae stay wae his family?" Arthur asked eventually.

"Naw, he's ne'er asked and, e'en if he did, she wouldnae hear o' it. Couldnae leave oor Maggie tae go awa' doon there."

Keeping her face turned to the hearth, Maggie was not so sure. She was happy, of course, as everyone's lives glided forwards while all she could do was reach out, grab the cards, and keep on playing the game.

The Munroe flat regularly became as busy as Sauchiehall Street so, when Penny took over the Bennie family mantle one Saturday afternoon, she brought Willie with her to swell the numbers. He was welcomed formally in the big room and eased onto the settee like he was one of the cushions, and from all of the letters that Maggie had read over the years, he may as well have been.

He shook her hand courteously and settled down, unaware of how well she knew him.

"How are ye?" he asked politely.

The first thing she noticed was his light hair, a shining bright contrast to the thick city air, but his rich voice was native.

"Ah've heard a lot aboot ye but ye're no' whit ah thought," she said, not sure even as she spoke what she had imagined.

On his left, Penny widened her eyes, trying to get Maggie to stop before it was too late.

"Whit huv ye heard?" Willie asked, sitting up and shuffling forward.

"Och, this and that."

It was time for Penny to launch the ultimate distraction.

"O lordie, whit's that?"

Maggie stared at her friend, who was rubbing her nose emphatically with her left hand. Willie grinned sheepishly and grabbed hold of it so tightly that he almost squeezed the ring right off. Suddenly, everything else was forgotten and the room was filled with joy.

"Ye took yer time! When'll the weddin' be?"

Before either could answer, there was a loud bang in the hallway. Arthur had returned.

"Maggie, hen!"

"In here, Daddy."

"Maggie, hen – oh, hello Penny. Is that you?"

He did not pause for an answer and was so agitated that he failed to see Willie, at all.

"Weil, Maggie, hen, ye'll ne'er guess wha ah've jist seen. Whit ah think ah've seen. If it wisnae oor Margaret."

"But she lives oan the south side."

"Aye, aye, ah know. But ah'd swear it wis her. She hus that walk, jist like yer mammy. And she hud a laddie wae her. Oan crutches."

The room was silent.

"Weil?"

"Wis it James?" Maggie asked.

"Aye. Ah think so." Her father was agitated. "Look, we huvnae heard onythin fae her in years. Ayeways a strange wan, and noo she goes and turns up right oan Maryhill Road. Oot by the Cooperative. Is there no' a furriers oot that way?"

"Aye. A' the way oot here fir a shoap and she doesnae get in touch wae ony o' us," Maggie growled. Arthur was silent. "Ah cannae believe this."

"Weil, we cannae dae nothing. They're family. And he's oan crutches."

"Did he hae twa legs?"

"Ah couldnae see."

"Richt. Ah'll write them a letter."

Fumbling with the bureau, she pulled it open and groped for the writing paper. Her fingers stumbled through dookits of ledgers, photographs and files while her mind tumbled in every direction of likelihoods and possibilities. And probable repercussions.

The paper she found was plain and durable, without the elegance that the Hepburns were accustomed to, but it would do the job and she leaned in further to grab a pencil.

"Whit should ah say?" she asked eventually.

"We'll gang awa'," Willie said softly, rising to leave with Penny's hand firmly clasped. Penny dragged herself to her feet and lent forward to give Maggie a kiss on the cheek while Maggie tried to think of something to keep them there. It was all too quick; there was so much left unsaid.

"Ah'll see ye themorra efter the kirk," Penny promised, turning to leave.

"Oh, hen, ah didnae e'en get tae hear aboot yer news. Daddy, Penny and Willie here are getting mairried."

"Och, sorry laddie." Arthur was chastened. "Ah didnae notice ye in a' the commotion. So ye're Willie, eh? It's braw tae finally meet ye."

"And whit huv ye heard tae date?" asked Willie, raising his eyebrows and winking at Maggie.

"This and that. Listen, it's jist bad timing wae ma sister-in-law, but ye huv tae come back o'er wae Penny. How about the morra?"

"Aye …."

The noise of thudding fists crashed through the house as someone banged on the front door. It was ferocious and demanding, and completely unnecessary when the storm doors were lying open. She wanted to stay in the big room to write her letter but the beats were impossible to ignore. Willie smiled over at her in reassurance, happy to lend his support.

As the pounding knocks intensified, her stomach clenched. It was an unrelenting sound and its memory would hammer away just as loudly in the years to come. With the others close behind, she walked towards it.

TWENTY-FIVE

Discord

A few weeks later, Maggie sat with a book hidden on her lap, tilted towards the light behind the clutter of her desk. Papers were piled high in their proper place and her filing system was a display of organised chaos; the waiting room was empty and the afternoon sun streamed merrily through the windows. Everything else could wait.

She was really getting into the yarn, the perfect escape from the letter to Margaret which still sat unfinished on top of the bureau. As the story spun more out of control, it made her own world seem more normal, her love life paling in comparison to that of the heroine. She was not a peasant girl stowing herself away on a pirate ship, cutting her hair or sailing the seven seas while saving the life of her secret love. It made the hairs on the back of her neck stand on end. She turned the page with trepidation, to the captain's confession. Unaware that his rescuer was a woman in disguise, he told her of his love for a plantation owner's daughter, who was faceless in all except her beauty. The poor stowaway could do nothing but listen behind her cropped hair and breaches, a solitary tear running down her flushed cheek. The course had been set to guide her away at daybreak on a relentless tide; and they would remain mere ships passing in the night.

"Awright."

The voice made her jump, dropping the book to the bottom of the ocean.

"Och, ah didnae mean tae startle ye."

"Naw, yer grand. Whit a lovely surprise."

237

She smiled up at the towering figure of John. He filled the open doorway and blocked the sun.

"Ah can see ye're working hard there."

He looked down at her with one arm resting on the frame.

Laughing, she picked up the book and threw it at him. It was a lame throw from weak wrists and the story stumbled through the air, but John was no sportsman and he fumbled it. His face reddened as it hit the floor.

He walked to her desk, fists clenched, ignoring the book that lay on the ground between them. Neither spoke, both waiting for the other. Eventually, Maggie cracked under the silence.

"Ah wis only playin' wae ye."

She got up to retrieve it. Bending down, she felt stiff and awkward, but his back was towards her anyway. It was sweet, she thought, the way he scowled in on himself; the way he cared so deeply. It would be unfair to expect any soldier to return unchanged, or perhaps he had always been that way. Perhaps she had just not noticed. His knock on her door had been as strong and intense as he was, and Penny had looked scared to death, but the first thing Maggie had done was to look past him, to see who else was there. It was never one without the other, until now.

When he had said that Tommy was not coming back, Penny and Willie left immediately and Arthur sank into the background while Maggie was given the bare bones of a story she would rather not have heard. Taking her hand in his, he gave her the support that she appreciated but did not need, keeping hold until she gently removed herself to go and make them a pot of tea. Since then, he had not mentioned his friend at all.

Her memories bound him to another world and, slowly, he was carving a position in the new one. He visited often with a spontaneity that was very unlike the reserved man he had once been; to the cinema, the cafe, and sometimes just to walk around the neighbourhood talking. It had been over a bowl of broth, about a week after his return, that it transpired he wanted to expand his uncle's business whenever the economy sorted itself out, and sharing his ambitions had prompted him to take her hand. As her hand turned clammy in his, she had berated her body for its unreasonable urge to pull away.

Sometimes she caught him staring into space, the large black pools of his pupils swimming into the past, and she felt like the cat that curiosity had killed. He was keeping darker things in his head than daydreams but the minute their eyes met and she smiled the look would pass and he would come into the world again. Just like that, she could help him with only a smile, his own personal doctor.

Her heart did not flutter when she saw him, her mind did not constantly picture his face; but what a relief when this old friend showed up in her life, broad and flushed and eager. Which was why, once she had returned to her seat to look at him over the cluttered reception desk, she willed herself to feel more.

He gazed back dolefully as if he could read her thoughts. Gone was the cheeky visitor who had appeared in her doorway a few minutes before, all because of some stupid book.

"It's rubbish onyway."

She tossed it into the top drawer but was itching for a moment by herself to read the next instalment – the kind of fairytale romance which could raise expectations of love to unobtainable heights.

John sighed and shuffled his feet, patiently waiting to find out what else he could guilt out of her. As the clock struck the hour, the door to the inner office opened and Doctor Bowman's bald head appeared, followed by the rest of him. He looked around his empty waiting room and shook his head. It was the first time in twenty years that he had seen the place empty; no screaming children, no gabbing women, no postulating men.

"Away home, now, Maggie." He templed his fingers to stave off an argument. "Really, you've been working so hard and the place is dead. Go and take the afternoon off."

Maggie desperately wanted to argue. Medically the doctor was brilliant but, administratively, she did not want to think what would happen if a single patient came in and he needed to find anything. She started to protest but all he saw was a young couple eager to be alone. At that moment, the heavy skies bowed and cracked, giving way to torrents of grey rain. Very soon the street would face a cascading avalanche from the top of the hill, all the way down to St Georges Cross. Perhaps, if she hurried, she would get home and only be soaked to her jumper.

"If ye're sure then, Doctor."

She shrugged into her jacket and fastened her scarf tightly beneath her chin, underprepared to meet the elements. Doctor Bowman nodded at John and disappeared back into his office.

"Where dae ye wannae go?" she asked politely.

As usual, he shrugged and led the way outside. She followed but stopped short by the door, casting her eyes towards heaven. The water cracked down on her soft skin and she was drenched instantaneously. The drops were heavy on her eyelids, threatening to tap right through to the sockets. It was sore. She wanted to hide.

"Let's go back tae ma hoose, eh? It's close!"

She had to shout to be heard over the cascade and he ran across the road to shelter under the awning of the butcher's shop. Considering this implicit agreement, she took off after him, leaving one sanctuary for another. Her footfalls and the torrential rain disrupted the film of water that lay on the street, sending glass droplets flying, each ricocheting piece stinging as if she were shattering a sheet of glass. Careening into John beneath the flimsy green canopy, she huddled down to drive away the cold but the wet chill penetrated deep. The rain fell straight into her peep toes and seeped through her stockings, and overcame gravity to flow upwards into her sleeves. Hiding was useless. Standing around was only making her wetter.

John watched as she tottered in front of him, too cautious to comfort and too rigid to laugh, so she laughed for both of them and took off at a sprint. She felt the full force of the weather as she ran unprotected down the street. It bore down on her and she pelted along as fast as the rain, and faster than her slingback shoes could carry her. She ran alone. John still stood in the semi-dryness of the shopfront, his face puffy and indignant, his brows furrowed close. His chest rose and fell as he steeled himself for the flight ahead and his fists twitched in anger as he was left to make the journey alone.

Yet Maggie saw none of this as she continued on. She had the giddy, wonderful feeling that she was flying free and fast towards the grey horizon, and felt she could keep on running until she left the smoke and tenements far behind. In their place would be green fields and stretching plains of sunlight, more a scene from one of her novels than from reality. All that she needed to get there was to run a wee bit faster.

Her wobbling inch-high heels were liberating as she rounded the corner and hurried past a hoard of children that was just then jostling out of the primary school gate. The noise was like a hundred tramcars crashing from the sky, an indecipherable cacophony of elated shrieks, but nothing could interfere with her peace. She beelined through them, on to Wilton Drive. Two puddles had slowly formed inside her shoes, personalising her plight and adding sound effects to her progress. Her shedding acted as a trough to catch droplets from the sky and carried them down her forehead and face to finally drip off the end like a second-rate waterfall. It made her scalp cold and tingly. She liked it.

So nearly home. The cobbles were treacherous and slick underfoot. Twice she nearly slipped to the ground. The sky clapped thunder and menace, and she watched a lightning fork split the sky a few miles to the west. The street was almost deserted. Almost, except for a solitary man who walked deliberately towards her, his hands clasped behind his back and leaning into his long strides. Even with his bent head covered by a flat cap, his grin shone out from underneath like the sun waiting to burst from the clouds as he, too, revelled in the awesome force of nature. The rain was too loud to be certain, but Maggie would have sworn that he was whistling to himself. It was only once he passed, his rolled cigarette saturated to nothing but paper at the corners of a smile, that she remembered the face under the hat. It was Alec McLean. Clearly, he had not seen her; had not once looked up from some invisible target on the ground. The guilt came crashing over her all over again but the War had shown her the importance of moving on, and it was never too late to get back in touch. Ignoring the rain and the roaring sky, she turned around to call after him, just in time to see him round the corner out of sight. Then John materialised, walking as fast as he could move while pointedly refusing to run. When he saw her looking over her shoulder, he brightened slightly.

"So ye decided tae wait on me efter a'?" he shouted, his voice almost lost in the racket of the storm.

He was unable to hide his satisfaction and she saw no reason to contradict him: let him believe what he liked if it kept a smile on his lips and the day feeling fair. She twirled gleefully on the spot, waiting for him to catch up.

With a man by her side she felt like a film star, skipping down the street and kicking up the puddles she passed without care or consequence. When she sprayed him lightly by accident, she hid her laughter behind his disgruntled sighs, and when they finally reached the close, neither was in a rush to go inside. They were already freezing and saturated; the weather could do no more harm.

"Is yer daddy in?" John asked.

"Aye, where else'd he be?"

241

"Och, ah wis jist wonderin if we'd hae some privacy. He's ayeways here, an' when we arenae wae him we're awa' tae Jaquonelli's or the dancin' or some other place we cannae git a moment's peace."

"Ah didnae realise it wis such a problem fir ye." Maggie scowled. Perhaps he was still angry at her for running out in the rain without him, or embarrassing him by throwing that book in the doctor's surgery.

"Is it an awfy bad thing ah'd like tae be alone wae ye fir a wee bit?"

"Naw, but ye *dae* get time alone wae me. Look at aw them walks we go fir. Roon' and roon' the block like a couple o' lost weans, naebody botherin' us. Or at Jaconelli's. It's no' like oor Mario's staundin o'er us, he's tae busy fechtin wae Amelia and daein white'er Teresa tells him. Really Johnny, ah dinnae know whit else ye want."

"Of course ye dinnae. An it's John, no' Johnny."

"Whit's that supposed tae mean?"

She turned to face him but he avoided her gaze, and she would not stand around just to be ignored. Stomping into the close and up the stairs, she could feel her hackles rise. It was murky and cool and the hard footsteps echoed loudly over the noisy rainfall outside. She hiked up her skirt so that she could stomp harder, her good humour snuffed out in an instant. Now the storm only filled her with rage.

John kept on coming behind her, sulking and tenacious like a child. When she shouted to let Arthur know she was home there was no answer, and no pipe smoke lingered in the air, so she busied herself by the range, fumbling and slow and hardly able to lift the heavy iron kettle. In her anger, she secretly waited for the apology that would never come.

Moments later, John stood in the doorway, hands in his pockets as he watched her struggle. "Ye cannae be mad at me fir wantin tae spend time wae ye, Maggie."

"That's no whit ah'm mad aboot and ye know it."

"Dinnae speak tae me like that. Efter aw ah've been through, dae ah no' deserve a bit o' respect?"

Maggie looked up sharply.

"Ye huv ma respect, and ye'd dae weil no' tae lose it!"

The War was not a weapon to be used lightly, or the world would suddenly be full of heroes who could not be questioned. She stood with one hand on the kettle and one on her hip, sizing him up.

His face reddened and his jowls trembled. "Ye're tae smairt fir yer ain gid. Most folk hae that smacked oot o' them as a wean."

"Ah guess ah'm used tae things bein easier when it comes tae ma daddy," she started, then thought better of it and made her voice soft and diplomatic. "When Tommy wis comin roon here, they used tae sit thegether an it ne'er seemed tae bother either wan o' them. Dinnae get me wrang, we were soon oot o' here daein oor ain thing in a', and it ne'er wance crossed ma mind that thir might be a problem."

He stood watching her with peculiar intensity, his gaze filling her with nerves. It was the blackness that she could normally dust away. After two weeks, her magic must have worn off. Even when she turned her back, she could feel his eyes burning into her spine and she did not realise how she was trembling until she spilled the boiling water on her fingers.

"Bugger!"

He did not flinch. The patter of torrential rain against the window pane thudded behind thin lace. Where it had once soothed her, now it rang out of oppression and discomfort, and still he stood straight and still, the silence filling the air between them and pressing into every crack and crevice until the small space was filled by all the things left unsaid.

"Ah guess it'd be the wrang time tae suggest takin' oor tea intae the big room?"

Her joke fell flat, so all she could do was stand there nursing her cup and her burnt finger. She considered asking him to leave, but the whole situation was too ridiculous for that. Instead, she took a deep breath and put on her most conciliatory smile.

Placing a cup directly in his hands, she led him to the wicker chair beside the fireplace and sat opposite so they could rest for a while. There was no coal to burn and the hearth stood cavernous and cold. The room began to grow dark and the deep night chill seeped through the grey walls like a ghost. Nonetheless, his impenetrable gaze slowly morphed into something more human and his body gravitated towards her.

"Dae ye think ah'm daft, Maggie?" he finally whispered.

"Of course ah dinnae."

The silence dragged on and she fought the urge to break it. The more she felt John relax across from her, the more her own tension slipped away. It was their first argument and it felt unnatural and strange, but surely it would be more strange if they did not argue at all, especially if Jess and Paul's relationship was any indication. Thinking of her cousin, she even managed to smile.

"Ah remember Tommy ne'er used tae drink tea," she reminisced. "It wis ayeways a wee drop whisky or a glass o' wine. Kept him strong, he said. Dae ye mind?"

But that was not the right thing to say. John jumped from his seat so fast that he shattered the calm she should have known was too tentative to last.

"Ah dinnae wannae talk aboot Tommy!" he bellowed. "That's aw it is when ah see ye. Tommy, Tommy, Tommy! How could ye be so callous, Maggie?"

She moved to get up but he put his hand up quickly to stop her, almost knocking her off her feet. She grabbed at the fireplace for support but her burnt fingers protested and all she could do was sink back down and stare at John in confusion.

"He wis ma best friend! Noo he's gone an he's aye ye wannae talk aboot! As if *you* hae a bloody clue! Of *course* ah remember. Ah know more than *you* e'er will, Maggie Munroe!"

"I wis jist...."

"Och, I shouldnae hae come o'er the night."

"But...."

"Just go oot and play in the rain or something."

Seconds later, it was he who left.

The deluge was soon over and spring hatched early, spreading light and warmth into the darkest fracture. Finally, the recovering city blossomed. When Maggie opened the door, it seemed like a new man had materialised. Bright and jaunty, John stood with a shopping bag and his shirt unbuttoned enough to reveal a tuft of sandy hair. It was warm outside and he had a coat of sweat on his upper lip to prove it.

"Come oan, Maggie, the day's wastin. An ye winnae be needing this!"

He tried to tug the jacket from her shoulders but she hung on fast. When he pulled harder, she stepped back and won. The March sun was glorious but she could no more rely on it than she could on a man.

"Ah'm cauld blooded."

"Let's be gettin aff then."

He turned unceremoniously on his heel.

"Where're we gaun?" she asked, hurrying out the door behind him.

His flat feet were already pattering down the stairwell so she called a hasty farewell to her father and slammed the door in her hurry to keep up.

"Fir a picnic in Kelvingrove. Ah thoucht it'd be nice."

Maggie stopped in her tracks. The coincidence was too much. He had to know. They had been good friends, after all. They must have talked about such things. And here was his great revenge.

"Ah prefer the Botanics."

The words escaped into the day unnoticed. He was already out of the close. She ran to catch up with him and he smiled down at her, his eyes reflecting the wonderful day and the beautiful girl on his arm. His brow would furrow if she made eye contact with another man but he did not say a word. It made her feel wanted; it made her feel whole.

It was a short walk to Kelvingrove and he was in no rush. Letting the shopping bag swing from one arm, he threw the other around her shoulder. Allowing herself to be swept up in the sparkle of the day, she let him enjoy his surprise without brushing him off and, as the afternoon progressed, she kept private counsel with her mammy. There was the tree she and Tommy had sat under, almost unrecognisable now in full glorious bloom; there was the fountain where children played for as long as summer lasted and where Tommy would jump in winter when the water ran dry; the same imposing homes on the hilltop that she had stared at uneasily, which made him laugh and call her a scaredy cat; and the river Kelvin gurgling past as it had since Glasgow found root, a witness to it all. The importance of respecting the dead through remembrance could not be sullied within the privacy of the mind.

"Whit're ye smiling at?" John asked, tightening his arm around her and shaking the cold from her shoulders. He was grinning.

Maggie pointed. Two red squirrels were chasing each other vigorously around the thick trunk of an oak. Their feather-duster tails swept at the air with the joy of freedom, completely oblivious to their spectators.

"See them wee squirrels o'er there? They'll be the first oot o' hibernation."

"Aye, they're no wastin any time gettin Spring stairted." He giggled behind his hand like Rachel would have done and sat forward to watch the female lead an endless chase. "There he goes, efter her again, usin up a' his winter energy jist tae get a wee touch, but she's nae interested in the poor de'il."

His voice was so animated, his face so expressive, that Maggie started to laugh and laugh.

"Ah'm happy if you're happy, Maggie hen," he said, oblivious.

His picnic was cheese sandwiches and crumpets, yet it was delivered with such gusto that it tasted as good as any of the tarts and fancies that Tommy had ever presented. Sitting there as he licked his fingers, Maggie realised she was growing fond of the man – a big boy from the country who had been forced to do a lot of growing up.

TWENTY-SIX

Civilisation

It was the summer when Scotland was on an outbreath. Not quite time to dust itself off, but to take stock and prepare.

"Ah dinnae like this." Maggie muttered, stepping slowly from the train.

She cast an eye up the steep, deserted mountain tracks, distrustful of the sudden stillness. After the bustle of Glasgow, they may as well have alighted on a different continent.

"Thir's a road jist past them hedges right there an' a village twa seconds walk doon there. However," Penny paused, sensing the anticipation of her audience, "we're no' *gaun* doon that way. Follow me, lassies!"

She took off uphill at a sprightly march, swinging her shopping bag with ease and leaving the others to scramble in her wake. Her legs were strong – those of the country girl she longed to be – and her small body soon disappeared amongst bush and bracken. Only the soft sound of her singing called the others to where she eventually stopped, waiting patiently for them with a smile.

"The route we're gaun should be rare. Gid scenery but no' tae tough fir a' you city sticklers," she called out gaily.

Maggie hobbled forward, her bones feeling stiff despite the fresh country air and the fact she was only thirty-two. Sunny without the stark glare of summer, fresh without the deep chill of winter, it was a perfect day, but she was a foreigner in strange lands.

"Ah ne'er knew Penny cid blether," Rachel muttered unkindly but no one was listening.

Each plant and bush they passed captured Penny's attention and she called the names with an expert eye. She knew the birds overhead from the sound of their call long before they swooped into view. Her three friends were unusually silent as they concentrated, more on avoiding the tremendous tree roots and bracken that lunged up like sentinels to bar their way than to understand the information she shared. They continued up and up until the train station became a brown speck in the distance.

Soon they found their stride. Only Rachel struggled along at the rear on feet that were used to solid city cobbles. Maggie kept a careful eye on Jess; if there was any sign of her struggling then she would turn her round and take her straight home.

Suddenly the narrow path opened to reveal a shocking panorama, out over a deep glen with only one small bothy signalling refuge. Slopes rose sharply on each side; up they climbed to ragged peaks which were centuries of rock tilted inwards at a precarious pitch and, sandwiched between, a shimmering loch that pushed outwards with a power all of its own. Steep slopes cast crimson reflections of blooming heather and infiltrated the aqua blue of its still veneer; a deep pool of beauty caught in a stranglehold that it was too still to shake away. It was further into the wilds than Maggie had ever wished to venture, and it took her breath away. Far off, a wooden boat drifted on the ripples, no bigger than a matchstick. There were lives being lived and stories being made, when at first it had appeared that there was nothing.

"Ah cannae believe this," she admitted.

"It maks ye proud," Jess agreed.

"Aye, as if ye created aw'thin wae yer ain twa haunds." Rachel rolled her eyes and untucked the pleat that had become wedged between her cheeks.

"Come oan, it's a wee bitty further yet."

Penny was off down the slope to another, wider path that circled the loch. She had warned them all to wear flat shoes but they hadn't matched her tough boots and nothing could have prepared them for the detour. Curious sheep watched their progress as they clambered across their patch beneath the cyan sky that formed the perfect canopy over the world.

They followed a winding trail north for half an hour while woodland fell in tight around them and they began a sharp ascent. The mud was hard and compact, but each undulation tested the strength of their soles and their willpower. The trodden earth was slippery underfoot and Maggie felt herself sliding backward more than once. She did not welcome the lack of control, not one little bit. She concentrated on each footfall, grunting as Jess powered easily past her to fall into step with Penny. It was the kind of problem that she did not have in Maryhill.

Abruptly, they came out into a large clearing. Surrounded by the forest, a scattering of small huts lived, indistinguishable with their box windows and thin net curtains set behind fresh painted fences.

"Here we are. Whit dae ye think?"

Penny held her arms out in welcome and Maggie walked forward, leaving Rachel leaning forward onto her knees, alone.

"It's awfy bonnie. Where are we?"

"Carbeth!"

"What's that, then?"

"It's ma new wee hoose. Willie's aunt bought it fir a weddin present."

Penny swept her arm up to a small hut that was keeking out from between two larger properties like it knew it was not supposed to be there. Its small garden was trimmed neatly round the narrow path that crawled up to the sunshine door, all white paint with yellow, a celebration cake good enough to eat.

Maggie looked past the picket fence to the well-worn road beyond. It pushed through the trees and down the slope, and was wide enough for a car. She cast an eye back to the path she had been dragged up, her mud-caked shoes and laddered stockings. Penny was having a laugh.

Rachel threw herself onto the ground, unimpressed. "So're ye movin aw the way oot here, then? These arnae hooses. Thir isnae e'en a shoap!"

"Naw, we hae Willie's work tae think aboot back in Glesga, and his aunt's gonnae help pay fir ma nursing so we hae tae be in the city. This is jist fir the holidays."

"Whit's that gottae dae wae me?"

As Rachel whined on, Maggie sauntered further away. Penny, however, was far more forgiving.

"Ah wanted tae bring ye here while ah can. Things're changin so suddenly, can ye no' feel it? Ah'll be a married woman afore lang wae a new joab, and Jess's a' settled doon wae Paul."

"Dinnae be daft!" Maggie cried.

She spun back to her friends to capture everything exactly as it was in that moment: Jess with her eyes like saucers, drifting towards the big hut on the left, Penny adopting a wide stance with her hands on her hips, a Peter Pan ready for takeoff, and Rachel blurred in the background, where she belonged. For the first time in a long while, life was good, and she could not bear to see it disappear.

"Och Maggie, things are changin. Wha knows whit's roon the corner."

The sadness that suddenly came over Penny was at odds with the beautiful spring day and her hand splayed across her throat as she drew the thoughts down. She pushed open the creaking gate and beckoned everyone forwards.

"Whit a bonnie garden!" Maggie said, first through the gate and giving her friend a quick hug on the way past to make melancholy the most fleeting of guests.

"Aye, but ah dinnae hae the keys yet."

So they sat on the lawn, sharing a tartan blanket and sandwiches from the bag. The ham tasted moister in the country, the eggs fresher, the bread more sweet and, before long, everyone was laughing. She kicked off her shoes to enjoy herself fully and ignored Penny's gloomy foresight, absentmindedly rubbing at the hard lumps that were forming on her soles. The bunions were as much reality as she needed.

On her left, Jess finished her sandwich and lay back on the grass.

"Ye're affy quiet," she whispered, but her cousin just smiled and stretched out further.

For a long time, no one spoke. The bees buzzed and the birds sang, but it was the quietest Maggie had ever heard the world.

"John Anderson's stuck aroon weil. Ah didnae expect him tae last this long." Rachel said finally from her spot on the path, thoughtlessly squashing a buttercup between her fingers.

"Nice o' ye tae say."

"He disnae seem yer type," Jess added.

"Really? Why no'?"

Jess shrugged and patted a curl behind her ear to avoid making eye contact. Maggie tried a different tac.

"Ah'll grant ye, he wis a big oaf years ago. But the war seems tae hae knocked it oot o' him."

"An' ye like that, dae ye?"

"Aye, it's interestin."

"And ye're happy," Penny said, swiftly cutting off another question from Jess.

Maggie paused. The girls looked at her expectantly. *He's ayeways in a wee world o' his ain, shut up in his ain heid,* she thought, wondering what they would say to that. *Suddenly he's aff somewhere else, and ah wannae reach intae his mind, fish oot his thouchts and splat them across the table so ah can see.*

But she could not imagine their advice. If she could have, she would have acted on it long before.

"Aye, ah'm happy," she said, thinking about their picnic. "Like ah said, he's interestin. It wis gid o' him tae come o'er tae tell me aboot Tommy, and he remembered aboot that hip flask. That's funny, ae no?"

Rachel sniffed and threw the flower onto the grass. "Men ayeways fa' aboot yer feet like ye're Miss Queen Bee."

Maggie felt her fingers curl into her fist and sat on them.

"Ye ayeways tak somethin and twist it," she said, so quietly that even Rachel could sense the danger.

"Dae ye hae ony advice fir me 'boot married life, Jess?" Penny asked quickly.

"Oh aye, ye're gonnae love it. Thir's nothin like sharin yer life wae somewan special."

"Miby she's no' the richt person tae be askin'," Rachel commented.

Jess wouldn't be drawn and grew thoughtful, contemplating the truth of it.

"Ah cannae lie, it isnae ayeways easy. Paul's right stubborn when he wants tae be. Like, e'ery time we hae a disagreement."

"Aye, as if ye're ony better."

"Awfy funny, Maggie. Seriously though, ah know ye've a' heard the twa o' us at each other's throats. He's as deif as a doorknob and cin be moody as hell but ah widnae change him. He's exactly whit Maggie wis talking aboot. Interestin. In fact," she hesitated, looking around. "Ah'm pregnant."

Rachel's shrieks scattered birds from a neighbouring tree. Scooting over to Jess, she put her hand out to touch her stomach.

"Should we be huggin' in yer condition?" Penny asked.

"It's awright. Dinnae worry aboot me. Ah'm no' that delicate."

In response, their tight embrace rocked Jess gently onto her back. "Ah wouldnae hae dragged ye up here if ah'd known."

Jess laughed. "Please. Ah'm awright. Paul's bad enough, tiptoeing roon me. Ye know how stupit he's gotten? He's haudin back on yon hoochmagandy 'til the wean comes oot, guy fiert o' daein some damage – and ah've still got six months tae go! It's drivin me daft! An dinnae go sae red in the face as if ah said some dirty wurd, Penny Sinclair. It'll be Penny Grant soon enough, an' then ye'll know exactly whit ah'm talkin aboot."

"It must've bin a braw twa months so far, then," Maggie said, trying to save her friend's blushes.

"Ye've known that lang! And ye've telt Maggie awready?"

"Dinnae blame Maggie. Ah telt her no' tae say onything,"

"Ah've been watchful, like, and she's been climbing yon braes better than me."

Penny was flushed. "Ye should hae telt us sooner and we could hae got ye some presents."

Jess shook her head, adamant this time. "Ah dinnae want ony presents. They're bad luck. When the wean's oot kickin an screaming, then ye can buy me onythin ye want. Ah'll be sticking aroon fir a while, at least."

"Awhile jist?" Maggie played with the hem of her dress, mindful not to jump to conclusions. After all, she kept Jess's secret for months; if there was a bigger secret, she would know about it.

"It'll be gid tae hae Aunt Agnes aboot. Yer mammy will hauf the hard work fir ye. She'll be indi...indi...whit's that word?"

"Nae idea," Penny said. "Ah cin jist imagine Minnie's reaction next time she's visiting and sees ye wae a wee bundle. And Paul, he must be so happy."

"Aye, both o' us are. But we're awfy nervous." Jess's voice changed. "Ah jist want this wean so much. And ah'm thirty-nine noo, girls. It's ma last chance."

"Dinnae cry, hen." Maggie knelt on the cold grass by her cousin's side, wrapped her in both arms and kissed her cheek. "Ye need aw yer strength tae tak gid care o' yersel and yer wee bundle. Indispensable. That's the word ah wis thinking o'."

She looked around at them all. "We're gettin auld."

"Wee Ena and Stevie are the young wans noo." Jess rubbed her eyes and stood to help Penny pack up. "But inside ah'm the same as ah wis back when we used tae head doon Barrowlands wae a bottle o' whisky hidden in oor haundbags."

Maggie left them and wandered over to the dusty windows of the hut, feeling a new heaviness in her bones. It was so sparse and dark that she could not imagine what the future had in store for the tiny home in the forest, and the dim reflection of the girls tidying up and talking was only a window into the past.

When the shadows lengthened and the sun began to slip over the ceaseless sky, they set off down the hill on the main road that led directly to the promise of home; and as they turned a bend in the fading light and were greeted by Glasgow flickering in the distance, Maggie cried out, "Civilisation!"

She bounded towards the cherished sight of home. It was a beacon calling to her. Yet, in days and years to come, she would often wish for that quiet afternoon. For the company of her friends and the memory of her youth.

TWENTY-SEVEN

Behind Closed Doors

Back in the city a few weeks later, Paul and Jimmy decided to take Arthur to the Garscube for a rare treat and Maggie accompanied her daddy as far as the Menzies house. From the kitchen, she could hear Aunt Agnes shout out the window to Wee Ena and Stevie, whose replies blended with the squeals of the other children playing in the back court. The drama was ongoing so the men left and she and Jess had the living room to themselves.

In the dappled afternoon light, Jess scrutinised her closely from behind her darning, the sock lying limp in her hands. Her face was a patchwork of sunlight and shadows through the filter of the thin lace curtains, but her concern was unobscured.

"Whit's wrang?" she asked. "Ye've got a richt look on yer face."

"It's jist the wan ah wis born wae."

"Dinnae gie me that. When a lassie hus a face as lang as a pulley rope, guaranteed it's o'er a laddie. So? Whit's he done?"

Maggie did not want to have that conversation.

"Still watters run deep. That's how the saying goes."

"Ah."

"And how are ye feelin'? Is the wean movin' aboot yet?"

"Naw, naw, Maggie. We're talkin' aboot you."

"No ye'r no'. Ye'r talking aboot John Anderson."

"And?"

She shrugged easily but her stomach clenched around all the things she did not want to share.

"Ye're ayeways an open book, Maggie Munroe. It isnae a gid feelin when that changes o'er a man."

The room was closing in, hot and as uncomfortable as the Spanish Inquisition.

"When ah know anything, ah'll tell ye," she promised.

"Richt, whit hae ah missed?"

Finally, the interruption she had been waiting for. She gave silent thanks to Agnes, who hobbled slowly through the door and wiped her hands on her apron like she had achieved a great feat. Jess pulled herself up to help, cleaning carefully between each of her mother's fingers while the woman gasped but held her ground. She was far too used to the painful routine. All Maggie could do was launch a distraction.

"Whit're the weans up tae?"

"Stevie's climbing up the midden, e'en when ah've telt them no' tae and he's far tae auld fir that cairry oan."

Agnes tutted and sank into a chair, folding in on herself before continuing.

"Wee Ena's sitting oan the grass in her gid dress reading books and bossin the weans aboot wae that bloody Gillian, although they know ah can see them fae the windae. She should be aff speaking tae laddies, no the weans."

"Maybe she's dreaming o' weans of her ain," Maggie muttered, then, "Right, ah'm awa'. Ah've got some chores t'dae."

"Can ye no' stay a wee bit longer?" Jess asked, manoeuvring herself and her bump delicately back into her chair.

"Ah'd love tae but ah'll see ye the morra. No, no, dinnae get up! You twa keep comfy and ah'll let masel oot. And if ah see those weans up ony midden, ah'll skelp them fir ye."

She walked to the door, with Jess grumbling, "Daddy'd better no' be steamin when he gets in," as it swung slowly shut.

Outside, she could hear their laughter through the window, Aunt Agnes deep and vehement, and Jess beside herself. The shrieking of happy children soared over the tenement block and the more distance there was, the more she wanted to claw herself back inside.

"Are ye a'right, hen?" Mr Henderson, the milliner, asked as he passed on his lunch break.

The most well dressed man in Maryhill, he managed to look at ease whatever skin he was wearing that day, and her throat tightened when she answered. Everything was fine. It was.

He carried on his way. She continued on hers. If she turned the corner onto Wilton Drive, John may well be standing at her close. If she turned the corner onto Wilton Drive and John was at number ten, he would not be gone until late in the evening.

She stopped. But she liked him. Really, she did. It was just that temper of his. Like walking on eggshells. She knew when it was coming; in that brief moment when his face stilled like the placid Sandler's Pond, out by Carbeth, before a storm. And heaven forbid she mention Tommy.

Her fingers clenched around the pleats of her skirt while she formed a plan. If he was there, she would make sure to mention Tommy. In any way possible. Single-handedly, she would keep his memory alive.

Straightening up with conviction, she walked around the corner and onto her street, then stopped just as suddenly. It was not John who stood there but Big Stevie, darting out of number five in broad daylight. She had expected him to be with the other men at the pub but there he was, freshly shaven, glancing up at the darkened windows of number ten and straightening his tie.

There was no time to jump back to safety. Instead, she stood afloat on the corner, fingers splayed like a lizard trying to blend in. The street was deserted, nobody there to see, but that was little comfort when it meant there was nobody else she could hide behind. She waited as he hesitated then turned up the street and walked away… jaunted… skipped… Maggie threw up her hands and gave up trying to analyse that walk. The only thing she knew for sure was that it came from a very satisfied man. And she saw the viper inside with her white feather and it made her sick.

Only once he had safely rounded the corner did she move for home, impulsively looking up at Sarah Gibb's second-storey windows as she passed. The curtains were drawn. The white feather was a story she had not shared with her uncle, hesitant to reopen a wound that ran deeper for someone else. If this was to be the outcome, she would forever regret that decision. The brash woman who would trade off any chance of decency to ensure all eyes were on her would be back at it soon, flitting around until it was another man standing outside her close.

The shadows were growing long up the brick walls and creeping into any home that left itself open. If only she had been a few minutes later, she would not have had to see, but it was too late to turn back the clock. When night descended, she would keep her eyes open and see if Big Stevie returned.

"Yer feet sound awfy heavy, so they dae," Mrs McNulty called from the close entrance.

"Aye, aye."

She traipsed up the stairs with her handbag knocking against the bannister and her mind whirling somewhere else. Between John and Big Stevie, only one thing was certain: each survivor who returned from the war had their reason damaged.

"Whit dae ah dae. Whit dae ah dae?"

Without Arthur, the flat seemed large and empty. She threw herself into his favourite chair, crossed her legs beneath her and willed some of his wisdom to permeate. Her mind flitted back to settle on the worries she had woken up with. He would have his own opinions on that, but so far she had been too afraid to ask. He knew what it meant to be a country boy, straight off the train from Strathaven with big dreams in the city, but now the Lanark laddie's naivety had left him and there was something hard in its place.

Her mother filled the space that Arthur left. *He's changed, Maggie. It wis bound tae happen.*

"Whit if he gets worse?"

"Whit if he gets better?"

Poking the cold fire with her stocking soles, she could find neither answer nor distraction. Instead, all she could see was John's throbbing brows as his mind took over and, in the background, Jess's ill-concealed look of concern.

Her head began to throb as she turned over every conversation that had gone sour. The most recent was when he had stayed for dinner, a spontaneous guest served nothing planned or special, just mince and tatties. Everything had been going well until the tatties came out lumpy, just the way she liked. It was not, however, the way that he liked them. She remembered his snarl, the curl of his top lip like a mastiff ready to bite, and the satisfaction she felt when she spotted it and managed to whisk them away in time; but when she returned to the table with them mashed smooth in the bowl, it was her interference that caused the storms to come.

Ah wid hae been fine the way they were. His voice barely laced with calm. *Fine, jist winnae dae fir a guest,* Arthur said jovially from the head of the table, oblivious to the threat. Maggie had held her breath, unsure what was about to happen. If he erupted, her daddy would not sit by and take it, of that she was certain. He would react in the way that perhaps she should have done all along, and the only certainty was that her relationship with John would not survive. Perhaps John sensed it, too, because he glared at her but kept quiet.

As the men's conversation continued, she racked her brain to understand how the whole thing could have been avoided. Nothing came to mind other than she had mashed his potatoes. Maybe, if she had not done that, things would be better. At the very least, she would have the tatties that she liked. But that was selfish...

Walking him to the door, she would have apologised if only she could think of what to apologise for.

Don't treat me like a bloody guest, he had snapped when they reached the hall, raising his fists to his elbows and looking ready to jab out. *Have yer tatties yer ain way.*

He left her there, storming down the stairs with his rage echoing after him. It was a sourceless gust of anger and she knew that if the same thing were to happen in the future then she would be unable to sidestep it and the whole cycle would start again.

By, that wis gid. Whit a braw laddie, Arthur remarked when she returned to the kitchen, and she did not have the energy to contradict him. There was so much that they still had to discuss about her visit to Margaret; a conversation that had been placed to one side for a man who blamed her for his dislike of lumpy tatties.

John faded into the background as one memory led to the next: further back in time to the train shuddering to a stop at the strange station on the south side and her aunt's face as she realised they had arrived.

And she hus nae idea we're comin? Aunt Agnes had asked, adrift. *This is a big mistake, hen.* Maggie did not need to hear that. *Aye, but daddy telt ye whit he saw. And they're family. If thir's ony kind o' problem, we cannae jist leave her.*

Each time the subject was broached, Maggie found herself clinging to family duty, the only argument she had left. Agnes squared her shoulders and nodded.

She helped her aunt up and off the train, taking care with each step, and they alighted onto a central platform where ivy still grew up the wall of the embankment in a blanket of green, just as she remembered from her last visit back in more auspicious times. She offered her arm as they made their way to the street above, the arthritis something else that Margaret was unlikely to notice.

They hobbled past an ice-cream parlour with a queue that reached the pavement and turned onto a broad street, lined with trees and an affluent splattering of vehicles. The brass numbers left no uncertainty. *This is it. Number Eighteen.*

The house was on the ground floor and the garden was immaculate, complete with a small bench where the family could sit out and bushes where flowers would bloom. It was in the same position as the Menzies' flat but the outlook was out of this world. They got to the wally close just as the skies broke properly and they hurried inside. The space was opulent, all orange and gold, and Maggie felt a jealous churning of resentment that she would rather have left alone. *Should we jist go?* she whispered. Agnes did not say anything but her pursed lips spoke plenty.

They had already started to turn when the door burst open and Margaret appeared. She wore a long fawn dress, woollen with black trimming, and small heels. She did not wear a coat or Maggie would have assumed she was going out. Her carefully-coiffed hair was as dark as it had been ten years previously and her perfume reached out to draw them forward, but it was the deep frown accentuating the cleft of her chin that took Maggie's breath away. This was how her mother would have looked had she lived so long, albeit with a housecoat and baffies.

Margaret had not let them through the door. *Thank you for coming but please make an appointment next time.* All thoughts of leaving left Maggie's mind. *But ah wrote ye a letter, twa weeks ago now. Ah telt ye when we were coming, jist tae pop in like.* The woman wrung her hands in the fitful gesture common to her Bennie heritage, but her face remained implacable. The soft tip-tapping of a stick on wood came from the hall. Someone was tucked away just out of sight but Margaret did not move aside. They had come all this way so there was no harm in asking. *How's James?* Margaret put her hands on her hips, making herself wide. *Fine.* Silence. *That's no' very polite. Are ye no' gonnae ask efter oor Donald?* It was Agnes, addressing her sister for the first time. Arm in arm, the trembling was impossible to ignore. Maggie turned and her aunt had no choice but to follow.

We shouldnae hae come wae oot yer say-so. Ah'm sorry. We'll be headin aff. Margaret did not say anything. Agnes waited and waited until she was at the entrance. Still her sister did not ask after Donald.

It was an uncontrolled detonation. She whipped round, faster than she had moved in a long time. *He's deid!* she cried, her voice echoing up the close. *Sssssshhhhh!* Margaret responded, terrified the neighbours would hear. Maggie could not believe it. *Can ye no' hear her? She said he's deid. And a' ye dae is tell her tae be quiet?* It was not how she had been raised to speak to her elders, but Margaret remained erect and hard-hearted. And just behind, Maggie could see the stooped shape of a shadow in the dim light of the hall. Whoever was there, either cowed or disinterested, they were silent.

Come oan. That's no sister o' mine. Agnes led the way, hobbling fast through the door and out into the rain. For once it was Maggie who followed, her heart thumping. *Ah'm sorry, ah'm sorry, ah'm sorry.* Tears streamed down Aunt Agnes's face unchecked, washing away her strength. At each turn, they expected to hear footsteps over the pattering drizzle behind them; it was only once they reached the train station that they accepted Margaret was not going to follow. No reconciliation that day. The gulf which had once been unspoken was now staring them in the face.

Despite all that, weeks later it was John who was the last image on her mind before she fell into a fitful sleep, a mass of restrained anger over lumpless mashed potatoes. When she awoke, darkness had fallen but the unsettled knot in her stomach remained. Her crooked elbow was a dead weight under her head and the rush of blood when it moved was unbearable, and she wished she could roll over and slip back into sweet oblivion. Dreams had been of her mammy, a woman living by her side with sage advice and a heartening embrace, but with the opening of her eyes, the nearness and the comfort was slipping away fast. She woke up with more of her missing than when she had gone to sleep. In the waking world, the house grew cold in its emptiness and there was no one to cry out to so she waited for the pain to subside. Each spasm of her muscles reawakening caused her to jerk awkwardly. She was getting old.

When it was finally over, she walked to the big room to draw the curtains. She looked briefly across the street at Sarah Gibb's bedroom. Everything was dark – small mercy.

Shivering with fatigue, she headed back to the kitchen. The fire took quickly and soon the kettle was brewing on the range. That was one thing she could control.

There was a shift in the air; a thickening around her that mirrored the tightening inside when the leg cramps had hit. The room was saturated with intent and she was viewing it through a kaleidoscope that dealt only in shades of grey. Instantly, she knew that it was her mother behind her. Not a vague memory, or echoed words, or a pale replica in the form of a distant aunt, but the solid form of someone she thought she had lost. She knew it as certainly as she could see every memory that they had shared. All she had to do was turn; to move her feet or glance over her shoulder. They would talk about so many things; real things that mattered, not boys or neighbours. Or maybe they would talk about everything, including boys and neighbours, and analyse Margaret until she was nothing more than a caricature in their heads. They would decide how to put it all right. Together. All she had to do was turn and she would not be alone. All she had to do. The closeness, the proximity, the thudding heart. She hesitated.

In those few seconds, the moment vanished. All she could feel was the fear of disappointment, that she would turn and there would be nothing there. Her mother had left before she found her courage. The air lifted and her hope was swept away.

There would never be another chance to see Clara and that was not something she could blame on John. For the first time in years, she sank to the ground, hugged her knees and wept, but she could cry all she wanted; she would never be able to fill what had been ripped from her the moment she chose not to turn around. The kettle whistled on but no one was there to hear it.

TWENTY-EIGHT

The Sidelines

In the late summer of 1946, time sped up and Annie Munroe was a casualty of its haste – it dragged along her battered body and left her mind behind. Arthur went as soon as he heard his oldest sister was failing. His new cane did not slow him down. Surrounding himself with those who loved her best, he made his way to her side before it was too late.

Wee Ena held Stevie's hand, unable to recognise that it was okay to show her heart was breaking. Arthur had led the way and had already disappeared over the threshold but she was reluctant to follow. Ushering gently from behind, Maggie felt herself in their place, too young to fully understand but too old to escape from reality. She had the experience to know that things would not get any better and she would not patronise them by pretending otherwise. Just as well, for the parcel of bones inside was wrapped in sallow paper and had already begun to fade. From beneath a thick bundle of blankets, it rattled shakily with each hard-earned breath and no one voiced the truth, that it would be far less painful if it were just to stop. There, with her loved ones huddled around the bedside, it was Flo who Annie whispered to in those final moments. As she slowly slipped away, her sister was left with a rueful smile, and Maggie wondered who would smile for her when she left the world.

Jess's bump grew and grew, but the bigger she got, the less she spoke about the changes. It would be easier to bear the loss of something she had pretended she never had in the first place. Instead, she flung herself back in time to the army, visiting Dolly for some

Hyndland home baking and holding onto a photograph of young Rose in Wakefield. It had arrived in the post two weeks before and showed the girl on her wedding day to the attentive miner, Harry. He looked down at his wife, his face obscured, one of the great mysteries of Jess's Yorkshire life. She had heard it so often that Maggie could recite the story of the photograph verbatim although it meant nothing to her; the grainy image of a cake intricately designed as a ladies handbag, which Rose's father had made for her birthday one day and which had made it to the wedding party the next. It sat as if opened, royal-icing flowers spilling out into the table lavishly to show the maker's skill. She would never have been able to afford something so beautiful and intricate had it been shop bought, and the monochrome snapshot radiated light and intimated colour as bright as the bride's smile.

Rose was so proud of her father, Jess would say, sounding mighty proud herself; she had been with the two since the start and she had left some of herself there. Beyond the miner's likeness and the root of the father's culinary skills, the greatest mystery of all was whether Jess was reminiscing herself into amnesia. After all, Maggie thought, it was just a cake.

Jess took these memories to share with Dolly between tennis sets. She waddled to the heart of the West End and watched from the sidelines as her friend's tiny black head jumped tirelessly after flying balls, gorging on the cornflake clusters that had been made just for her as she spectated. The girl's wartime sergeant had moved down to Glasgow for her and joined Jess on the sidelines when he was not busy teaching, chatting in the sun and showing her what a happy life could look like.

Juxtaposed with these two girls, Maggie wondered what she had to offer her cousin, so she sat listening earnestly with her own questions tightly buttoned up inside. While Jess and Paul searched for their own happy memories without a family to tie them down, any wrong word from her would prove fatal. That made it even sweeter when, two months later, Jess gave birth to a healthy baby girl. Ten fingers, ten toes and round like a baker.

Suddenly Jess's grin came from the present, where Paul and wee baby Annie were the only stories worth telling and the crushing rock she had been living under was lifted. As baby Annie grew big and strong on chubby legs as pink and soft as rose-petals, she proved herself more hardy than a flower, for her tumbles were hard and many; something Jess would have done well to remember. She spent half her life with her heart in her mouth, and her whole life counting her blessings.

Not long after, Penny and Willie were married in a small ceremony at Queens Cross Church. It was a day fighting off the drizzle but spirits were high. The bride wore an ivory suit, all delicate sequins dancing like surface water, and the groom the mottled red tartan of the Grants, the blush of sunset on the glen. Afterward, standing outside amongst the bridal party, Maggie unwittingly caught the bride's bouquet and turned the same shade as the tartan. Dutifully accepting congratulations from the well-meaning and the lonely, she pretended not to see John's hopeful smile from the sidelines, his eyes on her as he lifted the small metal hip flask from his sporran and took a swig.

TWENTY-NINE

Reading Leaves

1948

He chose a blustery day at Penny's but and ben in late September, when the whole gang descended on Carbeth for cosy company on the back of an Indian summer. For the first time in two years, he had been invited along. It was what acceptance felt like.

"Ah want this side!" Maggie called excitedly, bagsying her spot in the flimsy double bed by throwing her bags nearest the wall. Penny and Jess dumped their cases nearer to the door, ready to top and tail, and Willie dragged in the children's cot from the kitchen.

"You girls get settled," he said.

"Whit dae ye think we're dain?" Maggie demanded.

"Thir were three in the bed and the little wan said…" he sang on the way out, joining the men to set up camp in the front room and leaving the women and children behind.

There was romance surrounding the bustling mountainside oasis, like something he had seen in a movie once but could not quite remember. He saw Willie approaching, but had been listening to their banter through the wall and did not approve. Still, he waited with willful procrastination for the perfect moment to arise. He watched wordlessly while the others built a fire in the garden and munched silently on the sausages they cooked for him; he lay awake all night on the hard wooden floor with only the ticking carriage clock and light rumbling snores for comfort and, in the morning, when the sun rose as strong and bright as ever, he did not say a word but promised himself that he would not rest again until the job was done.

Chatter floated around him and nobody noticed that his mind was elsewhere. Maggie barely seemed to notice him at all. There she was with Penny, frying some square sausage and beans for breakfast with everyone else crammed in the front room alongside them, splattering the tiles without worry or care. Willie and Paul shouted out their requests but only Paul had an excuse for the racket and, while Penny ran to it, Maggie shouted right back. That would all change once they were married.

Jess came in from the garden to report that the day was heating up nicely; she was certainly sweaty after running around with Wee Annie. Everyone moved quickly after that. Dragging his feet, he followed behind on the way to Sandler's Pond, watching Maggie closely. Willie led the way down the narrow path, through the woods like a great explorer, and Paul scrambled after him. The two men were overly gregarious for his liking, but Maggie was too busy to keep up, talking over her shoulder while Jess picked her toddling wean up over tree roots and stones.

Only Penny fell behind with him, carrying her sleeping baby in her arms while supporting the tiny black head to ensure it did not roll back and damage its spine, but it was preferable to the calamity of a pram on the uneven country paths, so Penny was telling him. John looked wonderingly at the infant and its mother smiled. He smiled back. His own children with Maggie would be just like that one, but even bonnier.

The group stopped to rest where the ground grew soggy and grass gave way to reeds. In the distance, squealing children could be heard splashing around amidst the distressed singing of a curlew. Maggie ran straight toward the water and disappeared into a tsunami of her own making and Paul followed, kicking off his shoes and diving through the mud. Before he went in after them, Willie ran back quickly to ensure Penny and Wee Maggie were safe. Only then did he speed off.

Slipping off their shoes, the two mothers kept their daughters close and paddled at the water's edge, chatting all the while. John watched as they satisfied themselves with shallow ripples and Wee Annie clapped her hands in delight. However, no matter how much they called and called he refused to join them. He sat on the blanket and waited. And waited.

The sky clouded, thick curtains that settled low to obscure the horizon. There was nothing else for him other than what was right in front of his nose. Rays of sunshine threatened to break through but he paid them no mind, losing track of time while he waited for Maggie to return, so lost in his thoughts that it may have been minutes or hours. The mothers moved closer to the reeds and he had the world to himself; knowing he deserved her, knowing the lines on her face were lengthening and her options were few, knowing that he had been dreaming of this moment for nine years.

As he planned what to say, the words tumbled around his head, and the more he tried to contain them, the more he lost their thread. Maggie was lucky he was spending so much energy on this. She was lucky and she did not even know it. Lucky and spoiled. Not the kind of qualities he had ever imagined in a wife, but marriage was a compromise and she could compromise for him just fine. Then she was back. There she was, with her girlfriends as she always would be, out of breath and laughing. Somewhere beyond the reeds, the others could be heard shouting to each other, oblivious that their best member had returned to shore. He sat conspicuously on this thick picnic rug and the world spun on around him, and he wanted to dive into Maggie's mind to discover what she was thinking. He called her over but she just laughed.

"Get o'er here and join me!" she yelled.

It sounded like an order so he looked past her, out towards the emptying pond. Shrugging, Maggie grabbed Wee Annie and birled her round and round while the water lapped at her ankles, and the child shrieked in delight. She was lifted half out of the water but still got a good dunking in her light strawberry dress, all merriment and oblivion. His hackles rose; the idyllic setting was marred and the storm clouds gathered.

It was mid-afternoon, yet the world darkened as if night was falling and a harsh wind whipped over the hills from the North. The boys swam into view with their eyes turned up to the elements. All around, people were leaving the water in droves and heading for safety. Paul waded towards Jess and the towel she held open, and only Willie was still in the pond when the thunderclouds finally broke. Within seconds, he was engulfed, and the heat of summer was washed away for good.

"Git oot o' there immediately!" Penny shouted at him.

Jess had already retrieved Wee Annie and was inching backwards up the path.

"Ah'm wet awready. Whit difference'll a few drops o' rain make?"

He quickly changed his mind when the darkness was broken by an electrifying fork of lightning that struck a nearby peak like a knife carving butter. The crash of thunder that followed was so loud that it even made Paul jump, and Willie leapt out of the water to join the mad dash to safety, scooping his daughter from Penny's thrust-out arms as he ran towards the but and ben. Jess had got there before him and Maggie, soaking wet in her bathing costume, snatched her towel to follow.

"Wait a minute!" John grabbed her waist and held her there.

Shifting impatiently, she pulled against him. Curling white strands were plastered to her forehead and moisture was beginning to run down the shed of her hairline and into her eyes. Penny threw her a curious look but got no response so took off with Paul.

He held her tight but she did not turn to face him until they were the last people by the water's edge.

"Whit are ye daein John? Can we no' go inside?"

"Ah think ye look bonnie Maggie. Ayeways dae."

"Weil, ye must need specs then. Come oan."

She grabbed his hand and tried to drag him up the path, but he stood firm.

"Let me talk tae ye. Ye're no' lettin me get ma words oot. Ah've known ye fir years and ma time wae ye's bin the best years o' ma life."

"Can we no discuss this inside?"

Her heart beat faster and it did not feel good.

"If it wisnae fir ye, ah'd hae gone back tae the fairm an' given up the butcher trade fir gid, but ah've stuck wae it and made ma livin'. A gid livin. Ah hae you tae thank fir that."

"Och, ah'm happy fir ye."

Repeatedly pulling against the arm that restrained her, she glared upwards as another fork of lightning split the sky. The hut was so close that she could make out the murky bright lights through the trees.

"Ye're more than a help tae me. Ye sustain me."

Fast lines of horizontal rain struck at all angles but the barrier did little to mask the solemnity that was etched onto his face when she finally turned. In that moment, with his eyebrows drawn and jaw set in earnestness, he appeared his most handsome, and a flush of embarrassment flitted quickly past. His confidence seemed to wane but he carried on regardless.

"Ah want tae marry ye, Maggie." Silence. "We'd make a wonderful life thegether. Get a wee place and hae naebody tae bother us."

"Naebody? Naw, ah couldnae. Dae ye mean ma daddy? Ow!"

His grip tightened on her wrist. "Weil, he's no' coming wae us. Ah know he disnae really like me. Bugger that. Besides, ye need tae mak yer ain life."

She wriggled but couldn't move. "And how could ah live wae masel if ah leave him? Let go."

"He loves ye and wants ye tae be happy, e'en if he cannae be a pairt o it."

It was desperate. With the storm crashing upon them, she felt the weight striking on her shoulders. It was a merciless force and she wanted to find safety more than anything else. Still, he talked on.

"Take a bit o time. Talk tae yer faither aboot it, if ye must. Ah'm no gonnae rush ye or force ye. Ah want ye tae luve me like ah luve you. Ye'll marry me in the end."

Maggie did not need time to think about it and, finally, she managed to squirm out of his grip.

"Ah cannae marry ye, John. Ah'm sorry."

"It's bin twa years, Maggie!"

"Ah know."

Two years with a split personality: one of love and affection and one of contemplative silence at best and tempestuous moods most of the time, each day bringing its own set of surprises and disappointments. A few weeks earlier, when she had given into sentimentality and mentioned Tommy in a rare attempt to keep his memory alive, she had been reminded of just what a stupid move that was.

'Ye're still in love wae him!'

"Ye're bein stupid. Ah've ne'er been in love wae Tommy. No' really,"

"Then that would make ye a dirty hoor," he had screamed, slapping a hand against the dining table and jumping out of his seat, "Either ye're a liar or a hoor. Whit am ah tae think o' ye now, Maggie?"

On the bed recess, Arthur had his eyes opened wider than they had been in years and spoke up, his voice sharp and uncompromising.

"Naebody talks tae oor Maggie like that. Awa' hame noo, laddie, and dinnae come back til ye've calmed doon and redded yersel oot."

And John wondered at his dislike, as if the old man should have sat there and taken it alongside his daughter.

"Is thir any point in me waitin fir ye?" he asked, tears mingling in the wetness of his face.

"If ah could answer that fir certain then ma answer wid be yes."

She had to shout to be heard over the worsening rain and her voice resonated loudly with frustration and dismay.

"Tell me, please! Whit can ah dae tae mak ye sure?"

"Can ye no' try tae let me in, John? Thir's this place ye go tae in her heid an' ah cannae get in. Show me wha ye really are an then ah'll marry ye."

"Maggie, are ye oot here!" Jess called from afar, sounding distant and muted behind the torrential downpour.

"Ah'll try," John promised.

"Maggie, where ur ye, hen?"

"If tryin isnae gid enough? Whit if ye cannae prove tae me whit kind o' man ye are?"

"Ah dinnae want tae loose ye."

"Maggie!"

"Ah cannae expect ye tae stay."

"Maggie, there ye are."

"Sorry Jess, we were jist … ."

"Weil, that's enough noo. Come oan in oot o' the wet. There's a nice pot brewin."

Under the shelter of a large umbrella, Jess steered her up the path and inside, leaving John to trail behind. There was no need to respond to the chatter about Agnes's growing aches and Paul's frustrations; all she had to do was keep silent and pretend to listen. If she had looked behind her, Maggie would have seen the familiar dark veil slip over her man. Instead, she leaned against her cousin, letting her feet be guided while her mind reeled.

That night, she whispered her secret, hiding her embarrassment under the blanket of the rickety double bed. Neither Jess nor Penny was particularly surprised but they kept their opinions to themselves and they all waited to watch what would transpire. It was a long wait.

THIRTY

Slipping Away

The long summer finally left them and winter came in fast. From her position in the kitchen, she could hear the grandfather clock chime the hour in the hall, a window rattled in the wind and the distant voices on the wireless crackled through in the big room. She stood silently in darkness, trying to remember Jess's face. Already, it was slipping away. It had stood so often by the range while tea was brewing that its features should have been etched into the plaster but it was floating out of reach on wisps of intangible steam. Like a drunk looking for the next level of inebriation, she told herself that the memories would come back stronger next time.

She took Donald's stool into the scullery and sank down beside the pile of clothes that had gathered beside the sink. How many times she had complained about this housekeeping to her cousin's sympathetic ear. Slowly, carefully, she put the clothes through the mangle, expecting each item to break. Her mind should have been full of memories, but instead it was blank, like a slate that had never been written on in its entire thirty-five years. It was a stalled engine that she could not kick into gear. All she could focus on was the next item, the next movement of her hands.

She awoke with her head on her arms. For the first few, precious moments her memories truly were wiped clean but then the pain crashed in anew. For so long, her happiness had hung on where Jess was going to be, on what she was going to do; then, just as everything seemed settled and she would stay in Glasgow, she was gone.

Maggie knew that the best she could hope for was to wait it out so she continued like that, head down, praying for sleep to come and free her again. Finally, her prayers were answered.

"Come oan, hen. It's time tae get up."

Arthur shook her gently, waking her for a second time.

"It's the middle o' the night, daddy," she said.

"Naw, it's the back o' ten. They jist said so oan the radio."

Her eyes flew open. "Och, ah'm late!"

"Where fir?"

"Ma work!"

"But it's Saturday, Maggie."

"Is it?"

She sank back down.

"Miby ye should go talk tae John."

She looked up at him in surprise. His eyes were fixed straight ahead in the gloom, at a row of utensils hanging on the wall.

"He came o'er yesterday. Ah forgot tae tell ye. Says he'll be at Jaconelli's this mornin' fir elevensies if ye can mak it."

"Dae ye think ah should?"

"It micht be gid fir ye tae talk."

"Tae John?"

Arthur laughed and, thoughtlessly, she laughed, too.

"Weil, at least he's gid fir something," he said.

His wee girl stood up and kissed him on the forehead. He felt his way to the hall press, collected her coat, and her fate was sealed. She slipped inside, feeling it tight against her day-old clothes. Her jumper was thick but she grabbed a navy scarf, one that Jess had knitted for her, tucking it deep inside to fill the gap.

"Take care o' yersel," he told her.

Nodding, she headed out into the snow. It whipped around her as she crunched up the street towards the cafe, the thick sky crushing down with a darkness more akin to nighttime than a quiet winter's day. When she got close, the light from the low table bulbs was a sanctuary up ahead and she pushed her way quickly inside.

There was John, just as he said he would be, sitting in the booth at the back. He beckoned to her as she stomped her feet on the welcome mat and rose when she did not go straight to him. The place was surprisingly quiet with only one other table occupied. There, a young couple rocked their sleeping baby, whispering so quietly that

Mario's voice carried over from the kitchen as if he were in the room with them.

"Can ah hae a knickerbocker glory, Mrs Jaconelli?"

"Oan a day like this?" Amelia laughed, filling the sweetie jars instead.

"Ah'll bring it o'er, hen," Teresa promised, lifting herself from her stool.

John took her coat and hooked it to the end of the table.

"Ye're here," she said.

"Aye, ah am. Where were ye yesterday?"

Sitting back down heavily, he motioned for her to do the same. She held her ground.

"Whit dae ye mean?"

"Ah went tae yer hoose and there wis naebody there."

"Aye there wis. Daddy says he talked tae ye."

"You werenae there."

"Ah wis oot."

"Weil, ah dinnae like it when yer oot. Whit am ah tae think? Where huv ye gone tae? Afore, ah'd think ye were jist oot wae Jess, but … ." He trailed off.

Giving up, she sank into her seat, worn out and ready to go home.

"Ah dinnae mind if ye talk aboot her."

"It's no' her ah'm bothered aboot. She's deid."

Maggie sat very still. "There's naebody else," she whispered.

"Weil, ah'm no surprised, really. Colin came in the shoap the other day and said tae me, 'Ah think ah've jist seen Maggie. Ah thought she wis an auld wifie and then she turned roon'. That's whit he wis thinkin. Naebody can see whit a braw lassie ye are past aw yer white hair, Maggie. They see ye as ye'll be in thirty years, no' how ye are the now."

"Is that you tryin tae mak me feel better?"

"Better aboot whit?"

Just then, Teresa came round the counter, hobbling slowly to keep control of the huge ice cream.

"Here ye go, hen." She put it between them. "It's free. Have it fir Jess. It wis a mighty brave thing she did fir the wean. It's jist a shame it didnae work oot."

"We still hae Annie," Maggie answered.

"Aye, but ye'd hae hud her onyway." Teresa leaned against the table and looked at her earnestly. "It wisnae e'en a proper fever, like she thought. It broke twa hoors efter Jess died, so ah heard. If she hudnae panicked at the first wee sign and ran oot like that ..."

"Aye, or if Doctor Bowman had been in when she got there ... Ah know. But Jess wis ayeways a careful mammy and she'd hae done onything tae protect oor Annie. She'd hae run tae hell and back tae keep her safe."

"E'en run herself intae a grave," John added.

"She died thinking her daughter widnae survive. Thinkin she couldnae find a doctor tae help. And at the very last door, when she banged and Doctor Crawford answered, then her hert gave oot and she jist fell doon deid. Is that true, Maggie?"

Maggie nodded and focused on the table top.

"That's jist the cruellest."

With a shake of her head, the old woman patted Maggie's shoulder and headed back behind the counter. For her, the tragedy would end at close of business. For John, it had ended already.

"So onyway, jist let me know if onywan says onything tae ye."

"Aboot whit?"

"Aboot yer looks. Let me know if ye want me tae sort them oot fir ye."

She patted her hair around her ears. Nothing had changed overnight. A few extra lines rung her eyes but her spirit remained the same, or so she thought.

"Ah've no heard onywan talkin aboot me."

"Weil, ye wouldn't, would ye?"

"Ah cannae believe we're huvin this conversation. No' the day."

"Ah'm jist trying tae look oot fir ye. Dinnae get so defensive." He lent forwards and helped himself to the knickerbocker glory.

"Lookin oot fir me?" Her voice rose but she did not know how to continue.

"Calm doon, calm doon. Ah cannae talk tae ye when ye're like this."

"Like whit?"

"The way ye'r being, makin it awfy hard tae talk tae ye, taking awthin as an insult, treating awthing like it's my fault when ah'm only tryin tae help. Dinnae be so aggressive, Maggie."

Teresa glanced over from the counter and the other couple was silent. All they could hear was John. All they would know is what he was telling them. She saw herself through their eyes and wanted to object, but anything she said would just fuel the fire. She felt sick.

"If ah'm a problem right now, ah'll ne'er be ony better than this."

Her soft voice fooled no one. Pulling the ice cream towards her, she started eating. If it had not been given for free, she would have stood up and left right there. John watched her.

"Ah think it's best if ye tell me wha yer speaking tae. Jist so ah can mak sure they're decent."

It was not in Maggie's nature to watch her words. Without letting them out, they sat in her throat until she nearly choked. Each time they were swallowed, they jarred against his heavy sighs. When he started folding the napkin over and over again against the edge of the table, it was all she could do not to rip it from his hands and throw it at him. The ice cream slid down so quickly that she gave herself a paralysing headache, starting just below her left ear and running the full length of her side. Those freezing spasms were usually a chuckle to be shared in the comfort of an ice cream parlour but, that day, the lack of control was nothing to laugh about. Until the ice cream was done, she just had to sit there and bear it.

"Wir lucky we hae each other. Wir a team."

She wanted to dab her mouth with her napkin but he had taken it from her. Using her thumb instead, she kept going, one bite after another, racing to the end.

"And yer daddy wis awfy nice the other day, tellin me aboot ye. Miby ah cid come o'er tae dinner again sometime. It's been awhile."

There were only a few spoonfuls left. She scooped them high and slid them down in a oner.

"Thank you, Mrs Jaconelli," she called whenever it was gone, slipping out and grabbing her coat.

"Next Thursday?" John called after her.

"Aye, aye," she answered. The next Thursday she would make him some mince with lumpy tatties.

Feeling the burn of the young couple's eyes on her back, she wondered if it was her aggressive behaviour or white, white hair that drew their stares. She was almost outside by the time she pulled on her jacket and tucked in her scarf, well aware of how stooped she was as she braced against the cold. There was nothing left to do but pull open the door and hobble through the snow. Not that it mattered; no one would be looking at her anyway.

She had to speak to Jess. Finally she was ready to share everything and get a good second opinion on the illustrious John Anderson. She had walked two blocks in the direction of Lyndhurst

Gardens before she realised her cousin was not there. Too late, she remembered the difference between true pain and hurtful words.

THIRTY-ONE

High Tide

1950

Rachel had been on her way out to accidentally bump into Maggie in the Botanics when the letter arrived. She did not recognise the curled, intricate handwriting and the postage stamp was unfamiliar, despite bearing the King's head. Her curiosity was aroused as she took a seat and carefully prised a thin square of paper from the envelope. She unfolded it and held it up to the light, struggling slowly with the faded writing. Once she had read it, she read it again, and once more, and was found minutes later by her mother staring blankly into space.

Nothing extraordinary had ever happened to Rachel Campbell until that moment.

"Why'd ye bring the wean?"

"Oor Annie's no' the only wean aboot," Maggie retorted, nodding at Wee Maggie who sat demurely on Penny's lap.

"Aye, but that's *her* wean," Rachel huffed, sounding more like a child than anyone else in the room.

"And it's a Wednesday efternoon. Haud yer wheesht. It's tradition."

Maggie turned to Annie, who was looking between the two with her hands clasped over her pinafore and the pensive expression of a child who had done something wrong.

"Dinnae listen tae her, hen. She likes a gid moan because she doesnae know whit else t'dae. It's an affliction. Now, dae ye want tae go and order twa ice creams?"

"Aye!"

The change was instantaneous. Wee Annie sprang up, ran to the counter and jumped up and down in her excitement to be seen. Maggie loved to see her happy but Rachel had summoned her to Jaconelli's that morning, calling it a celebration although she could not remember the occasion and, despite herself, she was intrigued to know why.

She slid into the booth beside Penny, forgetting the proper greetings. Wee Maggie grabbed a long spoon and smeared herself a thick moustache of ice cream before turning to the entertainment of the studded upholstery. Battling against her placid nature, Penny spoke harshly, but that was not enough – Wee Maggie just clapped and giggled in delight as her namesake tried to stop her, unwittingly sending some synthetics flying like a projectile onto the shiny wooden floor.

Aghast, Maggie sprung down and tried to lodge them safely back into the seating again, shouting apologies to a distracted Teresa Jaconelli while Wee Maggie just laughed and laughed. Then Rachel picked up her spoon and hit the side or her ice-cream cup with such authority that even Wee Annie looked back from the counter in expectation.

"Lassies, thanks fir a' comin' the day. It's important tae me that we a' meet cause ah've got some excitin' news."

"Ye're knocked up."

"Ye've finally decided tae go blonde."

"Carey Grant's comin tae toon."

"Ah'm flittin tae Canada!"

No one stirred, no one blinked, no one opened their mouths. Wee Maggie squirmed but her mother held her fast, not in the mood for games. Annie arrived with the ice cream, climbing back into the booth. No one glanced her way and she swung her feet loudly against the wooden panels. Maggie could not take it.

"It seems a bit o' a strange decision, hen. Canada's a big cauld place tae sail aff tae oan a whim."

"It's no' a whim. Ah'm aff tae get mairried."

This time, Maggie was silenced completely. Wee Annie looked between her and Penny, scowling as she tried to understand the sudden change in the room.

"Och, y'eejits. Mind Joshua, ma soldier fae Winnapeg?"

"Whit wan?" Penny snorted.

"Ma Canadian soldier! Joshua! You met him, mind? At the Locarno?"

"'Course we dae," Maggie assured her. "He wis the wee ginger laddie wae the funny teeth."

The memories suddenly came flooding back and Penny lost all control, laughing long and hard until tears rolled and Wee Maggie started crying for real. Annie started laughing, too, eager to fit in and oblivious to Rachel's glower of murderous rage. Her round face beamed and her cheeks flushed a pretty pink, and she had absolutely no idea why she was laughing. Something in all of the mirth struck Maggie as the wrong kind of justice.

"He wis awfy nice," Penny managed after a moment. "A right friendly laddie wae gid conversation. He was tellin awebody aboot the bears they have, and how he can fight them aff and keep ye safe."

"That's him awright. He sent fir me. He wants tae mairry me!"

"But that wis, whit, six, seven years ago? An' he wis only here a few weeks. Does it no' seem a bit strange?"

"He explained it aw in his letter." She produced a creased wad of writing paper and brandished it around like a weapon against all those who stood against it. "Joshua Jarvis is an honourable man. He said he luved me, he promised he'd come back fir me and that's jist whit he's done."

"Then why did he no' dae it sooner?"

"His mother, ye see?"

Looking across at them, it was clear that nobody else *did* see.

"He planned oan sendin' fir me the minute the war wis o'er, but when he got hame tae the fairm that bloody mammy o' his widnae hae it. She insistet that he work hard and find a Jewish gurl. So he waited and waited, and then a few months ago that auld bitch died! The first thing he did wis get in touch wae me an' ask me if ah still luved him; if ah'd waited oan him."

"Does he know yer answers tae those twa questions are awfy different?"

"Haud yer wheesht, Maggie Munroe. Ah sent him a telegram straight back and telt him that aye, ah still luve him. It's settled. Ah leave next month!"

"But ye hate the country. Ye widnae e'en come wae us fir a weekend at Penny's but and ben. Dae ye really think ye'll fair ony better as a fairmer's wife, way o'er yonder?"

"Ah know whit ye're thinkin. But it's ma wan chance tae be happy. He remembered me a' this time and he really luves me. Can ye imagine that? Someone luving *me* that much?"

"But what aboot Mrs Campbell?" tried Penny. "Are ye no' worried aboot how she'll cope oan her ain."

"Bring yer mammy, he says. She's coming wae me!"

"Really? Huv ye telt *her* she's flittin tae Winniebooboo?"

"Dinnae be funny, Maggie. Ah'll admit, she took a bit o' convincin. Miby ah'll call ma first laddie Isaac."

Maggie sat forward to read the crumpled letter for herself, slowly deciphering the faded words. The marriage was to take place immediately.

"And wae ma mammy as chaperon, his intentions are honourable. Ah can see yer suspicious mind fae here, Maggie Munroe."

She sighed. "If ye're sure this is whit ye want then ah'm happy fir ye."

She folded the paper carefully back up and handed it across to Rachel, hoping that the vicious bitch would not get more than she deserved.

Born and raised in the biggest city in Scotland, Maggie expected the steady stream of migrants that shuffled into her daily life but had never expected anyone to waltz out. When she arrived on the dock, it was packed with families, many of whom would not be taking to the ships but would be waiting right there in Glasgow for news of their loved ones to trickle through. Hankie in hand, she joined them.

Fragmented moments entwined to leave an impression of the last few harried weeks: the small flat growing empty as slowly the boxes filled, the arguments and shouting over what to take, the tenuous speculation about what the colonies would bring; and eventually the tears, from Rachel.

Pacing around the Dunard Street park at the start of the week, Penny had given up watching the girls play and confided, "Ah can feel a weight at the base o ma tummy. It's been growin e'er since she telt us and noo it's the size o' a rock. I'm scared it's gonnae fade alang wae Rachel."

Surprised at the sentiment, Maggie tried to muster some of her own but the only feelings she could channel were those she had long repressed, torn between wishing Rachel an enthusiastic farewell on a one-way ticket or reaching catharsis through verbal annihilation, but she had remained indecisive for too long. With the day of departure upon them, time had slipped by without resolution, and all she could do was dab her dry eyes and focus on the small group congregated around Rachel's small brown travel case.

"Ah'll be seeing ye, Arthur love," Mrs Campbell said coyly; then stepped forwards and planted a ferocious kiss on the old man's lips.

His walking stick fell to the ground hard, attracting unwanted attention from strangers who really should have been preoccupied elsewhere. Attached to her lips, muffled giggles reached his aged ears but all he could see was the end of her wide nose.

Finally, she drew back, leaving him flushed and floundering.

"Ah've been waiting tae dae that fir years noo and tha' wis ma last chance!"

Before anyone had a chance to say goodbye, she shuffled lightly up the gangplank and out of sight. Rachel grew teary and picked up her suitcase.

"That's me aff then."

Penny sobbed and hugged her, and Maggie watched life thrash around her like fish in a bowl. Rachel's one chance had come; the chance she had always dreamed of; the chance to be a part of something. Her heart soared higher than the gulls as she gave Maggie one last squeeze and headed to join her mother on the splendid vessel which would bear them safely west.

Alighting the tram at Queen's Cross, they split like the opposite points of a star, Penny heading north, and Maggie and Arthur south at an easy stroll.

"Ah cin jist imagine wee Rachel up tae her knees in cattle shite."

"Be kind, daddy."

"Uch, she'll be grand. A big braw lassie like her wis built fir that life. Gid fir her but a loss fir Glesga." He grew thoughtful. "She says

Joshua's pals are aw jealous o' his Scottish lassie. Ye'd better no' get ony ideas aboot joinin her."

Maggie laughed. "And leave aw this? From whit ah saw back oan yon dock, miby it'll be you wha's headin o'er tae dae some weddin' o' yer ain."

A mischievous breeze whipped around them as they turned onto their street. Arthur wobbled on unsteady feet and Maggie's summer bonnet lifted clean off her head. It spun to the ground, twirling down the pavement like a football kicked by an omnipresent child. She ran to catch up but it taunted her, rolling along, always just out of reach; her fingertips grasping at nothing but air.

Arthur was left behind. That damned wind lifted and bellowed up her short dress as she bent and shuffled her way down the street, and the sound of deep laughter carried over the crest of the draught as she struggled against frustration.

Then, as suddenly as it had started, the wind stopped. So did her bonnet. It sat innocently on the pavement waiting for her, wondering what was taking her so long. Falling on it with both hands, she felt mistrustful of the sudden calm. Only slowly did she become aware that it had stopped right outside the entrance to her close, and that she was in the shadow of a tall man who was staring down at her with raw amusement.

"Jesus bloody Christ!" she gasped.

"Hello, Maggie."

She reached out tentatively to squeeze his calf. Her fingers met his trouser leg; felt the texture of nylon against skin. He was real. And, as she looked up into the dark, glittering eyes of Tommy Gunn, she was swept away for a moment by the storm of her undoing.

THIRTY-TWO

The Bad Yins

"Ye're a ghost."

"Obviously I'm not. I am standing right here, amn't I?"

He bent towards her, hand extended but obscured as a dark shadow under the harsh midday sun.

She heard the clunk of his stick on the cobbles close behind and sprang to her feet unaided.

"There ye are, daddy. Ah got ma hat back. Here, can ye take it up the stairs fir me? Ah'll be up in a wee minute."

"Tak yer time, hen."

Arthur strolled past and nodded a greeting to the tall shape silhouetted before him. There was something familiar about the easy and confident stance – something he could not put his finger on. Maggie was glad, for had he recognised the visitor, he might have collapsed right there on the pavement. At thirty-six, she was having enough trouble of her own. On he sauntered, swinging his stick and whistling a merry tune, and she took the moment to still her shaking hands but less could be done about her racing heart. The strain was palpable.

She was painfully aware of Tommy's eyes on her, of how old she must look. For his part, he looked exactly the same. How funny that a face she had been scrambling to remember for years could spring back into focus with ease. Only the clothes had changed.

"Whit ... how? Ah dinnae understaund," she burst out the moment her father's back disappeared into the murky safety of the close. "Ye're deid. John telt me."

"I don't know why he told you a stupid thing like that. Feel how real I am."

Tommy shortened the gap between them, rolling up his shirt sleeves so she had to fight the impulse to grab hold of his forearms. He pinched her playfully and she yelped with delight. It was a joy that he was alive. When he took her hand, she did not pull away, only looked deep into his knowing eyes in the hopes that some of that knowledge would pass her way.

"How long huv ye been waiting?"

"Only a few minutes. I met that neighbour of yours, Mrs McNulty."

"Ye spoke tae Mrs McNulty?"

"Oh yes. She was as surprised as you to see me here and filled me in on my death. I must say, I'm surprised at John. He was very much aware of my existence when we parted ways in Paris. February nineteen-forty-six. I remember it well because there was a storm that day. Quite unusual. And he was able to recollect all that perfectly well when he met me off the boat last month."

"He saw ye last month? Ye've been here fir a whole month?" She could not decide which point was most important.

"Oh Maggie, he told me you did not want to see me, otherwise I would have come straight over."

"Then why are ye here noo?" She could not keep the suspicion from her voice.

"I can feel you in every crevice of this city, Maggie. It was impossible to forget you were here, right on my doorstep and I had to come and hear your answer directly. Tell me to my face. Are you still my girl?"

"Urgh! Ah wis told ye wir deid."

"I *was* dead, in a sense, without you."

Whistling cut their conversation short, a warning floating up the street from the direction of Woodlands. They froze. Then John walked into view, sauntering leisurely in their direction. He halted about ten feet away, struck dumb by the sight of his friend and his lover reunited. He noticed their incredulous expressions and the hand that Tommy still held tight in his own. His eyes narrowed and his round face reddened, a watery rash of sweat broke out across his forehead and his clenched fists threatened to hit out, if there had been anything near enough to hand. Time was suspended. Then, with a gargled yell, he turned to leave.

"Where dae ye think ye're gaun?" Maggie broke free from Tommy and ran after him, digging her nails into his arm. "Get yersel' back here an' act like a man. Ye've goat a fair bit o' explainin t'dae."

Mrs McNulty's thin lace curtains fluttered. God knew how many unseen spectators lay witness behind the dark windows that encompassed her from all sides and high above, but Maggie was glad. She wanted them to see. It would serve as a lesson for anyone else who planned to treat her like a fool.

"Weil, ye both look awfy cosy," he spat. "Look at ye!"

"Why did ye tell me he wis deid?" she demanded.

She was half his size yet a force to be reckoned with and she strained towards him. Stepping forwards, Tommy put a hand on her hip to restrain her. She still could not believe he was really there.

"Ah didnae. Ah telt ye he wisnae coming back fae France. Ye drew yer ain conclusions fae that."

"Ye let me! And we discussed these conclusions at length! Ye knew whit ah thought – whit ah wis telling awebody! Are ye daft?"

"It wis fir the best. Why waste yer time oan somewan wha bided in France tae shack up wae some fuckin hoor."

"That is not exactly what happened …"

"So whit? Ye thought it wis better ah grieve as if he wis deid?"

"Aye, so ye didnae waste yer time thinking he'd come back fir ye."

"Whit made ye think ah'd *want* him tae come back fir me? Naw, ye jist wanted me fir yerself. Whit's sadder, ye didnae hae the courage tae see if ye were enough. Ye used yer bloody trickery instead. Bloody coward! Bloody coward piece o'…."

"I agree. That was appalling behaviour John. I would never have expected …"

"And *you*!" She turned on Tommy now, who did not have the decency to cower under her glare. "Ah dinnae e'en want tae hear fae ye. Awa' biding wae some lassie fir years and then swannin back here, expectin tae pick up where ye left aff. Ye mak me sick! Both o' ye!"

She froze, unable to decide who was most culpable. In the end, her only option was to flee, but regardless of how fast she marched, the two men kept up. They stayed on her heels, yammering over each other to make themselves heard as she stomped up Wilton Drive. Her skirt beat an angry rhythm and her lips pressed together in indignation, but there was liberation, too. At last, things were becoming clear.

At the top of the street she took a sharp left, past the school to the park which lay unusually deserted. At least that was something to be thankful for. She was in every way alone, walking up and up past the ghosts of swings and relics of good times. The sky seemed to recede against inner-city grey; birdsong faded behind the incessant drum of their excuses. The wall she built against their lies was strong, but it was too robust to let out the confusion and anger that ripped around her brain. Eventually she slowed. The boundary wall was approaching and if she wanted to go further she would step onto the road.

John whined in exhaustion, ready to collapse, and Tommy took the opportunity to state his case.

"I never stopped thinking about you." His pale eyes were small darts as they searched hers for compassion, "A girl, she tricked me so I would stay when all I wanted was to come home to you."

"Fine story."

"She told me she was pregnant so I would return to her and when I did, for the baby's sake, her father coerced me into marriage before I knew what was happening. He was huge, moustached, a tyrant of a man really, and I couldn't refuse."

A pause to see if she was still with him.

"My son was two years old when we lost him to scarlet fever. It was the worst day of my life."

He inched forwards.

"And there I was, left alone in a loveless marriage. All I could think of was you. It grew unbearable, the memory of my sweet, unwavering Maggie always first and last thing on my mind."

She cried out incredulously. He used the interruption to light a cigarette.

"So, I cracked. I left and came back here to get you, only to be told by John that you didn't want to see me."

John flailed his arms in protest but was still in no state to argue. Maggie rolled her eyes.

"The rest I've told you already; my feelings for you, so strong that I didn't listen to John and had to come over. From the lies he's been telling you, I am very glad that I did."

"Whit's her name?"

"Who?"

"Yer wife."

"Marie-Ann, but I'm getting a divorce."

"Ah widnae get a divorce if ah wir you. She's the only wan stupit enough tae put up wae yer shite."

"He met her in a Parisian slum, and she wisnae the only wan," John rasped. "No by a lang shoat. Ye wernae furst in his mind then, doll. Dinnae let him fool ye."

"And how am ah supposed tae believe onything *you* tell me efter aw the years o' lying, ye utter wee gobshite?"

She jabbed a finger towards him in accusation but his voice remained soft, almost pitying.

"Ah know. Ah'm sorry ah wisnae honest wae ye fae the stairt. But ye know deep doon why ah did it. Ah jist wanted tae protect ye. Ah love ye so much."

"Is that not something, Maggie? An admirable liar."

"That's enough."

She stood back to study the impressive mess in front of her. John's hair flopped wildly as he struggled for breath and he looked at her with pain and longing entirely of his own creation. He had built his own prison of deception, which barricaded him from the one person he wanted most in the world. Tortuous years of half-truths, self-doubt and betrayal had left him empty. And from now on, alone.

Tommy remained a picture of confidence and composure. An outward construction of experience, wrinkles of refinement etched on a sun-leathered face, inwardly he was the same boy who had swaggered up to her reception desk over ten years before. He had the charm then of a young man rising to the challenge of life. Now nearly forty years old, the charm had turned sour; he had failed to grow with the experiences he had been given and failed to appreciate the lessons that were laid at his feet. What a waste. At last, the shock of their meeting was subsiding and she could see him clearly; the man he had failed to become.

"Mind years ago, when ye left fir war oan that train? Ye ne'er did gie me the chance tae answer ye. Ma answer noo is the same's it wis then – no' a chance in hell. Ah ne'er hae, an ne'er will be, ony girl o' yours, Tommy Gunn. That's final."

He looked incredulous and started to speak so she grabbed his cigarette, took a drag, and threw it at his face. There was small consolation when he jumped back and she did not meet John's lying eyes, ignoring him completely as she strode into the rising wind towards home. It was unfathomable, almost ten precious years wasted in a heartbeat.

"Ah love ye!" he yelled after her, as if she did not know that. As if it would somehow help. As if that were not entirely the problem.

PART THREE

The End

THIRTY-THREE

Living

1952

It was a multi-tasking mess. One chubby hand brought food to her mouth while the other broke it into the crumbs that fell all over the patchwork rug. It was her birthday and Wee Maggie would compromise for no one. She was three years old and understood perfectly that all the fuss was for her. Grown-up Maggie stood beside Penny with her own piece of dumpling to watch the total destruction in tiny toddler hands. A cousin from the Sinclair side sat stiff on the settee beside the birthday girl, vigilant as ever in a stiff-pressed burgundy suit. She had been charged with looking after Wee Maggie for the day and took her duties seriously, but had no idea what to do to stop her.

When Penny had asked to use her flat to celebrate, Maggie had been delighted but it had ended up being terrible timing. The letter rested uncomfortably at her side, pushed mercilessly into her pocket out of sight. Perhaps she should have hid it in her room, but resting it down in a drawer would set it free, and she was not ready for that. The curling scrawl was a page of incrimination, beckoning her to a life she had not asked for, with a woman she did not like. Besides, Aunt Flo was using her bed to rest while the house was full of guests and would not be disturbed.

Both the kitchen and the big room were full to bursting, but there was no hosting to be done; everything had been prepared beforehand

and laid out on the table. Aunt Agnes pottered about filling tea cups unnecessarily, determined to make herself useful, and Jimmy kept close watch by her side. Only her left hand functioned so she used her right wrist to keep the pot upright as she did her rounds, and no amount of coercion could make her stop. She flitted from blether to blether, filling her ears and her mouth just like Davie would have abhorred.

"She hus yer luve o' cake," Penny noted, raising an eyebrow archly and drawing Maggie back to her namesake.

"And yer fair hair."

"Willie's jist as much tae blame as me."

"Weil, at least she didnae get it fae the milkman, then. Look at it staundin oan her heid like an airmy o' sojers. She's gonnae be a right wee cracker when she's aulder."

"Jist like her Aunt Maggie."

"Och, awa!"

Wee Ena approached them from the hall, her emerald green gloves wrinkled in the middle and dragging a reluctant Annie behind. The younger girl was subdued at last, red-rimmed eyes telling a sorry tale. She had deserved a good leathering, and the cries and yells which had echoed into the flat could still be read on her long face.

"Are ye o'er yer daily tantrum?" Wee Ena demanded. Her niece blew hot air and rubbed her eyes. "Whit de ye say tae yer Aunt Penny?"

"Sorry fir causin a scene," Annie sniffed, more sorry for the red mark on her bottom than anything else.

"It's Wee Maggie wha needs the apology. It's her pairty ye've spoilt."

Looking closer to tears than ever, Annie slunk away to join the other children and help herself to some dumpling.

"She's a wee torag."

"It's jist a phase," Aunt Agnes told her daughter, coming up to pour them more tea. Penny sighed.

"Ah hae ma fingers crossed oor Maggie misses it."

"If no, it's you wha'll be left tae deal wae it."

Aunt Agnes nodded to where Willie nursed his dram at a precarious tilt. He and Paul were over by Arthur's armchair, surrounded by friends and in the midst of an epic tale. Paul swayed in concentration, lip-reading through heavily bloodshot eyes, and

Arthur nodded along, happy to be amongst family. While the point was not lost on Maggie, she was warmed by his contentedness.

"We should leave them alone wae the weans and see the smiles get wiped aff thur faces."

"Ye dinnae know how lucky ye are tae hae a gid man like that."

"There'll be a gid wan oot there fir you in aw, hen." Penny hugged her as if she and Wee Maggie had swapped bodies.

"Miby, miby no'. Men can mak ye happy or mak ye miserable and when ye hae a habit o' attractin the latter, weil, ye're better aff on yer ain. And ah'm happy. Ah widnae hae ma life ony different, staundin here, right now, wae you twa beside me."

She looked at Wee Annie and Wee Maggie and smiled.

"Ah ayeways thought ah'd hae weans o' ma ain, but the biggest waste o' ma life'd be shackin up wae a philanderer or a liar.

"Ah'm no' including you in that," she told her Uncle Jimmy, who had just then been approaching but slunk back from the group, trying to disappear.

"Jist as weil." He laughed in relief and turned to Penny. "Here, ah brought this wee thing fir the birthday girl."

He whipped a wooden figurine from behind his back; a beautiful horse with a long, curved horn on its head. Bending down, he held it out to Wee Maggie who clapped her hands in delight, dumpling forgotten.

"Mammy, mammy, mammy!" she cried excitedly.

"It's a unicorn," he told her. "It's the national animal o' Scotland, so miby yer mammy can get ye a real wan someday."

The birthday girl grabbed it in both hands and dropped it on the floor. Penny wiped crumbs from her pinafore and bent to pick it up.

"Thank ye so much, Jimmy."

"Och, it's nothing. If Donald wis here, he'd dae it much better."

"Hello!"

It was Sarah Gibb, announcing herself and her self-importance to the room. Even the sound of her voice made Maggie shudder.

"Och, Uncle Stevie, ye made it," she said, moving back to welcome him into the fold and leaving a bit more room to accommodate Clara and Jess. She could feel them close by and needed all the support she could get with that woman invading her home.

He made straight for them, his jolly face flushed and healthy, and pride in his new wife, Sarah, emanated unashamedly. Since Maggie had chosen not to speak up about all she had witnessed, she could not begrudge him that.

"Stevie hud tae work the day," he apologised. "Either that or meetin a lassie. But he sends his love tae the wee yin."

"Dae ye still love me, Paul," Sarah called over to the fire.

Seeing her watching him, he saluted casually and turned back to his friends. It was almost funny but Maggie's skin crawled. Oblivious that she could be seen, Wee Ena rolled her eyes and Maggie counted her blessings that she had finally found an ally. Still, she said nothing.

"Maggie wae troosers oan? Wha'd hae thought it. A modern wuman, eh? And a new hairdo, in a'?"

Sarah moved into the centre to plant a kiss on her cheek and stayed there, playing with the short white curls that fell to her chin. She took another step back and changed the subject, trying hard to pretend the toxic judgement, and the person who wore it, didn't exist.

"Dae ye mind ma girlfriend, Minnie?" she asked Big Stevie.

"Aye, aye. The wan in Skye."

"Weil, no' fir lang. She's passin through Glesga next month oan the way tae Canada."

"Tae Winnabooboo?" Penny asked, lifting Wee Maggie off the chair so she could run around with her friends.

"It's Winnipeg. It means muddy watter in Cree," Maggie corrected, then caught herself. There was no reason for her to know so much and Penny's interest was piqued.

"Aye," she tried again, "and Davie's sister's gaun wae her."

"It's an awfy lang way tae go when ye cannae come hame," Aunt Agnes grumbled.

"They're jist game fir a change."

"When did she tell ye this?" Penny asked suspiciously.

"She didnae. Ah hud it fae Rachel. Is it hot in here?"

"Naw, but yer going a bit red."

"No' ah'm no. But ah cannae open a windae wae a' these weans aboot."

The first chance she got, moving quietly so as not to wake Aunt Flo, she changed into a skirt that hung just above her knees. No one said a word. She transferred the letter from one pocket to the other but it did not sit any better there. Hours later, once the children had worn themselves out and lay curled in a pile of debris, the old clock struck three, signalling to everyone that it was twenty-four minutes past the hour and the adults were left to clean up the carnage. Wee

Ena organised them all, shouting at her mother not to do too much and at Uncle Stevie and Paul to help her daddy with the dishes. Rocking his sleeping daughter in his arms, Willie trotted after them to keep them company and, when the last cup was hung in its rightful place, the last crumb swept from the floor and the final sundries thrown back into the bureau, Maggie excused herself from her own house.

It was late afternoon and long shadows were cast across her favourite time of day. Her skirt was light and her blue cardigan unseasonably warm, so she wrapped it round her shoulders and set off into the mellow warmth of May. The smell of hops bellowed up from the distant Clyde in pungent waves and children filled the streets, playing tig and ball with the energy of those drunk on the season. She wound her way through, smiling a greeting at the familiar faces who knew her from the surgery or from playing in those same streets with her decades earlier. It was with heavy sentiment that she passed them by. She could have stopped to join their frank conversation as they communed on the pavement next to the rose bushes, but for once she needed to be on her own.

The long shadows were her companions. They reached hungrily for the waning light overhead as the sun dipped across an angry orange sky. Hypnotised, Maggie longed to follow its flight over the horizon to an unknown end. Without thinking, she kept walking in the direction of the sun and barely noticed when she left Maryhill. The roads broadened and there were no more careening children, for now they played in large communal gardens where mothers could watch their games from the dignity of high wooden benches while talking in discreet whispers behind gloved hands. Maggie surveyed them critically, knowing their parental love did not come close to that of Penny or Paul; it was not how much they had but how they chose to show it.

She walked past bomb damage on Queen Margaret Drive that remained as a lasting memory of bad times so recently lived through, and the wrought-iron gates of the Botanic Gardens relented with one push, allowing entry to the lush and vibrant world that had been her comfort since childhood. The pond was a reflection of green foliage but, as usual, it was the sparkling beauty of the Kibble Palace that dominated the scene. Under the glowing sky, it ignited as if it were on fire. Drawn to it like a moth, there was nothing to trouble her, nothing to occupy her thoughts, and the letter and the proposition it contained melted away.

Throughout her life, sadness had been immediate and left her gasping, anger had bubbled up over time and anxiety had hit her like a train, but real contentment had crept up slowly, polite and quiet, then sat back and waited for her to take notice. Maggie took notice that day amongst the peonies and rhododendrons. There was a group of people made just for her, inside her house right at that moment, who would be there for her no matter what happened, for as long as she lived. Whether they were filling her days with excitement or frustration, she could not be without them. As she approached the entrance to the Kibble Palace, her heart beat fast and her breathing became shallow, overcome by everything she felt for the world.

The familiar humidity hit her as soon as she entered the greenhouse and the pungent aroma of the tropics hit her full force. An exotic jungle was alive in front of her and her eyes were wide open to see it. The immense mass of plant life that rose in front of her had been there since before she was born, but that day she sank down onto the low stone wall surrounding the goldfish pond at the palace entrance to experience everything as if it were new.

All of the atmosphere, nane o' the danger.

The orange glow outside was turning red. Soon it would deepen, all would be dark and the park would be shut for the night, but she did not want to leave. Not quite yet. Instead, she stretched her legs out lazily and leant back to look deep into the reflective waters.

Where are ye fish.

They were being elusive, melting into the dappled shadows cast from foliage overhead. The only clear image on the still surface was that of her own face. Once a curvy adult, those curves had filled out and softened with age and her curling hair now only accentuated the years which gathered on her pale skin. Nonetheless, she smiled at the reality of herself and was met with the crinkling welcome of a humorous grin and mischievous gaze, timeless remnants of the girl she had been.

Taking the letter from her pocket, she smoothed out the crumpled pages and glanced briefly at Rachel's shallow words. Apparently there was a life of promise out in Winnipeg; of men and a mother waiting for new connections, but all the colour of the West sat flat on the page when compared to the life she had seen at Wee

Maggie's party. She loved everything in front of her far, far too much to throw it away.

Slowly, deliberately, she tore the paper into tiny pieces and set them afloat on the fishpond. The goldfish materialised instantaneously, coming close to the surface to flip-flop over each other and nibble the edges. Their noisy splashes lasted moments before they found the words distasteful. They quickly submerged and swam away as suddenly as they had arrived, and her laughter echoed after them.

A low whistle from behind startled her. She jumped as its echo harmonised with her laughter, bouncing around the deserted interior of the Kibble Palace like wayward children on a Sunday.

"Maggie Munroe."

"Wha's that?"

The voice was behind her, coming from the entrance door. She had been so preoccupied by the threat of the jungle that she had forgotten what lay behind. Spinning around, she had to squint against the horizontal rays of sunset to find the silhouette and with it she answered her own question: that recognisable stance, balanced evenly on both feet with hands clasped behind his back. His head was slightly bowed and he looked up at her through round, rimless spectacles. His face was tanned from the early summer sun and his high cheekbones were flushed. The smell of soft leather reached gently across the space, a subtle undercurrent to the pungent abundance of plants.

"It's Alec McLean. Sorry ah startled ye, hen."

"How did ye know it wis me?" *God, ah staund oot like a sare thumb.*

"Ah ne'er forget a face or a cracking pair o' legs."

"Och, away. How are ye? Ah've no' seen ye in years." *Ye're looking good, by the way.*

"Still working at the leather shop up the road. Whit aboot yersel?"

"Still working at the doctor's doon the road." *Awfy convenient.*

"Fancy that. And yer daddy?"

"Awright, ah suppose." *Apairt fae his airm, his eyes, and a' the rest.*

"That doesnae sound tae gid. Can ah sit doon, hen, and ye can tell me aboot it?"

"Better yet, why no' come up fir dinner and he can tell ye aw aboot it himself?" *And dinnae rush awa efterwards.*

~

Did ye hear aboot yon Maggie Munroe? Naw? Weil, she went awa and got hersel' mairried, so she did! Didnae know the laddie fir five minutes and the next thing they're walking doon the aisle, so they are. Ah mean, they knew each other *years* ago but only mild acquaintances like so that disnae really count, neither it does. He looked proud as punch when he saw her at the manse, no' in white like wan o' the young wans but a' dressed up in blue, wae a hat o' midnight and a brim as wide as ma airm, so it wis, like somethin fae the Thirties. Fir as lang as ah can remember she's ayeways hud a laddie in tow, that wan, ayeways gien them the run-aroon and ne'er gien the 'I do', so she wis. Naebody cid understaund it and it must hae bin a richt worry tae her faither getting auld and knowing he may no' be here much longer and a' that, wae naebody tae look efter his only wean, neither thir wis. Onyway, it's done noo and a lovely man he is, richt enough. The three o' them are living on Wilton Drive, the flat above me, happy as Larry, so they are, and ah jist found oot she's up the duff awready! There wisnae ony time tae waste wae her age and a' but it wis still awfy fast work if ye ask me, so it wis. Ah said as much tae her the other day and she says tae me, 'ma wean's due in May, Mrs McNulty, eleven months efter ma wedding, so ye'll see it wisnae *tae* fast'. Jist like that she came oot wae it, so she did, as if *AH* wid imply onything o' the sort. Some lassie's are affy touchy, so they are. Did ah tell ye she was proposed tae three times already? So she wis. Three times in as many years and she turned them a' doon flat. The hale block wis convinced she wis going tae end up an auld maid, so she wis. It jist goes tae show whit ah've been saying ma hale life lang; whit's fir ye will no' go by ye and wha's fir ye will no' go by ye. Neither they will.

The End

Author's Note

I have written this novel to bring to life the stories I heard throughout my childhood and capture the essence of the most important woman (besides my mammy) that I've ever known. From the outset, I've tried to reflect her voice as closely as possible so that I can hear her in my head, telling me funny stories that cross decades. The Scots language should have status and recognition equal to other languages globally, but the strength of its dialects vary depending on context as they come under pressure to conform to English language norms. This fluctuating usage is evident in the novel and all I can do is keep all my fingers crossed that I'm doing my gran justice.

The Reverend and Doctor depicted in this novel were a real life brother and sister. Their father was the local minister during the 1930s and 40s, but Elizabeth Barr was the first ordained female presbyterian minister in Scotland in 1935 and went on to sit on her church's General Assembly. A truly remarkable woman, she married Marion McCrae and George Johnstone on 28th March 1952, and Marion would work as her brother's receptionist for 50 years.

A mention should be given to the Garscube Bar which is such a favourite of the Munroe/Bennie/Menzies men and used to sit at the corner of Garscube Road and Lyon Street. During its time, there was a plaque of dedication on its outer wall to commemorate the men of Lyon Street who died during WWI. More men are reported to have died there than from any other street in Glasgow (perhaps Scotland) and, between the wars, it is said that the bar honoured the dead with their own piper and bugler on Armistice day - an important part of the area's history lost to time and redevelopment.

The American youngster, mentioned by Tommy Gunn, who gave his first speech when meeting survivors at the Beresford Hotel in Glasgow was JFK, as documented in the Glasgow Times. At least that's one thing Tommy isn't lying about! The influenza which took Daisy Bennie in Ruchill hospital is a fictionalised account but based on family memories of the flu and Cerebro-spinal fever epidemics in the early 20th Century, and the novel is set in the North Kelvinside subdistrict of Maryhill. Thanks for joining me for a wee look into the past.

Acknowledgements

An acknowledgement is not enough to give Maisie Johnstone for all of the stories that shaped this novel. I waited two years too long to write it so she never got the chance to read it herself but, unlike me, she lived it all in the first place so she wins. I would also like to thank her daughter, Betty, for reliving the stories with me regularly and being open to minor deviations from the truth in the early years and major shifts later on.

To the farsighted and masterful Dan, whose skills went beyond design when dealing with a rookie client - thanks for telling me, at every step, that the journey would be worth it. To Alisdair, for reading over the words to ensure they aren't gobbledygook - hats off for doing this despite having celebrated the end of your proofreading duties when I left university the first time round.

It's been a team effort and I think I have managed to pop out the other side sane.

Thanks to Mike for highlighting the history of modern landmarks, Calum for being such an invaluable support during the book launch, James for your description of Jaconelli's in the early days, Brett for feedback on how Scots translates to a North American tongue, and to Lovina Roe, without whom my love of Scots literature would not have become so ingrained during my high school years.

Thank you Nancy Barr, Margaret Scollon, Dr Margaret Russell and Marion Luke for the first-hand accounts of war-time Glasgow in 2023, long after the threat has passed. Your histories are injected with such personality and perspective that they prove much more colourful than fiction.

A quick mention for the Glasgow North/West community groups who keep the enduring spirit of Maryhill alive. Rowena, June, Robbie, Margaret and Sheryl, Juniper and Kathryn had particularly useful background information for this novel, but countless others had great anecdotes and help these networks flourish every day. One of the many things this city is good for is a blether.

Graham, and John, Jacqui, Jill and Jack (a.k.a the Johnstone clan) - thanks for your support and understanding while I mess with your mum/gran.

Most importantly, here's to Dorrie, Ruby and Maisie. For the stories.

Research Credits

- Glasgow Times

- OldGlasgowPubs.co.uk

- The National Archives

- The Mitchell Library, Glasgow

- Maryhill Burgh Halls *(maryhillburghhalls.org.uk/blog/2020/5/8/1941-the-luftwaffe-bomb-kilmun-street-maryhill)*

- Nextdoor.co.uk

- Old Maryhill Facebook Group

JJ Scott was born in Glasgow, Scotland before she was abruptly removed from the city at the tender age of 5 and taken to a small village for a 12-year stint, much to her chagrin. But JJ wasn't one to let a little thing like being stranded in the countryside get her down. She spent her days dreaming of her return to the city and plotted her escape by studying for an LLB at the University of Glasgow.

JJ channelled her love for the city to finally bring her debut novel, The Making of Maggie Munroe, to life. Inspired by stories from her childhood when she and her brother would sit around the card table in Wilton Drive to play auld maid and listen to their gran weave stories of the past - including the revelation that she had been proposed to by four different men (talk about a plot twist!) - JJ poured her heart and soul into this deeply personal project.

Despite being based firmly in Glasgow, much of the writing of 'Maggie' took place during the years JJ spent backpacking around the world. These travels have provided endless inspiration and introduced her to a diverse cast of characters, some of whom will rear their colourful heads as her literary journey continues.

Find out more at **jjscottauthor.com**